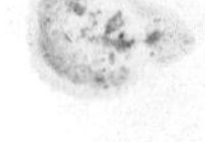

PENGUIN CANADA

NEUROPATH

SCOTT BAKKER is the author of *The Darkness that Comes Before, The Warrior-Prophet*, and *The Thousandfold Thought*, a trilogy that *Publishers Weekly* calls 'a work of unforgettable power.' He spent his childhood exploring the bluffs of Lake Erie's north shore, and his youth studying literature, languages, and philosophy. He now lives in London, Ontario, with his wife, Sharron, and their cat, Scully.

Also by Scott Bakker, writing as R. Scott Bakker

THE PRINCE OF NOTHING SERIES

The Darkness That Comes Before,
Book One

The Warrior-Prophet,
Book Two

The Thousandfold Thought,
Book Three

NEUROPATH

SCOTT BAKKER

PENGUIN
CANADA

PENGUIN CANADA

Published by the Penguin Group

Penguin Group (Canada), 90 Eglinton Avenue East, Suite 700, Toronto, Ontario, Canada M4P 2Y3
(a division of Pearson Canada Inc.)

Penguin Group (USA) Inc., 375 Hudson Street, New York, New York 10014, U.S.A.
Penguin Books Ltd, 80 Strand, London WC2R 0RL, England
Penguin Ireland, 25 St Stephen's Green, Dublin 2, Ireland
(a division of Penguin Books Ltd)
Penguin Group (Australia), 250 Camberwell Road, Camberwell, Victoria 3124,
Australia (a division of Pearson Australia Group Pty Ltd)
Penguin Books India Pvt Ltd, 11 Community Centre, Panchsheel Park,
New Delhi – 110 017, India
Penguin Group (NZ), 67 Apollo Drive, Rosedale, North Shore 0745, Auckland,
New Zealand (a division of Pearson New Zealand Ltd)
Penguin Books (South Africa) (Pty) Ltd, 24 Sturdee Avenue, Rosebank,
Johannesburg 2196, South Africa

Penguin Books Ltd, Registered Offices: 80 Strand, London WC2R 0RL, England

Published in Canada by Penguin Group (Canada), a division of Pearson Canada Inc., 2008
Published in the U.K. by Orion Books, an imprint of The Orion Publishing Group Ltd., 2008

1 2 3 4 5 6 7 8 9 10 (WEB)

Publisher's note: This book is a work of fiction. Names, characters, places and incidents either are the product of the author's imagination or are used fictitiously, and any resemblance to actual persons living or dead, events, or locales is entirely coincidental.

Manufactured in Canada.

LIBRARY AND ARCHIVES CANADA CATALOGUING IN PUBLICATION

Bakker, R. Scott (Richard Scott), 1967-
Neuropath / R. Scott Bakker.

ISBN 978-0-14-316871-3

I. Title.

PS8553.A3884N48 2008 C813'.6 C2008-902748-5

Typeset at The Spartan Press Ltd, Lymington, Hants

British Library Cataloguing in Publication data available

Visit the Penguin Group (Canada) website at **www.penguin.ca**

Special and corporate bulk purchase rates available; please see **www.penguin.ca/corporatesales** or call 1-800-810-3104, ext. 477 or 474

To my Fall 2003 Popular Culture class.
For remaining honest in the face of complexity,
and humble in the shadow of mystery.

ACKNOWLEDGEMENTS

This book was born out of a bet with my wife, Sharron, whose sharp eye and loving skepticism have shaped the story at every turn. If a book this dark could have godfathers, they would be my brother, Bryan Bakker, who held the rope as I crawled down the rabbit hole, my agent, Chris Lotts, who despite the Argument insisted on asking 'But why?' at every damn turn, and Gary Wassner, who taught me, among so many other things, that complicated fathers were the best fathers of all.

Those who have been instrumental in finessing the book include, Jon Wood at Orion Books, Barbara Berson at Penguin Canada, Roger Eichorn, Frank Cameron, Chris O'Brien, and Chris Viger at the University of Western Ontario, who was gracious enough to let me attend his graduate seminar in the spring of 2006.

Among the innumerable friends and acquaintances who have left their mark, I should mention Karl Schroeder, Rick O'Brien, Lisa Rusal, Brian Ribeiro at the University of Tennessee, Nandita Biswas at the University of Western Ontario, Nick Smith at the University of New Hampshire, Danielle Gagne at Alfred University, and the painfully erudite members of my reading group, especially Whitney Hoth, who prefers 19th century literature for a reason – good or bad nobody seems to know.

Thanks to you all.

AUTHOR'S NOTE

The following story is based on actual trends in neuroscience, psychology, and cognitive science. Despite all the controversies (and there are many), one fact has managed to rise above the fray: we are not what we think we are.

From whence did Dante take the materials for his hell but from our actual world? And a very proper hell he was able to make of it.

SCHOPENHAUER

You should know better.

After all, you're watching it on the news: the diagonally parked cruisers, the milling officials who glance and scowl in your direction. You see the cordons, the lengths of sagging tape, and without thinking you know that there, *on the far side, lies something horrific, the residue of something too wicked for general consumption. There, you understand, is the crime scene.*

A place where human meat turns chill.

'The Chiropractor,' the newsmodel says, 'continues to terrorize New Yorkers.'

You shudder when you hear that, because you are a New Yorker. The image flickers to Mrs Alvarez, the generic neighbor, who weeps at the loss of someone so special, so beautiful. She looks like a good woman, so you empathize. You do the mental math, calculating the distance between Mrs Alvarez and your house, and you think of calling a friend. Didn't you go to a restaurant just around the corner from there?

You look at the phone lying next to your keys on the kitchenette. You want to call someone, *but you curl your feet into your hands instead, run your thumbs over the polish on your toes.*

The poor girl, you think. You scowl, trying to envisage the horrific truth behind the NYPD spokesperson and her facade of euphemisms. Multiple lacerations. Blunt force trauma. But there is more. There has to be a twist to make things twisted. The stuff about the spine – that's just to juice the ratings, surely. What about the other stuff? The sex stuff. After all, it isn't just the murder, it's the aim.

The poor girl, you think, pressing your knees tight. Just like you, she had secrets, tender secrets, that vicious others wanted to know. You glimpse images, nude and rude and wet. You taste something metallic. You smell the goat of unwashed groins. For an instant, you hear her scream . . .

Troubled, your gaze drifts from the screen to the thumb petting your toes. You decide your feet look cute.

I agree.

You wonder if it's something about the male species. It really wouldn't surprise you. Your last boyfriend was sick – not sick *sick, but sick enough – always trying to talk you into gagging on his you-know-what. And the one before that, well, we best not go down that road.*

You blink, run two fingers down your temple and cheek in a way that would make your father recall your mother. Your eyes – vultures that they are – come circling back to the coverage. The detective to the left of the spokesperson, you decide, brings home copies of the crime scene photos. He has that grizzled look.

Like meat plucked too late from the fire.

You chuckle and sigh, feeling warm, safe, and lonely. This is stupid, *you decide. You change the channel, move to the make-me-laugh section of the store.*

That's when you hear the tapping at your window.

You become very still.

There's no code, no tempo or beat, only the arrhythmia of things waving in the wind.

Only me.

You mute the television, try to peer through your lovely reflection, but end up reviewing your appearance instead. You stand, bronze in the lamplight, breathless with indecision. Your spine arches.

You come to the edge of the fishbowl.

CHAPTER ONE

August 17th, 6.05 a.m.

Love dies hard.

Two years they had been divorced, and still he dreamed about her . . . Nora. As slender as an intake of breath, shining with the light of all those admiring eyes. It had been her day – her day first – and Thomas had made it his own by giving it to her wholly. The music thumped. The floor swayed with smiles and grand and flabby gestures. The grandfather from North Carolina, shaking his hands like Sunday revival. The cousins from California, wowing the women with their MTV moves. The aunt from *WeightWatchers*, striking this or that *Cosmopolitan* pose. The spectators laughed and cheered, continually glanced at the little illuminated screens they held in their palms. Catching his wind at the bar, Thomas watched them all. He beamed as his best man, Neil, broke clear of the fracas to join him. He looked like an actor, Thomas thought, dark-eyed and erratic, like Montgomery Clift celebrating the world's end.

'Welcome!' Neil cried in a tone meant to cut through the jubilation, 'Welcome to Disney World, old buddy!'

Thomas nodded the way people do when friends say inappropriate things, a kind of reflex affirmation, chin here, eyes over there. He could never leave things alone, Neil. That was what made him Neil, Thomas supposed – what made him extraordinary.

'Give it a rest,' he said.

Neil threw his hands out, as if gesturing to everything in all directions. 'C'mon. You see it as clearly as I do. Courtship. Pair-bonding. Reproduction . . .' He grinned in a manner that was at once festive and conspiratorial. No man living, it seemed to Thomas, could put so much contradiction into his smile. 'This is all just part of the program, Goodbook.'

'Neil . . .'

'You don't have an answer, do you?'

Thomas saw Nora making her way toward them, laughing at an uncle's one-liner, clutching old hands. She had always been beautiful, but now with the pomp and attention she seemed something impossible, ethereal, a vision who would shed her gown for him and only him. He turned to scowl at his friend, to tell him that she – *she* – was his answer.

His new conclusion.

'Time to grow up, don't you think? Time to put the Argument behind us.'

'Sure,' Neil said. 'Time to *sleep*.'

Nora danced between them, staggered Thomas by swinging from his arm.

'You guys are freaks!' she cried. She could always tell when they were talking shop, and always knew how to draw them back to the rough ground of more sensible souls. He held her in the rocking way of drunken lovers, laughing so hard he couldn't speak. Another Tom and Nora giggle session. At parties, people would always comment how only they seemed to get each other's jokes. Isn't that what it meant? 'Getting' somebody?

They were just on the same drugs, Neil would say.

'Can't you feel it?' she cried, rolling her eyes out to the drunken yonder. 'All these people love us, Tommy! All these people luv-luv-luvvv—'

The alarm clock crowed as remorseless as a reversing garbage truck. Thomas Bible swatted at it, squinted at the spears of sunlight. He felt like a scrap of something drawn from a forgotten pocket: too crumpled for too long to ever be smoothed. He was hungover – well and truly. Running his tongue over his teeth, he winced at the taste.

He sat hunched for several moments, trying to muster the peace-of-stomach he'd need for the long lurch to the bathroom. Fucking dreams. Why, after all these years, would he dream of his wedding reception? It wasn't so much the images he resented as the happiness.

He was too old for this shit, especially on a work day – no, even worse, a work and kid day. He could already hear Nora's rebuke, her voice cross and her eyes jubilant: '*What's this I hear . . .*'

The bathroom reeked of whiskey, but at least the toilet lid was down. He flushed without looking, then sat down in the tub and turned on the shower. The embalming water felt good, so much so he actually stood to wash his hair.

Afterward, he pulled on a robe and trundled downstairs, shushing his dog, an affable black lab named Bartender. He collected the whiskey tumblers and beer bottles on his way through the living room and thought about checking in on the den, but the partially closed door buzzed with awkwardness. Just inside the door, a pair of blue jeans lay crumpled across the carpet, legs pulled inside out. He considered barging in and committing some petty act of vengeance – bellowing like a drill sergeant or jumping up and down on the fold-out or something similarly stupid – but decided against it.

The Advil was in the kitchen.

His place was old, one of the original farmhouses built long before the rest of the surrounding subdivision. Creaky hardwood floors. Tall ceilings. Smallish rooms. No garage. A concrete porch just big enough for two Mormons. 'Cozy,' the real estate agent had said. 'Claustrophobic,' Nora had continually complained.

Even still, Thomas had grown to love the place. Over the years he had invested quite a bit of time and money in renovations – enough to make the Century 21 guy right. The kitchen, especially, with its period fixtures and porcelain-rimmed walls, radiated character and homeliness. In the morning sunlight, everything gleamed. The chairs cast ribbed shadows across the tile floor.

Now if only Nora hadn't taken all the plants.

By the time he started the coffeemaker he was feeling much better – almost human. The power of routine, he supposed. Even half-poisoned, the old brain appreciated routine.

The previous night had been nothing if not crazy.

He wolfed down a couple of stale Krispy Kreme donuts with his coffee, hoping to settle his stomach. After sitting for several minutes listening to the fridge hum, he pulled himself to the granite counter and began preparing breakfast. He knew the kids were awake before he heard them. Bart always clicked out of the kitchen and bounded upstairs moments before the muffled cries began. Like all labs, he adored his tormentors.

'No!' Thomas heard his daughter, Ripley, shriek. Tumbling footsteps along the hallways, then, 'No-no-no-no!' all the way down the stairs.

'Dad!' the eight-year-old cried as she barrelled into the kitchen. She was thin and willowy in her Donna Duck pyjamas, with a pixie face and her grandmother's long, raven-black hair. She swung into her seat with the strange combination of concentration and abandon that characterized everything she did. 'Frankie showed me his you-know-what again!'

Thomas blinked. He'd always been an advocate of early childhood sex education, but he could see why most parents were keen to keep the genie in the bottle for as long as possible. Shame was a lazy parent's way of teaching discretion. Or so he told himself.

She made a face. 'His *thing*, Daddy. His' – she screwed up her face as if to give the official word an official female expression – '*peeenis.*'

Thomas could only stare in horror. *Dammit, Tom,* he could hear Nora say. *They need their own rooms. How many times* . . . He called out upstairs, wincing at the volume of his own voice. 'Frankie! Do you remember what we said about your morning—' He caught himself, looked askance at Ripley. 'Your morning . . . you-know . . .'

Frankie's petulant 'Yes' floated down from the nethers of the house. He sounded crestfallen.

'Keep your pecker in your pants, son. Please.'

Of course Ripley had been watching closely. '*Pecker,* Daddy? Eeww!'

Thomas grabbed the bridge of his nose and sighed. Nora was going to kill him.

No shame, he told himself. The world was lesson enough. Ripley was already fretting over what clothes to wear, talking about how L'Oréal was better than Covergirl was better than whatever. Soon they would wince at photographs of themselves, at the sound of their voices on the answering machine, at the rust spots on the rockers of their car, and so on, and so on. Soon they would be good little consumers, buying this or that bandaid for their innumerable little shames.

Not if he could help it.

Several minutes afterward, little Frankie shuffled across the tiles, squinting against the sunlight. Thomas was relieved to see his Silver Surfer pyjama-bottoms intact. The four-year-old rubbed his puffy eyes, flapping his elbows as he did so. Though impish and compact, Frankie exaggerated all of his movements – even his facial expressions. He waved more than he needed to wave, stepped more than he needed to step; he even sat more than he needed to sit. He took up a lot of room for such a little kid, spatially as well as emotionally.

Ripley regarded him, her expression one of glum boredom. 'Nobody needs to see *that*,' she said, pointing at his crotch.

Thomas cracked another egg, smiled ruefully.

'So?' Frankie replied.

'So it's weird. Showing your *thing* to your sister is weird. Ugh! It's sick.'

'Is not sick. Daddy said it's healthy. Right, Daddy?'

'Yes . . .' Thomas began, then grimaced, shaking his head. 'I mean *no* . . . And yes.'

What was the problem? Hadn't he taught a graduate seminar on child sexuality at Columbia? Didn't he know the 'developmentally correct' swing for most every curve-ball a kid could throw? He held up both hands and stood over the table, trying to appear both stern and clinical. His children, however, had forgotten him. Mouths half full of toast, they bickered with the obstinate whininess that characterized so much of their communication.

'Come on. Listen up, guys. Please.'

They were both chattering at the same time now. 'No, you!' 'No, *you*!' Christ Almighty, his head hurt.

'Listen up, jerks!' he cried. 'The old man has had a rough night.'

Ripley chortled. 'You got drunk with Uncle Cass last night, didn't you?'

'Can we wake him, Daddy?' Frankie asked. 'Can we wake him, *please*?'

What was it with the apprehension? *Just a bad night*, he told himself. *I'll sort it all out this afternoon.*

'No. Leave him be. Listen up! As I was saying, the old man has had a rough night. The old man needs his kids to cut him some slack.'

They both watched him, at once wary and amused. They knew what he was, the clever little fiends. He was a Hapless Dad. When they angered him, they simply pretended he was shamming until it seemed he *was* shamming. Manipulative little buggers.

Thomas took a deep breath. 'I said, the old man needs his kids to cut him some slack.'

They shared a momentary glance, as though to make sure they were both on the same mischievous page, then began laughing.

'Serve oos owr breakfust, wench!' Frankie cried, mimicking some movie they'd watched not so long ago. It had become their Breakfast Joke.

With this, Thomas was undone. He conceded defeat by ruffling their hair and kissing their heads.

'Don't say "wench",' he murmured.

Then he got back to breakfast – like a good wench, he supposed. He'd forgotten how much he loved weekday mornings with his children.

Even when hungover.

Normally he saw Franklin and Ripley only on weekends, as per his custody agreement. But Nora had asked if he would take them for the week: some bullshit about a trip to San Francisco. Ordinarily taking the kids wouldn't have been a problem, but Nora had unerringly caught him at the worst time possible: the run-up to the new school year, when the kids had scaled the stir-crazy summit of their summer holidays, and when he was up to his eyeballs with committee and course prep work for the upcoming semester. Thank God Mia, his neighbor, had agreed to help out.

Mia's real name was Emilio, but everyone called him Mia, either because his last name was Farrow, or because of his days as a drag-queen. He was a great guy: an amateur Marxist and a professional homosexual – self-described. He was a technical writer for JDS Uniphase and usually worked out of his home. Though he constantly made noise about despising kids, he was positively maudlin when it came to Frankie and Ripley. He complained about them the way diehard sports fans complained about their team's winning streaks: as though offering proof of humility to fickle gods. Thomas suspected that his love of the kids was nothing short of parental, which was to say, indistinguishable from pride.

Running late, Thomas hustled the kids across the lawn. The neighborhood was young enough to sport winding lanes and a bewildering variety of trees, but too old to suffer the super-sized Legoland look. They found Mia standing on his porch arguing with his partner, Bill Mack. Mia had dark, Marine-cropped hair, and a face that shouted zero body fat. His build might have been described as slight, were it not for the obvious strength of his shoulders and arms. The man was built like an acrobat.

'So that's just great,' Mia was saying. 'Fanfuckingtastic, Bill.' He turned and smiled guilelessly at the Bibles assembled on the steps below. 'Hi, kids,' he said. 'You got here just in time to say bye-bye to the prick.'

'Hi, William,' Thomas said carefully to Bill. The previous month Bill had decided he wanted to be called William – the name had more 'cultural capital' he had said.

'Jeeeezus Christ,' Mia snorted, his inflection somewhere between Alabama wife-beater and California gay. 'Why not just call him Willy?'

' 'ee's goot a wee willie,' Frankie cried out in his Scottish accent. Another movieism.

Mia laughed aloud.

'Why hello, Thomas,' Bill replied sunnily. 'And how are the Bibles doing?'

'Dad's hungover and Frankie showed me his pecker,' Ripley said.

Bill's smile was pure Mona Lisa. 'Same ol, same ol, huh?' He crinkled his nose. 'I think that's my cue . . .' Sidling between the Bibles, he walked to his old model Toyota SUV – one of the ones eco-protestors liked to sling tar across. He looked like a blond Sears catalogue model in his three-piece. Thomas glimpsed Mia mouth *Fuck off and die* as he pulled out the driveway.

For as long as he'd known them, Bill and Mia had done all the things statistically doomed couples typically do. They made faces while the other was talking – a frightfully good indicator of impending relationship meltdown. They described each other in unrelentingly negative terms. They even smacked each other around now and again. And yet somehow they managed to thrive, let alone survive. They had certainly outlasted the Bibles.

'Nothing too serious?' Thomas said, checking as much as asking. Over the years he'd helped the two of them sort out several near-fatal communication breakdowns, usually by talking one of them from the brink without the other knowing. Guerilla therapy, he called it.

'I'll be fine, professor. Gay men love assholes, remember? Pardon my French.'

'Daddy speaks French too,' Ripley said.

'I'm sure he does, honey.' Mia nodded at the black minivan parked next to Thomas's Acura. He raised his eyebrows. 'Company, professor? L'amore, perhaps?'

Smirking, Thomas closed his eyes and shook his head. Mia was hopelessly nosy.

'No. Nothing like that.'

Thomas was a creature of habit.

Over the years since he and Nora had moved to the burbs, the hour-long commute into Manhattan on the MTA North had become a reprieve of sorts. Thomas liked the packed anonymity of it all. The literary types could boo-hoo all they wanted about the 'lonely post-industrial crowd', but there was something to be said for the privacy of vacant and indifferent faces. Countless millions of people all herded into queues, all possessing lives of extraordinary richness, and most with sense enough not to share them with strangers.

It seemed a miracle.

Thomas imagined some grad student somewhere had published a paper on the topic. Some grad student somewhere had published a paper on everything. Now that the big game had been hunted to extinction, all the little mysteries found themselves in the academic crosshairs, all the things that made humans *human.*

Usually Thomas read the *New York Times* – the ink and paper version – on the trip into Manhattan, but sometimes, like today, he simply stared at the passing Hudson and dozed. No river, he was certain, had been the object of more absent contemplation than the Hudson.

He had much to think about. Frankie's incestuous exhibitionism was the least of his concerns.

He glanced at the front page of his neighbor's *Times* and saw the headlines he'd expected.

EU SAYS US AID PACKAGE 'NOT ENOUGH'
DEATH TOLL COULD TOP 50,000 RUSSIAN OFFICIALS SAY

And of course,

THE 'CHIROPRACTOR' STRIKES AGAIN:
SPINELESS CORPSE FOUND IN BROOKLYN

He found himself peering, trying to read the hazy squares of text beneath. The only words he could make out were 'vertebrae' and 'eviscerated.' He blinked and squeezed his eyes, cursed himself for giving in to his morbid curiosity. Thousands of years ago, when people still lived in small communities, paying attention to random acts of violence actually paid reproductive dividends. That's why human brains were hardwired to pay attention to them.

But now? It was little more than an indulgence. Candy for a stone-age mind.

He thought about the previous night instead.

He was just screwing with me . . . Wasn't he?

Thomas emerged from the oily humidity of the subway onto Broadway and 116th. He leaned against the railing, overcome with what his father had always called 'jelly belly'. Fucking shooters. Why had he agreed to do shooters? The New York march of cars and people soothed him for some reason.

Columbia was surprisingly busy, given the school year had yet to begin. Dozens of students sat on the steps along the Low Plaza, cradling books and coffees and the ubiquitous palmtops. Thomas always enjoyed the walk to Schermerhorn Hall: the cobbled courtyards and bricked gardens, the contrast of grass and old stone, the humble academic grandeur. He passed through the shadow of St Paul's Chapel, and it seemed he could feel the morning cool radiating from its hunched walls. For all its logistical drawbacks, Schermerhorn was an ideal home for the psychology department. Apparently Columbia's designers had a yen for interior spaces, enclaves within enclaves. It seemed proper that the Schermerhorn should be hidden, just as it seemed proper that it should be old, the stone leached, the walls settling on uncertain foundations – a place built by men who could still take the soul seriously.

Perhaps because he was hungover, Thomas found himself pausing before the entrance, gazing at the latter half of the inscription above.

SPEAK TO THE EARTH AND IT SHALL TEACH THEE

A laudable commandment, he supposed. But what if humanity had no stomach for the lesson?

*

He ducked his head into the psychology department office to check his mail.

'Oh, Professor Bible,' he heard Suzanne, the head administrative assistant call.

Hanging sideways in the doorway, he smiled at her. 'Make it quick, Suzy; I'm feeling woozy.'

She grimaced and nodded toward three suits, two women and one man, loitering outside the department head's office door. They seemed to be watching him with peculiar interest.

'Can I help you?' Thomas asked. Their scrutiny felt vaguely offensive.

The dark-haired woman stepped forward and held out her hand. 'Professor Bible? Thomas Bible?' she asked.

Thomas didn't reply, convinced that she already knew who he was. Something about their demeanor said they had glossy photos in their breast pockets, and dossiers in their palmtops.

'I'm Shelley Atta,' she continued after an awkward moment. 'This is Samantha Logan and Dan Gerard.' Logan was tall, blond, and implausibly attractive. Despite the crisp professionalism of her suit, something about her demeanor spoke of tongue studs and ankle tattoos. With blue eyes and gallic brown hair, Gerard had the look of a washed-out football captain: packed with low-density muscle, indifferent to the faint mustard stains on his lapel. The kind of guy who made monkey faces when he peed. They seemed an unlikely pair.

'Is there someplace private where we might speak?' Atta asked.

'Preferably someplace with a BD player,' Logan added.

'What's this about?' Thomas asked.

Shelley Atta's eyes narrowed in irritation. She had a dense frame that could seem matronly or imposing, depending on her expression. She suddenly seemed imposing. 'We're with the FBI, Professor Bible . . . As I said, is there someplace private where we can talk?'

'My office will have to do,' Thomas said, turning on his heel like the busy man he was.

He demanded and studied their identification on the way to his office. He felt like a moron afterward. They certainly looked at him as if he were a moron.

Thomas distrusted 'law enforcement' in all its multifarious guises, for many small reasons. A cop with the NYPD had been his neighbor once – a total asshole. Narcissism. Borderline personality disorder. You name it. Then there was the shakedown he had experienced driving through backwoods Georgia years back. Somehow the local sheriff had clocked his crippled Volkswagen – which could manage what? sixty-four or sixty-five floored? – doing ninety-seven. He still remembered the way the man had leaned into his window: like he was hungry and Thomas had his Kentucky Fried Chicken.

But the big reason was that he knew how frail people were. It was his job, studying all the things people would rather not know about themselves. He knew how quickly and how thoroughly positions of power could distort them. He knew the behavioral consequences of such distortion, and he knew how often innocents suffered as a result.

Thomas unlocked the door and ushered the three agents into the papery silence of the cubicle that was his office. Unlike some of his colleagues, he had never made a 'home' of his office. He had no comfy chairs for graduate groupies, no prints of Nietzsche, Skinner or Che Guevara, just books and sticky-notes. The agents scanned his shelves. The attractive blond ran an appreciative finger down the spine of his first and only published work, *Through the Brain Darkly*. Agent Atta seemed to be looking for evidence of pornography or drug use. Either Dan Gerard was a restless man, or he was distressed by the chaos. A mild OCD perhaps?

'So what's this about?' Thomas asked again.

'We should watch the BD first,' Shelley said, producing a silvery disk.

Thomas's stomach tightened. They were purposefully denying him context, anything that might prepare him for what he was about to see. They were going to be watching him closely, he knew, looking for small, telltale cues in his reaction . . .

Just what in the hell was going on?

The FBI, here in his office. Surreal. He suddenly relaxed, even smiled as he turned on his computer. The kids were going to freak when he told them about this. '*The FBI, Daddy*? *No way*!'

It must be some kind of mix-up.

They waited for Windows to load – always an awkward moment, it seemed to Thomas, even when alone.

'Bible,' he heard Agent Gerard say behind him. 'What kind of name is that?'

He was trying to rattle him, Thomas supposed, using oblique

antagonism to make it more difficult for him to conceal any potentially incriminating reaction. But they had no idea just how hung-over Thomas was. He doubted a muzzle-flash next to his ear could make him jump.

Thomas turned in his swivel and looked Gerard dead in the eyes. 'Grab those chairs,' he said, motioning to the far side of his office. 'We should all sit.'

Agent Gerard glanced nervously at Agent Atta, then did as he was told. One down. Two to go.

Thomas dropped the disc in the tray. They were all sitting now.

The screen was black.

'Do those work?' Agent Atta asked, pointing at his desktop speakers. Thomas clicked through a couple different windows.

'YOU LIKE THAT?' blared from the speakers.

The voice sounded male, but it was electronically distorted – deep, as though gurgling through a synthesizer's version of the ocean bottom. Thomas's skin pimpled. What was this?

'What are you doing?' A female voice, breathless and undistorted. She sounded confused, as if she wanted to be terrified but . . .

'DO. YOU. LIKE?'

'Nnnngha . . . Oh God, yesssss.'

But was too aroused.

There was a tussle of lights on the screen, then Thomas saw a home video shot of a woman's torso. She was sitting in some kind of black leather chair, and wearing a patterned-pink shift so soaked in water or sweat that it clung to her like a semi-translucent condom. She was panting like a dog, her back arched, her nipples hard. Her face remained off camera.

'YES . . . YOU LIKE,' the rumbling voice declared. Whoever was speaking, Thomas realized, was also holding the videocam.

'What . . . Wha-what are you doing?'

'MAKING AN ARGUMENT.'

'Oh, Jeeeeesussss . . .'

The camera dipped, and Thomas glimpsed her naked thighs swaying. She seemed to be grinding her hips, but nothing was touching her. Nothing he could see.

'MAKING LOVE.'

'Mmmm . . . Mmmm,' the faceless woman moaned, her voice curiously childlike.

'MORE?'

The camera jerked upward, and Thomas saw her face. She was bleach-blond, with the pouty-lipped, harem-beauty of a Hollywood starlet. Her right cheek was thrust against her shoulder. Her eyes were glassy and unfocused, her lips pulled into a pained O.

'Pleeeeaaase,' she gasped.

Her body stiffened. Her face slackened. For a moment, her lips hitched into an Elvis curl. Then she started writhing in ecstasy. Gasps became howls, and for a mad moment, she shrieked, until the tendon-baring intensity strangled the possibility of sound. She convulsed, jerked to the plucking of inner strings.

Then suddenly she was back, whimpering, 'Oh-my-gawd-oh-my-gawd—'

'AGAIN?'

'Oh-please-yes!' Swallow, then, 'Yes-yes-yes-yes!' with every quick breath.

Then she was coming again, and the camera jerked yet farther up.

Thomas exploded from his chair. 'Are you fucking kidding me!'

The woman's braincase had been sawed open. A flea-circus of pins and wires formed a scaffold over the convoluted neural tissue. Lobes glistened in the light.

'Calm down, Mr Bible,' Agent Atta said.

Thomas clutched his scalp, fairly yanked his hair. 'Do you realize I could fucking *sue you* for showing me this . . . this . . . What the fuck *is this*?'

'WOULD YOU LIKE THE CONTROLS?'

'The disc arrived by mail in Quantico, Virginia, the day before yesterday.'

'So this is your fucking *mail*? What? You belong to the rape-of-the-month club or something?'

'As far as we can tell,' Shelley Atta said hesitantly, 'the woman in the video was not sexually assaulted.'

'YOU ARE FREE,' the ocean-voice croaked. 'YOU KNOW THIS? YOU MAY LEAVE ANY TIME YOU WISH.'

Thomas clicked pause. An image of the woman biting her lower lip froze on the screen. He found himself looking away, around the claustrophobic confines of his office. The air seemed thick with exhalations. Someone smelled like coleslaw.

'Tell us,' the other woman, Samantha, said, 'do you know the whereabouts of—'

'No,' Thomas interrupted. 'I'm not saying anything until you tell me what this is about. I'm a psychologist, remember? I'm familiar with informal interrogation tactics, and I refuse to cooperate until you stop playing games and tell me *just what the fuck is going on.*'

Agent Atta scowled at him. Agent Gerard stared blankly at the frozen screen.

'Let me tell you what we do know,' Samantha Logan said. 'According to Biometrics, the woman is Cynthia Powski, or "Cream", a porn starlet from Escondido, California, who was reported missing last month. Our analysts assure us the images are real, and the neurosurgeons we've consulted insist the level of . . . manipulation depicted is quite possible. What you just witnessed is real, Professor Bible. As bizarre as it sounds, someone is abducting people and screwing with their brains.'

'People?' Thomas asked, his ears buzzing. 'You mean this woman isn't the first?'

Agent Logan nodded.

Suddenly Thomas understood. 'You're looking for a neurosurgeon . . .'

He thought of the previous night.

'According to our research,' Shelley Atta said, 'you were roommates with Neil Cassidy at Princeton, weren't you?'

'Of course I was— You think *Neil* did this?'

'We're almost certain of it.'

Thomas waved his hands wide, as though warding away something with more momentum than his world could handle. 'No. *No.* Look, you don't know Neil. There's simply no way he could have done this. No way.' Even as he spoke, he could see him, Neil, grinning in the porch light, his teeth Crest-commercial straight.

'And why do you say that, professor?' Agent Logan asked.

'Because Neil is sane. When my life goes crazy, when I have difficulty distinguishing up from down, I call Neil – that's how sane he is. Whoever's doing this has suffered some kind of psychotic breakdown. Statistically, the chances of something like that happening to men my age is almost nil.'

'So you and Neil are close?' Agent Gerard said.

Numb nod.

'How close?' Agent Atta asked.

'Bum-buddy close. What fucking business is it of yours?' Thomas paused. He was letting his temper get the best of him – and letting these Feds push his buttons. *Think clear*, he reminded himself. *Think straight.* But he couldn't squeeze the writhing images of Cynthia Powski from his thoughts. He could still hear her moan, it seemed. He could even smell her sweat.

'Look,' he continued evenly. 'Your primary suspect is a very close friend of mine. And you know what? If we were talking about somebody I didn't know, say the chief of neurosurgery at Johns Hopkins, I'd probably be more than willing to play this game with you. But I know how these things work. You're fishing for something. It could be general information, or it could be something specific. The bottom line is that I have no way of knowing just what you're fishing for, which means I have no way of knowing whether I'm helping my buddy or digging him a deeper hole.'

'You don't trust us?' Agent Logan asked.

'Are you kidding me?'

'We're the good guys, Professor Bible,' Agent Atta said.

'Sure you are. Do you have any idea just how *bad* people are at reasoning? It's terrifying. Add to that the contradictory interests typically generated by hierarchies, like the FBI, where career-friendly decisions are so often at odds with truth-friendly decisions. Add to that the emergency repeal of the constitutional provisions guaranteeing due process—'

'It would be stupid to trust us,' Atta said, her tone tired and disgusted. 'Irrational.'

'Exactly,' Thomas said flatly. 'One might even say insane.'

CHAPTER TWO

August 17th, 9.38 a.m.

Except for two young girls with piercing eyes and pierced eyebrows, the train was empty. When they glimpsed him watching them, Thomas looked away, at once discomfited and scornful. He studied the eternal Hudson instead, trying to think away the fear that churned his gut.

'Perhaps when the next person dies,' Agent Atta had said before leaving his office. Thomas had thought of calling Neil then and there, to warn him, to question him, something, but had stopped short of actually punching the number. He needed to see him, he realized. He needed to see his reaction.

Perhaps when the next person . . .

It was strange how easily the obvious escaped people in the press of events. So much was seen without seeing, understood without understanding. Thomas had overreacted in his office, had dismissed something that had screamed for careful consideration. But how could anyone think clearly after watching that . . . that neuroporno or whatever it was?

Besides, Neil was his best friend. Closer than even his brother, Charlie.

It had to be some kind of mistake.

Even so, something in Agent Atta's look haunted him. *Not another one*, her eyes had said. Another intimate of another perp, claiming there was no way their buddy/son/husband could do something like that. And she was right. As a rule, people judged themselves according to their intentions and others according to results. In study after study, individuals ranked themselves as more charitable, more compassionate, more conscientious than others, not because they in fact were – how could they be when they were just as much others as they were selves? – but because they wanted to be these things and were almost entirely blind to the fact that others wanted the same. Intentions were all important when it came to self-judgement, and pretty much irrelevant when it came to judging others. The only exceptions, it turned out, were loved ones.

That was what it meant to be a 'significant' other: to be included in the circle of delusions that everyone used to exempt themselves.

And then there was Cynthia Powski, trembling, gasping, squirming as though rolling a squash ball between her thighs.

MORE?

Pleeeeaaase . . .

But what was he supposed to say? 'Neil? Oh, *that* psychopath . . . Yeah, we polished a forty of whiskey at my house last night. In fact, he's passed out on my fold-out couch right now.'

Was he supposed to say that?

No. They hadn't earned his trust. There was no way he would turn in one of his oldest and closest friends, not without hearing his side first.

There were always sides.

The doorbell had rung at exactly 7.58 the previous evening. Thomas knew this because Ripley and Frankie had been begging him to watch *Austin Powers*, which was on at 8.00, all through dinner. He had just finished loading the dishwasher, and Frankie was throwing a tantrum in the living room, demanding he unlock the parental controls.

Thomas had swung open the door while telling Frankie to hold his bloody horses, and there was Neil, waving at the moths and midges twirling about the porch light.

'What the hell are you doing here?'

Neil beamed his best panty-remover smile, held up a brown paper bag. He was dressed at his nondescript best: khaki shorts, hindu sandals, and a black nano-T-shirt with a panel playing and replaying some clip of Marilyn Monroe swimming naked in a black-and-white pool. Thanks to his lean build and the jaunty, jockish way he carried himself, he looked more like an undergraduate hoping to score some weed than a respected neurosurgeon. Only his face advertised otherwise. No matter how expressive, it always seemed to flex about something inveterate and imperturbable, as though he had been a boxer or a Tibetan lama in his most recent previous life.

His minivan loomed in the driveway behind him.

'Found myself in need of some liquid therapy,' he said.

'Dad!' Ripley cried out in her snottiest voice. 'It's, like, *starting* already!'

'Austin Powers,' Thomas said in explanation.

'Smashing, baby,' Neil said, clapping him on the shoulder.

An hour later, Thomas realized he had become quite drunk. Ripley was curled around cushions, fast asleep between him and Neil. Frankie was sitting avidly on the floor in front of the screen, laughing as Austin dodged booby-bullets.

'Aren't you tired?' he asked his son.

'Nooooooo.'

Thomas looked apologetically at Neil. 'I promised I would watch it with them.' Ever since the divorce, the kids had become particularly exacting when it came to promises. He sometimes wondered how many penny-ante pledges it would take to dig him out of the hole he and Nora had shoveled together.

Neil laughed, nodded at Frankie who rocked like a heroin junkie beneath a close-up of Austin. 'Just think,' Neil said. 'Right now your son's brain is being rewired by signals from outer space.'

Thomas snorted, though he wasn't so sure he found the comment funny. It was an old college game of theirs, describing everyday events in pseudo-scientific terms. Since science looked at everything in terms of quantity and function instead of quality and intention, the world it described could sound frighteningly alien. Neil was entirely right, of course: Frankie's brain *was* being rewired by signals from outer space. But he was also just a kid enjoying something silly on TV.

'And,' Thomas replied, 'any minute now molecules from my large intestine will trigger nerve impulses inside of your nose.'

Neil frowned at him, his eyes luminous with reflected screens. Then he gagged and laughed all at once, pulling his nano-T over his nose. Black-and-white Marilyn kicked across the sides of an oblong pyramid.

The room thundered with machine-gun fire. Frankie turned with what he called his 'squishy face' and cried, 'You *stink*, Daddy!'

'Shhh,' Thomas admonished. 'You know how mad Ripley gets.'

'I have mallcools in my nose too!' Frankie chortled to Neil. 'Stinky ones.'

Instead of humor, there was a flash of anger in Neil's gaze, so quick that Thomas was certain he had imagined it.

Thomas had shrugged, flashed his son and his friend a dopey guilty-as-charged smile. 'I had KFC for lunch.'

After putting down the kids – or the little Gideons as Neil liked to call them – Thomas had found Neil checking out the books on the living room shelves. The overhead lights glared, making a ghost of Marilyn and her naked breast-stroke across his chest.

Thomas nodded at the shirt. 'Kind of sexist, don't you think?'

Neil turned and tilted his head, his trademark one-shoulder shrug. 'So is biology.'

Thomas made a face.

'Where's your book?' Neil asked, running his eyes across the landscape of titled spines. Some of them were beaten and battered, others shiny new.

Thomas grimaced the way he always did when his book was mentioned. 'In the basement with the others.'

Neil smiled. 'Been demoted, huh?'

Thomas returned to the couch, eyed the full shots of whiskey Neil had poured, decided to take a swig of beer instead.

'So what's up, Neil? How are things at Bethesda?'

As much as he loved the guy, it irritated Thomas the way he always had to press him for the details of his life. It seemed part and parcel of a more sweeping inequity that haunted their relationship. Neil had always been elusive, but not in a secretive or suspicious way. It was more aristocratic, as if something in his bloodline exempted him from full disclosure.

Neil turned from the shelves. His face looked pale and blank in the lights. 'Actually, there's nothing at Bethesda.'

Thomas cocked his head, not quite sure whether to believe him. 'You quit? Neil, you should've—'

'I didn't quit.'

'You were fired?'

'I never worked there, Goodbook.' He paused as though out of breath. 'Bethesda was, ah . . . Jesus, I don't know how to say it without sounding cheesy. Bethesda was, well . . . just a cover.'

Thomas scowled. 'Now you're screwing with me.'

Neil shook his head, laughing. He held out both hands, like a prophet or a politician or something. 'No. I'm serious. I've never even set foot in Bethesda.'

'But then . . .'

'What have I been doing?'

Thomas stood blinking. 'Are you kidding me? All this time you've been *lying* about where you worked? Neil . . .'

'It's not like that, Goodbook. It's not like that at all. Lying about Bethesda was part of my job.'

'Part of your job?'

'I was working for the Man. For the NSA. When they tell you to lie, you lie, no matter who it is, and God help you if you don't.'

'The NSA?'

More laughter. 'Unfuckingbelievable, huh? I was a spy, Goodbook. A fucking science spook! Reverse-engineering God's own technology!'

Thomas laughed as well, but like someone bullied into doing so. It was strange the way the company of intimates could make lunacy seem almost normal. Or maybe not. They were the baseline, after all; what we all use to sort the mad from the sane.

'I knew this would freak you out,' Neil continued. 'Which is why . . .' He scooped up the bottle of whiskey and banged it on the coffee table.

Thomas flinched.

What was it about lies that made them seem so pedestrian? Everyone lied all the time – Thomas knew the statistics, knew that men lied primarily to promote themselves, while women lied to spare others' feelings, and so on. But it was more than a matter of typical patterns or brute frequencies. There was something *essential* about lies, something that ranked them alarmingly low on the list of slights and injuries. A toolbox wasn't a toolbox unless it had a pair of pliers – something to twist or bend with.

'But why did you do it?' Thomas had asked. 'Why join . . . *them.*'

Neil had this peculiar way of smiling sometimes. 'Sly' was too small a word to describe it. Even 'conspiratorial' seemed to lack the requisite number of syllables.

'For the love of my country,' he said. 'Gotta protect the Fatherland.'

'Bullshit. You a patriot? Please.'

'Hey, man,' Neil crowed, 'my high school is, like, way, *way* cooler than your high school.'

Thomas refused to laugh. It was an old joke of theirs, referring to the way patriotism was simply 'school spirit' writ large, a mechanism used to generate solidarity, to enforce consensus and conformity, particularly during times of crisis or competing social interests.

'So why did you do it?'

Neil slouched back into the couch. 'For the freedom.'

'Freedom?'

'You have no idea, Goodbook. The resources. The lack of constraints.' He paused as though debating the wisdom of his next words. 'I now know more about the brain than any man alive.'

'More bullshit.'

'No. I do. I really do.'

Thomas snorted. 'Prove it.'

Neil had flashed that self-same smile.

'Patience, Goodbook. Patience.'

'So what were you doing?'

'You wouldn't believe it. It was straight out of Mengele 101.'

Thomas swallowed, struggling to absorb this. 'Try me.'

'It started small fry: experimentation with sensory deprivation interrogation techniques. They gave us this theo-terrorist, let's call him Ali Baba, who they thought could be key to unlocking several American-Muslim cells. We interviewed him several times via a sham fellow inmate, discovered what he thought his execution would look like, and more importantly, what he thought *paradise* would look like. Then we arranged his execution—'

'You *what*?'

Neil shook his head. 'Always so literal . . . We arranged his *sham* execution, making sure he recognized it by providing the cues he expected. But instead of killing him we simply put him under – *deep* under. Then we transferred him to a specially prepared sensory deprivation tank, pumped him full of MDMA variants and opiates, gave his body some time to acclimatize, then woke him up.'

'So what happened?'

'He awoke to nothingness, no sound, no light, no smell, no touch, and higher than a fucking kite. He tried screaming, thrashing, and all that – a brain in sensory limbo automatically attempts to generate feedback stimuli – but we'd induced motor paralysis to better prevent him from sensing himself. Besides, he had no choice but to feel good with the mickey we'd slipped him. When the MRI showed us his visual centres spontaneously lighting up, we introduced him to God.'

'You what?'

'We introduced him to God, this ultra-slick intelligence specialist from Bahrain. Ali Baba literally thought he'd died and gone to heaven. Let me tell you, when God's asking the questions, people answer.'

The horror had to be plain on his face. That and the confusion. Neil always seemed to speak to different parts of your head, to broadcast on multiple frequencies – it was one of the things that made his company at once so entertaining and nerve-wracking. But this?

'And . . .'

'And nothing. The guy was a dud. But after we refined the techniques, especially when we began channelling their hallucinations with VR interventions, we learned plenty, trust me. From the theo-terrorists, at least. The eco-terrorists were tougher nuts.'

'So that's what you've been doing all these years?'

'Christ no! That's how I started. After the preliminary success of the SenDep program, I was identified as a rising star. They transferred me from the psychomanipulation division to the neuro. They opened the vault, good buddy, and let me wander the wonderful world of black ops.'

Thomas lowered his beer. 'The NSA has a neuromanipulation division.'

'You're surprised? Why do you think places like Washington or Beijing are infested with spies? *Because that's where the decisions are made.* Wherever important decisions are made, you find spies. And ultimately –' he tapped his temple with a finger – 'this is where *all* the decisions are made. So why not?'

Thomas poured two more shots and handed one to Neil. 'Because it's immoral,' he said. 'And just plain creepy.'

'Immoral? *You* think it's immoral?'

'Fucking A, I do.'

Neil scowled and smiled at once. 'Weren't you the one always arguing that morality was a sham? That we're simply meat puppets deluded into believing we live in a moral and meaningful world?'

Thomas had nodded. 'Ah, the Argument.'

The Argument. Its mere mention seemed to open a pit in his stomach. Evidence of an old atrocity.

'Well,' Neil had said, 'we *are* talking about terror suspects here.'

'Bullshit again. That's just part of the Paleolithic dreamworld people live in. They estimate threats as if they still live in a stone-age community of a hundred and fifty people rather than a world of billions. Terrorism is theatre, you know that. Slippery bathtubs are more of a threat. Christ, campaigns against autoerotic asphyxiation would save more lives! The powers that be are just milking our psychological vulnerabilities to secure their agenda.'

A derisive glance. 'And what about Moscow?'

'That has precious little to—'

'You know,' Neil interrupted, 'it's hard not to feel sorry for them, sometimes, even when you know for a fact that they've had a hand in dozens of deaths. Our heads are just filled with so much crap. The older ones, in particular, think they're Captain Kirk or something. Our evil mind-scanning technology is no match for the *human spirit.* I even had one old theo-terrorist tell me that his soul was his citadel, and that God guarded the gate.'

He paused for a moment, as though pensive with regret. His face was drawn.

'What did you say?' Thomas asked lamely. He still couldn't believe he was having this conversation.

'That I could give a rat's ass about his spirit. That it was his brain I was interested in. That his will was simply one more neural mechanism, and that once it was offline, he would quite happily tell me everything our field operatives needed to know. And I was right. We had moved far beyond sensory deprivation interrogations by that time. Using all the imaging data on the brain's executive functions – you know, Roach's famous experiments on the differences between weak-willed and strong-willed individuals – we simply isolated the offending circuits and shut them off. It was as easy as flicking a switch.' His laugh was more a breath-filled snort. 'Who would have guessed, huh?'

'Guessed what?'

'That all that evil mind-scanner stuff would be so laughably far from the truth. Why design a machine to read thoughts when all you have to do is shut down a few circuits and have your subject read them out for you?'

Dumbstruck, Thomas stared at him. Neil, his best friend, was saying that he was one of the bad guys.

Wasn't he?

'I . . .' Thomas began in a thin voice. 'I don't know what to say . . . let alone think.'

'Fucked up, huh?'

Thomas studied the shot-glass before him, the ring of hard light across the rim. 'It's not so simple.'

'But it is, Goodbook. Desires arise from the deepest of the brain's mechanisms. It's like plastic surgery. There's what? *Five* high-production channels entirely devoted to plastic surgery on the web now? Evolution has hardwired us to assess the fitness of prospective mates in terms of visual appearances. Once our tools and techniques allow us to manipulate skin and bone, desire does the rest. The old taboos are gradually rinsed away, and before you know it, the cosmetic surgery industry is producing a quarter of the country's bio-waste, and makeovers require bone-saws instead of dainty little pencils and brushes. Where once we used to paint ourselves to conform to desire, now we *recarve* ourselves. Same with designer babies. Or gene-doping in sports. You name it. Neuromanipulation. Neurocosmetic surgery. Are you telling me you don't think it's inevitable?'

Thomas glared at him, breathing evenly. 'No. I'm telling you I don't think it's right.'

Neil shrugged. 'If you mean that most people would *disapprove*, then you're correct.' He had looked away while saying this. Now his eyes flashed dark and menacing. 'But why should I give a fuck?'

Thomas belted down another shot, not because he wanted it, but because it seemed safer than replying. It was funny how easily a lifetime of learning could be forgotten, how all the layers of sophistication could be stripped away, leaving a wounded boy, a hurt and mystified friend.

'Have you an arm like God?' Neil suddenly asked, obviously quoting something. He laughed.

'I don't understand.'

'It's *his* program,' Neil had said. 'So why not just enjoy the ride?'

Booze was never a good thing when having conversations like this. The content came through loud and clear; it was the emotional significance that was filtered. Booze had a way of making sharp things fuzzy and fuzzy things sharp.

'Why tell me this now?' Thomas asked.

'Because,' Neil said, reapplying his mischievous smile, 'I've quit.'

'But . . .' Thomas paused. Suddenly it dawned on him that Neil was doing far more than breaking a nondisclosure agreement, or even committing a felony for that matter. This stuff had to be *classified* – which meant his friend was committing treason. They were treading water in the deep end of the pool.

Death-penalty deep.

'Just like that?' Thomas asked.

'Just like that.'

'I didn't think they let you guys quit.'

'No. They don't.'

'But they're making an exception for you.'

Another smile, a second coat of mischievousness. He ran a finger along a dark braid in the couch's upholstery. 'They have no choice.'

'No choice,' Thomas repeated, looking with dread at the brimming shot of whiskey before him. 'Why?'

'Because I've covered my bases,' Neil replied. 'I've been planning this for a long time.'

Despite the booze, Thomas suddenly felt very alert. Something told him he needed to be careful.

'So you *do* think it's wrong . . . what you did, I mean.'

Neil leaned forward, elbows on knees like a basketball coach.

'The world is on the brink, Goodbook. I'm simply the first to cross over.'

Thomas knew what he was talking about, but for some reason found himself pretending otherwise. 'Brink. What brink?'

Neil wasn't buying. 'Is it the kids?'

'What are you talking about?'

'Are they the reason?'

'The reason for what?'

'The reason you moved back into Disney World?'

The confusion, the double-take disorientation, evaporated, and

Thomas suddenly felt focused the way only whiskey and outrage could make possible. 'You're drunk, Neil. Leave them out of this.'

Disney World was their pet term for the world as understood by the masses, one papered over with conceit after comforting conceit. A world anchored in psychological need rather than physical fact. A world with a billion heroes and happy endings, where the unknown was irrelevant and confronting your own weaknesses was the breakfast of losers.

'You know, I find it hard to remember what it's like living with one foot in both worlds. To know, on the one hand, that paternal love is simply nature's way of duping us into perpetuating our genes—'

'It's not *duping* . . . Look, Neil, you're really starting to piss me—'

'Not duping? Hmm. Then you tell me, why do you love your son?'

'Because he's my son.'

'And that's an explanation?'

Thomas had glared at his friend. 'The only one I need.'

'Evolution wouldn't have it any other way,' Neil had said. 'It takes a lot of commitment to raise a child to reproductive age.'

Thomas tossed back his shot, clenched his teeth in revulsion and dismay. What the fuck was going on?

'Because you love your kids,' Neil continued, 'you expend tremendous resources on them, you train them, feed them, protect them, you would even die for them. You do all the things that *your genes happen to require*, and for reasons that have nothing to do with the harsh realities of natural selection.' Neil frowned, leaned back into the cushions. He hooked his toes on the coffee table. 'And that's not duping?'

'They're just different descriptions of the same thing,' Thomas said. 'Different angles.'

Neil paused to slam back his whiskey. 'C'mon,' he continued, gasping. 'This is *your* argument I'm making, Goodbook. Didn't you spend an entire chapter listing all the ways we bullshit ourselves to feel better? And how about your cognitive psych classes? Didn't you tell me that you spend the first two weeks discussing the relationship between gut feeling and socialization? How all those movies urging people to "follow their hearts" were simply another way for culture to reinforce the status qu—?'

'Enough!' Thomas cried. 'What are you saying, Neil? Are you actually trying to talk me out of *loving my children*?'

Again the one-shoulder shrug. 'Just saying,' he had said, his manner both offhand and nightmarish. Marilyn swam ethereally across his broad chest.

'Just reminding you what you already know.'

Speechless, Thomas did what most men did when at a loss for words: he turned on the TV. The lights automatically dimmed. The quiet seemed to sizzle beneath the television blare.

He could feel Neil sitting on the couch to his left, watching him. That annoying Coca-Cola pop-up – the 'gurgle-gurgle' one his kids loved – flashed onto the screen. Surgical white flickered across the room. He clicked through the news sites, letting the fragments of info-chatter seal the hard moment that had passed between them. An update on the French eco-riots. A retrospect on the causes of the Chinese economic crisis. A tasteless story about Ray Kurzweil's recent death. Accusations that Wal-Mart had installed hidden low-field MRIs to monitor their employees.

Neil reached out to pour them two more shots of whiskey. 'I guess you have no choice,' he said.

Thomas gingerly raised the shot-glass, downed it. He was drinking mechanically now, a talent he had picked up in the final days of his marriage. 'What do you mean?' he asked, pretending to watch the screen. The high-definition images seemed to drain away all his anger, make his world as small and trivial as it actually was.

'To rationalize. To set up shop in Disney World.'

Thomas shook his head. 'Look. Neil. All this stuff was great in college. I mean we were soooo radical, even in Skeat's class, mopping the floor with lit majors, freaking people out around the bong . . .' A pained grimace. 'But *now*? C'mon. Give it a rest.'

Neil was watching him carefully. 'That doesn't make it any less real, Goodbook.' He gestured to the TV, where lines of Muscovites stretching out into a haze of grey snow shared the screen with talking heads and warm studio lighting. 'Just look. It's *ending*, just as Skeat said it would. No virulent pandemic, no mass environmental collapse, no thermonuclear Armageddon, just mobs and mobs of people, hominids pretending to be angels, clutching at rules that don't exist, feeding, fighting, fucking . . .'

Thomas snorted. 'Neil . . .'

'So where are your knockdown arguments? Outside the threat of coercion, why should anybody play along? Why should we help granny across the street? Because it *feels* right? Please. Anyone can train a cat to shit in a box. Because of what philosophers say? Double please. We can blah, blah, blah forever, come up with an endless stream of flattering bullshit, redefine this and redefine that, and in the end all we've done is confirm you cognitive psychologists and your Christmas catalogue of ways we bullshit to make ourselves feel better.'

Thomas laughed. Emotionally, it always felt like standing on marbles when he was drunk. Annoyed one minute, amused another. In balance, and out.

'So,' Neil pressed, 'where are your knockdown arguments?'

'I have two,' Thomas said, raising the same number of thick-feeling fingers. 'Frankie and Ripley.'

Neil shook his head and smiled. Now it was his turn to feign interest in the images tumbling across the TV. He cradled his beer between steepled fingers. For the first time, Thomas saw past his own irritation and disbelief, and realized just how much stress his best friend must be suffering.

The NSA . . . unbelievable.

On the screen, images of armed men shooting into the sky floated beneath a GE corporate banner: Islamic fighters in some breakaway Chinese province.

'Theo-terrorists,' Neil said.

'I think,' Thomas replied, 'the technical term would be "insurgents."'

'Whatever. You know how we dealt with them in the Neuromanipulation Division?'

Marilyn tittered at the edge of the pool on his T-shirt.

'How?'

'Love,' Neil said. 'We made them love us.'

Thomas had stared blankly at the screen.

'As easy as flicking a switch.'

This had been the pattern, since their first days rooming together at Princeton. Neil with his questions. Neil with his demands. Neil with his mocking replies, his outrageous claims. All of it hedged with *just-fucking-with-you* glances and a *what's-your-problem* tone. Just as no two people are exactly equal in terms of capacities, no friendships are perfectly mutual. Neil had always been quicker, better looking, more articulate – inequities that had always expressed themselves through the complicated weave of their relationship.

And Thomas had always been more forgiving.

'But hey,' Neil drawled after a moment, 'I came here to celebrate, not to break your balls.'

Thomas shot him a humorless look. Black-and-white Marilyn seemed to be drowning across his chest, but it was just a trick of the angle. 'I was beginning to think the two were indistinguishable.'

'I'm sorry, man. Just a mood, you know. Here.' He splashed two more shots of whiskey, then raised his in a toast. After a reluctant heartbeat, Thomas raised his in turn. He could feel himself sway ever so slightly.

'I've escaped,' Neil said. There was something embarrassingly direct about his blue-eyed gaze. 'I've completely escaped.'

Thomas had been too afraid to ask which . . .

The NSA or Disney World?

CHAPTER THREE

August 17th, 11.15 a.m.

Plagued by a curious breathlessness, Thomas crowded off the MTA North with a dozen or so others, most of them chatty octogenarians. He'd lost count of how many times he'd shaken his head and pinched his eyes, but images of Cynthia Powski, her desire turned inside out, returned with every blink. Again and again, like an adolescent dream. He didn't begin shaking until he started crossing the hot-plate asphalt of the parking lot.

Sunlight glared across a thousand windshields.

Everything had pockets, hidden depths that could be plumbed but never quite emptied. A look, a friend, a skyscraper – it really didn't matter. Everything was more complicated than it seemed. Only ignorance and stupidity convinced people otherwise.

There was something unreal about his house as it floated nearer around the curve. In the final days of their marriage, it had been a curious image of dread, a white-sided container filled with shouts and recriminations, and the long silences that cramp your gut. It had occurred to him that the real tragedy of marital breakdown was not so much the loss of love as the loss of place. 'Who are you?' he used to cry at Nora. It was one of the few refrains he meant genuinely, at least once the need to score points had climbed into the driver's seat. 'No. Really. Who are you?' It began as an entreaty, quickly became an accusation, then inevitably morphed into its most catastrophic implication: 'What are you doing here?'

Here. My home.

To drift across that final, fatal line was to be locked in a house with a stranger. Or even worse, to become that stranger.

He could remember driving back the evening after she had moved out, rallying himself with thoughts of how peaceful it would be, how nice to finally have his *home* back. Kick back and crank the stereo. But when he opened the door, the bachelor bravado had dropped through the soles of his feet – of course. For a time he simply sat on the living room floor, as vacant as the rooms about him, listening to the eternal hum of the fridge. He remembered shouting at the kids to pipe down, even though they were gone. He had cried after that, long and hard.

Home. Life to the pale of property lines.

He had struggled hard to build something new, another place. It was partly why stupid things like plants or appliances could strike him with teary-eyed pride. He had worked so hard.

And now this.

He slammed the car into park, fairly ran across the lawn.

'Neil!' he shouted as he burst through the doorway. He hadn't really expected anyone to answer: Neil's minivan was gone.

Bartender growled and yawned, then trundled over to him, tail flapping. An old dog's greeting.

'Uncle Cass is gone, Bart,' Thomas said softly. He peered across the living room gloom, at the showroom tidiness. The smell of spilled whiskey bruised the air.

'Uncle Cass has fled the scene.'

He stood motionless next to the sofa, the static in his head roaring loud, thoughts and images in parallel cascades, as though boundaries between times and channels had broken down. Cynthia Powski, as slick as seals, moaning. The Ocean Voice mentioning an argument. Neil saying, *As easy as flicking the switch . . .*

The Ocean Voice mentioning an argument . . .

It can't be. No way.

He thought of Neil working for the NSA, rewiring living breathing people, cheerfully lying for all these years. He thought of their Princeton days, of the fateful class they took with Professor Skeat. He thought of how they used to argue the end of the world at parties, not the end that was coming, but the end that had already passed.

He thought of the Argument.

Ocean Voice. Neil. The FBI. Cynthia Powski.

No fucking way.

Thomas nearly cried out when the door bell rang.

He peered through the curtains, saw Mia standing impatiently on the porch. Thomas opened the door, doing his best to look normal.

'Hi, Mia.'

Over his neighbor's shoulder, he glimpsed a white Ford – a new Mustang hybrid – driving slowly down the street.

'Everything OK?' Mia asked. 'The kids saw your car in the driveway. I thought I should—'

'No. Just forgot a couple of important things for a committee presentation this afternoon.' He leaned out the door, saw Frankie and Ripley standing on Mia's porch.

'*Daddeee!*' Frankie called.

Strange, the power of that word. Pretty much every kid used it, the same name on millions of innocent lips, over and over, and yet it seemed to thrive on this universality. You could feel sorry for all the Wangs and Smiths – who wanted to be one among millions? – but somehow 'Daddy' was different. Thomas had visited colleagues whose kids called them by name: 'Hey, Janice, can I have supper at Johnny's? Please-please?' There was something wrong about it, something that triggered an exchange of slack looks – a premonition of some budding rot.

Dad. A single name on a billion lips, and nothing could undo it. No court order. No lifestyle choice. No divorce.

Thomas blinked at the heat in his eyes, called back laughing to his son, asked him if he was being good for Mia. Frankie bounced up and down, as though he waved from a distant mountaintop.

Maybe there were heroes after all.

As much as he longed to spend a moment with his boy, he apologized to Mia and climbed back into his car. Among the wild peculiarities of the previous night's drinking session was something Neil had said about Nora, a throwaway comment really, about talking to her or something. But of course that was impossible, given that Nora was in San Francisco, which was why Thomas had the kids on this, the busiest of all summer weeks.

What was it he had said? Something. Something . . . Enough to warrant sharing a word or two.

He called out her name to his palmtop as he accelerated down the street, but all he got was her inbox recording. He told himself she might know something. At least that was what he allowed himself to think. The real concern, the worry that clamped his foot to the accelerator was altogether different.

Maybe she was in danger.

Think clear, he reminded himself. *Think straight.*

The Argument.

Ocean Voice had said he was making an argument, as well as 'making' love. But what argument? Was it *the* Argument?

Was it Neil holding the camera? Was he the shadow behind the occluded frame?

The Argument, as they would come to call it, was something from their undergraduate days at Princeton. Both he and Neil had been scholarship students, which meant they had no money for anything. Where their more affluent friends bar-hopped or jetted home for the holidays, they would buy a few bottles of Old English Malt Liquor, or 'Chateau Ghetto' as Neil used to call it, and get fucked up in their room.

Everyone debated things in college. It was a reflex of sorts, an attempt to recover the certainty of childhood indoctrination for some, a kind of experimental drug for others. Neil and Thomas had definitely belonged to the latter group. Questions – that was how humans made ignorance visible, and the two of them would spend hours asking question after question. Grounds became flimsy stage props. Assumptions became religious chicanery.

For a time it seemed that nothing survived. Nothing save the Argument.

Like most, Thomas had moved on. Humans were hardwired for conviction, thoughtless or otherwise, and had to work to suspend judgment – work hard. He had taken the low road, allowing the assumptions to crowd out the suspicions. The years passed, the children grew, and he found himself packing all the old questions away, even as he continued playing Professor Bible, destroyer of worlds in the classroom. Nothing killed old revelations quite so effectively as responsibility and routine.

But Neil . . . For whatever reason, Neil had never let go. Thomas humored his ramblings, of course, the way you might humor old high school football stories, or any reminiscence of irrelevant glory. 'Oh, yeah, you sacked him real good.' He even wondered whether it was a sign of some hidden distance between them, an inability to connect outside of on campus residences and off-campus bars.

Last night had simply been more of the same, hadn't it?

He was trying to talk me out of loving my kids.

Peekskill glared beyond the windshield, whipping this way and that as Thomas gunned the straightaways and squealed around the turns. He peered like a pensioner over the steering wheel when he turned down Nora's crescent. The sight of her black Cherokee in the driveway made him numb.

So much for her trip.

His heart sucked ice-cubes in his chest.

'San Francisco my ass,' he muttered.

Special Agent Samantha Logan put her white Mustang into park and let it idle. She flicked her cigarette outside, watched Thomas Bible through the windshield. He trotted up to the front door of a grey-brick bungalow. He looked agitated.

Somehow she'd known he was heading home. She'd followed him from Columbia to the West 116th subway station, then raced north to beat him to Peekskill – halfway to fucking Poughkeepsie! Somehow she'd known there was more to Thomas Bible than met the eye.

If it wasn't for Shelley Atta and her insistence that Bible see the BD, they might already have what they needed. But *no*, the idiot thought Cynthia Powski would rattle the man into compliance. As if anyone with two marbles to rub together would be anything other than outraged by Neil Cassidy's little 'sitcum', as her sometime-partner Danny Gerard had wickedly dubbed it. When Atta had mentioned her plan, the first thing Samantha had wondered was how she herself would react. But that was the problem with pricks like Shelley Atta: they just couldn't step outside their own skin. Or didn't care to.

Samantha Logan had understood why Thomas Bible had kicked them out of his office. She had even secretly applauded him for doing it. But why had he raced home afterward? And why had he raced here immediately after that?

Just where was *here*, anyway?

*

Thomas paused in the shade of the porch. He'd been to Nora's 'new place' more times than he could count, picking up the kids, delivering the kids, and once to help her carry in a new refrigerator – something he still alternately congratulated and cursed himself for doing (they had ended up screwing on her tacky living room couch). And yet despite the frequency of his visits, nothing about the place felt familiar. He was an interloper here, an unwelcome passer-through. The long low porch with its impenetrable windows, its bustling planters and sun-hanging geraniums, its whitewashed railing and black aluminum door, had always seemed to personify Nora somehow.

And Nora no longer loved him.

But there was more to his hesitation; there was Neil and the FBI as well. Why had Neil mentioned her? And what was it he had said? Something. Something . . . Thomas rubbed his face in frustration.

This isn't happening.

He simply stood and breathed, stared like an idiot at the closed door. The house seemed preternaturally quiet. When he blinked, he no longer saw Cynthia Powski, he saw *inside.*

Signs of struggle. Lines of blood roped across hardwood floors . . .

No way. No fucking way.

A fly buzzed in the corner of the window's concrete sill, caught in a dead spider's woolly webbing. Another bounced across the opaque glass, summer quick. Sunlight streamed through the railing, casting oblong bars of brilliance across the floor. One of them warmed his left shoe.

Nora. Even after so much bitterness, so much dismay and disbelief, he continually worried about her living all alone. Patronizing concerns, he knew, but . . .

After so long. After trying so hard.

This is crazy!

He rapped the door, his knuckles lighter than air.

He waited in silence.

A dog barked from some neighbor's backyard. Kids squealed through a series of swimming pool explosions. *Poosh . . . Poosh-poosh.*

No one answered the door.

Thomas pressed thumb and forefinger against the bridge of his nose, tried to massage away the ache. From over fences, a masculine voice shouted at what must have been the swimming children. Thomas could almost see the water making oil of sunlight. He could almost smell the chlorine.

He knocked again, harder and faster.

Quiet.

She probably *was* in San Francisco. She probably took a cab to the train station. Or maybe she went with what's-his-face, that young intern at her agency – didn't he live somewhere in Peekskill? He probably picked her up. Maybe Neil hadn't said anything about seeing Nora. There was no—

Thomas grasped the cool knob, twisted . . . only to have the door yanked out of his hands.

'Tommy—' Nora said, blinking at the ambient brightness beyond the eaves. She had a nimble brunette's face, with a model's pillow lips and large, hazel eyes that promised honesty and a shrewd accounting of favors. Her straight, short hair was as Irish fine as her skin was Irish pale. Staring at her, Thomas suddenly remembered dreaming of their wedding reception that very morning, and it seemed she had looked the way she looked now, like yearning, like sanctuary and regret . . .

Like the only woman he had ever truly loved.

'I-I can explain,' she said.

'Have you been crying?' Thomas asked. Beyond the confounded emotions, he felt relieved to the point of sobbing. At least she was safe. At least she was safe.

What the hell was he thinking? Neil a psychopath?

She itched an eye. 'No,' she said. 'What are you doing here? Where are the kids? Is everything okay?'

'The kids are fine. They're with Mia. I came . . . ah . . .'

She watched him.

'I came because Neil stopped by last night. He mentioned something about seeing you.' Thomas smiled, finally finding his stride. 'Since you'd told me you were going to San Francisco I thought I'd swing by to make sure everything is alright. *Is* everything alright?'

The question seemed to catch her off-guard, or perhaps it was the intensity of his concern. 'Everything's fine,' she said with a sour *what's-this-really-about* smile.

A strange moment passed between them as he stepped into the foyer, a memory of forgotten intimacy, perhaps. Their eyes locked.

'The San Francisco trip was bullshit, wasn't it?'

'Yes,' she said.

The exchange had been completely involuntary, or so it seemed to Thomas.

'Why, Nora? Why lie?' Resentment was back in the driver's seat.

Not like this . . . C'mon, you know better.

'Because . . .' Nora said lamely.

'*Because* . . . Christ, Nora, even fucking Frankie could do better than that.'

'Don't say that. Don't say "fucking Frankie".' You know I hate it when you say that.'

'How about San-fucking-Francisco? Or does that get under your skin too?'

'Screw you, Tommy,' Nora said. She turned toward the kitchen. She was wearing a light cotton dress, the kind that made men wish for gusts of naughty wind.

Thomas glanced down at his hands. They trembled ever so slightly. 'So what did you and Neil talk about?' he called.

'Not much,' Nora replied bitterly. She turned to address the granite counter-top. 'He didn't come to talk . . .' She laughed, as though marveling over carnal memories. Then she dared his astounded gaze, her expression tight with shame, resentment – all those things people use to digest their sins. 'He never does.'

Thomas stepped into the air-conditioned gloom.

It was funny how natural such things could seem, how easily you could convince yourself you knew all along. Even as he recoiled at the impossibility, buzzed through the slow-assembling implications, part of him whispered, *Of course.*

He forced the words past the hornet sting in the back of his throat. 'How long?' There was no certainty, no breath in his lungs, so he repeated himself just to be sure. 'How long have you been fucking my best friend?'

Nora and Neil . . . Neil and Nora . . .

Her eyes were swollen. She blinked tears and looked away, saying, 'You don't want to know.'

'While we were married,' Thomas said. 'Huh?'

Nora turned back, her expression somewhere between anguish and fury. 'I just . . . just needed him, Tommy. I just needed . . .' She struggled with her lips. 'More. I needed *more.*'

Thomas turned to the door, grabbed the handle.

'Have you seen him?' Nora called, her voice half-panicked. 'I m-mean . . . do you know where he is?'

She loved him. His ex-wife loved Neil Cassidy. His best friend.

He turned and grabbed her. 'You want to know where Neil is?' he cried. He cuffed her on the side of the face. He clenched his teeth and shook her. She would be so easy to break! He started pressing her backward. But then, in some strange corner of nowhere, he could hear himself whisper, *This is a jealousy response, an ancient adaptation meant to minimize the risk of reproductive losses . . .*

He dropped his hands, dumbfounded.

'Neil,' he spat. 'Let me tell you something about Neil, Nora. He's fucking snapped. He's started killing people and making videos to send to the FBI. Can you believe it? Yeah! *Our* Neil. The FBI visited me this morning, showed me some of his handiwork. Our Neil is a fucking monster! He makes the Chiropractor or whatever they're calling him look like a choirboy!'

He paused, struck breathless by the look of horror on her face. He lowered his hands, backed toward the door.

'You're crazy,' she gasped.

He turned to the door.

'You're lying! *Lying*!'

He left the door open behind him.

The ground seemed to pitch beneath his feet. The walk to his car seemed more a controlled fall. He leaned against the door to catch his breath. The metal stung his palms, and he found himself thinking how when it came to heat, the whole world was a battery, sucking it up, then releasing it in a slow burn. A convertible rolled past, filled with teenagers shouting over subwoofers. He glared at them in a disconnected-from-consequences way.

Neil and Nora.

The Acura's interior was amniotic, the air was so hot. He placed trembling hands on the steering wheel, caressed the leather. Then he punched the dash five times in rapid succession.

'FUCK!' he roared.

It seemed the world was ending. That the Argument—

'Professor Bible?' he heard someone call. A woman.

He squinted up at her beautiful face. 'Agent Logan,' he managed to reply.

She smiled cautiously.

'Professor Bible, I think we need to talk.'

CHAPTER FOUR

August 17th, 11.56 a.m.

Thoughts like wasps at the beach, nagging, threatening, never really stinging. That's what it had been like. Of course he'd worried about Neil and Nora on occasion, but he had always decided to err on the side of trust. Trust.

And now look at him: stung beyond sensation.

Agent Logan had followed him back to his house so that he could drop off his car. Now he sat beside her in her Mustang, numb in more ways he would have thought possible. A wool-haired kid with a squeegee cleaned her windshield at an intersection, and Thomas found himself comforted by the sight of her rummaging through her purse for loose change. He even smiled at her gentle curses.

'Why you?' he asked after she had handed the kid several dimes and quarters.

'Pardon?'

'Why send *you* after me?'

'The boss thought I was your kind of people.'

'And what kind is that?'

'Honest,' she said with a wry smile. She looked away to make her left turn. 'Honest and confused.'

The bar was local, the kind of place that depended on the ebb and flow of the work day as much as the regularity of blacked-out sporting events. A TGIF, or something similar – Thomas literally couldn't remember. They paused at the entrance so that Sam could slip a five-dollar bill into a plastic Salvation Army donation bubble. Inside, one waitress stood at a faux-antique till, chatting with a woman who looked like the manager. It was completely deserted otherwise. Thomas followed Agent Logan to a front booth, feeling like an intruder despite all the signs of heavy human traffic. Compared to the sunny clamor of the street, the place seemed like a cave with dropped ceilings. It smelled of beer and sour cushions.

'So what happened back there?' Agent Logan asked, propping her elbows on their table.

Through the tinted window to her right, a parade of consumers marched along the sidewalk. A middle-class soccer mom. A brown-suited sales rep. A working-class *New Jersey Devils* fan. And on and on. Thomas pretended to be interested in them as he spoke.

'You know, I still remember what Neil told me at our wedding reception. He pulled me aside and pointed to Nora – she was dancing with her father, I think. "Now *that*," he said, "is a fine piece of tail, my friend." ' Thomas ran a hand over his face and stared across the bar's murky expanse. His laugh was pained. 'He was speaking from experience, I guess.'

When he closed his eyes he could see them together. Neil and Nora.

Agent Logan studied him for a moment, her eyes wide and full of sympathy. 'You know, Professor Bible, the systematic deception of intimates is a red flag for—'

'No,' Thomas exclaimed. 'Please . . . spare me your FBI profiling crap. You know who I am, what I do. There's no need to insult me with half-remembered course notes from Quantico.'

Agent Logan turned her face to the window, her expression unreadable.

Thomas shook his head. 'Look, I'm sorry. I really am. It's just that . . .'

'Just what, Professor Bible?'

'Call me, Tommy. Please.' He paused as the waitress, a pink-faced blond, set down coasters and beers.

'Do you know what dreams are, Agent Logan?'

'I must have dozed through that part at Quantico,' she said drily.

'Well our brains are plastic networks.' He paused, then added, 'Plastic like "malleable", not like your shoes.'

'Ouch,' Samantha said, grinning.

'All the behaviors generated by our brains arise from different neural configurations. In turn, these configurations arise in response to different stimuli from our environments – it's kind of like mini-evolution: those behaviors that allow us to successfully cope with our environments are reinforced. Reproduced. Those that do not are discarded, at least ideally.'

Even as he said this, he realized he was speaking more for his own sake than for hers. Pain had a way of bending your words into circles. Had it really come to this? Sitting with a stranger in a franchise bar, spilling his guts. Was he really this alone?

'So what does this have to do with dreams?'

Thomas shrugged. 'Well, some say that dreams allow our neural networks to reconfigure themselves in *possible* as opposed to actual circumstances. By dreaming of different situations, our brain actually prepares itself for different possible eventualities. Dreams allow our brain to cope.'

'Like training simulations?'

'Exactly.'

Samantha frowned. 'So what does that have to do with anything?'

Thomas wiped angrily at his tears. 'Because I never, not once, dreamed that anything like this could happen.' The fist he raised to his forehead somehow became a wrist pressed against his temple. '*Fuck . . .*'

Neil and Nora.

Thomas excused himself to make a call on his palmtop. He turned to watch Agent Logan from the middle of the abandoned dance floor. She stared out the window, the very picture of impatience and ambition – and all the more striking for it. Listening to the ring in the receiver, Thomas found himself wondering whether she had a significant other. Careerists tended to stay single—

'Hyu,' a rough voice answered.

'Hi, Mia,' Thomas said.

'Tommy, Jeeezus. I've been trying to reach you!'

A host of parental instincts came clutching. 'Phone was off. Why? What's wrong?'

'Nothing, really. It's just that Nora called and said she was coming to get the kids.'

'What did you tell her?'

'That I needed to talk to you first, and that I would call her back after.'

He heard Frankie shouting '*Daddy-Daddy-Daddeee!*' in the background. He imagined Ripley sitting by Mia's picture window, coloring, then an image of Cynthia Powski blotted her out.

'Forget she even called.'

'You sure? She sounded all weirded out on the phone. Wasn't she supposed to be in San Francisco?'

'She was. It turns out she was fucking an old friend instead.'

So easily spoken.

'Oh . . .'

'I have to go, Mia.'

'Are you okay, Tommy?'

'Can't talk now, Mia.'

He clicked the palmtop shut, slipped it into his blazer pocket. When he glanced up Agent Logan was watching him, her smile the sad smile of those stranded at the perimeter of painful events.

'Just had to check up on the kids,' he explained as he slid back into the booth.

Samantha smiled. 'Beautiful kids.'

He looked at her sharply.

'You need to ease up on the paranoia, Professor Bible. I followed you from Columbia, remember? I saw them on your neighbor's porch. Like I said, beautiful kids.'

Thomas scratched the back of his neck. 'Forgot about that. Why *did* you follow me, anyway?'

'I was desperate. Desperate for leads. I wanted to tell you, by the way, that I loved how you dealt with us in your office.' She laughed. 'Showing you the Blue-ray like that was a mistake. I told Shelley she'd regret it.'

'Agent Atta strikes me as a hard ass.'

Samantha shrugged. 'She has to be. Not easy being an Arab-American woman in the FBI . . .' She trailed to take a healthy swig of beer, then with a guilty grin added, 'My dad used to say the only thing worse than a bitch was a woman angry for good reason.'

Thomas laughed. Either Samantha Logan was real people or she was trying to present herself as such. Was this a tactic of some kind?

'Are you always so open with your views, Agent Logan?'

Pained smile. 'I figure it's useless to BS someone with a PhD in bullshit.'

'*That* would be a philosopher,' Thomas said. 'Me? I'm a psychologist.'

Thomas found himself laughing with her, struck by how quickly she had managed to turn his mood. There was something about her smile, a kind of open-mouthed honesty, that spoke of loving, irreverent parents and a childhood spent joking around the dinner table. He couldn't help but wonder how much they had in common. '*The boss thought I was your kind of people.*'

'Which is *why*,' Agent Logan said, ducking her head as she lingered on the word – an oddly endearing gesture, 'we could use your help on this case.'

He snorted skeptically. 'What you guys need is a neurologist.'

'A psychologist isn't close enough?'

Thomas shrugged. 'Neurology is the science of the brain. Psychology is the science of the mind. Simple enough, I suppose, but things get very complicated very fast when it comes to understanding the relationship between the two.'

'The relationship of the mind to the brain?'

Thomas nodded into his beer. 'Some say the mind and the brain are actually the same thing, but at different levels of description. Others say they're entirely different things. And still others say only the brain is real – that the mind, and therefore psychology, is bunk.'

'What do *you* say?'

'I honestly don't know. The scary thing for me is that as the years pass and neuroscience matures, the relationship between the two disciplines starts to seem more and more like that between astronomy and astrology, or chemistry and alchemy.'

'And why's that?'

He paused, struck by the selfless candor of her expression. In his never-ending effort to engage his students, he had memorized innumerable little 'factoids' regarding this or that freshman preoccupation. As a result, he knew far too much about the myths and details of attraction. He knew, for instance, that Sam possessed all the features that men in Western cultures found appealing: large eyes, slender nose, high cheeks and delicate jaw. He knew that, no matter what the circumstances, simply looking at her would light up the reward centers of most men's brains.

His own included.

'Because neurology is a *natural* science,' he replied after a glutinous cough. 'It looks at human behavior and consciousness as natural processes like any other process in the natural world. It actually provides causal explanations for what we are.'

'And psychology doesn't?'

'Not really, no. Psychology also involves something called "intentional explanations", which are pretty tricky from a scientific point of view.' He found himself breathing deeply, as though steeling himself for some arduous task. 'For instance, why did you take a sip of your beer just now?'

Samantha frowned, shrugged. 'Because I wanted to,' she said lamely.

'There you go. That's an intentional explanation. A *psychological* explanation. This is largely how human beings explain and understand themselves: in terms of intentions, desires, purposes, hopes, and so on. We use intentional explanations.'

'And they're not scientific?'

Her foot brushed his leg and a jolt passed through him. She was just kicking off her shoes, he realized.

'Not comfortably,' he replied, 'no. Before science, we largely understood the world in intentional terms. From the dawn of recorded history pretty much all of our explanations of the world were psychological. Then along comes science and *bang*: where storms were once understood in terms of angry gods and the like, they're understood in terms of high pressure cells and so on. Science has pretty much scrubbed psychology from the natural world.'

The disenchantment of the world. In his classes Thomas was always at pains to convey just how extraordinary this transformation was – is. Homeric Greece, Vedic India, biblical Israel: in terms of structure, these worlds were cut from the same cloth as Tolkien's Middle-earth. Sanctioned by tradition, yes, anchored in the assent of masses, certainly, but projections of human conceit all the same. Magical. What fact could be more extraordinary? The entire human race had spent the bulk of its tenure living in various fantasy worlds, pleading, kneeling, murdering, avenging, all in the name of make-believe. The whole of humanity deluded. And if Neil was right, precious little had changed.

'Until science,' he continued, 'we humans really had no way of distinguishing good claims from bad claims outside of tradition and self-interest. So why not confabulate? Make stuff up? Why not elaborate belief systems that cater to our vanity, to our need to keep everyone in line? It's no accident we've cooked up thousands of different religions, each peculiar to some distinct culture.'

Sam paused to take a drink, and to reorient herself, Thomas supposed. 'So then why have I always thought psychology was a science?'

'Because it is, in a sense. It uses many of the same tools and standards. It proceeds by hypothesis. The problem lies primarily in its subject matter.'

'The mind.'

'Yep. To put it bluntly, the mind's, well, *spooky*. The ancient Greek roots of "psychology" are *psūkē* and *logos*, literally "the discourse of the soul". The roots of "neurology", on the other hand, are *neuron* and *logos*, or "the discourse of the sinew". This pretty much sums up the crucial difference: neurology deals with the mechanics of the meat, whereas psychology deals with the syntax of the ineffable. You tell me which is more scientific.'

She laughed. 'You were wrong, professor.'

'About what?'

'You *are* a philosopher.'

He found himself laughing a little too hard – an out-of-joint response to out-of-joint circumstances. At some level, it was simply too absurd to take seriously: Neil a madman, Nora screwing him, and this FBI agent plying Thomas with beer in an effort to track him down. *Ha-ha, Neil is fucking Nora. Ha-ha, Neil is murdering innocents. Ha-ha-ha . . .*

Agent Logan's look told him that she understood this, if not explicitly, then at the level of obscure bodily cues. Suddenly he felt close to this stranger, even though he didn't know the first thing about her.

Go slow, Goodbook. It's been a long day.

Something about her had stirred that anxious, adolescent tickle – that almost desperate desire to be liked. It seemed he could hear Neil laughing in the background.

'*Have you an arm like God?*'

Samantha's eyes flashed as she took another drink. 'You really need to work with me on this, professor.'

Thomas shook his head, his thoughts immersed in a fog of competing demands and confusions. Too much was happening too fast. 'Like I said, I'm not a neurologist. I'll tell you anything you want to know, but otherwise, I'm just a frumpy academic.'

'Professor—'

'Tom. Call me Tom.'

'Tom, then. Look, with everything going on . . .' She hesitated. 'Did you know that since the North Atlantic Drift collapsed, the number of eco-terrorist attacks against American targets has tripled?'

By coincidence, Thomas had glanced at the television over the bar as she said this: CNN images of the freak blizzard in northern France. A blizzard before September. Of course everyone was blaming America and her former love affair with SUVs.

'The Bureau's resources,' Samantha continued, 'were already stretched to breaking point by the anti-terrorism campaign. And now the Chiropractor is loose in the city – worse even than the Son of Sam. How many agents do you think Washington has assigned to hunt down Neil Cassidy?'

'I have no idea.'

'Eighteen, most of them part time. There's only the three of us – Shelley, Danny, and myself – here in New York City, along with some loaners from the NYPD. Everyone else is working on the Chiropractor case. We need your help, Tom. Honestly.'

So there it was, her motive for this friendly beer. She wanted him to profile his best friend, provide a framework they could use to explain, and perhaps even anticipate, his moves. Thomas studied her face, this time trying to look past the hum of her beauty. She looked all of twenty-five, but something about her demeanor said she was at least thirty.

'Look, Agent Logan, I—'

'What about vengeance, professor?' she asked sharply. 'What about nailing the man who nailed your wife?'

There it was. She had taken the shortcut.

He should have been offended but . . . He seemed to have no room for more fury.

'The Argument,' he said, his eyes drawn once again to the TV.

She scowled and shook her head. 'I don't understand.'

Images of snow plows were replaced by that of rioters in frozen Paris streets. Howling Gallic faces, collars up, their fear and anger condensed in their exhalations. The more pessimistic climatologists had been right: global warming had tipped the climatic equilibrium, flooding the oceans with fresh water from the ice-caps, and the North Atlantic Drift, which had warmed Europe from Lisbon to Moscow – or what was left of Moscow – had simply disappeared. Given its latitude, Europe was slowly turning into a version of the Canadian Arctic.

What have we done?

'Yoo hoo, professor?'

Thomas cleared his throat, drew a sweaty hand across his cheek and jaw. 'On that BD you guys showed me this morning. When the girl asked him what he was doing, the voice – Neil, I suppose – said he was making an argument.'

'Yeah, so?'

'Well, I think I know what that argument is. I think I know Neil's motive.'

'You gotta understand: Neil and I were close in college. Real close.'

'No offense, but I have to ask: were you lovers?'

Thomas smiled. 'He punched me in the asshole once while playing "drunk WWE", but that's pretty much as romantic as it got.'

Samantha laughed. 'I've had worse dates. Trust me.'

'We weren't lovers,' he said, 'but only because the physical attraction wasn't there. We were like brothers, twin brothers, who just knew what the other was thinking, who just . . .' Thomas shook his head. 'Trusted.'

Even then, Neil? Were you fucking me over even then?

'So what does this have to do with the argument?'

He took a quick drink, more to organize his thoughts than anything else. 'Well, Neil and I weren't fascinated so much with each other as we were fascinated by the same things – the same topics. We used to debate stuff endlessly, from nuclear weapons to NAFTA. Then we took this philosophy class on eschatology – on all things apocalyptic – taught by this Vietnam-era burnout who was obsessed with the end of the world: Professor Skeat. Professor Walter J. Skeat.' He told her about the course, how it moved from the nuclear to the biblical to the environmental apocalypse, remembering as he did so all the youthful flares of insight that had made the class into a kind of religious experience. Everything became fraught with significance when the world was on its deathbed. Every word became a last word.

'But what really caught our attention,' he said, his gaze lost between memories, 'and what old Skeat spent half the time talking about, was something he called the *semantic* apocalypse, the apocalypse of meaning.'

'Why did it interest you so?'

Thomas took refuge in another drink, suddenly conscious of her scrutiny. Did she find him anywhere near as attractive as he found her? Women were just as keyed to facial symmetry as men, but their preference for infantile versus masculine features tended to vary with their menstrual cycle – which was to say, fertility. Thomas supposed he had the symmetry nailed – he liked to think he was a handsome dog – but he was definitely on the juvenile end when it came to his features. A true blue baby face.

Was that why Nora had betrayed him? Had Neil simply caught her ovulating?

'Because,' he said, struggling to recover his previous train of thought, 'Skeat claimed the semantic apocalypse had *already* happened. That was how the Argument started.'

Samantha frowned. '*The* Argument?'

'That's what we called it.'

'So what was it?'

'Remember how I said science had scrubbed the world of purpose? For some reason, wherever science encounters intention or purpose in the world, it snuffs it out. The world as described by science is arbitrary and random. There's innumerable causes for everything, but no reasons for anything.'

'Sure,' Samantha said. 'Shit happens. There's no . . .' She paused and cocked her head, her look appreciative. 'There's no meaning to what happens. What happens just . . . happens.'

Thomas smiled, impressed. Of course she was nowhere near agreeing with him – the Argument cut across the grain of too much hardwiring and socialization for that – but she had the versatility to at least entertain the idea. He could see why her superiors would grant her the latitude for something like this, sharing a beer with a possible material witness. A true professional, she was bent on understanding rather than forcing her own views. The *truth* of the Argument was irrelevant, here.

Wasn't it?

'Exactly,' he replied. 'The "will of God" or what have you is indistinguishable from dumb luck. That's why car insurance companies don't give a damn how much you pray – let alone to whom. It often seems otherwise, but once you factor in our penchant for self-serving interpretation and cherry-picking, it becomes painfully clear that we're deluding ourselves.'

'You mean with religion?'

Thomas paused over his beer. People were painfully credulous, capable of believing anything. And once they did believe, they had innumerable strategies for skewing and dismissing, all the while convinced they were the most open-minded and even-handed person they knew. They rewrote memories. They made up rationalizations, then believed them with religious conviction. When they didn't miss counter-evidence altogether, they warped it into further proof of their own cherished views. The brain was a spin doctor, plain and simple. The experimental evidence for this was out and out incontrovertible, but thanks to a culture bent on pseudo-empowerment, scarcely a peep could be heard above the self-congratulatory roar. Nobody, from truck drivers to cancer researchers, wanted to hear how self-absorbed and error-prone they were. Why bother with a scientific tongue-lashing when you could have a corporate hand-job?

'Everyone thinks they've won the Magical Belief Lottery, Agent Logan.'

'Which is?'

He nodded at the parade of passers-by beyond the plate-glass window. 'Everyone thinks they more or less have a handle on things, that they, as opposed to the billions who disagree with them, have somehow *lucked* into the one true belief system.'

Her face crooked into a rueful smile. 'I've seen my fair share of delusions, trust me. The people we hunt burn them for fuel.'

'Not just the people you hunt, Agent Logan. *All* of us.'

'All of us?' she repeated. Something about her tone told Thomas that the distinction between her and her quarry was important to her. No surprise there, given the things she must have witnessed over the years.

He leaned back, holding her gaze. 'You do realize that every thought, every experience, every element of your consciousness is a product of various neural processes? We know this because of cases of brain damage. All I have to do is press a coat hanger past your eye, wriggle it around a little, and you'd be utterly changed.' This description never failed to provoke expressions of disgust in his classroom, but Agent Logan seemed unimpressed.

'So?'

'You're right. In a sense it's a trivial point. Every time you take an aspirin you're assuming you're a biomechanism, something that can be tweaked with chemicals. But think about what I said. Your *every experience* is a product of neural processes.'

It seemed he could sense Neil leaning over his shoulder as he said this, a grinning aura, knowing full well the destination, but morbidly curious as to the path old Goodbook would take. Neil looked at heads the way ill-tempered children looked at toys – as things to be fucked with.

'I'm not following you, professor.'

Thomas hooked his shoulders and palms in a professorial *you're-not-going-to-like-this* gesture. 'Well, how about free will? That's a kind of experience, isn't it?'

'Of course.'

'Which means free will is a product of neural processes.'

A wary pause. 'It has to be, I guess.'

'So then how is it free? I mean, if it's a product, and it *is* a product – I could show you case studies of brain damaged patients who think they will *everything* that happens, who think they command the clouds on the horizon, the birds in the trees. If the will is a product of neural functioning then how could it be free?'

Frowning, Sam suddenly swigged her beer, head back, the way a truck driver might. Thomas watched her slender throat, as white as a barked sapling, flex as she swallowed.

She gasped and said, 'I just *chose* to drink, didn't I?'

'I don't know. Did you?'

For the first time her face crinkled into a look that was openly incredulous. 'Of course. What else could it be?'

'Well, as a matter of *fact* – fact, unfortunately, not speculation – your brain simply processed a chain of sensory inputs, me yapping, then generated a particular behavioral output, you drinking.'

'But . . .' She trailed.

'That's not the way it feels,' Thomas said, completing her sentence.

'It's pretty clear that our sense of willing things is . . . well, illusory. It started with a variety of experiments showing how easy it is to fool people into thinking that they're willing things they actually have no control over. That laid the groundwork. Then, when the costs of neuro-imaging began to plummet – remember all the hoopla about low-field MRIs several years back? – more and more researchers demonstrated they could actually determine their subject's choices *before* they were conscious of making them. Willing, it turns out, is an add-on of some kind, something that comes to us after the fact.'

Now she seemed genuinely troubled. Thomas had seen the same look on a thousand undergraduate faces, the look of a brain, Neil would have said, at odds with itself – one whose knowledge could not be reconciled with its experience.

The brain, it turned out, could wrap itself around most everything but itself, which was why it invented minds . . . souls.

'But that can't be . . .' Sam started. 'I mean, if we don't really make choices, then how could . . .'

Thomas grimaced in sympathy. 'How could anything be right or wrong? Good or evil?'

'Exactly. Morality. Doesn't morality mean we *have* to have free will?'

'Who said morality was real?'

She worked her bottom lip for a moment, then added, 'Bullshit. It's gotta be . . .'

A crimson eighteen-wheeler roared down the street outside the window, hauling who knew what to who knew where. Its diesel roar faded into the sound of a crowd cheering through the tin of television speakers. The Braves, a canned voice said, were on the warpath once again.

'I mean, I make decisions, all the time.'

She was arguing now, Thomas realized, not simply entertaining academic claptrap for the purposes of tracking down Neil. The Argument had a way of doing that to people. He could remember the horror it had engendered in him years ago in Skeat's class. The sense that some kind of atrocity had been committed, though without date or location. More than a few times he and Neil had made the mistake of debating it while catastrophically stoned – a mistake for Thomas, anyway. He had simply sat rigid, crowded by paranoias, his eyes poking and probing the tissue that had once been his thoughtless foundation, while Neil had laughed and chortled, pacing the room as if it were a cage. Thomas could see him, hair askew, ducking to peer into his face. 'Whoa, dude . . . Think about it. You're a *machine* – a machine! – dreaming that you have a soul. None of this is real, man, and they can fucking *prove* it.'

Thomas rubbed his eyes. 'In controlled circumstances, researchers can determine the choices we make before we're even conscious of making them. The first experiments were crude and hotly contested – pioneered by a guy called Libet. But over the years, as techniques improved and the fidelity of neuro-imaging increased, so did the ability to pin down the precursors of decision making. Now . . .' Thomas trailed with an apologetic shrug. 'What can I say? People still argue, of course – they always will when it comes to cherished beliefs.'

'Free will is an illusion,' Sam said in a strange tone. 'Even now, everything I'm saying . . .'

Thomas swallowed, suddenly apprehensive. He had been carefully folding his napkin as he talked; now he set it like a tiny white book on the table before him. 'Only a small fraction of your brain is involved in conscious experience, which is why so much of what we do is unconscious. The bulk of your brain's processing falls outside what you can experience; it simply doesn't exist for your consciousness, not even as an absence. That's why your thoughts simply come out of nowhere, apparently uncontrolled, undetermined . . . Yours and yours alone.'

Samantha yanked her hands out in a warding gesture, shook her head. 'Come on, professor, this is just too crazy.'

'Oh, it goes deeper, trust me. Everything falls apart, Agent Logan. Absolutely everything.'

Sam watched the streamers of bubbles in her beer. 'So it has to be wrong, doesn't it?'

Thomas simply watched her.

'Doesn't it?' she repeated, her tone somewhere between wonder and irritation.

He shrugged for what seemed the hundredth time. 'Free will is an illusion, that much is certain. As for other psychological staples like the now, selfhood, purpose, and so on, the evidence that they are all fundamentally deceptive continues to pile up. And if you think about it, perhaps this is what we should expect. Consciousness is young in evolutionary terms, a jury-rigged response to a perfect storm of environmental circumstances. We're stuck with the beta-version. Less even. It only seems slick because it's all we know.'

'You mean,' Sam said drily, 'as far as *science* is concerned.'

Thomas took a long drink, exhaled heavily out his nose. In his freshman classes, attacking science was hands down the most common response to the threat posed by the Argument – as well as the weakest.

'And science is a mess, sure. But it's the only mess in recorded history that has had any success at generating and deciding between theoretical claims – not to mention making everything around us possible as a result. In historical terms, it is absolutely unprecedented. What are you going to believe? A four-thousand-year-old document bent on tribal self-glorification? Your own flattering intuitions on the fundamental nature of things? Some hothouse philosophical interpretation that takes years of specialized training just to understand? Or an institution that makes things like computers, thermonuclear explosions, and cures for small-pox possible?'

Samantha Logan stared at him for a long and lovely moment. Someone jacked up the volume on the flat-screen above the bar. A silky whisper fanned across the tables, extolling the wonders of Head & Shoulders.

'*Because when your hair shines,* you *shine . . .*'

'But there're truths outside of science.'

'Are there? I mean, there's a lot of non-scientific *claims* floating around, that's for sure. But *truths*? Is the Bible more true than the Quran? Is Plato more true than Buddha? Maybe, maybe not. The fact is we have no way of knowing, even though billions of us jump up and down screaming otherwise. And the more science teaches us, the more it seems we're just duping ourselves altogether. Our internal yardstick is bent, Agent, we know that for a fact. Why should we trust any of our old measurements?'

Most people simply nodded and dismissed the Argument. Most people found their fables too flattering to seriously challenge. A thousand sects, cults, religions, and philosophers agreeing on nothing, and yet each thought their ticket held the winning number of beliefs. Why? Because *they* held it. Somehow their personal experience of speaking in tongues, of remembering past lives, of having this prayer answered or that premonition come true was the *only* experience that mattered, the only one that made true . . .

So few could crawl into the Argument's belly and truly comprehend. The trick was crawling back out again.

Thomas watched as various expressions struggled for mastery of Sam's face. A dismissive scowl, a sarcastic retort, a plea for reassurance. It seemed he could glimpse all of them.

'I have to say, professor, that this, without a doubt, is one of the most depressing conversations I've ever had. I feel like drowning myself in a tub.'

Despite the sorrow that welled through him, Thomas smiled a mock winning smile. 'Welcome to the semantic apocalypse.'

Sam breathed deeply, enough to blow aside the odd strands of hair that had fallen across her face. 'So you think this is what Cassidy is up to? You think he's simply making the Argument in the most dramatic way he can?'

Thomas paused, troubled by the hollow in his stomach. 'For the ancient Greeks, puppets were *neurospastos*, "drawn by strings". I think this might be what Neil is up to.'

'You mean showing us the strings?'

'Exactly. He wants the whole world to share his revelation.'

Even as he said it, Thomas somehow knew that it couldn't be true, that something far more terrifying was at stake. But as so often happens in the course of making arguments, it didn't seem such a bad thing cutting corners here and there, allowing what was convenient to trump what was true. What mattered was that she *believed.*

'Think about Cynthia Powski,' he continued. 'Think of that BD as the first premise in an argument. What does it say? What conclusion does it point to?'

Sam nodded appreciatively. 'That he's in charge. That he can force her to do, and more importantly, to *feel*, anything he wants.'

'Is it? Then why does he surrender the controls to her?'

'I dunno. To show that he can make her *want* to be raped? Isn't that the rapist's credo? That all women secretly want it?'

Frowning, Thomas let his gaze wander the bar. The number of people now hunched over drinks and tables surprised him. He glanced at a waitress marching with a steaming plate of fries. 'Maybe. But remember what Atta said? What we witnessed wasn't rape. Neil – supposing it was Neil – forced a woman to experience something akin to multiple orgasms. Be he didn't *touch* her – not sexually, anyway. No. I think he's pointing to something more abstract. From his standpoint, I think he thinks his position is incidental to the BD, not at all important.'

'And why's that?'

'Why? Ask yourself: if you were in that chair, if you were Cynthia Powski, would you want it?'

'What kind of question is that?'

'An important one. Would you *want* it?'

'Fuck, no.'

'If Cynthia Powski were here right now, what do you think *she* would say?'

Samantha looked at him angrily. 'The same.'

'Exactly. Perhaps that's Neil's point. We all think we're free, that no matter what the circumstances, we can freely decide to do things differently. Neil's arguing otherwise. He's simply showing us what the brain is: a machine that generates behaviors which are either repeated or not depending on how the resulting environmental feedback stimulates its pleasure or pain systems. How can he do something against her will when there's no such thing?'

Samantha's eyes fell to her empty beer glass.

'Strike that,' Thomas said. 'He's going one better. He's *demonstrating* otherwise. He's committing a crime that proves that there's no such thing.'

'No such thing as what?'

Thomas raised his brows. 'Crime.'

'So what's wrong with him then? I mean in psychological terms, what's wrong with him?'

Staring at her, Thomas found himself wondering what it would be like to *be* her. Studies had shown that beautiful people lived happier, longer, and more successful lives. 'The halo effect', researchers called it. Because beauty generated positive social feedback, beautiful people tended to develop the positive attitudes that everyone from sales gurus to Baptist preachers associated with health, happiness, and success.

How many doors had Samantha Logan's beauty opened?

'But that's what I've been saying,' Thomas replied. 'It's conceivable there's *nothing* wrong with him.'

A thoughtful frown. 'Sure, but only because you know about this semantic apocalypse thing. Just pretend you're an average psychologist, someone unscarred by Skeat. What would you think?'

It was a good question. Thomas breathed deeply, glanced across the dim interior. More and more people were arriving, filling the silence that lurked at the bottom of all busy places.

'Well,' he began, 'obviously, I'd suppose Neil was suffering from some kind of antisocial personality disorder – I mean, only a psychopath could do what we saw this morning, right? After building a case history, though, I'd be troubled by the fact that Neil doesn't fit the standard profile for severe antisocials.'

'There's your wife,' Samantha said abruptly. 'That certainly fits the profile.'

'Just because all antisocials are bastards, doesn't mean all bastards are antisocials. No. As much as I would like to chalk this betrayal up to some kind of neurophysiological deficit, there has to be a pattern of some kind . . .'

He trailed, found himself blinking back the heat in his eyes. For a moment, he'd almost forgotten.

Neil and Nora.

'Sorry,' Samantha said.

Thomas pulled his hands into his lap, pretended to cough. He knew that he had to be careful. He could feel it, lurking like a scarcely suppressed alter-ego behind his words, his thoughts – the need to prove himself to this beautiful woman. But there was more to be wary of – far, far more. People chronically attributed emotions generated by their circumstances to the people they happened to find themselves with. Couples meeting for the first time on high suspension bridges reliably ranked their opposites as more exciting and attractive than couples meeting for the first time on a footpath. And this situation with Neil was nothing if not precarious.

'I'd also suppose he was suffering from some kind of extreme depersonalization disorder, either something—'

'What do you mean?' Samantha asked.

Thomas stared, tried to will away the buzz of excitement that seemed to hover around her. There was something about Samantha Logan. Klutzy and ambitious. Crude-talking and intelligent. Earnest and urbane. He tried to blink the shine from his eyes, to remind himself of the madness that encircled him. But there she was, front and center, humming with promise and focused entirely on him.

But then there was what Neil would say – and what Thomas-the-professor knew. Thanks to a potent blend of hard-wiring and socialization, men were far more likely to read sexual cues where none were to be found. They constantly confused female attention for sexual interest. The sad truth was that false positives paid better reproductive dividends. Assuming that every woman wanted to jump your bones was just another way of covering your odds at the evolutionary craps table.

'I don't think,' Thomas finally said, 'Neil sees himself as a person anymore.'

Samantha crinkled her nose in disbelief. 'Not a person? Then what does he see himself as?'

'A brain. A brain among brains.'

'I'm having difficulty wrapping my head around this one.'

'I'm a philosopher, remember? It's all bullshit.'

'It's gotta be.'

Thomas looked down to his thumbs. 'If you think of a way out, be sure and let me know. I mean, I *love* my kids. I really *love* them. I don't think I knew what love meant until Ripley was born. And Frankie was double trouble. That simply *has* to mean something, doesn't it?'

Or is it just another lie? Like my marriage.

Samantha stared at him.

'What's wrong?' Thomas asked.

'Ah, nothing. It just didn't hit me until now.'

'What didn't hit you?'

'When you were going through the Argument and all that . . . I guess I just assumed there had to be some kind of catch. Some kind of trapdoor you weren't letting me in on. But there isn't, is there? I mean when you asked for . . . for a *way out* a couple of seconds ago, you really were asking, weren't you?'

'I suppose I was.'

Long silence. 'So what if he's right, Tom?'

'Neil?'

'Yeah, Neil. What if he wins his argument?'

Thomas shrugged. She looked like Nora, he thought. She looked like Nora when she was frightened.

*

'We should go,' Samantha said, rooting through her purse. She looked up and smiled girlishly. 'I'm barely fit to drive as it is. How about you? You okay?'

'I'll just take a cab home.'

'Home? The day's just beginning, professor. You're coming with me.'

Thomas smiled, more relieved than annoyed. The thought of returning home made him feel hollow. 'You think so, do you?'

'I know so,' she said to her purse. 'You need to tell Shelley all this.'

She stood abruptly and Thomas found himself following. There was something about her manner, a breezy certainty, that demanded he acquiesce. 'Tell me,' she said as they walked to her white Mustang, 'when was the last time you saw Neil Cassidy?'

And like that, the spell was broken. He was just another tool in her investigative kit, he realized, a way of nailing his best friend.

'About six months ago,' he inexplicably replied.

CHAPTER FIVE

August 17th, 1.54 p.m.

The lie nagged him so much the most he could do was stare out the windshield at the flash and glare of passing vehicles. Why hadn't he just told her the truth?

They think he's a serial killer, for Christ's sake!

And Nora was making love to him.

'Where are we going?' he asked numbly.

'Back into the city. To the Field Office.'

'Things will be crazy, I imagine,' he said lamely.

She cocked her head. 'Crazy?'

'You know, with the Chiropractor and all.' In these days of broadband it was rare for anything non-political to rise above the disjointed din of millions pursuing millions of different interests. The niche had become all-powerful. The Chiropractor story was a throwback in a sense, a flashback to the day when sitcoms or murders could provide people a common frame of reference, or at least something to talk about when polite questions gave out.

'Actually things will be quiet,' Sam replied. 'The NYPD's hosting the Chiropractor Task Force.'

Thomas said nothing, stared at two kids in SUNY sweatshirts waiting at a bus stop.

Tell her the truth! Neil's gone off his fucking rocker! You sensed it last night. You just knew something was wrong. He could see them, Neil and Nora making love. He thought of her little 'yoga trick', the one they would laugh about on Sunday mornings. She had always been so hot, so frank with her lust. He could almost hear her whisper in his ear . . .

‘*So goooood . . . So good, Neil . . .*’

His hands were shaking. He took a deep breath.

Tell her!

Sam was turning right on a street he didn’t recognize. ‘Are you sure you’re okay, professor?’

‘Call me Tom,’ he replied, ignoring her question. ‘Someone, either you or Agent Atta, said you were *certain* that Neil was responsible for what we saw on that BD. How? How do you know?’

His tone had been sharper than he’d intended.

Agent Logan glanced at him apprehensively. ‘Ten weeks ago the NSA informed us that a low-level researcher of theirs, a neurologist, had gone AWOL. They gave us his name, his biometric data, and just asked us to keep an eye out, which we did as best we could.’

‘Neil? But—’

‘You thought he worked at Bethesda.’ Sam shook her head.

Thomas *had* been about to say that Neil was far more than a low-level researcher. ‘Bethesda was just his cover?’

‘Bingo. So anyway, since the matter had been pitched as a potential espionage problem – and a low priority one at that, the case was given to the Counterintelligence Division. A week afterward, the Criminal Investigative Division caught a break in the Theodoros Gyges abduction . . . Did you ever hear about that?’

‘Not much.’ Thomas did know about Gyges – everyone did. In his short-lived activist days, Thomas had actually organized a boycott of one of the guy’s New Jersey Target stores. ‘Just the *Post* headline,’ he said. ‘ “Brain-damaged Billionaire,” or something like that.’

‘Exactly. Missing for two weeks, then he just pops up in Jersey, his head wrapped in bandages. Aside from some disorientation, he seems perfectly fine, until, that is, he’s reunited with his wife.’

‘What happened?’

‘He doesn’t recognize her. He remembers her, and everything else, perfectly, but he can’t recognize her. According to the report, he demands that she stop impersonating his wife’s voice, and when she continues pleading – she *is* his wife, after all – he freaks out and hospitalizes her. Big mess. The media would have loved it if their plates weren’t already so full.

‘So they run some tests, and it turns out that Gyges can’t recognize any faces, not even his own. Creepy stuff.’

‘Sounds like some kind of prosopagnosia,’ Thomas said. Face

blindness had been known since antiquity, but it wasn't until the nineties that damage to the fusiform face area in the visual cortex was identified as the culprit. In his classes, Thomas regularly used it as an example of how the brain was a grab-bag of special purpose devices, not the monolithic soul machine that so many undergraduates assumed it to be. 'I'd like to see the file.'

She flashed him a triumphant grin. 'Welcome to the good guys, professor.' As though unable to repress herself, she reached out to bop her fist against his.

'Anyway,' Sam continued, 'a couple of weeks ago someone in the Counterintelligence Division – I have no idea who – reads about this in the *New York Times*, and immediately draws the connection to their missing neurologist, Neil Cassidy. They send someone up from Washington with Cassidy's picture—'

'Which was useless, of course.'

Sam smiled and wagged a finger. 'Not at all. Like everyone else, the Bureau's up to its elbows in the Great Wetware Revolution. Haven't you read *Time* magazine? It's revolutionized forensics.'

Thomas nodded. 'Lemme guess. You showed Gyges Neil's picture while scanning him with a low-field MRI. The neuronal circuits dealing with facial recognition lit up.'

'Exactly. Gyges's *brain* recognized Cassidy just fine, and in a manner consistent with a traumatic encounter. Just the circuitry relaying this information to his consciousness had been damaged. It turns out that Cassidy isn't quite so clever after all.'

Thomas said nothing. They had no idea whom they were dealing with, he realized.

It is you, isn't it, Neil?

'And that,' Sam continued, 'was when the gears started turning. The Chiropractor investigation was gobbling up resources at every jurisdictional level, so the NYPD brass were only too happy to turn over their ongoing investigation to the Bureau – especially now that it carried a National Security stigma. Shelley, who was the NCAVC coordinator for the ongoing NYPD circus, was made Investigator-in-Charge of our meager Task Force. As it stands now, everything is pretty much ad hoc. Our Department of Justice and State's Attorney advisors are little more than interns, and as far as I know, our public affairs officer is a moonlighter from the Chiropractor Task Force. Our organizational flowchart looks like tossed spaghetti.'

She paused, as though troubled by her own cynicism. 'But we have a suspect, a known subject. Things tend to straighten themselves out when you have a SUB.'

Thomas listened to the *hum-ker-chunk* of wheels over pavement, wondering how it could sound so ancient, so this-is-the-way-it's-always-been. The world beyond the tinted windshields seemed autumn sunny and surreal. Oblivious.

None of this could be happening.

Nora and Neil.

'It's him, professor,' Sam said softly. 'Neil Cassidy is our man.'

They swept off the entry ramp and merged into traffic. The first I-87 sign that Thomas glimpsed sported a rust-rimmed bullet-hole.

'I just need to check up on the kids,' Thomas said, fishing through his blazer for his palmtop.

He let Mia's phone ring five times. He hung up rather than leave a message.

They're probably out back.

'No luck?' Sam asked, her eyes fixed on the road.

'I seem to be batting a thousand.'

She spared him a mischievous glance. 'Me too.'

Thomas could think of nothing further to say, so he stared at his thumbs for several pointless moments, studied the bruised nail he'd earned playing squash the week before. *Gotta work on those sidewall shots*, he thought inanely.

If Sam found the silence awkward, she didn't show it. She whisked them down the freeway, bobbing in and out of traffic. Thomas found his eyes darting between the digital speedometer and the encapsulated drivers surrounding them. She drove like a veteran commuter, playing slim margins of error in order to slowly advance. She leaned on those slowing her down by riding their ass, and punished those riding her ass by slowing down. She also – intentionally it seemed to Thomas – lingered in others' blindspots.

'You drive like my ex-wife,' Thomas finally remarked.

Sam grinned wickedly. 'She was that good, was she?'

'She was an asshole,' he heard himself snap. 'Could you ease up a bit, you think?'

Sam shot him a blank look. Without warning, she yanked the Mustang behind a rust-laced U-Haul in the right lane, then braked so hard that Thomas's belt locked. For a moment, she seemed to study the van's giant $79.95 decal reflected across the hood of her car. 'You know, professor,' she finally said, 'I've been holding back because I knew you were upset.'

Thomas tried not to look at her. 'No need to pull your punches, Agent Logan. I'm a big boy.'

'There's several things that have me puzzled.'

Thomas's stomach lurched. 'Such as?'

Why did you lie?

'Why did you rush home immediately after speaking with us this morning?'

'I wanted to call Neil. No, I *needed* to call him. To confront him. I thought I had his number at home.'

'Did you?'

Thomas shrugged. 'I couldn't find it.'

'Some close friend.'

'He moved about three months ago,' Thomas explained. 'When he called to give me his new number I wrote it on a scrap of paper. What can I say? I guess I am a bad friend.'

The part about the move was true. At least, Neil had *said* as much. Who knew what was true anymore?

'So why did you rush over to your ex-wife's house immediately after that?'

'Because when I tried calling her for the number, she hung up.'

Stupid thing to say, he realized. They no longer needed warrants for phone records. Ever since the drought, when a cadre of home-grown Islamic extremists had criss-crossed the Southwest setting wildfires, the American public had enthusiastically surrendered their constitutional scruples. Thomas had been all for it back then, watching the parade of hellish landscapes night after night, not to mention the satellite photos, where it seemed the very map of America was being burned. The smoke had reached the high atmosphere, turning several days into crimson nights, even as far away as New York. He had been too young to fully appreciate 9/11, but Burning Hills . . . It had rattled something deep.

'Hung up, huh?'

Thomas stared hard at her beautiful profile, understanding that she had become Agent Logan again. People were like polarized glass, transparent and opaque by turns. Cooperators one minute, competitors the next.

'Nora thought I was making it up. Your visit. The Blue-ray. She accused me of playing another sadistic head game.'

Sam frowned. 'Why would she think that? Neil's *your* best friend, isn't he? Why would she think you'd make something like that up?'

'My question exactly. I was dumbfounded. Which is why I drove to her place.'

How could it be so easy? How could he just look into her eyes and make shit up? With a kind of numb wonder, he realized that he was actually good at it. The dead look, as though simply reading the script of his memory. The tilt of the head, as though to say, *It sounds strange I know, but what can I do?* For his entire life Thomas had always pegged himself as someone who would choke in clutch situations.

Choke for the truth.

Sam glanced at him apologetically. *Just doing my job*, her eyes said. *Business . . .*

'When I arrived,' he continued, 'she was more frightened than furious. She thought I was making it up because I'd found out the two of them had . . . had been . . . When she told me as much, the shit well and truly hit the fan.'

He knew he sounded convincing. Even still, his chest tightened, his thoughts buzzed. Sooner or later they would interview Nora. After all, she was banging their perp. *I'm fucking myself.*

'Sorry, professor,' Sam said. She looked at him searchingly, as though afraid she had lost something. 'I mean, Tom.'

He nodded as though to reassure her.

When had he developed such a facility for lies?

Everybody's fucking everybody.

Sam spent the rest of the drive into Manhattan briefing Thomas on the details of the Gyges and Powski abductions. Gyges, a retail magnate, had simply never returned from an early morning jog in Central Park. Witnesses reported seeing him chatting to someone in a silver BMW, nothing more. When Thomas asked how it was a billionaire like Gyges would do anything without some kind of security, she replied, 'He was one of *those* guys.'

'What kind of guy is that?'

'You know, the kind of guy who pisses two paces back from the urinal.'

Thomas laughed. 'Because he's got a big dick?'

'No. The exact opposite. Because his dick is small.'

'I'm not sure I understand.'

Sam's smile was dazzling in the sunlight. 'Having a small dick is one thing. Not giving a damn about it is something different altogether. Broadcast your weaknesses, and people think you strong.'

'Or,' Thomas added, 'that you suffer delusions of penile grandeur.'

Sam cackled. 'That describes most men I know.'

Cynthia Powski, 'Cream' of Vivid Digital fame, had disappeared in the parking lot of her luxury condominium complex after visiting 'friends'. No witnesses. The lot security cameras had been knocked out by supposed vandals the previous night. They knew she made it to the parking lot – or at least they thought they knew – because her Porsche was parked the way she always parked it, kitty-corner across two spots. They knew she never made it to her condo because of her boyfriend, whom the Escondido authorities had considered their prime suspect until the BD arrived in Quantico.

Though Thomas listened patiently, and even asked several pointed questions, dozens of worries and recriminations bubbled through his thoughts. After teaching for so many years, he'd found he could listen to, even answer, his students' questions while remaining entirely distracted. He never realized just how functionally distracted he could be until his divorce. How many anti-Nora zingers had he hatched while explaining this or that staple psychological concept to his class?

Special Agent Samantha Logan talked and he listened, all the while wracking his brains.

Why lie?

To protect Neil?

But why? Not only had the guy flipped his lid, he'd been screwing Nora. Screwing *him.* Why protect Neil now?

Back in Princeton, he and Neil had once rented *The Exorcist* as a lark, expecting to be more amused than anything else. The movie had scared them shitless, even though neither believed in God, demons – or even priests for that matter. After smoking several bowls contemplating the contradiction, they came up with what they called the 'Exorcist Effect', the disconnect between knowing and conditioning.

They knew demonic possession was bullshit, but they had been conditioned to be terrified – habitualized. So much of therapeutic psychology, Thomas would later discover, involved resisting the Exorcist Effect.

So much of what it meant to be human.

My closest friend . . .

He protected Neil out of habit. Goddamn habit.

And yet, even after he realized this, he continued listening to Sam rattle off fact after fact. Amiable. Attentive. Once, when a pinch in traffic forced her to fall silent, he fairly screamed at himself to come clean. *Just tell her!* he inwardly cried. *Just say, 'Samantha, I lied . . . Your SUB just happened to pop by last night.'*

Instead he said, 'Traffic's a bitch.'

Somehow they had found their way to the West Side Highway. As they paced the Hudson River, Thomas stared at the far shore, watched Jersey sulk beneath a senescent sun. It seemed impossible that mere centuries ago that shore marked the limit of literate civilization. The limit of *knowledge.* He could see them, the Dutch and then the English, wandering into the emerald deeps, between trees like temple pillars, across a continental Karnak.

How many had gone mad? How many, like Neil, had repudiated everything they had known, had adopted first the ways and then the horrors of what lay beyond knowledge?

Neil as Kurtz, he thought wryly. *Me as Marlowe . . .*

How flattering was that?

Not very, he realized a moment later. Not at all.

'You were only able to identify Neil,' Thomas found himself saying, 'because he wanted you to.'

'What do you mean?' Sam asked.

'What you said before, about Gyges's brain remembering Neil, even though Gyges didn't. I'm no neurosurgeon, but my guess is that it's far easier to wipe out face recognition altogether rather than selectively.'

'So what are you saying?'

'That Gyges is part of Neil's argument. He's saying something.'

'Saying something. Saying what?'

'You've read Gyges's statement, I take it.'

'Only about fifty fucking times.'

For some reason it thrilled him every time she swore. Probably because he'd spent his entire adolescence chasing chicks who swore. Or trying to, anyway.

As bad as people were at unconscious first impressions, studies showed they were astonishingly accurate when they paused to actually think about the stranger before them. Special Agent Logan, Thomas knew, had been raised in a working-class household. Non-religious. Stable. She had become conscious of her sexuality at a young age – had probably lost her cherry to a neighbor kid in her early teens. Like him, she was part of the so-called 'Webporn' generation, that crop of sex-desensitized kids who found wanton intercourse an irresistible short-cut to status and adulthood – giving rise to the recreational promiscuity that Thomas's Gen-X father had openly envied, and destroying what used to be sound psychological generalizations regarding teen sexual activity.

She was a post-party-girl woman, Thomas decided, goal-oriented and rule-averse, cynical and hang-up-free, who would use the tools God gave her, tradition-be-damned. That was the role that she had chosen from the rack of identities modern society offered. Even still, there was a reserve to her manner, an earnest anxiousness that belied her brassy talk. A whiff of naive idealism. For whatever reason, being cool and conscientious never seemed a comfortable fit.

'Does Gyges recall any mention of the Argument?' Thomas asked.

'No. But then we never asked.'

'So there's a chance . . .'

Her eyes probed her mirrors, and she tapped her blinker. 'There's one way to find out,' she said.

Gyges, it turned out, lived in The Beresford, on the Upper West Side overlooking Central Park. Thomas found himself craning his neck like a yokel as they walked to the entrance, intrigued by the uneasy marriage of industrial dimensions and Italian renaissance motifs. When Sam flashed her FBI badge, the doorman simply shrugged as though he were a palm-reader confronted by yet another extraordinary inevitability. People were hard to surprise, nowadays.

'Do you get air miles with that?' Thomas quipped as they marched through the posh lobby.

Sam smiled, once again rummaging through her purse for charitable change: a UNICEF box had been set on a table between the lifts.

'Just miles,' she replied, punching the elevator pad with pennies in hand.

The air was scented – the smell of rich wives, shopping to and fro, Thomas imagined. He studied his distorted reflection in the elevator's brass doors, wondered whether the motto set into the ornamental shield, *Fronta Nulla Fides*, wasn't some kind of joke on the residents. A screen in the elevator featured CNNet clips of all the top stories, from the chaos in Europe, the Iraqi civil war, to the latest Chiropractor details. Apparently another spineless body had been found, this time in Queens. Live. On-the-scene. It was like watching murder through a fish tank, Thomas thought.

The man who greeted them at the penthouse door was short, barrel-chested, and sported one of those dark, heavy beards that always made Thomas think of hairy backs. His eyes were red-rimmed. He wore his blue jeans pulled up too high on his waist. Thomas knew instantly he was one of those guys who spend far too much time sucking in their gut in front of the mirror.

'Thank you, Mr Gyges. I know—'

'Hello, Agent Logan.'

Thomas raised his eyebrows. He hadn't been sure what to expect – certainly not decisive recognition.

'I never forget a voice,' Gyges said, reading his mind. 'Otherwise, I've never seen her before in my life.'

'But you have,' Sam said.

Gyges shrugged. 'If you say so . . . And you? Have I seen you before?'

'No, Mr Gyges. I'm Thomas Bible.'

Gyges nodded warily.

'Dr Bible is a psychology professor over at Columbia, Mr Gyges. He has a few questions he'd like to ask.'

'Do you now? Forensic or therapeutic?'

'The two can sometimes be the same. But I'm not a boo-hoo grief counsellor, if that's what you mean.' Thomas paused, licked his lips. 'I'm a friend of Neil Cassidy.'

Gyges's face went blank. 'Please come in,' he said.

They followed him through a marbled foyer into a palatial living room designed and decorated in the archipelago style all the rage among the rich and famous: monumental rooms broken into various 'intimacy convergence zones'. But the effect – whatever it was supposed to be – was undone by the trash scattered about the furniture. The man certainly liked his local Subway outlet.

'You must forgive the Spartan inhospitality,' he said, motioning to a U-shaped sofa. 'I dismissed all of my staff. I found them . . . unrecognizable.'

Thomas joined Sam opposite the ailing billionaire. There was something anti-climactic about the moment, as if the billionaire and his environment had fallen short of his expectations. Too many movies, no doubt. The whole world fell short now that CGI was waving the cinematic yardstick. Not even the super-rich could measure up.

'Drink?' Gyges asked. 'All I have is Scotch, I'm afraid.'

Sam waved no. Thomas asked for one on the rocks.

'So,' Gyges asked on his way to the bar, 'what questions could a friend of Mr Cassidy have for me?'

Thomas breathed deep. Given Sam's description in the car, he had decided to strike a conciliatory note, something that would set the man at ease. 'Many. But I thought you might have questions of your own.'

Gyges smiled bitterly. *So it's therapy after all*, his look said. 'And what might those be?'

Thomas shrugged. 'Why? For starters. Don't you want to know why he did this to you?'

The man turned back to the drinks. 'Oh, I know why.'

'You do?'

'But of course. I'm being punished.'

Thomas nodded carefully. For some reason he said, 'For your sins . . .'

'Yes. For my sins.'

'And what sins are those?'

Gyges gave the Scotch a curious swirl, as though soaking the ice cubes. 'Are you a priest?' he asked as he handed Thomas his drink. For the first time Thomas noticed how assiduously the man avoided looking at either of their faces.

'No,' Thomas replied.

'Then my sins have nothing to do with you.' He turned abruptly, not toward Sam, but in her general direction. His mannerisms were beginning to remind Thomas of a blind man. 'Psychologists,' he said, with easy contempt. 'They want all your sins to be symptoms, don't they?'

'I apologize, Mr Gyges,' Thomas said, setting down his drink. 'Would you prefer—'

'Professor Bible thinks Cassidy is making some kind of argument,' Sam ventured. 'We need your help, Mr Gyges.'

The billionaire finally looked her full in the face. His eyes reflected a peculiar horror. 'Argument? What kind of argument?'

Sam glanced at Thomas. 'That nothing has meaning,' she said. 'This might sound hard to believe, but Neil Cassidy believes that there's no such thing as . . . as . . .'

'People,' Thomas finished for her. 'He thinks that much of what we believe, things like purpose, meaning, right and wrong, are simply illusions generated by our brains.'

Gyges's eyes glistened with tears. 'Well he's certainly wrong there, isn't he?'

'Wrong where?' Thomas asked.

'About none of this having meaning.'

'I'm not sure I understand.'

'Of course not,' he snapped without explanation. He shook his head. 'Just what is it you want?'

Thomas and Sam exchanged a nervous glance. The man possessed a peculiar presence, something at once awesome and pathetic. Thomas thought he finally understood what Sam had said earlier regarding men who piss two paces back from the urinal. 'Did Neil say anything to you about a . . . about a *premise*?'

'Neil?'

'I mean Cassidy. Did he?'

Gyges stood quietly for what seemed a long while.

'I want to say, yes,' Gyges finally said. 'But I really can't remember.'

'Are you sure?' Sam asked.

Gyges scowled. 'Do you know where my favorite place is, Agent Logan?'

Thomas put a hand on Sam's knee – whether to warn or to reassure her, he couldn't say.

'No,' she said. 'Where?'

'The subway,' the man replied with a pained smile. 'The fucking subway is where I feel the most at home. The most . . . normal. At first it was just a . . . a comfort, you know? But it's become far more.

Far, far more. Now it feels like Christmas with dead relatives or something. Just sitting there, swaying with strangers.'

He turned to refill his tumbler. 'Pathetic, huh?' he called over his shoulder.

'Would it be better,' Thomas ventured, 'if we did this by phone?'

'Oh, now he humors me,' Gyges said to the vaulted ceiling. He turned, hesitated, then looked at them as though on a dare. He smiled warmly and said, 'Get the fuck out.'

Thomas and Sam could only stare.

'Which word seems to be the problem?' Gyges asked. 'Get? Fuck? Out?'

The two of them hurried to their feet. 'Can we call you, Mr Gyges?' Sam asked. 'We really—'

'Jeeesuss!' the burly man cried. 'Get! The fuck! *Out!*' With each word he stomped forward, like a silverback broadcasting an imminent charge.

Thomas stumbled on the curled edge of a Persian. Sam steadied him. His arms wide, Gyges herded them toward the foyer. They paused before the door.

Thomas looked up, saw the three of them reflected in a heavy, rococo-framed mirror.

'Three strangers,' Gyges said with a calm that seemed frightening given the savagery of moments before. 'Do you know what it's like, Dr Bible, to live nowhere? To look and look and find yourself nowhere?'

In a curious sense, Thomas did, but he wasn't about to say so. 'You're standing right here, Mr Gyges.'

'Am I? I'm not so sure.' A contemplative scowl. 'But you don't realize what it's like, do you? You think I see you, that I know you, that the problem is that every time I look away I forget who you are. But it's not like that. Not at all. When I stare at you – like this, like I'm staring at you right now – I don't recognize you from one second to the next. And it's not like your face becomes something *new* every moment, something that I've never seen before. It's just unknown. Unknowable . . .'

Gyges turned from the mirror to Thomas.

'When I look into the mirror, Dr Bible, I'm not there. But the kicker is that *you aren't either*. For me, there is no *you*. Just a voice. A voice from the dark.'

For a moment Thomas could only stare at him. 'You're suffering a brain injury,' he said lamely. 'You need to underst—'

'Brain injury?' the bearded man replied. '*Brain injury*? Is that what you think this is?' Shaking his head, he strode past them and yanked open one of the oak-stained doors.

Thomas turned as he crossed the threshold. 'Then what is it?'

'You're not a priest,' Gyges snapped.

The door pounded shut, swallowed the world before Thomas's face.

Neither of them said anything until the elevator doors closed.

'What do you make of that?' Sam finally asked.

'I don't know. He was drunk, for one. But beyond that? Could be he's suffering some post-traumatic stress . . .' he trailed, struggling to make sense of what had just happened. 'One thing's for sure.'

'What's that?'

'Did you notice how he behaved around us? The utter absence of any eye contact. His body language. Almost cringing from our presence.'

'So?'

Thomas breathed deeply. 'So, we were monstrosities to him. Faceless monstrosities.'

'What are you saying?'

Thomas found himself looking at his hand, at the missing wedding band on his ring finger, thinking of all the neural machinery churning away underneath, making this experience possible. *That* was where Neil was striking. Not at the heart, but at the soul.

'That Theodoros Gyges lives in a world of boogeymen.'

Other than in the back seat of a taxi, Thomas so rarely drove through Manhattan that he found the trip downtown to Federal Plaza vaguely disconcerting. Manhattan had always (and there was no other word for it) flummoxed him. The scale was nothing short of geological, as though the streets and avenues were river beds sunk canyon-deep into some ancient Martian plain. But the *feel* . . . At once archeological, like a vast inscription with Central Park the indent of some God-King's seal, and yet statistical, like a great 3-D bar graph, charting the sum of human hopes against the GDP of nations – a Powerpoint presentation frozen in monumental stone.

New York, Neil had once told him, was braille for a blinded God – the one place where the bumps of human ingenuity towered high enough for divine fingers to read. When Thomas had asked what it spelled out, Neil had replied: 'Three words: "*Fuck. You. Too.*" '

'So what do you think, professor?' Sam asked. 'If Gyges is Cassidy's first premise, what is it?'

'I'm not entirely sure,' Thomas said absently.

Nothing made sense. That was the heartbreaking truth. Nora fucking Neil. Neil murdering innocents. Sam pursuing him, career hound that she was. Europe freezing to death. Moscow gone – or a good chunk of it, anyway. Even a fool could see there was no plan, no hidden author. Everything shouted indifference. *Everything.* And those who thought otherwise, who embraced their hardwired weakness for simplicity, certainty, and flattery, simply made it worse. Voting for hardline rhetoric. Killing in the name of x, y or z.

Why couldn't they just play the game and let the world die?

Neil's words . . . from the previous night.

'Well, we need to come up with something,' Sam said. 'Something to wow Shelley. We're not going to catch this guy without your help, professor.'

Is that what he wanted? To hunt Neil?

He's hurting people.

What did it matter?

'Did you hear me, professor? Professor Bible? *Yoo-hoo . . .*'

'Call me Tom,' he said.

Think clear. Think straight.

He had already decided he was suffering some kind of dissociative stress response. The wan feeling of dislocation. The sense of self-estrangement, as though he shammed every smile, every word, every breath. Classic characteristics of the 'crisis phase' of critical incident stress.

Thomas Bible's world had been turned upside down. Like Gyges's staff, it had become unrecognizable.

'Recognition,' he said abruptly, suddenly seeing the answer to Sam's earlier question.

'Go slow, Tom. It's been a long day.'

He looked at Sam and smiled. 'I'll be okay. My brain is more plastic than most.'

'Like my shoes,' Sam replied.

*

The click of Sam's heels possessed an oily echo as they hustled across the Federal Building's basement parking garage. 'Neil's saying something about recognition,' he explained. 'He's saying recognition – self or other – is simply a matter of wiring.'

Sam frowned in the exhaust-stained gloom. 'I don't get it.'

'Think. Without recognition, there's nobody, just like Gyges said. There are no *people*, only buzzing brains bumping into buzzing brains.'

Sam pondered this over the course of several more clicks. 'So what would Powski be?' she asked as they approached the elevator. 'That pleasure is simply a matter of wiring?'

'Why not?'

Sam scowled, as though struck by something she should have thought of earlier. 'It almost seems as though he's arguing with you. You in *particular*, not the world.'

Thomas felt his stomach clench.

'Why do you say that?'

Her look was penetrating, almost manic in its intensity. 'Because you're the only person who could possibly decipher his message. Without you, he'd be talking over everyone's head, don't you think?'

Why *had* Neil come over last night? Why the confession? He had banged Nora shortly before – her bullshit trip to San Francisco made that clear enough. So what? He screws Nora, then drops by unannounced to drink and break bread with his old buddy, Goodbook? On his way between murders, no less. And on the night before the FBI is sure to start hunting down his old contacts.

Neil Cassidy was probably the most brilliant, most *premeditated* man Thomas had ever known. Sam was right. Neil was playing a game only Thomas knew, which meant he simply *had* to be playing *with* him. But why? Did he simply need him to teach his real opponents, the FBI, how to play? To bring them up to speed? Or was he doing all of this for Thomas's benefit?

Does he hate me that much?

A pang stuck him in the chest. For a moment, he felt like a schoolboy, all alone, abandoned by his only friend. *He's been screwing Nora all this time . . .* And smiling, clapping him on the back afterward. Didn't that speak of a fixation of some kind, of a pathological hatred?

Not necessarily, Thomas-the-professor had to admit. Friends banged friends' wives all the time, even friends they genuinely loved and respected. If they hated, it was usually to rationalize their betrayal. *Looks good on the prick*, or *Serves him fucking right*. Otherwise, such peccadilloes had surprisingly little impact on the suite of expectations and attitudes that made up friendship. It was as though the two behaviors worked on a different frequency.

'Could be,' Thomas replied, looking away from Sam.

She needs to know! Tell her!

'What's wrong, professor?' Sam asked. Just then, the elevator chimed open.

'Cynthia Powski,' he said, as the doors closed. 'Do you think she might still be alive?'

What have I done?

'Might . . . But we doubt it.'

'Why's that? He spared Gyges, didn't he?'

'In a living-death sort of way, I suppose he did. But you missed the rest of Cynthia Powski's performance this morning.'

Thomas swallowed. It hadn't occurred to him there might be more. 'What do you mean? What happens?'

Sam hesitated – her face looked all the more beautiful for its concentration. 'There's a break, and when he starts shooting again, Cynthia's still in the throes of passion, but something's changed. The neurologists we consulted think he somehow attached a transmitter to the primary pain pathways to her brain—'

'The spinothalamic and spinoreticular pathways?'

'Exactly, and used it to replace the pleasure control panel or whatever the hell it is he uses in the beginning of the BD.'

Thomas could only stare.

'Then he hands her a piece of broken glass.'

Images of Cynthia – memories from this morning – flashed before his mind's eye, her writhing now soaked in blood and scored by weeping gash after weeping gash.

Sam continued. 'The pain input generated by the resulting tissue damage, they told us, was probably stopped before it reached her brain, and translated into a signal that directly stimulated her pleasure centres. He rewired her like a basement rec-room, professor, then watched her slice her way to ecstasy.'

'My God,' Thomas whispered.

He made her cut herself. He made her want *to cut herself . . .*

Sam blinked rapidly. 'Wait till you see it, Tom. There's no God, trust me.'

Churning in his gut.

What the fuck is happening? Wake up . . . Wake up!

'But then that's Cassidy's point, isn't it?'

Thomas clutched his hands to keep them from shaking.

The Field Office was smaller than he expected, and except for cleaners, apparently abandoned.

'Hard to believe I run the FBI, isn't it?' Sam said, as she gestured to her cubicle.

Thomas smiled, cataloguing – as much out of habit as anything else – the various identity claims and behavioral residues that every workspace sported. The things that said *I belong to this*; *this is what I do*. Nothing surprised him, except, perhaps, the blue-headed pins arranged in the shape of a heart on her tackboard. He nodded to a NY Rangers cap hanging from a tack. 'You a fan?'

'Fucking A,' she said, settling into her chair. She cracked her knuckles, then began tapping at her keyboard. 'You?' she asked.

'Too much heartbreak.'

'One of *those*, are you?'

'One of those who?'

Sam sorted through a succession of bright windows on her flat screen. 'One of those who think games are about winning.'

'I guess I—'

'Here it is,' Sam interrupted. 'Neil Cassidy's brain.'

The screen was tiled with neural cross-sections, day-glo colored and shaped like chestnuts. For an instant, it seemed impossible that these images could be in any way related to his best friend, let alone to what he had seen on the BD earlier this morning. They seemed too abstract, too clinical, to be the engine of today's events.

But they were.

'According to the appended assessment,' Sam said, 'there's nothing to suggest that Cassidy is missing shame or guilt circuits. He's definitely not a garden variety psychopath, whatever he is.'

But Thomas already knew this. Neil lacked the behavior crucial to psychopathy, or to antisocial personality disorder more generally. He and Neil had been close for a long time, and as good as psychopaths were at bluffing conscience in the short term, they always showed the heartlessness of their hand sooner or later.

'Scary smart though,' Sam added. 'You want me to print these files up for you?'

'Please,' Thomas said. He felt numb. Meeting the FBI was one thing, but coming here, walking the halls of the bureau, was altogether different. It reminded him that it was an institution he was dealing with, with all the perils and pitfalls that represented. You could generally depend on individuals to be rational, but an organization? Especially one as enormous as the FBI. No matter how reasonable the decisions made at this or that labyrinthine juncture, the sorry fact was that you simply could not trust them to add up to anything sane.

'How did you get these?' he asked as the first pages began slipping from the laser printer.

'From the NSA.'

Speaking of monstrous institutions.

'And how did they get them?'

'Low-fields are pretty much part of any government biometric scan, nowadays, especially at sensitive locations.' She shot him her peculiar but endearing slanted smile. 'Would you like to see *yours*?'

'You gotta be kidding me.'

'Nope. Check it out.' She flashed through an array of windows, entered a code, then scrolled through what looked like dates and times. Another graphic of a brain, this one three-dimensional, popped onto the screen, animated by shifting colors like the temperature contours on a weather map. 'When I logged you in, this snapshot of your noggin was automatically taken.'

Thomas cursed under his breath.

'Pretty creepy, huh?'

'But this is useless without analysis,' Thomas said. 'What can it possibly tell you?'

A pained smile. 'Analysis comes included. It's a package deal. Look.'

A small window of text opened in the bottom left-hand corner. Thomas swallowed.

'So let's see,' Sam said. 'Subject is agitated: fear and anxiety, mostly, little aggression and absolutely no murderous intent. Whew – that's a relief. The subject also shows signs of grief and disorientation, with – oh, this is interesting – with a strong possibility of deception.' Sam leaned back to look up at him. 'You hiding anything from me, professor?'

Tell her!

Thomas laughed. 'Not consciously, no.'

Sam smiled. 'That's the thing with these things. All hints and probabilities. I've been told that the software improves every year, though.'

'No doubt,' Thomas said grimly. 'Context mapping seems to be the only thing people in my biz are doing any more – that and parallel behavioral testing. That's where the real money is.'

'Context mapping?'

'Yeah, where they correlate different behaviors, emotions, mental tasks and so on to various imaging results across populations. Basically mapping what these patches of color mean in terms of our real-world experience.'

'Mind reading,' Sam said.

'Worse.'

'So then why is the money in – what did you call it?'

'Parallel behavioral testing.' Thomas scratched the back of his neck, trying his best to cultivate a look of almost-boredom. 'Remember how a couple of years back the government made it illegal for corporations to use low-fields on their customers and employees? Well ever since, big business has invested heavily in attempts to bring together the results of various behavioral tests – written, verbal, task-oriented, stuff like that – to various fMRI types. So, if you respond in such and such a way to such and such a test, they can roughly *infer* your low-field, and consequently what kind of customer or employee you'll be. Basically it's given them a crude way around the law. And it's meant big bucks for many a mediocre psychologist.'

People were almost universally shocked when he explained this. But what did they expect? They lived in a social system devoted to the pursuit of competitive advantages. The very structure of the society they so prized, even prayed to, was devoted to getting them to do what others wanted, short of outright coercion.

You were only allowed to push the buttons that people couldn't see.

'Does it work?' Sam asked. Apparently she was more pragmatic.

'You know,' Thomas said with a shrug. 'Less than they hope, more than they admit. You wouldn't believe the bullshit.'

'I work for the FBI.'

'Even still.'

Sam grinned. 'Enough fun for now,' she said, gathering up the printed sheets and handing them to Thomas. 'We need to see if the boss is still lurking around.' She smiled triumphantly, as though anticipating brownie points.

Sam led him through a carpeted warren of workstations, some completely dark, others illuminated by kooky screensavers. Something like shock accompanied his first glimpse of Agent Atta. She stood in a glass-enclosed conference area, talking to a tall black man in a stylish suit. It seemed hard to believe that just this morning she'd swept into his office bearing madness. Special Agent-in-Charge, Shelley Atta, destroyer of worlds . . .

Thomas paused in the gloom.

'Logan still hasn't called in,' Atta was saying. 'She doesn't have a clue what's going on.'

A tingle always accompanied eavesdropping, as though words could be bedrooms. He and Sam both froze in their tracks, intent on the conversation they had stumbled onto.

'What's her story, anyway?' the black man asked. 'Who'd she fuck to get sent up so quickly?'

'You mean you haven't hear—'

A vacuum hummed to life from the back of the office. Cleaning staff.

Thomas turned and saw Sam pale-faced and motionless at his side. It was always like this. No matter how much he reminded himself that the lives about him were every bit as impacted as his own, he found himself faintly astonished whenever he confronted that complexity. Of course Sam had skeptics and detractors – enemies even. Of course she had made one sketchy decision too many. Everyone was in the same boat. They just lacked the eyes to see past themselves.

'*Fuck*,' she whispered.

'Don't read too much into it.'

'Into what?' Her voice cracked. 'Having my reputation dragged through the mud?'

Thomas pulled her aside.

'People gossip. It's just part of being human. Some think it's the evolutionary key to our intelligence.' He fell silent, feeling slightly abashed. Nora had always laughed at his habit of thinking that knowledge could see people through difficult moments. A pensive moment passed. 'Who's that Atta's talking to, anyway?'

'Dean Heaney. Our DoJ advisor.'

'Do they know each other? Are they old friends?'

'No.'

He knew he was doing it again, but he couldn't stop himself. 'Well, there you go. The more slight the acquaintance, the more likely the person hearing accusations of deficiency will attribute those deficiencies to the accuser.'

'Really?' Sam said in a strange tone.

'Really,' Thomas replied, even though he knew he'd somehow caused more harm than good. Why? Why were facts so helpless in the face of pain? 'They call it trait transference.'

Sam stared at him angrily. A tear rolled down her left cheek. 'And what if they're true?' she asked.

'What if what's true?'

'The accusations,' she said, turning on her heel.

'Sam!' he called, following her. 'Sam, I didn't me—'

'*Bible*?' someone incredulously cried. Agent Atta. Sam stopped and whirled.

'Bible!' Atta bellowed from behind him. '*Freeze*, asshole!'

Thomas stopped in his tracks.

'Hands up. Over your head.'

Thomas did as he was told, too stunned to feel anything, let alone think.

'Now turn slowly.'

'Shelley?' Sam shouted. 'He's here to help!'

'Help? I don't think so.'

Thomas had turned as she said this, but his protest was quashed by the sight of Agent Atta's gun levelled at his chest. A red dot swayed across the breast of his sport jacket. A wave of heat flashed through him. Terror.

'Th-this is insane,' he croaked.

'I'm afraid your professional opinion means squat around here, professor. You're suffering something of a credibility crisis.'

'Shelley!' Sam cried.

In the dark Agent Atta's look was hard and handsome in the way of solid women. Something in her eyes told Thomas that she enjoyed pointing her gun. 'Your professor friend,' she said to Sam, 'has been what you might call less than forthcoming. It seems that while we were interviewing him in his office this morning, our SUB was sleeping off a hangover in his house.' She paused for an instant to let the significance of this sink in. 'Gerard's over at his place now. The Evidence Response Team is en route.'

Sam approached her boss warily, casting a searching look at Thomas as she did so. The DoJ advisor, Dean Heaney, sat on the corner of an unoccupied desk just behind Agent Atta. He smiled as though watching a skirmish between family members he equally despised.

'Ask him,' Atta said to the junior agent.

'Is it true?' Sam said rigidly, her look somewhere between stunned and devastated. Very unprofessional.

'Yeah,' he said.

'That's why you rushed home this morning.'

'I *wanted* to tell you, it was just that—'

All at once her demeanor became hard and cynical–professional. For some reason Thomas found this almost as disconcerting as Agent Atta's gun.

'Wanted?' she said. 'Then why didn't you?'

Where did you go? Sam?

'I'm not sure.'

'This guy's a psychology professor?' Dean Heaney chortled from behind. 'Remind me not to send my kids to Columbia.'

Between the gun, the accusations, and Sam, Thomas felt he might have a heart attack. 'He was my best friend for eighteen years,' he said hotly. '*Eighteen years*! What did you expect me to do?'

'The right thing,' Agent Atta said.

'And handing him over to the Feds is always the right thing, is it? Talk about fucking credibility crises. No. I had to know for sure.'

Agent Atta pulled out her handcuffs.

'Tell me honestly, Agent Atta,' Thomas said quickly. 'If the Feds were after someone you loved, how quickly would you roll over?'

The question seemed to catch her off guard. She glanced nervously at Sam.

'Careful,' Heaney said. 'It could be a Jedi mind trick.'

'What do you think, Samantha?' Atta asked.

The sudden, irrational fear that Agent Atta was about to execute him seized Thomas. *Gun-gun-real-gun!* reeled through his panicked thoughts.

'I think we need him,' Sam said hastily. 'He *knows* what Cassidy's doing, Shelley. And he thinks he knows why. He's given us a motive – a *real* motive, for Christ's sake.'

'A motive?'

'Better than anything those NCAVC jokers have come up with. Better by far.'

Atta's large, chocolate eyes lingered on Thomas for a moment. 'Speak,' she said.

'It's a long story,' Thomas replied.

Atta holstered her Glock. 'Then you ride with me,' she said.

CHAPTER SIX

August 17th, 7.01 p.m.

Thomas felt a flare of embarrassment when he saw the vehicles congregated in front of his house: two Peekskill cruisers, a couple of unmarked cars, and a black van probably belonging to the Evidence Response Unit. Flashing lights splashed comic-book colors across the white siding. Contrails roped the sky above, fading into violet fans as night tightened its grip. They had driven to the very edge of daylight.

Shelley ran her car onto his lawn and pulled it into park. 'Look, professor, you're not out of the woods yet,' she said, staring at him intently. 'As it stands, we could charge you with obstruction, harboring a fugitive, maybe even accessory after the fact. You're too smart to think we'd nail you, but you're also too smart not to know how these things go. Anything can happen.'

'Don't bother with th—'

'Hear me out,' Atta interrupted. 'Now you've taken responsibility for your foolishness – which is a rare thing in this business. I've dealt with so many assholes that I sometimes feel more like a proctologist than special agent. You're not an asshole . . . I can see that.'

'So you believe me?' Thomas had spent most of the drive giving her an abbreviated account of what he'd told Sam earlier, about Skeat's class in Princeton, about the Argument – and of course, Nora. The entire time Atta had simply stared at the road, only rarely glancing at him to let him know she listened. Otherwise, he felt as though he were arguing the virtues of water to a stone.

'I believe yours is the most plausible interpretation of this madness I've heard. Don't get me wrong. I think all that stuff about the semantic apocalypse is bullshit, plain and simple. But the question is one of whether Cassidy believes it.'

'You'd make a good psychologist, Agent Atta.'

Atta actually smiled. 'Men do tend to shrink in my company,' she quipped. She shouldered open her door, saying, 'Now let's see how you do as an investigator, professor.'

There was something matronly and more than a little condescending about her demeanor, but Thomas decided that he liked Shelley Atta. She radiated stability, something he desperately needed given all that had happened, never mind the fact that he was about to help the authorities ransack his house . . . his *home*.

Could the day become any more nightmarish?

'Tommy!' he heard someone cry as he crossed his lawn. Mia, leaning over the railing of his porch. Ripley and Frankie were crowded at his side, Ripley tall enough to imitate Mia's lean, Frankie gripping the wrought iron spindles with a convict's resignation. They both looked terrified.

Ignoring Agent Atta's angry call, he trotted over to them, doing his best to look more sheepish than stunned. The fact that neither of them said anything brought his heart to his throat.

'So what did we have for dinner?' he asked lamely.

'Are you under rest?' Frankie asked, wide eyed. His face seemed impossibly round in the clicking lights – and defenceless, utterly defenceless.

'He doesn't have handcuffs on,' Ripley said, her tone of sisterly reprimand as forced as Thomas's. 'I told you he wouldn't have handcuffs on.'

As though to confirm the fact, Thomas reached up to place a hand against each of their cheeks. He did his best to chuckle and smile. 'Exciting, huh?' he said glancing back over his shoulder. He managed to resist an apologetic look at Mia.

'They have *guns*,' Frankie said.

'They're not going to shoot Bart, are they?' Ripley blurted.

'They're the *good* guys,' Thomas explained. He could feel his parental instincts roil, spin with urges to protect, to mislead, to reassure. A father was supposed to be a bulwark, someone who turned aside worldly intrusions, and yet here he was, feeding his children lame apologies. 'Just like the movies . . .'

'Then where are the bad guys?' Ripley asked.

'Far away,' Thomas said. 'Daddy's just helping them find . . . directions.'

Agent Atta's voice fell hard across the evening air. '*Professor*!' Frankie fairly jumped.

'Look,' Thomas said, caressing each of their cheeks with his thumbs. 'I won't be long. You two just hang tight and I'll come get you in no time, okay?'

But both of them were staring at the shadowy woman behind him. 'Why's she hollering at you, Dad?' Frankie asked in a small voice. His eyes had the look of having crawled across the first of many scary facts. Their home had been cracked open. Could the world be big enough to break anything?

Rather than answer, he looked to Mia. 'Would you mind? At least until . . .' He gestured helplessly to the surrounding commotion. He glimpsed Agent Atta waiting impatiently beside the bushes that flanked his porch.

'Sure thing,' Mia said with an understanding blink. 'C'mon, kids. Let's go see if your house is on the news. You could be famous!'

Thomas was almost overwhelmed by a feeling of invasion when he stepped inside. Strangers, everywhere he looked, strangers going through the pockets of his home. Two uniformed cops were in his kitchen, leaning against his counter and apparently shooting the breeze. Sam, Gerard, and Dean Heaney stood in an expectant cluster in his living room. Behind them, two women wearing Evidence Response Team jackets seemed to be scanning his carpet.

'Well, Gerard?' Agent Atta asked.

The agent looked at Thomas for a sour moment. 'Still sweeping,' he said to his SAC, 'but other than kiddie porn on the computer' – he graced Thomas with a contemptuous wink – 'I don't think we'll find anything.'

Thomas grinned his best fuck-you grin. Scarcely a month passed without some story of some reform-minded political figure arrested on child pornography charges. Just the previous week Thomas had found a leaflet in his department mailbox accusing the government of 'politically motivated cyber-planting'.

'Why would Cassidy come here?' Sam asked, frowning. 'He must have known we'd show up sooner or later.'

'Could be he was simply being sociable,' Atta replied, staring from point to point around the living room, looking for all the world like a disgusted interior decorator. 'Could be he wasn't . . .' She turned to Thomas. 'You said you passed out around 2.30 or so last night?'

Thomas shrugged. 'That's when I *think* I pass—'

'So he had the run of the place for about five hours, then.'

'Could've done anything,' Gerard said. *To you or your kids*, his expression added.

Thomas felt faint. This was not his home. These people were not hunting his best friend.

'I want you to do a walk through, professor,' Atta said, 'check to see if anything is amiss – you know, out of place. Whatever game Cassidy is playing, he seems to think you're an important player. Gerard, Logan, you give him a hand. Make sure he's thorough.'

'You gotta nice dump, here,' Gerard said as they stepped into the den – what used to be Nora's workout room. 'Here's your copy of the warrant, by the way.' He slapped a document against his chest.

Thomas glared at him, trying to decide whether his hostility was real or procedural. 'It's not signed,' he said, scanning the document.

'We'll get our janitor to sign it tomorrow.'

Thomas looked to Sam, who simply shrugged. *You brought this on yourself*, her look said.

He found himself clutching the paper, as though it were the only shred of whatever it was that would see him through this. Here he was, standing in his den, helping strangers turn his life inside out. The room seemed smaller for some reason, the ceiling dingier. Cobwebs hung like bells in the corners. A peculiar shame suffused him – not that of secrets exposed so much as that of recognition: his home was simply one of millions, little more than a shell, dressed to give the pathetic illusion of individuality.

Just another monkey, Neil would say, *hiding in your hole.*

'Hockey fan, huh?' Gerard said, glancing at a vintage Bruins jersey Thomas had pinned to the wall.

'You're not?'

'Too Canadian.'

'What's wrong with Canadians?'

'They're just Americans who think they're better than Americans.'

Thomas snorted. 'As opposed to what? Americans who thi—'

'You should know I almost shot your dog,' Gerard interrupted, gesturing to Bart on the fold-out couch. Thomas wasn't sure whether he'd ever met someone who oozed quite so much *I-don't-give-a-shit*. It was all an act, of course, the sign of someone preoccupied by dominance hierarchies. Classic Freudian compensation. Gerard so regularly communicated his power because he was so uncertain of it.

'Why would you shoot my dog?' Thomas asked.

'Too friendly. I never trust anything too friendly.'

'What? He hump your leg or something?'

Only Sam laughed. 'Big dog, Gerard. You'd be wearing diapers for weeks.'

Thomas found himself glancing at her in thanks, then looked ruefully at his sad old dog. Bart yawned, and then, as though to prove Sam right, rolled over and showed his belly – among other things.

'*Bart*,' Thomas said.

'Gawd*damn*,' Gerard said, his look appreciative. 'That dog deserves his own website.'

'Ignore him,' Sam said, shaking her head at her partner. 'Do you see anything, professor? Anything out of place?'

'Www,' Gerard cackled, 'dog-got-a-bone.' Evidently he found himself quite hilarious.

'I'm not even sure what I'm supposed to be looking for,' Thomas admitted. 'Are you?'

'I'm not sure about anything any more,' Sam replied.

'Or how about,' Gerard continued, 'www.canine.com? You get it, Logan? Kay-*nine*. Look at it. That's gotta be nine inches in dog years!'

'Have you been smoking crack?' Sam asked, nevertheless smiling. 'Nine inches in dog years,' she repeated to Thomas. Then, as though all bound in the same wires of tension, the three of them burst out laughing.

Madness, Thomas found himself thinking. Everyday life was madness.

'Bart!' Thomas cried. 'You're distracting the special agent!'

As though finally shamed by their laughter, Bart whined and rolled off the mattress. He trotted from the room.

Thomas wiped tears from his eyes.

'It's good to clean the pipes,' Sam said from his side. 'Especially after a day like today.'

'Remarkable animal,' Gerard said, shaking his head.

'C'mon,' Sam called, following Bart out the door, 'let's at least pretend we're looking for wild geese.'

Thomas lingered behind to take one last look. A strange vertigo haunted the room, like the delayed reaction to a near miss on the freeway. He had a drunken memory of Neil disappearing through the doorway. Not his friend Neil, but the Neil looming behind the frame of Cynthia Powski's final porn. Neil the shadow. Neil the knife.

'So he had the run of the place . . .'

Thomas found Agents Logan and Gerard in his office. Sam was studying his giant satellite poster of the Earth on the far wall, framed by high-resolution whorls and continental land masses.

'Space buff?' she asked.

He suddenly felt embarrassed by how juvenile it looked. 'When I was a kid,' he explained. 'I put it up to cover the tacky panelling more than anything else.'

'Still, nice picture,' Sam said, as though she understood the wonder of such things.

'No tits,' Gerard chimed, leaning back to peak behind a bookcase.

Despite their earlier laughter, something about their carefree attitude sparked resentment in Thomas. Then he realized: when you lost a trail, you followed a search pattern, which was little more than a systematic attempt to squeeze dumb luck out of an indifferent world. For the human mind there was precious little difference between looking for something unknown and looking for nothing.

So they were going through the motions. Same as him.

He walked over to the oak desk that he and Nora had spent a laborious summer refinishing. Everything seemed to be where he'd left it. A stack of draft course outlines. Sticky notes with meaningless reminders. He turned on his desk light – the green glass one Neil had given him for Christmas years ago in college. What he saw punched the breath from his lungs.

'Sam,' he said numbly.

'Nine inches in dog years,' she was saying in a *you-take-the-cake* tone.

'Sam,' he repeated. 'Come here.'

He pointed to the light.

'What about it?'

'That wasn't there before.'

'Shelley!' Sam shouted. 'You're going to want to look at this!'

In a blue marker all but invisible against the green glass when the light was off, someone had written

www.semanticapocalypse.com

Not someone. *Neil.*

There could be no doubt, Thomas realized with horror.

He was part of the game.

He stood by woodenly as Sam sat at his desk and fired up his computer.

You already have Nora, was all he could think. *Just leave me alone.*

Within moments, his office was crowded with people, and Thomas was numbly explaining how he found the web address. Atta had Gerard chase all the newcomers except Dean Heaney from the room, then call someone named Lamar at 'CI'.

'And tell him to keep it under his hat,' she snapped. Gerard nodded, frowning in concentration.

'Got it!' Sam cried.

They all crowded around the flat panel. Gerard muttered on his palmtop behind them.

A small black window had opened in the centre of the screen. No, not entirely black. Grey shapes – *moving* shapes. Legs scissoring across . . .

'Low-res webcast,' Sam said.

'Realtime?' Agent Atta asked.

'Impossible to tell.'

They saw booted feet kicking something.

'Is that a hand?' Dean Heaney asked. 'Someone dead?'

A bright flash, as though a floor lamp had been rolled around. A glimpse of a prostrate body. Shining blood? Then . . .

'Fuck me,' Sam muttered.

It was over. Whatever it was Neil had broadcast, it was over.

Special Agent-in-Charge Shelley Atta turned to Thomas with baleful eyes. *Your fault,* her look muttered.

'Wait a sec,' Sam said. 'It's starting over. He's probably been replaying this all day.'

She was right. The window was still black, but something in the character of the gloom had changed. A pale smear near the center seemed to gain resolution. A face, like that of a drowning victim rising through black waters. Then suddenly the picture was bright – there had been some kind of cut. It was a talk-show clip, something like the old *Charlie Rose*, showing a handsome, middle-aged Latino man wearing a suit and seated in studio lighting. He appeared to be listening.

'Is that who I think it is?' Sam asked.

'*Zarba*,' Agent Atta hissed. At first Thomas thought she was naming the man, but then he remembered that *zarba* was Arabic for shit.

'Who is it?' Gerard asked.

Sam rolled her eyes. 'It's Peter Halasz. You know, the congressman who went missing two days ago.'

Thomas realized he'd been holding his breath. 'It's him all right,' he said. He and Nora had actually voted for him when he was running for city council years back when they had lived in Brooklyn. He heard himself say, 'What the hell you up to now, Neil?'

'Nothing good,' Atta said darkly. She raised a hand and started snapping her fingers. 'Someone? Dean . . .'

'Already on it,' he said, holding his palmtop. 'Sorry to bug you, Jeff, but you ain't going to believe what I'm—'

'Look,' Sam said, 'he's saying something.'

'Sound!' Agent Atta exclaimed. 'Doesn't this thing have sound?'

Thomas dropped to a crouch and rather indelicately pushed past Sam's bare knees. He'd connected his computer to an old amplifier, which he kept beneath the desk. He cranked the volume.

'. . . as for the implications of the so-called "Wetware Revolution" ' Halasz's voice boomed from the speakers, 'I really think it's a tempest in a teapot.'

Thomas turned the volume down some. Sam greeted him with a quick, nervous smile as he pressed himself free.

'God has imbued each man with a free soul,' Halasz was saying, 'and it's that free soul that makes each man – excuse me, Felice, I meant to say, *person* – it's that free soul that makes each person responsible for their fortune good or bad, and more importantly, responsible for their *crimes*.'

'But surely—' a female voice began, but was cut off. The fishbowl scene freezed. A heartbeat passed and the window went black.

'I saw that interview,' Heaney said, holding his hand over his palmtop. 'It's from this spring, I think, when Halasz was campaigning against neurological courtroom pleas.'

'He taped it,' Thomas said, thinking of Cynthia Powski. 'It's part . . . part of his argument.'

Why did that word 'his' feel so wrong?

Suddenly the window brightened, and they saw Halasz again, this time crouching on the floor of what looked like a cage, his head wrapped in bandages. He held a little girl with matted blond hair cradled in his arms. He seemed to be wearing a disheveled version of the same suit he'd worn in the interview. The little girl wore a plaid skirt with white stockings – some kind of school uniform. She wasn't much younger than Ripley. They both stared at the camera in abject terror.

'Is Lamar getting this?' Atta barked to Gerard.

'Loud and clear,' Gerard said, his palmtop to his ear. 'He's running biometrics on the girl right now.'

'This is an outrage!' Halasz snarled at the camera. 'An *outrage*!'

The girl starting *cooing* – a sound that made Thomas tingle with horror. It was like watching a psychotic nightmare through a pipe. Suddenly Thomas wanted to run, to be anywhere-but-here.

'Roberta Sawyer,' Gerard said, repeating an inaudible voice. 'Goes by "Bobbie". Reported missing last week in West Virginia.'

'Our boy gets around,' Atta muttered.

'Shush,' Halasz was saying to the girl. 'Shhhh . . .' He pressed his cheek against her matted locks. Low-res tears spilled from his eyes when he closed them. They popped open, seemed to search the blackness somewhere off behind the camera. 'Hush,' he whispered.

Then he bit into her cheek as though she were an apple.

Her shriek was inhuman.

'*There're boundaries*!' Halasz wailed. '*Limits*!'

The girl flopped like a deep-sea fish in his arms. People fought, Thomas numbly realized, as frantic and as vicious as any wild animal.

'NO, CONGRESSMAN,' Ocean Voice said. 'ONLY CIRCUITS AND BEHAVIORAL OUTPUTS. WHAT DOES IT MATTER WHETHER THE INPUTS COME FROM ME OR FROM THE WORLD?'

Halasz shook his head, like a dog rending tendon from bone.

'*God's* circuits!' he cried, spitting blood like spittle. '*Your* perversion!' he sobbed, leaning back to the twitching girl. 'This isn't me! God made me!'

'BUT YOU FEEL IT. YOU CHOOSE.'

Drenched in hot blood, Halasz laid the girl on the cement floor before him, weeping.

'*Pleeaase*,' he hissed, as he started taking off his clothes. '*Pleeeassse*!'

'YOU WANT THIS. YOU ACHE.'

Thomas simply turned and walked from the room. He could hear Halasz muttering, '*But . . . but . . .*' He went to the bathroom and sat in front of the toilet for a while. He stared at the rind of dust rimming the faux-brass register, wondered about germs. '*No! Just a little longer, please . . .*' floated down the hall, followed by noises too human . . . too human to be animal.

He did not vomit.

'*Soooo good . . .*'

He could not think. He could not feel.

'*Soooo . . .*'

When he returned to his office, all was ashen-faced silence. The computer was off.

Sam began softly sobbing.

'That is some fucked up shit,' Gerard was saying.

The four of them, Thomas, Sam, Gerard, and Dean Heaney milled around the living room. Agent Atta was in the kitchen, talking on her palmtop after having chased away the locals and the Evidence Response Team.

'Did he hypnotize him?' Gerard asked.

Thomas ran a slow hand over his scalp. 'No. Hypnosis doesn't work that way. The notion of the all-powerful hypnotist and the all-compliant subject is a myth.'

A scowl flexed across the agent's pudgy-handsome face. 'But I saw this act in college once where—'

'Half-true, half-bullshit,' Thomas interrupted with a heavy breath. 'Researchers have discovered that many participants actually follow the hypnotist's instruction just to please the crowd, not the hypnotist.'

Gerard shook his head, wild-eyed and unconvinced. 'I know what I saw.'

'But then, you *are* an idiot,' Sam said. 'Didn't you see the bandages?'

The big man sneered. 'I was talking about college.'

'So you think it's another brain thing, professor,' Dean Heaney asked.

Thomas rubbed the back of his neck. Every time he blinked he saw . . . too much.

'Gotta be,' he said after a moment. 'Some kind of surgical intervention, probably in the anterior cingulate gyrus and the dorsolateral prefrontal cortex – but you'd have to ask a neurologist.'

'The anterior what?' Gerard asked.

'The parts of the brain involving executive functions.'

'Oh.'

'Just so you know,' Sam said, 'he means the *will* – the parts of the brain involving the will.'

There was poison in the air – Thomas could feel it – and they only had one another as targets.

'Good thing you clarified that for me, Logan. I thought he was talking about the president's last dump.'

'Sorry, Ger,' Sam said with mock contrition. 'I didn't mean to sound condescending – you know, *talk down to you . . .*'

Still on the phone, Agent Atta sauntered in from the kitchen, saying 'I got it, I got it, I got it,' in an irritated tone. 'Okay. Bye.' She clapped her palmtop shut, glanced at each of them in turn. 'Well,' she said, 'I've talked to some of the more expensive suits in Washington.' She fixed Thomas with a hard look. 'Just so you know, professor, from this moment forward, you're not to talk to anyone about what you witnessed here, understand?'

'What do you mean? Why?'

'National Security.'

Thomas blinked. It was funny how charged certain words could become. Thomas's father had always sworn aloud whenever he heard the phrase on old broadcast TV. During the Cold War, he would explain, back when nothing less than the fate of humanity was at stake, they hadn't required a fraction of the measures supposedly necessary for the War on Terror. '*There's always a lunatic fringe*,' he would rant. '*You might as well declare war on jacking off!*'

'Oh,' Thomas said. 'I get it.'

'I'm not sure you do.'

'Oh, but I do, Agent Atta. Neil *told* me he was NSA.'

'So then you understand. We're dealing with highly classified subject matter here.'

'Important weapons in the never-ending war against terror, I suppose.'

Atta scowled. 'Something like that.'

She had the cornered look of someone forced to resort to a threadbare rationale, to be earnest about words that no one took seriously anymore. A certain willful fanaticism was required to act contrary to the obvious, a determination to *make* true.

'Bullshit,' Thomas said. 'Terrorism is theatre, and if the government was really interested in *helping* citizens, instead of manipulating them, it would tear down the stage, remind people that statistically, owning a gun is a greater danger than terrorism. This is about political embarrassment. About illegal skunkworks projects. About the lack of judicial oversi—'

'That's not what my—'

'Your handlers tell you what you need to hear! Nothing more, nothing less!'

Agent Atta stepped into his personal space, jabbed a long-nailed finger into his chest. 'You want to get into a pissing contest with me, professor? Hmm? Right or wrong, how difficult do you think I could make your life?'

Thomas stared down at her apprehensively. Suddenly Gerard's earlier quip about child pornography seemed more premeditated than otherwise. Ominous.

'There's a madman out there,' he said, finding courage in the steadiness of his voice, 'abducting and killing innocent—'

'You must be talking about the Chiropractor,' Atta said, 'because as far as the world is concerned, Neil Cassidy does not exist.'

'This is insane. Absolutely in—'

'Go ahead,' Atta said, jabbing him in the chest yet again. 'Test me.'

'That's enough, Shelley,' Thomas heard Sam say from his periphery.

'You,' Atta snapped at her subordinate, 'shut your barbie-ass up.'

Thomas turned away and strode to the door.

'Where are you going?' Atta asked sharply.

'Next door to get my kids.' He paused, shot Sam an apologetic look. 'Just so you know, agent, I expect all of you to clear out before I come back.'

He slammed the door behind him.

Thomas saw the headlights through the kitchen window.

The kids were asleep upstairs – they probably wouldn't even remember him carrying them home from Mia's. He should have been asleep too, but for some reason he sat at the kitchen table, staring at the cold tiles across the floor, listening to the refrigerator hum.

He was walking to the door before he heard the timid knock. For a pulse-pounding moment, he realized it could be Neil – but his day had been too long, too traumatic for him to sustain any kind of alarm.

Numb, he simply pulled open the door, saw Sam standing on the darkened porch. She looked drawn, her face framed by too-much-has-happened hair.

'Crazy day,' she said, smiling nervously.

Thomas nodded. 'Crazy day.'

'Can I come in? Are you busy?'

'Look, I really am sorry for ly—'

'People do crazy things,' she said breezily. 'That's what makes a crazy day crazy.'

Thomas smiled, stepped aside so she could come in.

'Besides,' she continued as Thomas closed the door, 'I wanted to apologize for Shelley.'

Thomas turned, regarded her for a moment. She looked tired, yet frenetic around the edges, like someone venturing out on a dubious limb. She looked beautiful.

'You really got the hunger for this one, don't you?' he said.

She smiled, looked at him quizzically. 'Hunger for what?'

'For this case. You really want to crack this case.'

Playful frown. 'That obvious, huh?'

'Would you like a coffee?' Thomas asked.

'Sure. A decaf if you got one. My nerves are fried.'

He smiled, nodded. 'Crazy day.'

Sam cocked her head, smirking. 'Crazy, crazy . . .'

'Be-fucking-yond,' he said, as he walked to the kitchen. He loved the fact he could swear freely in her presence. He grabbed the glass pot from the coffee-maker, but paused when she failed to keep up her end of their goofy verbal game. He turned. She was leaning against the door frame, watching him, the toe of her left shoe hooked behind the heel of her right.

'Look,' she said. 'This . . . this isn't right.'

Thomas nodded. He suddenly felt pale and naked in the kitchen light. 'Yeah.'

'Why I'm here. I mean *really* . . .' She smiled, then laughed nervously. 'I should tell you.'

'Why are you here?'

'Tomorrow, I'm scheduled to interview this guy, Dr Mackenzie. Someone who worked with Neil.'

Neil. Everywhere he fucking turned, his life's new centre of gravity. Thomas suddenly felt like a fool. For a moment he'd thought she'd returned . . . well, for *him*.

'And?' He winced at the impatience of his tone.

'Well –' she swallowed – 'I've been informed that this guy can't mention Neil's work in any way – it's all classified – so the most he can do is give us his personal impressions.'

'So?'

'I could really use your help.'

'What about Shelley or Gerard?'

'Like I told you, we're stretched to the breaking point here.'

Thomas frowned. 'Why? I mean, what could I do?'

Her face went blank. The FBI, Thomas knew, underwent extensive training in tactical communication – or 'verbal judo' as they liked to call it in the media. The courses typically used words like 'managing', 'redirecting', and 'achieving', but *manipulation* was pretty much what it all came down to. A veneer of impersonal professionalism, as it turned out, was generally the best way for law enforcement to get what they needed, whether from civilians or suspects. The best way to win a pissing contest was to keep your dick holstered.

'Interpretation requires context, professor. No one knows Neil better than you.'

Thomas scrutinized her for a bemused moment. 'Have you always been so ambitious, Agent Logan?'

'C'mon . . . It's not so simple. You know that.'

No, it wasn't. There were lives on the line. Real honest-to-goodness people.

'I suppose not.'

'Then will you come?'

It felt wrong. He knew it in his bones – it felt so very wrong.

But she needed him.

'Call me in the morning, agent.'

And she looked so very right.

It took some rummaging, but he eventually found an old air mattress in the basement. He sat at the couch, his eyes fixed on the TV screen as he blew the thing up. Various news-models muttered in low volume. Apparently a bloody vertebrae had been found in a Long Island mail box, someplace far from the camera grid.

After finishing with the air mattress, he went upstairs and peeled some sheets and his comforter from the bed. Arms heaped, the air mattress bobbing back and forth, he went to the kids' room. Frankie and Ripley were fast asleep. Standing at the door, he paused to savor the magic of children bundled beneath blankets – warm, clean, and safe. Then he laid the air mattress on the floor between them, made his impromptu bed. He angled himself close to the rose-colored night-light, as if he planned to read. He stared at a broken crayon and the shadow it cast across the carpet. He tried to guess its color.

The little bubble in his gut suddenly yawned, became vast with fear and remorse and self-pity. Alone on the floor, he hugged his shoulders, clenched his teeth. He felt like a macaque monkey cringing desolate in the corner of some greater cage, watching the rest of the troop with wide, uncomprehending eyes.

Neil and Nora . . .

But his kids. He had his kids. They were the totem, the charm. Something his and not his – something all their own – which was what made having them so meaningful. Something to die for in a life, a world, where sacrifices had evaporated into commercial chatter.

Above, Frankie kicked and rolled in his sleep. Bart's tail thumped the mattress four times. Thomas smiled, thinking of their exultant faces when they found him in the morning. Here. Between them.

Daddeeeeee!

So long as he had them, he would never be alone.

Two strangers in a driveway, only one pretending to be human.

'My mother,' you say.

'What about her?'

'She's always telling me not to do things like this.'

People like you don't believe in people like me. Not on this side of the glass.

'I'll stay here, then. Really, it's no problem.'

'And what, bleed all over the sidewalk? Come come, don't be silly.'

I smile, neglect to tell you the blood isn't mine.

Instead I say, 'I feel so stupid.'

When you turn to lead the way, my eyes make maps of what comes next. You even hold open the door, such an eager, illustrated cow.

'You should know,' I say in a carefree-friendly way, 'I only fuck the meat.'

And now look at you.

I mean, I hate you, and at the same time, I really don't care. I think of Dahmer opening his fridge, arranging the baking soda just so. It's no longer a mystery to me, how he felt, what he thought, cataloguing his milk-cold trophies. I know he saw the horror the same as I do. He saw you, *the same as me, and some part of him recoiled, rolled knees to chest in remorse. Part of him cried,* What-have-I-done-what-have-I-done . . .

But you see, he just

didn't

care.

You were everything. Squirming, screaming, the human cut from the animal, the animal battered into the doll. You were everything that mattered. The spit of taste, the tingle of touch, the spark of sight, curved hot against his belly. The one true thing.

And he didn't care.

CHAPTER SEVEN

August 18th, 8.39 a.m.

'So it must be strange knowing people the way you do.'

These were Sam's first words as they pulled away from Thomas's driveway the following morning. She had arrived in the midst of the morning pandemonium. Frankie was in one of his more murderous, brattish moods, where his endless declarations of 'No!' took on Shakespearean dimensions. You might almost think he was shouting at God Almighty. Thomas fairly dragged him crying over to Mia's while Sam watched from the driveway, leaning against her Mustang. 'Just a sec,' Thomas called, glancing at her in exasperated apology. Ripley, of course, was at her angelic best. *She* was no Frankie, and she made sure Sam knew as much by beaming a sunny 'Why, hello!' while her brother wailed. Mia leaned out his screen door, entirely unimpressed with Frankie's tantrum. He made no secret of his interest in Sam as the kids hustled past him.

'Frankie's having a bad morning,' Thomas said, though Mia had yet to look at him. 'I mean *bad* bad. I feel like I should mow your lawn or something.'

'I feel like I should mow *your* lawn,' Mia said, scrutinizing Sam the way a horny truck-driver might. He smiled and waved.

'Um, it's on the wrong side of the fence, don't you think?'

Mia laughed. 'I still get drunk from time to time – shoo, shoo. Go be *investigated.*'

Thomas shook his head, smiling. 'She *is* a babe, isn't she?'

Frankie was yelling at Ripley from somewhere in the house.

'Oh no, not her. She's a *fox.*'

'So it's good I'm a chicken, you think?'

Mia had ignored him, calling out to Sam instead. 'Traffic-wise you might want to drive out to the 87!' Thomas had turned in time to see her smile and nod in dubious thanks.

Now, sitting in the passenger seat, he pondered her question, trying to look past her glamor. Sunlight streamed across her, shorn of its glare by the windshield. Bunched about her waist and hips, her charcoal skirt and suit jacket looked hot to the touch. She seemed fresh and new – even the fabric-in-sun smell of her tickled him with a sense of novelty.

'I'm not so sure that I do "know people",' he said, glancing out his window at a passing brick bungalow. A mother in gardening clothes whisked by. She was scolding a crying girl, who held a broken-necked flower. 'Not anymore.'

And just like that, he was depressed.

There was regret in Sam's smile. All verbal roads led to Neil; she had to know as much.

'Well,' she said lamely, 'there's knowing and then there's *knowing*.'

A nice thing about being a cognitive psychologist was that you could skip the questions that people typically asked in difficult situations – especially all the versions of 'How could I be so stupid?' Thomas knew exactly how: he was *human*, and humans were particularly horrible when it came to esteem-related beliefs. The tendency to believe flattering claims – that one pretty much knew everything they needed to know, that one was generally more intelligent than others, more moral, more skilled, and so on – was universal.

Thomas had never suspected Neil because he'd always thought he had one up on him. Everyone thought they had one up on everyone else, and they tended to get freaked when things seemed otherwise. As much as he loved Neil, Thomas had always felt sorry for him – *sorry*! Neil had seemed hapless with his misplaced self-confidence, his narrow focus on career, his inability to grow up. Like everyone else, Thomas had made himself into a walking, talking yardstick of what was right and true, and Neil, poor Neil, just didn't measure up.

What a fucking joke.

Peekskill slipped past the windows, a tubular panorama of tar and concrete, franchise signs like flyswatters against the sky. A wild urge to scream kicked through Thomas. This was crazy, throwing himself into the maelstrom like this. He couldn't blink without seeing

Cynthia Powski – or even worse, Peter Halasz and Bobbie Sawyer. What did you do when the world became unhinged? What did any sensible person do? You retreated, you hunkered down where you were safe – *home* – with those few souls you knew you could depend on, and who depended on you.

What was he doing here, anyway? Chasing a skirt? Was it as crass as that?

As stupid?

'Hell*oooo*?' Sam was saying. 'Umm, professor?'

Thomas cleared his throat, ran a hand across his face. He studied her profile for what seemed a long, frozen heartbeat. Her wide blue eyes regarded the road, flat with concern. In the sunlight, wisps of hair glowed like fiber-optic filaments over her slightly up-turned nose.

Thomas breathed. She smelled like cherries.

'Sorry, agent.'

I should've stayed with the kids.

'I'm afraid I need to pick your brain a bit more,' Sam said, staring at the sunny terrain before them. The satellite radio was turned low. A talk-show voice fluttered over the ambient sounds of the road: someone talking about the Chinese economic meltdown.

' . . . *self-regulating systems require transparency and flexibility.*'

'*You mean democracy.*'

'*Well . . . maybe* before *the information technolog—*'

Thomas idly watched an Exxon-Mobil station slide past, as bright and shiny as a child's toy beneath a dark crowd of conifers. Rather than replying, he found himself thinking about fossil fuels, dinosaurs, then archeologists tramping through the Gobi dust.

'Feel like some *Fritos*?' Sam asked in the wake of his silence. She fished a small, crackling bag from her oversized purse, dangled it like he was a sulky ten-year-old.

Good old Fritos.

'No thanks,' Thomas said.

'Are you *shooooor*?'

Thomas shook his head and chuckled. 'What would you like to know, agent?'

She set the bag down and shrugged. 'Neil, Neil, and more Neil, I'm afraid. What you shrinks call an obsession, we Feds call "paying the rent." She paused, as though realizing that her bantering tone was simply making things worse. 'I need to know the world he lives in,' she continued more seriously. 'I need to crawl into his headspace.'

'No easy feat,' Thomas said. After a moment's hesitation he added, 'You understand the Argument well enough, don't you?'

'I think so,' Sam said pensively. 'I just don't understand how anyone could . . . could . . .'

'Believe in it.'

Sam nodded. 'According to what you said yesterday, Neil sees himself as some kind of missionary bent on spreading the Bad News. That's why I was so excited. I mean, as important as motives are to you psychologists, they're pretty much the end-all-be-all for us investigators. Without a motive, nothing makes sense.'

'And so?'

'Well I was thinking last night . . . Neil can't be a missionary, can he? Wouldn't that mean he actually had a *point*? And isn't that what your Argument is all about, the fact that everything is pointless?'

Thomas watched her for a bemused moment, debating the futility of what he was about to say. People were hardwired not only to be biased and closed-minded, but to think they were the most unbiased and open-minded person they knew. Humans were literally designed to be easily and irrevocably programmed. Knowing this made precious little difference. No matter how much research you showed them, they continued to fault the other guy, the other claim, the other book, what have you, with the regularity you might expect from a machine.

He *wanted* to think Sam was different – almost as much as he wanted to think he was different.

'Like I said, crawling into Neil's head won't be easy.'

'It never is.'

Thomas paused, searching for the right words. The muttering voice on the radio said, '. . . *and that sparked the foreign reserve crisis.*'

'Remember what I told you in the bar,' he started, his tone thoughtful, 'about the brain and evolution?'

'How we should expect consciousness to be a deceptive mess? Because of its youth or something, right?'

'Exactly. Evolution's a messy, opportunistic process, one that requires eons to work out the kinks. As a relatively recent adaptation, you would expect conscious experience, or whatever it is you and I are sharing this very moment, to be a relatively crude, low-resolution affair. And like it or not, this is exactly what cognitive science is discovering.'

Thomas paused, mentally rummaging through the bag of tricks he used to make this point to his students. 'Just for instance, tell me how much of your visual field is in color.'

Sam frowned and shrugged. 'All of it. Why?'

Thomas fished one of his pens out of his blazer pocket. 'Don't look,' he said, 'just keep staring at the road and try to tell me what color my pen is.' He held it up in her periphery: a Bic made in India.

Sam smiled, staring with corner-of-her-eye concentration. 'It *is* tough,' she said, 'but I'm pretty sure it's blue . . . Yep. It's blue. It's gotta be.'

Thomas handed it to her. It was bright red.

'We actually live in a primarily black and white world, with a narrow ring of color immediately before us. Our brain fills in the rest.' He spent several minutes explaining how the discovery of things like inattentional blindness, change blindness, masking, perceptual asynchrony, processing lags, and so on had overturned millennia of speculation in just two decades. 'You could make a career out of cataloguing all the ways in which consciousness is either blinkered or outright deceptive,' he said. 'The gap between the environmental information we *think* we take in, and the actual information we have access to is nothing short of staggering. It's so bad that most cognitive scientists refer to the experience you're having now – your sensorium as they like to call it – as the "Grand Illusion".'

Just then an eighteen wheeler pulled onto the road a short distance ahead, forcing Sam to break to a crawl. Dust rolled over the car. 'If it's as bad as all that,' she asked, obviously irritated, 'then why doesn't it *seem* that way?'

'But how could it seem otherwise? It's the only frame of reference you have.'

He could tell from her gaze that she wasn't so much watching the eighteen wheeler's towering rump as she was watching herself *watching* it. He could remember his own reaction to these facts in his freshman psychology class. He'd always been a reflective kid, but for the first time he found himself staring at his experience rather than the things within it. He could remember probing his visual field in particular, trying to understand how it could simply 'run out' without having any visible edge. Everything suddenly seemed at once fictional and impossible, like paint splashed across something monstrous. And quick, terrifyingly quick. Psychologists called such episodes 'derealization'. The irony was that they used the term to describe a kind of disorder, when it was about as accurate as any conscious experience could get.

It had certainly freaked him out – so much so he had sworn off dope for three months.

'Consciousness is an end-user,' Thomas continued, 'and a poor one at that. Out of all the information our brains crunch every second, only a tiny sliver makes it to conscious experience – less than a millionth, by some estimates.'

Sam, her eyes still blank, shook her head. 'But it doesn't *feel* that way. I mean, here I am, in the real world, seeing everything I need to see, driving to meet Mackenzie, listening to your madness . . .'

'Have you ever heard of something called "blindsight"?'

She shot him a quick *Yes-I'm-an-idiot* grin. 'I saw it in a kung fu movie, I think. Blind people who can see, somehow, right?'

'It's a real phenomena, suffered by people with damage to their primary visual cortex. Some can navigate rooms despite the complete absence of visual experience, or duck if you throw pillows at them. There's even cases of people who can draw pictures *they can't see.*'

Thomas referenced these examples so often that they had come to seem commonplace. But every so often – like now – something deep within him balked. How could it be possible to draw something you couldn't see, or write something you couldn't read? The discipline was littered with examples like these: bizarre pathologies that cut against our deepest assumptions regarding self and experience.

'So you're saying their brains can see, even though *they* can't?' A plaintive note had entered her voice. 'Like the way Gyges's brain could recognize Neil's face even though Gyges himself couldn't.'

'Exactly.'

'Too, too weird.'

'There's other forms as well. People who tap their toes, even though they find music unintelligible. People who grimace in agony, even though they feel no pain.'

Thomas looked out his window, glimpsed several children disappearing beneath the bowers of the woods that made a canyon of the road. He craned his head to peer between the trunks, but the trail – or whatever it was they followed – dropped away too quickly.

'There's actually no one place where consciousness comes together in the brain,' he continued, 'but in terms of the information it can access, it's very localized. It seems particularly hard for us North Americans to swallow given our bogus can-do indoctrination, but if you really attend to the decisions you make, even things like dragging your ass off the couch, you can clearly see how *after the fact* conscious experience is. You wanna get off the couch, then suddenly you are off the couch, and you credit yourself after the fact. So much of what we do – all of it in fact – simply pops into conscious experience, where "we" take credit for it.'

'But it can't be as bad as all that,' Sam said. 'It just can't. I mean *I think*, therefore *I am*, right? I feel stupid saying it, but doesn't that *have* to be true?'

'I'll admit it certainly seems to be the case. But it's a philosophical claim, and scientific research suggests otherwise. Something like "*it* thinks, therefore I *was*," would probably be more accurate.'

Sam seemed to scowl in slow motion. 'We're back to the self again, aren't we?'

Her voice had an edge.

They drove in silence for several moments.

'So really think about it now,' Thomas continued. 'Everything you live, everything you see and touch and hear and taste, everything you think, belongs to this little slice of mush, this little wedge in your brain called the thalamo-cortical system. For you, the road is as wide as a country road should be, the sky is as wide as *can* be. But in fact your visual connection to these things is smaller than the nail of your pinky. When I clutch your hand, your experience comes hundreds of milli-seconds after the fact. And all the neural processing that makes these experiences possible – we're talking about the most complicated machinery in the known universe – is *utterly invisible.* This is where we stand in the Great Circuit that embraces us: out of sync, deceived, as fragile as cobwebs, entombed in a hardwired cage: powerless. This expansive, far-reaching experience of yours is nothing more than a mote, an inexplicable glow, hurtling through some impossible black. *You're steering through a dream*, Sam, through smoke and mirr—'

Suddenly they were slowing, veering onto the shoulder. Gravel popped and crunched. Tall summer grasses whisked along the composite panels.

'Ooookay,' Sam said as she pressed the car into park, '*that* was just a little too freaky.'

'You said you wanted to know how Neil thinks.'

'My brain may have said that,' she said, scowling. 'I'm not sure I meant a word of it.'

Thomas laughed.

She slumped back into her seat, raised a hand to her forehead. Sunlight flashed from her clear-coated fingernails. 'So all this – the highway, the trees, my pounding heart – is simply *in my head*?'

'Afraid so.'

'But . . . But doesn't that mean *my head* is also in my head?'

'Yep.'

Her eyes lost focus. 'None of this makes any sense.'

'Why should it? Why should we experience *experience* as it is? Given its complexity and consciousness's evolutionary youth, we should expect quite the opposite. As I said, we should *expect* experience to be profoundly deceptive. As far as nature is concerned, any old crap will do, so long as the resulting behaviors are effective.'

'And by "crap" you mean stuff like meaning and purpose and morality. You know, the *crap* crap.'

Thomas hitched his brows into pained arches, smiled. 'Well, it certainly explains why we humans are congenitally puzzled about them. Think about it. Thousands of years, busting our nuts trying to figure out our souls, both social and personal, and we're just as baffled as ever. Exactly what you would expect . . . Exactly.'

He couldn't believe he was making these arguments again after so many years. The return of the college bull session. He could even feel that aura of uncertainty, that out-of-your-depth tingle that had made those days so sharp, so young.

And somehow he knew this was exactly what Neil wanted.

Sam was shaking her head, her lips pressed into a cold line. 'You're saying there's no such thing as consciousness, aren't you?'

Thomas shrugged. 'Who knows? Certainly not as it intuitively understands itself.'

The car was still running – a sub-audible purr. The radio voices had given way to some inane NPR jingle. The blinker ticked like a cartoon bomb.

'It's all a dream,' she said, more to herself than to Thomas, it seemed. 'All of it, from the pyramids to Shakespeare to . . .'

Thomas didn't know what to say.

There was something genuinely sad about her smile. 'How about you, professor? Are *you* for real?'

Her eyes held him, wet and open.

'Only if you want me to be, Sam.'

Another one of her friendly, skeptical scowls. She began pulling back onto the road. The eighteen wheeler had become a toy in the distance.

No more lies, he promised himself.

They drove in silence for several moments. Sam stared blankly out the windshield, while Thomas hugged his shoulders in apprehension.

'So Neil . . .' Sam said, trailing.

'Is unlike anyone you've ever hunted, Sam.'

Her look was pure *you're-telling-me*. 'This is what you meant at the restaurant, isn't it? When you said that Neil thinks of himself as a brain rather than a person.'

'I guess so. I didn't really think it through until now, though.'

'So we're talking about a man *without motives*? Is that it?'

'No. Motives, goals, reasons – these are just ways we make sense of ourselves and each other. Even if they're deceptive, they still work, which means they're still applicable to him, probably. The difference is that *he* no longer thinks in these terms.'

'Then just how does he think?'

'My guess is that he sees himself just . . . *doing* things. That he's suffering some kind of extreme depersonalization.'

'Depersonalization,' she repeated. 'You say that like it's a disease, but it's not, is it? It's more like some kind of . . . *revelation* or something.'

'I suppose so.'

'So what? Should I be thinking of him as a machine executing some kind of aberrant program?'

'Perhaps.'

'Help me out here, Tom. Every time I start thinking I have a handle on this crazy fucker, you throw me another fuzz ball.'

She was being too insistent, trying to force something actionable out of paralyzing facts. 'You asked me what Neil's world was like. I'm trying to tell you that he's passed beyond the veil, that he thinks he's seen his way through the illusions of consciousness. Since I'm stuck in the Lie the same as you, all I can really do is speculate about what Neil *isn't.*'

She scowled, her eyes reading the road. 'C'mon, professor. Speculation only becomes a problem when you confuse it for fact. You of all people should know that.'

Thomas exhaled, pinched the bridge of his nose.

'Think of it in these terms, then. For him, this is all probably like one of those movies where everyone's trapped in a mansion with hollow walls, where he has complete freedom of movement even though *we* think the doors are all lock—'

'You're saying we should try to draw him out?'

'No,' he replied. 'My point is that he sees us – all of us – as innately deceived by a consciousness that is at once dim, deluded, and ad hoc. He sees us as crippled by our evolutionary inheritance, our reliance on selves and rules and purposes. He thinks we're waging war from a dreamworld.'

Disney World.

Just thinking about it filled him with a vague, aimless worry, like that twinge of manly inadequacy you feel when shaking a hand more callused than your own.

'So he's underestimating us? Do you think we could exploit this somehow?'

Thomas rubbed his face, waved a hand. 'No. Look, agent, I appreciate that your job requires you to squeeze something practical out of whatever I say, but I'm thinking out loud as much as anything else. Let's just try to brainstorm for a bit, okay?'

From her expression, Thomas expected some kind of angry retort, but she seemed to catch herself. 'I'm sorry. It's just that this case—'

'Is important to you, I understand.'

She pursed her lips. 'I was going to say that it's unlike any case I've worked before. I've never been so . . . freaked like this. Your buddy-boy has a way of crawling under the skin.'

Thomas scratched his head. 'Probably because that's exactly what he's doing. It's a truism to say that most psychopaths have their own peculiar logic, something that makes them tick, something that we can puzzle through.'

He watched the scenery fall through his reflection in the passenger window. He spent a listless moment imagining Neil and Nora 'ticking' in his bed.

'But for Neil?' Sam prompted.

Thomas glanced back at her. 'It's reason itself he's murdering.'

As a psychologist, Thomas knew well the unspoken agreements that governed so much of what passed between people. At some point, mentioning Neil simply ceased being an option for either of them. His end of the bargain was easy enough to figure out: who wanted to talk about the best friend who had banged his wife? But for Sam, Neil was the only reason to talk – why she would collect a paycheck at the end of the week. And yet, here they were trading jokes and childhood anecdotes, discussing everything but Neil.

She told him about a particularly troubling case she had worked in Atlanta: a serial killer who was dumping the corpses of his victims – prostitutes and crystal meth addicts mostly – across south-central Georgia. Some were missing their heads, others their arms or legs or even their genitalia. She had been instrumental in breaking the case, but only because she had linked it to the much larger local investigation of missing pooches in Conyers. It turned out their SUB had been making his own mythological creatures in a creative yet misguided attempt to father the Anti-Christ. And even though she had needed sleeping pills and several months of counseling afterward, the source of her enduring outrage wasn't so much what she and her partner had found as it was the way the missing dogs and not the missing sex-trade workers had dominated the local media during the investigation.

'Can you explain that to me, professor? Huh?' she asked, trying to smile around a hateful fact. 'How pets merit more airtime than mutilated women?'

'It's yet another reflex,' he replied, knowing full well how lame anything he said would sound. 'Pets start to seem like our children because our brains use the same inference systems to understand them. If you think about it in those terms – missing sons versus missing junkies – it makes more sense.'

'Of course,' she replied, her tone vigilante cold. She wiped at the outer corners of her eyes with a pinky, swore under her breath. She wished she was stronger, he realized – like pretty much everyone else in the developed world. Some social roles demanded far more than others, and Thomas could imagine few more exacting than the FBI. The only difference between her and a soldier, he supposed, was that she defended decency instead of geography, innocents instead of agendas.

It sobered him, somehow, seeing her in this broader light. She had seen things, *survived* things – more than enough to command his respect and admiration. But there was an emotional honesty to what she said, an almost confessional air, which turned it into more than an ordinary *this-is-what-I-do* story. It made part of him wonder whether she did in fact 'like' him.

Since he and Nora had separated, he had gone out on only a couple of dates, both of them with faculty members from other departments, both of them predictably intellectual – just enough to prevent any real communication from slipping through – and both of them simultaneously consummated and terminated with a bout of hasty, cold-handed sex. They were enough for him to realize that he was no ladies' man, even though he had seemed to get laid enough back in college.

Because of Neil, of course. Neil had pretty much had a finger in all of his fucking. Metaphorically and otherwise.

It had even been a joke of Neil's at one point, asking Thomas if he would like another 'Neil-me-down'. The man collected old girlfriends the way others gathered recyclables. Where everyone else talked about 'hooking up', Neil talked about 'plugging in', insisting that sex was the only circuit that mattered. According to Neil, men were bullets, fired from pussies at pussies. 'Time to meet your maker!' he would cry out at the bar, steering Thomas toward some new quarry. How could Thomas *not* be an avid accomplice? Insecure. Tipsy with testosterone. He even congratulated himself from time to time for 'anchoring' Neil's rather high-flying team.

One of their female friends, Marilyn Kogawa, used to rake them over the coals about their sexual habits and attitudes. Even though it was 'them', Thomas always understood that Neil was her real target, that she simply spread the blame to avoid making her personal stake too obvious. Neil had slept with her as well, several times, playing on the emotional margins of that wondrously ambivalent phrase, 'fuck-buddy.'

'What are you doing?' Thomas had asked him once (probably

because he was nursing his own crush – Marilyn, as it turned out, would be another 'Neil-me-down'). 'Can't you see that she *loves you*?'

'I don't make the rules,' he replied. 'I just play the game.' Apparently the whole 'fuck-buddy' thing had been Marilyn's idea.

'But you're *hurting* her.'

Neil had winked. 'Well, she does *howl* a lot.'

At the time, Thomas had chalked up this insensitivity to what he referred to as 'Neil's strange obliviousness.' But now he could see that this was what Neil had always done in every aspect of his life: worked the rules to his own advantage. Things like embarrassment, hurt, or the fear of confrontation were simply tools to him. If you could catch him on a technical violation he would apologize readily enough, and in a manner that made you feel like a hard-ass for crying foul in the first place. But he was utterly deaf to anything that appealed to the *spirit* of the game. If friends or lovers got hurt, then they should mind the fucking rules.

The more Thomas thought about it, the more he realized that Sam was probably right. Neil had been high-functioning psychopath, even back then.

And now, not even the rules mattered.

Sam and Thomas fell silent upon reaching Washington's outskirts, out of verbal exhaustion more than anything else. Thomas imagined that Sam, like him, was busy soaking in the underclass ironies of their nation's capital. It dawned on him that he knew nothing of her politics, but he decided that he didn't care. It all just felt like a futile reflex any more. He could remember reading somewhere that Martin Luther King Jr was the last true *citizen* to visit Washington, that it had been tourists and businesspeople ever since. Thomas imagined that he was no exception.

The bar where they were to meet Dr Mackenzie was just off K Street, not far from Georgetown University, in a neighborhood planners would have called 'medium density mixed residential and commercial'. Thomas could smell the Potomac gnawing on tin and granite when he stepped out onto the sidewalk.

Sam gave him a hasty briefing as they walked up to the bar. Thomas could tell she was angry at herself for not doing so earlier; he could sense a gestalt shift in her attitude toward him, as though she were remembering some promise she had made to herself. Suddenly she was brisk and professional, if a little harried. Even still, she found time to answer a panhandler's upraised palm – one of those bums straight out of the old movies, all stained whiskers and clothes leathered with grime. Once again, Thomas waited on the guilty sidelines while she pawed through her purse. She ended up giving the old man a five, pinching the corner of the bill as though she were feeding something with teeth that snapped.

Dr Mackenzie, she explained with mnemonic intensity, was 68, an employee of the NSA for sixteen years, a widower for eight. He had a reputation for brilliance, though oddly enough, he had no publications whatsoever. She cast him a lingering look as they trotted up the steps to make sure, Thomas supposed, he had absorbed the significance of that last tidbit.

'Remember,' she said, 'try to read between the lines.'

Thomas smiled despite the lump in his throat. Why was he anxious all of a sudden? He almost felt like one of Neil's newly jilted lovers about to confront the first ex-wife. Neil, Thomas realized, had likely betrayed Mackenzie every bit as profoundly as he had betrayed him.

Thomas recognized the man the instant they stepped into the pub-worn interior. The place had a quaint teahouse atmosphere that not only belied its name, *Blowhards*, but all the telltale signs of hardcore barroom crowds: the cracked panes of glass, the carved initials distressing the already 'distressed' decor, and the smell of spilled booze and – oddly enough – cigar smoke. In theory-speak he would have said that its identity-claims contradicted its behavioral residue. In normal speak he would have said that it looked like a place where the high and mighty got down and dirty.

Mackenzie sat in a high-backed stall to their right, pondering his palmtop. He looked like a bald, diminutive grandfather, someone who should be wearing overalls rather than a lobbyist's slick K Street attire, a black pin-striped Armani by the look of it, with a hint of zoot in the cut of the jacket. When he spotted them, his face fairly exploded with affable good humor.

'Good-good!' he cried. 'I was getting worried I'd confused the times.'

He seemed a very happy ex-wife.

After the obligatory introductions, Sam slid against the wall and Thomas settled next to her. She laid the tips of all ten fingers on the manila file folder she had placed before her. It seemed quaint, like something from the innumerable crime movies Thomas had watched as a child.

I'm actually part of an investigation . . . The FBI *for chrissakes!*

'My,' Mackenzie said, tilting his head in Sam's direction, 'aren't you a striking beauty.'

Ordinarily, a statement like this would have sounded sexist, but for some reason, his age and festive disposition seemed to render him exempt. It was like he had a 'dirty old joker badge' or something.

Rather than blush, Sam smiled and looked down. His expression mild, Mackenzie retrieved a pack of Winstons from the inside pocket of his suit jacket. The lighter he seemed to conjure from nowhere.

'A nasty habit I've never been able to shake,' he explained in the midst of billowing smoke. 'Lucky for me, this place casts a blind eye.'

'A speakeasy for smokers,' Thomas said, finding himself, despite all his earlier apprehensions, quite disarmed. Mackenzie, he realized, was a classic rogue, someone who used charm and impish good humor to run roughshod over even the most exacting social niceties.

'For every Prohibition,' the old man declared, 'there are a thousand blind eyes, I assure you.'

Sam raised her eyebrows, pursed her it-girl lips. 'I *do* work in law enforcement, Dr Mackenzie.'

'I suppose,' the impish old man replied. 'But then you need me far more than otherwise, Agent Logan.' He looked at Thomas, shot him a friendly blink. 'Game Theory 101,' he said. 'Strike, or be struck.'

Sam leaned back from the wires of curling blue smoke, clearly annoyed. Smiling, Thomas reminded himself not to be taken in by the old charmer. Given what this man did for a living – he quite literally 'hacked' brains (in both senses of the word) – there could be little doubt that he, like Neil, was some kind of sociopath. Lacking the circuitry for the social anxieties that plagued everyone else, he doubtlessly found putting people at ease quite effortless. A former colleague of Thomas's had spent a better part of her career studying psychopathy. The biggest challenge, she had said on more than one occasion, was immunizing her research assistants against their charms.

Sam pressed on. 'What exactly was the nature of your work, Dr Mackenzie?'

'I'm afraid that's classified.'

The expected answer. Sam continued without missing a beat.

'It says here that you were Dr Cassidy's immediate subordinate – his second-in-command, in effect. Is that true?'

An apologetic look, mawkish because of the agility of his face. 'I'm afraid that's classified as well.'

Thomas frowned, wondering how it could be at once classified and in Sam's FBI dossier. He was about to say as much, but was pulled up short by a small flash of insight. 'Tell me, doctor,' he asked, 'did Neil ever mention the Argument?'

The bright eyes dropped to the table. For a moment he looked like something between a smiling Buddha and an Irish drunk.

'Oh, *that*.'

Thomas could feel Sam stiffen beside him. 'So he *did* talk about it,' she said.

'On occasion.'

'Would you mind relating the substance of those occasions?' she pressed.

'I'm afraid that's classified.'

Thomas frowned. 'Is it now?'

Mackenzie raised his small hands as though in surrender. His grin was contagious. His eyes fairly chirped with glee.

'Well it *should* be.'

'And why's that, Dr Mackenzie?'

'Because it's true and because it's scary as all hell. What do you think secrets are *for*, Professor Bible?'

'In my experience,' Thomas said, 'truth is rarely as dangerous as people seem to think.'

'Ah,' Mackenzie beamed, 'so you're a *cognitive* psychologist.' Glancing at Sam's perplexed frown, he explained, 'Professor Bible doesn't think the Argument is dangerous because he doesn't believe the greater part of humanity is *capable* of believing it.'

'He's right,' Thomas said in response to Sam's questioning look. 'But not for the reasons you might think. It's not because people are too stupid—'

'Well,' Mackenzie interjected, 'not *all* of them, anyway.'

Thomas scowled and smirked. 'It's just that we suffer from so many biases. We like things to be simple. We have no stomach for uncertainty; just think of the way people throw snap judgments at their televisions. We're out-and-out addicted to praise. We cherry-pick evidence that confirms our beliefs and selectively ignore disconfirming evidence—'

'We *rationalize*,' Mackenzie interrupted once again, as though to simplify things for Sam's poor feminine brain. 'Why do you think science was so difficult for our ancestors to come by? It pretty much turns human psychology on its head, doesn't it, Professor Bible?'

You mean the soul, Thomas wanted to say. It turns our soul on its head. Instead he continued as though Mackenzie hadn't spoken – a petty punishment for his speaking out of turn. 'We do these things all the time – *all* of us. But the biggest thing, hands down, is that we confuse agreement with argumentative strength, or even worse, intelligence. Since we can only judge things in terms of our prior judgments, we make what we already believe the yardstick for what's right or wrong.'

Mackenzie chortled. 'Certainly explains the present political situation, wouldn't you say, agent?'

Of course the president was a Democrat.

Sam's face broke into an upside-down smile. 'I'm not sure I—'

'Oh *my*,' Mackenzie interrupted, turning to Thomas. 'You would love to know what we're working on, wouldn't you? A cognitive psychologist? We've been forced to completely abandon all the folk psychological assumptions. The old eliminativists were right! None of the traditional categories are adequate – things are much stranger than you can imagine! I mean, take language – oh-ho! We experience nothing but *smoke*, nothing but smoke!'

Dr Mackenzie, Thomas realized, had a true passion for his work; he simply assumed that Thomas must feel the same. As it happened, this was another common human bias, sometimes called the 'consensus fallacy'.

'Just for example, we've completely isolated the rationalization module in the left hemisphere.'

'Rationalization module . . .' Sam repeated dubiously. 'Huh?'

'If you shut down the mitigating circuitry,' Mackenzie continued, 'you wouldn't believe the confabulations it generates. Lies, lies, endless lies, each of them completely true as far as the subject is concerned. It's as though each of us has a psychopathic liar built right into our heads! Can you imagine? I mean the evolutionary rationale is plain enough: reproductive success is tied to social status is tied to verbal competition, and so on and so on . . .' With these last words, he rocked his head from side to side.

'So Ramachandran was wrong?' Thomas asked.

'Ramachandran?' Mackenzie exclaimed. 'Wrong? Please, that's like saying ancient Greek medicine was wrong. "Wrong" is entirely beside the point, at least at this juncture. We've moved so far beyond that, so—'

He suddenly stopped, his open-eyed enthusiasm narrowing into something at once shrewd and sly. He didn't laugh so much as snicker.

'You should be commended,' he said to Sam while waving a finger. 'Bringing another academic with you. You *knew* that I would be more likely to open up if I could talk *shop*, now didn't you? I imagine we eggheads are rather predictably vain, hmm?'

He stubbed out his cigarette with his thumb.

Sam smiled and shook her head. She seemed to make a point of avoiding Thomas's gaze.

Of course, Thomas thought. Why else would she bring him? For his legendary powers of observation?

He knew the resentment he felt was more a function of the past couple of days than anything else. Hadn't she told him to read between the lines? More importantly, didn't she have an obligation to use every means at her disposal to prevent another Cynthia Powski or Peter Halasz? Coddling Thomas wouldn't be high on her list of priorities simply because it couldn't be.

'Tell me,' Sam asked in a queer voice, 'did you ever *operate* on Neil, Dr Mackenzie?' It was a question that only seemed obvious after she had asked it. Something had to explain Neil's turn to the unthinkable.

Things were moving too quickly.

'Never,' Mackenzie said. 'Why do you ask?'

Thomas stared at him. 'That's the answer you have to give, isn't it?'

'Please . . . You and I know how this works.'

'Let's just cut to the chase, then,' Thomas said. He knew he was speaking out of anger, that he needed to keep his trap shut, but the words easily outran his horse sense. 'What *can* you tell us, Dr Mackenzie?'

Mackenzie leaned back into his seat, his appraising look shocking for its sudden seriousness. He reached out and withdrew another cigarette. One for the road, as it turned out.

'You know what?' he said, squinting as he ignited it. 'Now that I think about it, precious little.'

'Let me guess,' Sam said. 'It's *all* classified.'

A burst of infectious laughter, framed in roiling smoke. 'Not at all, Agent Logan. Not at all.'

'Then what's the problem?'

'Well, agent, here's the thing. I genuinely *like* Neil Cassidy. He's the most brilliant man I've ever known.' His eyes became round with apologetic surprise, as though he'd just stumbled across a disconcerting fact. 'And I've decided that I don't quite like you . . .'

'But don't you feel betrayed?' Thomas blurted. How had things turned south so quickly?

'Exactly,' Sam added. 'If any of this gets out, you could find yourself without a career, or even worse.'

'Perhaps that wouldn't be such a bad thing,' Mackenzie replied without missing a beat. 'But I think you and I know the chances of that are pretty slim.'

Thomas looked to Sam, not quite sure what to make of this last comment. Just who was talking shop with whom? But she simply stared at the man, as if weighing some kind of dreadful decision.

Without warning, Dr Mackenzie was on his feet, smoking no-hands, stuffing his Winstons into his suit jacket.

'Well, I'm off,' he said, speaking as though they had just shared a plate of fish and chips. He turned on his heel and made for the door.

Thomas was dumbstruck. 'Mackenzie!' he cried out. He paid no attention to the other faces in the bar, though he was sure they had all turned toward him. Mackenzie spun, crooked his face forward attentively, waiting to hear what he had to say. 'You do know that –' Thomas glanced nervously at the other patrons – 'people, real people, could be hurt if you walk out on us?'

Slow blink. Sad smile. And a response that completely evaded his question.

'Ask yourself, Professor Bible, if you're so certain that the masses have no hope of grasping the Argument, then *why is our friend Neil making it*? He never struck me as particularly optimistic.'

The old man turned to hustle out the entrance, but paused, dragged around by a wagging finger.

'Oh, and Professor Bible . . .'

'Yes?'

'You should know that I actually envy you, in my way.'

'How so?'

The roguish eyes clicked to Sam, then back. 'Everyone knows psychologists are simply madmen turned inside out. All that glamor. We neuroscientists, on the other hand; we're just mere technicians.'

Somehow Thomas knew it was another eye-twinkling lie.

'You envy me?'

Another draw on his cigarette, deep enough to rim the bags beneath his eyes with orange light. The glow shined across both irises.

'In my way.'

Then he was gone.

CHAPTER EIGHT

August 18th, 2.58 p.m.

Coming along had been a mistake, Thomas realized as they walked back to Sam's Mustang. He was too close to the principals to bring much more than an alienating intensity to the table. And Mackenzie? The man was obviously a player from way back – and connected as well. Sam might as well have been a mail carrier for all the respect he showed her position.

'So what the hell was that all about?' Sam said as she started the car. The way she kept her eyes fixed on the street made him certain she was thinking the same thing he was.

'A narcissistic demonstration of entitlement,' Thomas replied.

'Which means?'

'He blew us off to prove to himself that he *could* blow us off. By showing us he didn't need us, he was affirming a congratulatory self-image.'

'Well, he should trim the old nostril hairs before congratulating himself too much. Did you see how *orange* they were?'

Thomas hadn't noticed. 'I thought he was quite dapper.'

'It was like taffy or something,' she continued in a ranting monologue tone, 'only with nicotine.' Thomas imagined that this was how she sounded when driving with Gerard. This was *Sam*, he realized, uncut.

'Gawd,' she exclaimed, 'I hate fucking smokers.' With a quick glance at her mirrors, she accelerated toward K Street. 'And what was that "I-envy-you-in-my-way" bullshit about?'

Thomas cleared his throat. 'You . . . I think.'

'Me?'

A tingling suffused his face. 'I think he thought I was going to . . . you know.'

Sam looked at him in shock, then burst out laughing – far harder than was necessary Thomas thought.

'Sorry, professor,' she said without a wisp of embarrassment. 'I like you and all, but . . .'

'But *what*?' Thomas cried.

'I *love* my job.'

'Yeah, well, I have my moments, you know.'

Sam braked at the intersection. Against an embattled retail backdrop, traffic whisked through the sun's glare, flashing as though through a searchlight. Thomas found himself staring down the treed rows of a Wal-Mart parking lot, twisting in the absence of any reply.

'So what's the plan?' he asked when it became apparent she had nothing to say.

'I'm not sure,' she admitted after a pensive moment. 'I need to talk to Shelley, to see if there's any way to apply real pressure.'

'On Mackenzie, you mean.'

'The man knows way more than he's letting on, don't you think?'

By chance, Thomas glimpsed the dome of the Capitol above the sliding streetscape. It seemed impossible that the soap opera on the nightly news was playing out right now, *there*, with real people who had hangnails and itchy asses just like everyone else.

Neil had said it himself: whether it was Washington, Beijing, or the human brain, spies were drawn to the smell of decisions.

'Men like him always do,' Thomas said.

The drive back seemed far longer. They floated down the freeway, trading this cohort of vehicles for that. In the lulls between topics, Thomas found himself staring out the window, wondering whether he really had fumbled the ball with Mackenzie, and thinking about Nora . . . about the crash of anesthesia that had accompanied her confession, about the mechanical insincerity of his rage.

Revelations were strange things. They rewrote consequences, sure, but what really distinguished them from garden variety insights was the way they revised the past. True revelations never came all at once. No, they gnawed, and *gnawed*, working their way through the soft tissue of memory, redigesting everything relevant. Not an hour would pass, it seemed, without some memory of Nora returning, like some old piece of machinery requiring a retrofit in light of the latest technical information.

In the wake of Neil, everything about their relationship had been transformed. Nora had always been critical. After their divorce a number of his male and female friends had admitted thinking she was something of a bitch. But for whatever reason, he had never seemed particularly troubled by her complaints, perhaps because he had fooled himself into thinking he knew where they came from. There was nothing quite like 'understanding' when it came to plastering over character flaws for the sake of emotional convenience.

There had been no catastrophic turn in their relationship: it had seemed to shake itself apart rather than spiral down from the skies. But even before the divorce, in one of those rare, honest reveries that punctuate any marital breakdown, Thomas had put his finger on a crucial change in the character of her complaints. At some point, her criticisms had shifted from things he did to things he *was*. And now that Thomas knew she was using Neil as her measuring tape, the inventory of her accusations, which at the time had so bewildered him, became sinister with implication. Of course he couldn't 'make her feel desired'. Of course, he was 'incapable of meeting her emotional needs'.

How could he be when she was bobbing for apples in his best friend's pants?

It was like Mackenzie said: everyone had a little rationalizer in their head, a gob of neural machinery devoted to getting them off the hook. Their very own blame-thrower. If Nora found herself attracted to Neil, well then, it simply had to mean something was wrong with their marriage: after-all, *happily* married women never strayed. And if their marriage wasn't happy, then it had to be Thomas's fault, because the Lord knows how hard *she* tried to make it work.

Another man's cock . . . Now that was a revelation.

'How are you doing, professor?' Sam asked once they made the Jersey Turnpike. 'You're awfully quiet over there.'

'Neil,' he said, knowing it would be enough.

It was strange the way names could become explanations.

Thomas reflected how odd it was, the way the hooks of sexual attraction had carried him so far only to drop him like a rock when she had made her lack of interest clear. Everything seemed fogged with irrelevance.

They drove in silence for quite some time. At first it was the kitchen-table quiet after a night of bad dreams – a kind of willful silence. Sam sorted through several satellite radio stations, but gave up after sampling a half-dozen different genres, everything from bluegrass to death metal. Nothing, it seemed, could trump the whisking roar of the highway. The sound of nature. It wasn't until the sun bellied in the west, drawing eighty-mile-an-hour shadows across the lanes, that the funk, or whatever it was Mackenzie had tainted them with, finally lifted.

Gazing forward, Sam slowly reached between their seats. 'Would you like some *Freeeeeeetos*?' she cooed, once again dangling the shiny little bag between them. She glanced at him, her eyes round with mock wonder.

Thomas sputtered with laughter. 'You're a nut-bar, you know that?'

'Is that your professional opinion?'

And just like that, everything was back to normal. They rehearsed the Argument a la Neil once more, trying to graph his possible motivations in the ether of conversation. But they only managed to paraphrase their conclusions from yesterday: Gyges had something to do with recognition, Powski had something to do with pleasure and/or desire, and Halasz had something to do with free will. Neil was stripping away the illusions, trying to reveal the meat puppet within.

'What about your book?' Sam eventually asked.

'My book?'

'Yeah, you know, *Through the Brain Darkly*.'

'You been researching me, agent?'

She cocked her head like a teenager. 'Uh, like, it's my job you know.'

Thomas smiled, looked out the passenger window. Night had fallen. An eighteen wheeler towered over them, and he found himself peering past the running lights into its grime-greased recesses: the roaring wheels, as tall as his door; the black-iron linkages, clacking to the bounce and grind of impossible loads; the pavement, rushing like a crimson river beneath the tractor's taillights. He looked away, overcome by a peculiar sense of vulnerability, as though he had leaned too far over a balcony railing. All he needed to do was reach out his hand and he would be yanked from the world, stamped and spun into dripping oblivion.

'I don't know what to say,' he replied, scratching his eyebrow. 'I mean, the book got me tenure, but it was one of those things that only seem to impress the people who already know you. Hopes were high. The reviews were harsh. It went out of print. Now it's little more than a joke passed down through generation after generation of graduate students.'

'Bible's Bible,' Sam said.

Thomas would have laughed, but there was a note of genuine pity in her otherwise rueful tone. 'What do you mean?'

'That's what they call it. The grad students at Columbia.'

'You've been *interviewing* people about me?'

Sam looked at him for what seemed a perilously long time, given her 80 mph cruising speed. A conspiracy of lights from the HUD and the dash made her seem almost supernaturally beautiful. Shining lips. Swales of blue and yellow along her cheek and neck. Suddenly the truck's headlights flashed through the rear window, bleaching all the inviting tenderness from her look. For an instant, she seemed more statue than human, with wet marbles for eyes.

'This is *for real*, professor. You do understand that?'

'It's starting to sink in,' Thomas replied.

Her gaze clicked back to the floating corridor of taillights before them. Several moments passed in encapsulated silence.

'So why the sudden interest in my book?' Thomas finally asked.

Sam shrugged. 'Because I find it curious.'

'Find what curious?'

'Well, the Argument is actually *yours*, not Neil's.'

Thomas snorted through his nose. 'Not anymore.'

'Why's that?'

Thomas frowned and smiled. 'Maybe someday you'll have kids.'

Sam laughed and shook her head.

'What's wrong with that?' he continued. 'A gun-packing momma. For a single-parent divorcee like me, it doesn't get much hotter than that.'

Sam beamed, but continued shaking her head. 'What did you make of Mackenzie's question?' she asked, obviously trying to change the subject.

Thomas studied her for a mischievous, tongue-against-the-teeth moment. 'Which one was that?'

'About the Argument. I mean, he *is* right, isn't he? Why would Neil bother making the Argument if there's no chance of convincing anybody?'

'Yeah . . .'

'You don't sound impressed.'

Thomas shrugged. 'It's a perfectly reasonable question.'

'And that's a problem?'

Thomas sighed, disappointed by this sudden return to seriousness. 'We're in way over our heads here, Sam. Who the fuck knows what Neil's up to? He was *NSA*, for Chrissakes, a neuroscientific spook, rewiring brains in the name of National Security. That's crazy enough . . .' They were sailing past another eighteen wheeler, this one with lights proclaiming JESUS SAVES like a Christmas decoration. He resisted a strange compulsion to gaze into the roaring wheels once again. 'Now? He's off the map altogether, charting territory we probably can't even imagine.'

'Like an explorer,' Sam said, hitting the blinker.

They stopped at a Flying-J for fuel and dinner shortly afterward. 'My Dad was a trucker,' Sam explained as they pulled onto the exit ramp. 'Besides, I'm addicted to Krispy Kremes.' Once inside, Sam succumbed to the call of yet another donation box, this one for some obscure environmental coalition. Some celebrity whose name Thomas couldn't remember gazed up from the cardboard planes, the money-slot in the center of his forehead.

'I gotta ask . . .' he said as they trolled for a table. 'What's with all the impulse charity?'

She shrugged, seemed to make a point of avoiding his gaze. 'When you have a job like mine, mistakes have consequences.'

Something in her tone warned him not to pursue the matter.

They both spent thirty minutes or so on their palmtops, Thomas with Mia and the kids, who seemed to have fully recovered from the morning's mayhem, and Sam with Agent Atta, who seemed to be quite upset about Mackenzie turning into a dead end.

'I tried to blame you,' Sam said with an *okay-that-wasn't-so-good* grimace. 'But the boss isn't having any of it.'

His elbows on the lime-green tabletop, Thomas rubbed his temples. 'But it was my fault, wasn't it?'

Sam scowled. 'What do you mean?'

'I just, ah . . . assumed you thought it was my fault.'

'Mackenzie? Please. If the prick was stupid, I'd be inclined to assign blame – to *me*, not to you. But the fact is, he's smart, scary smart like you, and with people like that, it's either a total crapshoot or a foregone conclusion. Trust me.'

Thomas looked down to the table-top, began counting crumbs. She was right. Mackenzie *had* been a foregone conclusion, almost as though the interview had been scripted. He was meeting his fears halfway, he realized, or 'negative scripting' as some therapists called it. He heard Sam sigh affectionately.

'Feeling down on ourselves, huh?'

Thomas smiled. 'No, thank you. I don't need any Fritos, Agent Logan.'

She regarded him with good-natured impatience. 'You're a good man, professor. A *good* man, and in a world that doesn't make any sense.'

His eyes actually burned. He blinked, made a point of not looking up.

'Call me Tom.'

'Okay,' she said, but reluctantly, as though the prospect frightened her.

Thomas dared glance at her eyes. The honesty of her smile embarrassed them both into silence.

Something changed after that. Sam did start calling him 'Tom,' though she slipped back into 'professor' now and again. But there was more – an air of familiarity, charged to be sure, but wonderfully relaxed all the same. Their dialogue took on an eager, exploratory air. At times it almost seemed a race to say, 'I know! Exactly!'

Sam, it turned out, not only had a past similar to his – he'd guessed and confirmed as much already – but also shared many of the same attitudes. She was skeptical by inclination, and sanguine by dint of work. She blamed herself more readily than others. She believed in hard work. She had never voted Republican, never would, but she couldn't stand the Democrats.

Thomas wasn't surprised. The fact that he was attracted to her said precious little: she was a fox, after all, and he was in the middle of the most emotionally tumultuous episode of his life. But she was also attracted to him – he was certain of it now – even though she was an FBI field investigator and he was a material witness, or so he supposed. She was attracted to him *despite* their circumstances. The old adage about 'opposites attracting' was largely untrue; the vast majority of people tended to fall for versions of themselves. People were like gravitational fields: sooner or later everything fell back to the earth of selfhood – hallucination or not.

Which was precisely the problem. He was simply medicating, he realized, using her to suture the wound inflicted by Neil and Nora. He was being the greedy one, the inconsiderate bastard. He was using her to prove that he still had what it took, that the whole cuckoldry thing was just a fluke. Sam, on the other hand, was simply wandering off the beaten track one step at a time, hoping she would find herself too far gone to turn back.

This was no joke, he realized. She was gambling with her career.

Nevertheless, when they pulled up to the driveway and she offered to help him carry the kids over from Mia's, he found himself saying yes. Drawn by some neighborly sixth sense, Mia met them at the door. Feeling breathless, Thomas formally introduced him to Sam.

'Hallo,' he said with admirable restraint as they stepped into the kitchen. Usually, Mia found coloring his tone with innuendos irresistible. 'Long drive, huh?'

'Oh yeah.'

'The professor talk your ear off? Stuff your head with creepy facts.'

Sam's smile was dazzling in the overhead light. 'Ooooooh yeah.'

The kids were crashed on the couch in their PJs, bathed in cartoon illumination. Thomas peeled Frankie from the cushions and handed him to Sam. Though she looked wonderful holding him, Thomas realized that his kids were just as much a liability as Sam's job. Not once in the course of their conversations had Sam mentioned anything about motherhood, let alone surrogate motherhood. Parenting wasn't among her talking points, and whenever Thomas mentioned it, she always steered the discussion elsewhere.

It just wasn't going to work.

But then, after carrying the kids over and putting them down, after sharing several wide-eyed *this-is-too-conjugal* looks, Sam asked him for a cup of coffee.

'It's still a long drive down to New York,' she explained.

At once cursing and congratulating himself, Thomas left her rubbing her feet on the living room couch. He filled the kettle and was surprised by the sound of the TV when he turned off the tap: the homogenized drone of an anchorman's voice discussing the Nasdaq. The voice disappeared, and he heard Sam laugh as he rooted through his cupboard for the instant decaf.

'What's so funny?' he called out, suddenly feeling as though he were back with Nora. Suddenly feeling good.

'Movie on a porn channel,' floated back to him, 'called *Weapons of Ass Destruction 14*.'

Thomas laughed. He found the coffee. 'Starring Agent Gerard?'

'That would be *Ass with Destructive Weapons*,' Sam said with mock seriousness. 'What's your code?'

He shouted the numbers to her one by one as he prepared her cup. His heart racing, he thought about Mackenzie and his final, enigmatic look. He was a perceptive old asshole, Thomas had to give him that.

She was curled up on the couch when he came out with the coffees, flicking between different channels, most of them full penetration – and various combinations thereof.

'All they have is gonzo,' she complained.

'Ah, an old-fashioned gal,' Thomas said, feeling himself stiffen. Anything goes, he supposed, after a day like today. 'Did you know that gonzo was actually how porn started off in the 1920s? Money shots and all. They called them "loops".'

Sam laughed in a kind of anxious, this-isn't-happening-way, curled her feet beside her. 'When I was fourteen my boyfriend and I would skip out and watch my dad's pornos. Pretty tame compared to all this . . . cock-slave stuff. I mean *look* at it.'

Thomas smiled, his heart racing. The scene flashed to a graphic close-up.

'No internet?' he asked. He shuddered to think of all the dirty cookies his computer had accumulated when he was fourteen.

'Too poor,' she said, crinkling her nose at the screen. She brought her feet to the floor, leaned forward with a skeptical frown. 'Now *that* looks about as sexy as stuffing a turkey.'

'Yeah, but it shows the spoons. Very sexy.'

'The spoons?'

'Yeah, where the bum meets the . . .' He swallowed, then said, 'It would be easier to show you.'

Her knees drifted a finger's-breadth apart. 'Show me, then,' she said, her voice thick, her eyes bright with an *oh-my-God-I'm-doing-this* look.

Thomas pushed the coffee table aside and knelt before her.

A low-volume '*fuck-me-fuck-me-fuck-me-fuck-me*' floated through the living room.

He placed his palms on her knees. She sighed. Parting her legs, he slowly pressed his hands under her skirt, sliding his thumbs past her knees, across bare skin, down into the hollow of her inner thighs.

'There,' he whispered, resting his thumbs in the divits to either side of her panties. 'The sexiest part of the female anatomy,' he said. 'The spoons.'

Her look was at once drunk, playful, and terrified. She squirmed, as though seeking his thumbs with her heat.

'You learn something new everyday,' she gasped, her voice shaking.

Thomas hooked his thumbs beneath her panties, slowly rolled them down her legs.

This can't be happening . . .

He glanced at the TV screen. The scene had changed. Now a powerfully built man dressed as a priest was unbuttoning a veiled widow's blouse. Beneath the black gauze, her crimson lips pouted in sexual sorrow. Her breasts seemed shockingly white against the black silk, her nipples pubescent pink.

'Ever play sex-charades?' he asked, more joking than hoping. His face burned.

'You mean fuck-alongs?' Sam replied, joining him on the carpet. 'Growing up, all the boys I knew were porn freaks. Every one.'

Thomas laughed, then yanked her around – perhaps more forcefully than he intended. He tore her blouse open to catch up with the priest. Sam giggled as much as groaned through much of the foreplay, and Thomas found himself relaxing. She was honest both to her humor and her hunger, and she seemed entirely uninhibited.

They were here to play.

Finally the priest hoisted the widow, long pale legs askew, onto his bureau, and Thomas thrust deep into Agent Logan. It was like sinking into moist lightning. She was perfect.

'*Mmm, Jesussss,*' Sam moaned.

'*Now fuck me, Father,*' the widow gasped beneath her black veil. '*Fuck me . . .*'

Thomas hesitated. His whole body trembled.

'It's been a long time,' he said.

'What about all those perky coeds?' Sam murmured.

'They don't like my brand of birth control.'

'And what brand is that?'

'Scruples.'

She drew a shining finger along his cheek, as though tracing the path of a tear. 'It's the end of the world, professor. They don't sell scruples anymore.'

They kissed for the first time.

After he came across Sam's breasts, the camera focused on the widow. She smeared pearl across her nipples then lifted her veil to lick her fingertips. Her face was at once hooker-hard and high-school soft. Beautiful, yet plain in the way of abused children—

'My God,' Thomas whispered.

'What?'

'It's her . . . Unfuckingbelieveable.'

'Who?'

'Cream,' he replied in a dead voice. 'Cynthia Powski.'

Thomas woke with a start, his heart hammering. It was still dark. Sam was slender and warm beside him. His right ear ached. His pillow felt like an old woman's lap.

With his ears, he searched the dark hollows of his house for sound, heard nothing but hardwood quiet.

He closed his eyes, saw Cynthia Powski, her tongue trailing semen.

He felt a weight, as though a child stood upon his chest.

Shame.

Shame for weakness. Shame for stupid stupid lies. Shame for fucking a stranger while his children slept.

Shame for Cynthia Powski, for watching her as he . . .

With thumb and forefinger, he pinched tears from his eyes.

Shame for all those years. All those years!

All those years fucking. Being fucked.

Neil and Nora.

For a moment, it seemed he couldn't breathe.

Groaning, Thomas threw his feet over the side of the bed. He sat for a moment, slowly rubbed his chest.

He was a psychologist. He knew shame. He knew it was a so-called 'social emotion', that unlike guilt it involved one's self rather than one's acts. Shame was global, guilt local. This was why shame was typically unwarranted, a response all out of proportion to its situational triggers. Shame always had causes, but rarely any reasons. How many waifish, therapy-hungry undergrads had he told this to?

Knowledge – this was the heart of humanistic psychology. The faith that self-knowledge somehow made a difference. That knowing could heal . . .

Perhaps this was bullshit as well.

He stood in the darkness. His skin pimpled in the cool. He walked to the doorway, grasped the frame and leaned out as though over a balcony. The weight in his chest would not ease.

My heart is leaden, he thought inanely. Like people, it weighed more dead than alive.

The source of the shame – the real shame – was obvious enough. He was a cuckold. He'd had few illusions about his marriage with Nora, but fidelity was one of them. In their 15 years together he hadn't once cheated on her, and he'd simply assumed that this, which had been an unspoken point of pride for him, had been duly noted and reciprocated by her. Unlike so many men, he deserved her fidelity. Didn't he?

What had he done?

Betrayal was a funny thing. In tests, subjects consistently rated threats involving betrayal as more dangerous than threats involving happenstance, no matter what the degree of 'objective risk'. This was why people feared psychopaths more than driving to the corner store, even though the latter was thousands of times more likely to kill. Betrayal struck deeper than statistics. Perhaps because its losses had no measure. Perhaps because people were fucking idiots.

But Neil and Nora. Why should he feel shamed by *their* betrayal? Where was the self-righteous indignation? Where was the rage that blackened eyes and pulled triggers? The shame was theirs! Wasn't it?

How could they? he cried to no one. How could they, unless he had somehow deserved it? Was that it?

Still hanging from his door frame, he wept for a time. *What did I do?*

Then he gathered himself thoughtlessly, in the way of train wreck survivors, and walked down the hall.

Numb, he stared at his children in the night-light gloom. Bartender, who always slept with Frankie now, watched him with brown, infinitely wise eyes. His tail thumped the mattress.

Frankie had kicked his covers off and slept, as usual, with one hand shoved down the front of his pyjama pants. No kid alive was as protective of his balls. Ripley lay on her side, her hands folded as though in prayer. She looked frighteningly old with her hair undone and thrown across cheek and pillow. Like her mother.

Smiling, Thomas closed his eyes, and the thought – no the *warmth* – of them swept him away.

He could hear them breathe. Really truly *breathe.*

Could anything be more miraculous?

New tears branched across his cheeks.

'Who've I betrayed?' he whispered aloud.

No one. Not them, the only ones that mattered.

He'd been a fool, sure.

But no more.

You come home late.

While waiting, I peruse the books on your shelves. Freud and Nietzsche. Sedgewick and Irigaray. I like that you are educated. Will there be time for interpretation? I wonder. Will I be something more than what I am? A principle? A metaphor?

Am I broken, mutilated . . . or am I simply honest*?*

I find a photo tucked between Updike and DeLillo.

It's you. I know this because you're everywhere: on the television, blissfully unaware of the cleft in your panties; on the magazine racks, a playful thumb hooked in your bikini bottoms; on the billboards, your tongue testing your teeth. You are the center of the eye's gravity. The universal solvent.

White. Female. Skinny-as-a-rail.

I retreat at the sound of keys. I love the feel of your carpet between my toes. I grin the grin of children ducking in ambush.

Will you outrun me with concepts? Will you declare me a symptom or a disease?

I watch you undress from the gloom of your closet. I wonder what your theories think of your thong, of the razors you draw to the very edge of your skin. What would they make of your smooth-skinned glory, twenty-eight going on fourteen?

How could they know I would be watching?

You scratch your buttocks with clear-coated nails, curse your wool skirt. I catch my breath when you turn to my hiding place, striding with thoughtless candor . . .

Once I used to wonder how people could abuse their pets. Now I understand.

They turn them into little people.

CHAPTER NINE

August 19th, 7.20 a.m.

Thomas dragged a raw cheek across his pillow, snuffled and groaned. True to form, Frankie and Ripley were arguing in the bathroom. How early was it? Before his alarm, anyway, the little bastards.

'Ripley!' Frankie was complaining. 'When it's yellow, let it mellow—'

'You're a piglet.'

'—when it's brown, flush it down. That's what Mia says!'

So. Fucking. Tired. Why couldn't they *ever* sleep in? Just once.

He heard a breathy groan. A warm hand brushed his back.

That's right . . . Sam.

'Morning,' she croaked as she stumbled by naked, searching for her clothes. Thomas watched her through bleary eyes, wondered at her perfect, figure-skater ass. Sunlight streamed through the sheers, making marble of her skin, illuminating her edges with otherwise invisible hair. It seemed the shape of her had been stamped into him – a million years of evolution, a lifetime of social conditioning – this one perfect woman. There was something glorious about that.

In the daily headline of his life, he thought, today's would read:

HOT FEDERAL AGENT BANGS WORN-OUT ACADEMIC

Too cool.

He was still drowsing when she returned wearing her skirt and blouse. He watched as she craned this way and that before his full-length mirror, frowning as she tried to flatten a fabric crease across her bum, first by rubbing a palm across it, then by endlessly readjusting the waist. She murmured, 'Shit . . .' over and over, each time with the why-me contempt women reserve for uncooperative clothing and seditious body-parts.

A long blink was all he needed to fall back asleep.

But as he dozed worry shot threads through the drift of associations, then like a pyjama-bottom drawstring, began to cinch things up. He saw Neil reaching into the nethers of Nora's skirt, as though about to shake another man's hand. He saw Frankie hunched in the shadows at the top of the stairs, watching him and Sam in the bounce of pornographic lights. Then everything began to smear, flicker . . . Gyges scowling at his reflection. Mackenzie laughing like a gnome. Cynthia Powski shrieking, cooing, bleeding—

The alarm went off.

He felt nailed to his pillow by his sinuses. Moving as little as possible, he grabbed the phone and croaked, 'Work.' Suzanne's digital recording tickled his ear. 'Mental health day,' he said after the tone.

Dragging his ass out of bed, he found the upstairs deserted. He hoped Ripley and Frankie were playing nice with Daddy's new friend. He shuffled to the bathroom, anxious and awake in a still-lurching body.

It was obscene how good a hot shower could feel. His body exulted in the steamy downpour, even as his thoughts lurched in recrimination.

Frankie and Ripley. They were the only important thing.

Sam would understand. Wouldn't she?

He trotted down the steps, still toweling his hair. Sam, looking almost as smart as she had yesterday, came out of the den with Ripley, who was clinging to her hand. They looked good, if somewhat uncomfortable, together.

'What are you two up to?' he asked.

Sam flashed him a baffled smile. 'I guess we're looking for something called –' she grimaced – 'Skin-baby.'

'I can't find Skin-baby anywhere, Dad.'

'Did you look in Bart's corner?' Bartender had this corner in the basement where he liked to stash things from time to time.

'No.'

'Then go look there, sweetie. Bart's probably been chomping on him, her, whatever.'

'Bart!' Ripley shouted in the imperious manner of little girls playing cross mothers. 'Did you take Skin-baby, Bart?'

It was strange the way even the most natural moments could seem awkward in the presence of someone new. In the day-to-day routine of things, nothing felt self-conscious; all the edges were sealed by familiarity. But add a stranger to the mix and everything changed. With newcomers came the specter of judgment.

After Ripley disappeared, Sam said, 'Skin-baby, huh?'

'Bart! You mangy mutt!' floated up the basement stairs.

'One of those creepy real-as-life dolls,' Thomas explained. 'They started calling it Skin-baby after they lost its clothes. For all the world it looks like a warm, pink baby . . .' He pursed his lips in a sour line. 'Only dead.'

When Sam failed to reply, Thomas added, 'My kids are weird.'

'Ahh, so they take after their father, then.'

'Some days I think it has more to do with nurture than nature.'

She looked at him pensively.

'What's wrong?' he asked, even though he knew. The madness of the last couple of days had thrust intimacy upon them. Now, in the cobweb-calm of morning, that intimacy seemed a shocking thing, like mysteriously waking up without underwear. She was confused, perhaps even more so than he was, given that she was risking her career.

And confused people tended to beat a hasty retreat.

'I should—'

'Look,' he interrupted. 'Have some breakfast with me and the kids. Get a feel for the Thomas Bible animal in his home environment. Do a little fact-finding before making any decisions.'

She stared, her face all the more lovely for the small signs of their previous night. Puffy-vulnerable eyes. Slightly disheveled hair. Ad hoc cosmetics. He thought of the blue heart she had made on her tackboard back in her cubicle. *Don't . . .*

'Sound fair?' he asked.

She nodded nervously. 'Sounds fair.'

He cursed himself for a fool as they walked to the kitchen. What the fuck was he doing? She wanted him – he could tell that much. But he couldn't shake the feeling that she wanted his *help* more. For some reason, this case had gotten its hooks into her – deep hooks.

And he wasn't interested in package deals.

My kids are all that matter.

*

Breakfast on summer mornings never failed to remind Thomas why he loved his house, despite all the calamitous and claustrophobic memories of the divorce. It was shallow, he knew, but it seemed to have the character of a movie still. There was something poetic about the pose of things: the sunlight glowing off the panes, the kids awash in the waking glare, the gleam striping the fixtures, rolling across the clatter of knife, spoon, and fork. The shadow cast by the kettle's steam.

Now if only Nora hadn't taken all the fucking plants.

'Ah,' Frankie said to Sam in the best Scottish accent a four-year-old could manage, 'yew're a keeper, lass!'

Sam shot Thomas a *what-planet-is-he-from?* look. Her smile caught the sun.

Thomas refilled her tea cup, then asked who wanted the last piece of bacon before – as he always did – popping it into his mouth. The kids laughed, as they always did. 'Aww, you wanted it?' he cried to Frankie in mock astonishment. 'You should have said something!'

Sam's palmtop twittered from her purse. She swore softly after looking at the ID, then retreated into the living room. Thomas found himself admiring her buns yet again, this time through her skirt.

'Did you show her your thingy too, Dad?' Ripley asked.

Thomas nearly coughed up bacon bits. 'Did I show her *what*?'

'Do you flush when you pee, Dad?' Frankie asked. Obviously this was Relentless Embarrassing Question Hour.

'Okay, guys, this poopy-talk has got to stop. It's not cute anymore. Keep this up and you're going to get me arrested. No. More. Poopy-talk. Okay?'

'Was that why the FBIs was here?' Frankie asked.

He'd been dreading this one.

'No,' he started carefully, 'that's not—'

'They were here,' Ripley interrupted, 'because Uncle Cass is a psycho.'

'Not funny, Ripley.'

'What's a psycho, Dad?' Frankie asked.

He glared at Ripley, warning her not to interrupt. 'A psycho is someone whose thoughts are broken. Someone who's sick. But I don't want to hear you using that word. It's not a nice word, Frankie. That goes for you too, Ripley.'

'But aren't you a psycho?' Frankie asked.

Thomas smiled. 'I'm a psych*ologist*, son. I help fix people whose thoughts are broken.'

That was the idea, anyway. Aside from mentoring the odd student here and there, all he did was pontificate in front of classrooms and argue obscure positions in journals and in conferences. But technically he was still a healer. He was just at several removes from those who needed to be healed.

Until recently, that is.

'How do you know when they're broken? Do they bleed?'

'No,' he replied. *Other people do.*

'They act crazy,' Ripley said. 'They don't do what they're *supposed* to do. Like flush the toilet.'

'When it's yellow,' Frankie hollered with small-boy savagery, 'let it *mellow*!'

'That's *enough*!' Thomas shouted, hitting the table. Everything jumped, cereal bowls, cutlery, and children alike.

Scared witless, Frankie began to cry. Ripley glared.

Thomas shook his head and grabbed a cloth to wipe up the spilled milk and Cheerios.

'Sorry guys. Sorry-sorry. Your dad's just a little stressed, that's all.' At some point, he told himself, all this madness would end. He would invoice it, wrap it with flattering rationalizations, then store in the Do Not Scrutinize section of his brain. He knelt before Frankie, who leapt like a little monkey into his arms. 'Shush, sweetheart. I'm not mad at you.'

'Are you mad at Ripley?' Frankie sniffled.

'He's mad at Uncle Cass,' Ripley said. 'Aren't you, Daddy?'

Thomas turned to his daughter and caressed her cheek. Good God, she was going to be an extraordinary woman. How could he be part of such a miracle?

'Yes,' he admitted. 'I'm mad at Uncle Cass. I thought he was my friend. I thought that he loved me, you, and Frankie—'

'And Mom?' Frankie asked.

Thomas swallowed. The little buggers never made it easy, that was for sure.

'And Mom,' he added. 'I thought he loved all of us, but he didn't. Listen to me, both of you. This is very important. You have to promise me that if you ever see Uncle Cass, you—'

Just then Sam marched to her purse on the counter. She looked at them quizzically. 'Jeez, you guys, I was only in the other room.'

'We missed you, *babeeeee*,' Frankie chortled. Thomas tickled him, and he squealed with laughter. He let go his father's neck and danced backward, his hands out in warding, his elbows pressed against his tummy.

'Gotta go?' Thomas asked Sam.

'Yeah, that was Shelley. Duty calls.'

Moments later they were all congregated by the door, Thomas scratching his scalp, Frankie and Ripley acting like darling little hams. Sam seemed flustered by all the attention. She hitched a leg up, then leaned to pull on her left shoe. She glanced at Thomas, her eyebrows arched.

'Hey, Sam?' Frankie asked.

'Yes, honey?'

'Where's your underwear?'

Sam paused for a moment.

'Frankie!' Thomas coughed.

'The kid's short,' Sam muttered to herself. 'How could I forget that the kid's short?'

'Where did they go?' Frankie persisted.

'Good question.' Pained smile. 'Ask your Daddy, honey . . .'

'Me?' Thomas exclaimed. He almost asked her if she'd checked the cushions, but thought better of it.

Then it came to him. 'Bart,' he said, red-faced.

'Mmm, nice,' Sam said. 'Tell ol' Bart he can keep 'em.'

'I'll walk you to your car,' Thomas said. 'You two mouthpieces finish your breakfast.'

He and Sam shared a significant look. People were always testing their roles against their circumstances. It was an important social reflex. She was freaked out, Thomas knew, not because of what his kids had said or done, but because they were simply *there*, suggesting roles and possibilities far out of proportion to a single night of crazy sex.

'So *that*,' Sam said as they stepped into the morning cool of the porch, 'was a Thomas Bible animal in his home environment, hmm?'

She laughed as he struggled for words. 'It's okay, Tom. I had fun. I'm glad I stayed.'

Thomas could only shake his head. He hugged his shoulders as if the morning was chill, which it wasn't. He glanced down the street, struck by the way illuminated planes and complicated shadows could pinpoint an unseen sun.

'Never a dull moment,' he said lamely.

'I guess not.'

'I'm sorry about Bart,' he added, still shamefaced and bewildered. 'He must have run out of pig's ears or something.'

'Professor?'

Call me Tom!

'Yeah?'

'You should quit while you're ahead.'

Thomas sighed and laughed all at once. 'Good advice.'

Without warning, Sam kissed him full on the lips. Her tongue probed deep.

They disengaged after an anxious moment. Sam actually glanced toward the street, obviously worried that someone might be watching. They had broken rules, and after the night before last, Thomas was certain he would be the talk of the neighborhood. Celebrity was the last thing he wanted just now.

'So when can I expect you at the Field Office?' she asked, as though in passing. *This is crazy!* her eyes shouted.

Thomas hesitated.

'Ah. I've been wanting to talk to you about that.'

Her smile faltered. 'About what?'

'About what you said the other night. You know, how it seemed Neil was doing all this for my benefit.'

'Which is exactly why we need your help.'

Thomas scratched his brow.

'Maybe.' He looked at her intently. 'But I have more than myself to think about.'

Sam searched his eyes. 'You're afraid that—'

'Wouldn't you be?'

She paused. 'I suppose I would. But there's measures we could take. We could make it impossible for him to find you.' She hesitated, then said, 'Or your children.'

She felt it too, he realized, the superstitious paranoia that mere talk could turn horrific possibilities into horrific eventualities. Humans were hard-wired to see story-arcs where none existed. The hero had to suffer – everyone knew that.

'You don't know him,' Thomas said. 'Neil is . . . gifted. He has an uncanny ability to circumvent obstacles.'

'Yeah, well, he's met his match, don't you think?'

'In the FBI?'

'I was thinking of *you.*'

Thomas shook his head. 'Wrong answer, Agent Logan. For as long as I've known him, the guy's kicked my ass in everything from Risk to racquetball.'

'But you wouldn't be playing alone this time.'

There was something in her look that at once troubled and exhilarated him to the point of breathlessness. He could almost feel the dopamine flooding his caudate nucleus. He was falling for her, he realized – falling for her hard. And that was a problem. As Neil would say, precious little distinguished the neurochemical profile of love from that of obsessive compulsive disorder. And now, more than at any other time in his life, he needed to be *rational.*

'I'd like to say that comforts me. I really do. But the FBI . . .'

Sam blinked, obviously hurt. She brushed a lick of hair, as soft as floss, from her cheek. 'I was thinking of *me,*' she said, turning to her car.

'Sam?' Thomas called, following her down the walk. 'Sam.'

'It's okay, professor,' she said, tugging open the door to her Mustang. From her expression he knew she'd transformed into Agent Logan once again. 'You know Neil better than anyone else; you've got to protect your own. I can appreciate that. Believe me.' She squeezed his hand.

'I am sorry, Sam.'

'I know.'

Several awkward moments passed. She swung into the car, then with a blank forward look, turned the ignition. The sound of her car had teeth.

Frankie and Ripley were fighting at the kitchen table when Thomas came back in – something about Sam's underwear, of course. Thomas was about to intervene, but the phone startled everyone into silence. He glanced at the caller ID, cursed. He closed his eyes to gather himself, then picked up the phone.

'Nora?'

'Hi, Tommy. Listen, could you do me a favor?'

For an instant he had no idea what to say. A favor? After these past couple days?

He left the kids in the kitchen. He could hear Ripley say 'Uncle Cass . . . is a psycho*path*,' in her radio DJ voice.

'You gotta be fucking kidding me,' he said to his ex-wife.

'Da-ad!' Frankie called. 'Ripley said *psycho*!'

'Daddy's talking to Mommy,' he called, knowing that would shut them up. It did.

'I just need you to keep the kids for a bit longer,' Nora said.

Thomas paused, brought up short by the quaver in her voice. He found himself surprised by just how little he had thought about her since the previous night with Sam, and idly wondered whether this was a staple of male psychology, something 'pre-programmed to maximize reproductive possibilities.' A bird in the hand, as they say . . .

'Where are you calling from?'

'It's been horrible, Tommy,' she whispered, the way she always did before crying.

Terror flushed hot through his limbs, face, and chest.

'What's been horrible, Nora?' He turned his back to the kids. 'What are you talking about?' His throat ached saying this, as though he had forced the words through a more primal urge to cry out.

He was seeing Neil around every corner now.

Please-no-no—

'The FBI,' she said, her voice hitching. In a rush of relief, Thomas realized they must have taken her into custody, probably to scare her into cooperating. 'You-you told them about me and Neil, didn't you?'

'What did you expect me to do, Nora?' *Do the crime, do the time, bitch.*

'Look, Tommy. I don't know why I told you. I-I should never have told you. The last thing I want is for you to be hurt . . .'

Unfuckingbelieveable. She was apologizing for *telling* him that she was fucking his best friend, as though honesty were the only real sin here.

'Yeah, I was pretty shocked,' he said with breezy cruelty. 'I mean, imagine that. Finding out your whole life was—' A sudden pang pinched his voice silent. He squeezed hot tears from his eyes. Cursed himself for an idiot. 'Imagine,' he continued in a broken voice, 'finding out your whole life w-was a fucking sham.'

How could you do this to me, Nora? Please!

'You're bitter,' she said, as though naming some inevitable adolescent phase.

Fucking bitch! Fuck-fuck-fucking cunt-whore-bitch!

Somehow he managed to squeeze out, 'I'm sure it'll pass.'

A long, uncomfortable silence followed. Thomas realized that she was crying.

'Hey . . .' he said softly.

'What am I going to do, Tommy?'

She loves him. Loves Neil.

His sigh was as much the product of disgust as regret. 'Listen. You gotta get a lawyer, Nora. Don't mess around. You can be guaranteed *they* won't.'

'But who?'

'You need someone ruthless. Bloodthirsty and smart. What about that Kim guy you used with us?'

'He's a divorce lawyer, Tom.'

'Exactly,' he said, hanging up.

He leaned his head against the wall for a moment, afraid he might vomit. Being mean-spirited just wasn't in his nature – no matter how hard he tried.

Stupid. So fucking stupid!

What was he doing, feeling ashamed? Served her fucking right.

Besides, they were probably just bullying her.

'I wanted to say hi!' Frankie bawled from the kitchen. Ripley stared into her empty cereal bowl.

Thomas jumped when the doorbell rang, actually dropped the phone.

'*Fuck-fuck-fuck-fuck-fuck!*' he hissed under his breath.

'Where's Mommy?' Frankie cried.

Thomas crept to the window, glimpsed Mia on the porch, wearing cut-off shorts, a tank, and fluffy-white slippers. *Nosy prick*, he thought, unable to repress a grin.

He reluctantly opened the door.

'No work today?' Mia asked, leaning against the frame.

'I called in sick. Thought I'd give you a break from the kids.'

Mia nodded, his look one of cartoon-skepticism. 'So,' he said pleasantly, 'the FBI was here . . .'

'And then some,' Thomas said.

'They interrogate you all night?'

Thomas closed his eyes, smiled, then surrendered to the inevitable. 'C'mon in, Mia,' he said. 'I'll tell you all about it.' He couldn't resist adding, 'You're as transparent as a negligee, you know that?'

Eyebrows raised, Mia shot him the finger as he stepped inside.

'*Mia!*' Frankie and Ripley cried as one.

While Thomas exchanged his bathrobe and boxers for jeans, a shirt and a blazer, Mia managed to settle the kids in front of the TV. Thomas brewed some fresh coffee, then joined his Number One Neighbor at the kitchen table. They spent an hour or so discussing the previous two days. Though in many ways Mia had become his best friend since the divorce, Thomas avoided any mention of Nora's affair with Neil – or of his night with Sam. He needed to sort things out for himself, first – or so he thought.

Afterward, Mia breathed deep, then said, 'Wow.'

'Pretty intense, isn't it?'

'You think?' He pawed his face as though trying to scrape off the madness. 'Well, you know what Marx says.'

'Do I ever?' Thomas asked. Mia quoted Marx the way others quoted Dr Phil.

' "With man, the root of the matter is always man himself." ' He snorted as though at a half-funny thought. 'I don't think he meant *grey* matter, though.'

'Neil's sick,' Thomas said sourly.

'You don't sound convinced.'

Something about this comment made his scalp prickle. 'How can I be? He's simply walking the talk, isn't he? Shit just happens. Tornados wipe out trailer parks. Bombs go off in coffee shops. Cancers spread. Arteries clog. Every breath, every heartbeat, is a crap shoot. That's just the way the world works; it's only our psychological shortcomings that make it seem otherwise. All Neil's saying is that the same goes with our neurons. That our every thought, every experience is just another synaptic roll of the dice. Statistical, not meaningful.'

'Certainly doesn't feel that way.'

'Why should it? Our brains evolved to process inputs, perceptions and the like, into effective outputs – the things we do. We see oncoming cars and traffic lights, and our foot depresses the brake pedal. What we don't see are all the neurophysiological processes involved. Our brain is essentially blind to itself, far more geared to external events than internal.'

Mia toyed with a lock of hair, contemplative and cross-eyed. 'So?'

Thomas breathed deep, smelled sun-on-dust and the memory of breakfast bacon. 'So, when we choose, or decide, or hope, or fear, or whatever, it's the same as when we see or hear: the brain drops out of the picture. We don't experience what makes experience possible. All the neurophysiological machinery that generates choosing, hoping, hearing, and so on, processes without *itself* being processed. For us, each thought comes from nowhere, constitutes a kind of . . . absolute beginning, so that it seems we somehow stand outside the nets of cause and effect that entangle everything about us, including our brain. Consciousness is like a hamster wheel, always moving, but somehow stationary as well. For us, it's always *now*, always *here*. We always feel we could have done otherwise because our choices always seem to stand at the beginning of events, rather than the middle.'

'*Oooo*kaay,' Mia said dubiously.

'Here, look,' Thomas said, reaching back and dragging a quarter from the counter-top. 'Watch.' He opened his hands to show Mia they were empty, then closed them. When he opened them the second time, the quarter gleamed dully in the centre of his right palm.

Mia laughed. 'Cool,' he said.

'Seems like magic, right?'

Mia nodded, his expression suddenly thoughtful. 'Like you pulled something from nowhere.'

'Now watch,' Thomas said, doing the trick again, this time at a right angle so that Mia could follow the quarter the whole time. 'Our thoughts are no different. They seem to spring from nowhere, but only because of a neurophysiological sleight of hand, because the brain is baffled by its own tricks. They seem magic. Special. Supernatural. Spiritual. Pull aside the veil of bone, and that magic evaporates.'

'But there is a difference,' Mia said. 'We *are* our thoughts.'

Thomas nodded. 'Exactly. That's what *we* are. Brains glimpsing themselves through peepholes, seeing magic where none exists.'

Mia seemed to stare past him, as though testing his words against the immediacy of his own experience. 'So you and I, sitting here . . .'

'Are just two biomechanisms, processing inputs, churning out behavioral outputs, which in turn become further inputs. All the reason, the purpose, the meaning, is simply the result of the fact that the neural machinery responsible for consciousness has access to a mere sliver of what our brains process – a sliver that it confuses for everything. Outside that sliver, there's no reason, no point, no meaning. Just . . .' He shrugged. 'Just shit happening.'

Scowling, Mia regarded him for a long moment. 'So when I go to the mall, I'm surrounded by herds of . . . biomechanisms? They only *seem* like people?'

Thomas wondered what would Neil say. Would he tell stories of how he had played this or that alleged terrorist like a puppet without them having the faintest clue? Or would he simply grab Mia and give him a first-hand demonstration?

Thomas pinched the bridge of his nose. 'They only seem like people because you can't access the processes that make them tick. So they become floating instigators, things that can only be tracked and predicted via your own neural systems. Our brains are exquisitely attuned to one another, to the point where everything you do or say triggers the same patterns of neuronal activity in my brain as in yours. They network by continually mirroring each other's processes. But since consciousness can't access these processes, we simply "get it".' Thomas hooked his lips in a mock smile. 'People seem like people for the same reason we seem to be free thinking, act initiating selves.'

'Because our brains,' Mia said slowly, 'can't see what's going on inside themselves. Because they constantly confuse the middle for the beginning.'

Thomas nodded. 'Thus the illusion that we stand outside of the arrow of time. That we somehow transcend the statistical clockwork around us.' He watched his thumb trace the rim of his coffee cup, glanced back up at his Number One Neighbor. 'That we possess souls.'

Mia was no longer looking at him or through him or anywhere for that matter. He had fallen back in his chair, his hands poised between a gesture of warding and disgust. 'So all of this . . . *this* right here right now . . . is a kind of magic trick? A *dream*?'

Thomas stared down at his socked feet, cursed himself for wondering, once again, what Neil would say.

'Tommy? This isn't *true*, is it?'

'Neil certainly thinks so,' he replied without looking up. 'And no one knows the science like him.'

'It's just more reductive scientific bullshit,' Mia declared with an air of angry resolution. Like most Marxists, he possessed the unsettling ability to take abstractions personally. 'They can't even figure out what foods are fucking healthy.'

Thomas stared at him for a moment, fending the urge to argue, to press and pin. He could tell Mia it wasn't about what was more fundamental than what, but about which kinds of claims people could take seriously. He could remind him of Hiroshima, or any of the other horrors and wonders that so set science apart. He could remind him that other claim-making institutions, including those that reduced scientific fact to 'social constructs', 'language games', or the work of Mammon, had no way of arbitrating *any* of their assertions.

Instead he asked, 'How's your coffee?'

'No you don't,' Mia exclaimed. 'I know that look—'

'Daddy! Daddy!' Frankie cried out from the living room.

Thomas turned to see his son come thumping into the kitchen.

'I found Sam's underwear!' he proudly declared. He waved Samantha's white panties over his head, panty-liner and all.

'Herr *Doktor*!' Mia drawled in mock astonishment.

Thomas snatched the panties from Frankie and stuffed them in his blazer pocket. He flashed Mia a grim smile.

'So tell me,' his neighbor asked slyly. Mia always turned up the volume on his Alabama accent whenever what he called the 'devil' got the best of him. 'What's it like?'

'What's *what* like?'

'Getting nailed by the Law.'

Mia left shortly afterward, explaining that, contrary to appearances, he did have a '*jaawb*'. The rest of the day passed without incident, with the exception of Frankie cracking his bean on the barbecue. The three of them had been playing catch in the backyard. The little bugger had crawled under the side-burner to retrieve the ball, then simply stood up. Bam! Thomas had watched the whole thing happen, and though he knew it was nothing serious, there had been this moment of distilled horror . . . Frankie on his rump clutching his scalp, a line of blood falling from his maul of black hair. The backyard had roared with the sound of unseen collapses, of great pylons or piers failing, as though the world were but a floor in some building's fatal cascade.

How had everything become so fragile?

Though Frankie insisted he needed to go to the hospital for 'Sergio' (Thomas had no clue where that one had come from), he took them both to the park and hiked down into the gully. Despite his turmoil, the giddy swings between horror (the thought of Neil coming back), thrill (the thought of Sam wriggling out of her panties), and rage (the thought of Nora gasping against Neil's cheek), he actually managed to have fun with the kids. They cleaned up the dozen or so crushed beer cans they found amongst the ferns. In the grotto cool, they counted the waterbugs skating across the creek's rippled back, and he explained surface tension to them. 'Just like Jesus,' Ripley said with a pundit's certitude. (Thomas had no idea where that had come from either).

Small wonder so many parents were bent on cloistering their children. It out and out terrified Thomas, thinking of his two kids panning for gold in America's cultural river. There were just so many sewage pipes, so many shades of Neil. But with things becoming ever more fractured and sycophantic, sending them to private schools seemed like one more contribution to an even more deluded and tribalized future. There had to be some common ground, it seemed to him, no matter how fucked up. People had to relate.

After tucking the buggers into bed and kissing Frankie's 'owwie' a dozen times, Thomas kicked his legs up on the couch and watched an old *Seinfeld* on Nickelodeon. But he found it impossible to laugh. He browsed several personal channels, or 'perches' as they were called, as much to reassure himself of his sanity as anything else. A billion bewildered people, all pounding their fists in the simulacrum of certainty, each with their own peculiar menu of scapegoat cheese. Then he surfed the news-sites, flashing between commercial broadcasts that pandered to mainstream prejudices (information, like any other commodity, was primarily geared toward customer satisfaction) and cash-strapped PBS. Images flashed, and the living room gleamed, darkened, and changed color in three-dimensional counterpoint.

No matter how many times he flattened his palms across his thighs, he always caught himself wringing his hands.

Sam didn't call.

No mention, national or local, was made of Neil or his crimes. Thomas wasn't surprised. The Chiropractor had struck yet again, this time with a cryptic letter to the *New York Times.* Several senators crossed the aisle on the issue of gasoline subsidies. The Russian economy, teetering after the destruction of southern Moscow, seemed to be riding some kind of petrol yo-yo. Of course, there were more eco-riots in Europe – poor shivering bastards. And some 'good' news here and there: bumper crops in Texas, more miraculous rain in the Sahara, church attendance up worldwide.

The world ends here, begins there. But it was never, Thomas reflected, quite the same.

He heard a rattle in the kitchen, jerked his head up over the back of the couch. The kitchen was black. Pale blue danced across the walls. His heart hammered. He heard shifting. A click.

What the fuck?

Over the course of the day, his innumerable fears had roamed the baffles of whatever he happened to be doing. Now they focused on this one thing, became very intense. Heart hammering, he blinked, stared into the black maw of his kitchen, saw nothing. He knew, given the disposition of rods and cones across his retina, that the center of his visual field was less sensitive to light than his immediate periphery, so he tried staring slightly off to his right.

But all he saw was Cynthia Powski diddling herself with broken glass.

He almost yelled in terror when Bart ambled from the blackness. People might forget dogs were predators, but primates never did.

'Jeezus, Bart. I damn near shit myself.'

Bartender trotted to the couch and laid his chin on the fabric, his eyes limpid and imploring.

Thomas curled on the cushions and hugged his big, hapless dog tight.

'No Frankie tonight, Bart?' he murmured into the dank fur. 'Figured you'd chum with the old man?'

Bart's tail slapped against the coffee table, once, twice, then knocked over Thomas's Rolling Rock.

Cursing, Thomas sent his dog scampering away. The beer had been almost empty, but the mess was big enough to warrant a trip to the kitchen. He paused before the black entrance, realizing for the first time that the florescent light over the sink was out. Weren't those things supposed to last forever? At this time of night, the kitchen was usually a nook of illumination in an otherwise darkened house. Silver shining in sterile light.

There was a sharp rap on the door to his right.

This time he did cry out.

He clutched his chest as he peered through the window.

It was Sam.

He yanked open the door and she was on him. Fierce kisses. Desperate breaths.

'You let me down,' she gasped. 'Twice you've let me down.'

'Sorry,' he said.

'No sorrys,' she said, pausing to stare at him. She smiled mischievously. 'Reparations.'

These are the rules.

I watch.

You set your groceries down, rummage through your purse, looking for your keys.

A man on a bicycle glances at your skirt line as he labors down the street. He likes his legs long and pale.

A bird sings with consumer confidence.

The leaves wave deep green, slow as though underwater. One twitters to the ground, spinning like a dollar bill.

Your door opens into the blackness of air-conditioned spaces.

The sun pricks the eyes of the children playing next door.

You steer your groceries through the dark slot. Recycled plastic rustles against the frame.

I follow.

Closer than your shadow.

Farther than your bones.

Now you lie there, watching my shadow grunt on your back, listening to my animal glory. The blood pools around your lips, your nostrils, as warm as cooling engine oil. You smell it, your life, as pungent as any excretion, and just as slick. You can feel yourself raining across your cheek. Raining down.

You lie there dying, without recognition, without resolve.

Neck broken, you weep without your body.

Meat.

These. These are the rules.

CHAPTER TEN

August 24th, 8.55 p.m.

Why did Daddy have to go?

The air mattress beneath him felt cold and wobbly, unsteady like his belly.

'Why did Daddy have to go?' he asked Ripley.

'Because I *told* you,' was her pouty reply. 'There isn't room, Frankie. Daddy's too big for the tent.'

'There's room,' Frankie said in a small voice.

'You said you wanted to sleep out here alone.'

'No I didn't.'

Ripley beat her arms against her sleeping bag in frustration. '*Yesss*, you did. I heard you, Frankie. Now go to sleep.'

'But I change my mind, Ripley.'

'Frankeee!'

'But *why*?'

When Ripley refused to answer he wriggled away from his sister, stared wide-eyed at the shadows cast by the flashlight across the bellied ceiling. The air smelled end-of-summer cool. Soon he would go to preschool. But the outside was dark, big, and hollow, filled with great nothings and terrible anythings. He heard a dog barking in the distance. It sounded angry.

'Where's Bart?'

'In-*side*,' Ripley said in her dangerous voice.

She thought she was soooo big. But soon he would be bigger, and no one would tell him what to do, and he would save little kids from bad cornfields and booby bullets and dinosaurs. Even *psychos* would be afraid of him. Last week, Mia had fallen asleep waiting for Dad to come pick them up, and he and Ripley had watched a show on psychos – a *cool* show. They had even seen *crime scene* photographs, with blood hanging like spaghetti from the walls. Sickos, Ripley had called them. Bad-bad men, just like Uncle Cass.

Frankie giggled to himself, whispered 'Sickos!' He liked that word, he decided. 'Sickos!' he hissed again. 'Sick-sickos!'

Then he thought he heard a rattle beyond the nylon, and he was frightened again. What if it was a sicko? He swallowed, thinking how big and empty and dark the outside was. A sicko could be anywhere, and Frankie wouldn't know. How could you know if you couldn't see? Maybe that was what the dog was barking at, some sick-sicko hiding in the hole between buildings, waiting to make spaghetti of somebody.

Frankie didn't want to be spaghetti.

'I wanna go see Bart,' he said. Dad said Bart had super senses.

'Quit your whining!' Ripley said like a little Mom.

'You're not Mom,' he mumbled.

Then he heard it. The sound of feet swishing through dewy grass. *Swish-thump. Swish-thump . . .*

'*Ripley!*' he gasped.

'I hear,' she said, her voice now as small as his.

Shwish-swish-thump . . .

He turned to her horror-stricken face. The flashlight lay between them, illuminating her face from below. Earlier that night she had put the flashlight to her chin and tried to make scary faces. Frankie had only laughed. Now she looked scarier than any face in the whole world.

'I don't want to be spaghetti,' Frankie murmured. '*Riplee-eeeeee . . .*'

They heard a pop from the peak of their pup tent. Ripley clasped the flashlight with both hands, pointed it toward the sound.

Something pointy whisked across the orange nylon.

Frankie couldn't breathe. He wanted to scream, but something clamped his mouth shut.

Another pop. Ripley jerked the flashlight toward the entrance.

It was black-black beyond the mosquito-screen gauze. The zipper started dropping, tooth by shiny tooth.

Click-click . . .

Ripley screamed. The zipper ripped down.

Something dark exploded into the light. Frankie felt an iron hand clutching at his stomach.

'I'M A BEAR!' a voice boomed, and Daddy's laughing face bobbed into the light. Ruthless fingers tickled and tickled. Both Frankie and Ripley screamed with laughter and delight.

Crowded as it was, Thomas lay with his kids, joking and poking, until they both drifted asleep. Afterward, he turned the flashlight on its head so that it was little more than a ring of light against the ground, then carefully made his way from the tent.

'Aaaarh,' he softly growled as he did up the zipper, making a face he found funny because he knew how his kids would have giggled had they seen it. He walked to the back patio and took a seat.

He fished a Rolling Rock out of his cooler, popped it, then surveyed the dark expanse of his backyard: the bland fence, the lonely maple, the kids' swing set, the space where he and Nora had once talked about putting an in-ground pool. He felt at once sad and proud, the way he imagined many men felt when taking stock of their humble kingdoms.

Strange the way that word, *mine*, so often stirred shame when attached to things.

That shed is mine, he thought, taking a drink. *Loser-shed . . . Mine.*

The significance of small childhood traumas had been all but discounted in psychological circles. Kids were doughty little buggers, those in the know now believed, pretty much idiot-proof when it came to parenting. Only genes, the vagaries of peer socializing, or extreme parental malfeasance could ruin them. Everything else, the experts maintained, came out in the wash.

Thomas disagreed. The small traumas lived like spiders in the emotional cracks of adulthood, catching what they could, and leaving the rest to larger predators. His parents had been poor and alcoholic, but his friends at school had come from relatively affluent households. He'd grown up ashamed, of his last-year's-hit-movie-lunchbox, of his Wal-Mart clothes, of his bruised-apple-instead-of-a-Twinkie. He'd grown up being quiet at lunch time.

Now shame tainted everything he owned. Everything 'mine'.

But as Mia would say, that was the whole point of economic freedom. Shame.

Those kids, though, he thought to himself. They were a different story.

Heartbreaking pride.

He rubbed his eyes, jumped when he glimpsed the shadow floating along the back of his house.

'Who-the—'

'Just me,' Mia called, holding up his own beer. 'Thought I'd join you for a drink.'

'Jesus, Mia,' Thomas gasped.

'Jumpy, aren't we?'

'Shush,' Thomas said, nodding to the pup-tent in the middle of the black yard. 'The kids just fell asleep.'

Mia nodded and laughed. 'They've been babbling about the great expedition for days now.'

'I promised them before the shit hit the fan last week.' Part of him still regretted caving to their relentless pressure. Thanks to the divorce, it was a parental paradox Thomas knew well: it was hard not to be indulgent in times of family crisis, and harder still not to be stern. 'I figured with all the craziness it would be a good distraction.'

Mia nodded. 'Hear anything new about Nora?'

Thomas grimaced. 'Still refusing to talk. Still behind bars.' The nightmare triggered by Neil's visit had taken a couple of surreal turns in the following days, Nora's imprisonment the sharpest among them. Just thinking about it triggered a sense of disbelief similar to what he'd felt when the Twin Towers had imploded, the sense that someone had switched reels in the Great Projection Room, and now CGI and producer rewrites were running amok in the real world.

Nora refused to believe that Neil had anything to do with what was going on.

She loved him.

Neil and Nora.

'Pooor, pooor lass,' Mia said, mimicking Frankie's lame Scottish accent. He'd been squarely in the serves-the-bitch-right camp ever since Thomas had told him about her and Neil.

'I feel sorry for her,' Thomas admitted.

'You shouldn't. She's a back-stabbing slut.'

Thomas grinned, remembering an old tirade of Mia's on 'honest epitaphs'. 'I thought you wanted something like that chiseled on your tombstone . . .'

'So?'

'So, don't throw stones—'

'When you live in Israel. Yeah-yeah, so I'm a hypocrite. I've changed my mind about my epitaph, anyway.'

'So what's it now?'

He held up his hands marquee-style. ' "Not so funny after all." '

Thomas laughed, though something about the joke mildly repelled him – like glimpsing Q-tips in someone else's garbage. 'You're such an ass.'

A smile cracked Mia's deadpan stare.

'Speaking of getting laid,' he said, 'what's going on with Special Agent Samantha Logan?'

Thomas chuckled. Just hearing her name tickled him. 'She just got back from Nashville. Apparently some televangelist named Jackie Forrest went missing a few days ago.' Hearing about Jackie Forrest's abduction had sent Thomas sifting through the bookcases in the basement, where he kept all the textbook wannabes sent by academic publishers and whatever else he had been too lazy to throw out. He found the book relatively quickly: it was hard to miss, not only because of its garish, gold-embossed spine, but because it had found its way beside a vagrant copy of his own book, *Through the Brain Darkly*. Coincidences could be so cruel.

It was called *The New Hero: Why Humanism is a Sin*, by Jackie Forrest, an eight-year-old relic of Nora's brief flirtation with fundamentalism. He could still remember the rush of relief when she announced her return to agnosticism. At the time, Thomas had thought *he'd* shown her how dim the light of Jesus was compared to that of Reason, but now he imagined that her affair with Neil had been the deciding factor. When it came to her immortal soul, Nora had decided to err on the side of fucking.

'They think it has something to do with Neil?' Mia asked.

'From the sounds of it. Jackie Forrest fits the profile, at least. Half-ass famous.'

Mia shook his head. In the silent moment that followed, Thomas imagined he was either thinking of the preacher shrieking in some dingy basement, or like him, trying not to. Despite Agent Atta's injunction, Thomas had continued to brief him on the details as they arose. Mia wasn't simply nosy, he was relentlessly nosy, and with such I've-got-your-best-interests-at-heart curiosity that he was well-nigh irresistible. Thomas inevitably told him everything about everything, and felt better for it afterward. Mia had a keen eye, and perhaps most importantly, had no problem giving honest feedback.

But this stuff with Neil's personal semantic apocalypse . . . Sometimes even Mia seemed to regret it. '*When you said he'd gone psycho,*' he had admitted the day before yesterday, '*I thought of blood, knives, and titties in the shower. Not this. This is beyond sick and healthy.*' His Number One Neighbor had strayed into curiosity-killed-the-cat territory, and he knew it.

Mia cleared his throat. 'So, have you got Sam a red wig yet?' A clumsy way of changing the subject, Thomas thought, but a welcome one.

'Huh?'

'You know . . . To do the whole Agent Scully *thang.*'

'So you had the hots for her too, huh?'

'Huge,' Mia said, warming to the topic. 'If it wasn't for Fox Mulder, I might be straight. You and I would be sitting here talking pussy and football.'

Thomas laughed. 'Aren't we talking pussy now?'

'A privilege of growing up in a bilingual household.'

'Well, to answer your question, no, I haven't bought her a red wig yet. She packs a pistol you know.'

'Probably for the best. She's not Agent Scully hot, anyway . . .'

'Scuse me?'

'Doesn't have that "I'm-frumpy-let's-fuck" air about her.'

Thomas roared with laughter, then caught himself, remembering the kids.

'Sh-shush,' Mia said, laughing.

'Sometimes,' Thomas gasped, 'talking to you is like smoking a joint.'

Mia had done this many times before, especially during the darkest days of his divorce: distracted him from his troubles, reminded him what it was like to laugh. Thomas pulled two more beers from his cooler and tossed one to his Number One Neighbor.

'So you had a thing for what's-his-face . . . The guy who played Fox. David Duchovny?'

'Who didn't?' Mia replied. 'Why do you ask?'

'All the girls at Princeton were ga-ga over Neil because they thought he looked like him.'

Always getting laid, weren't you, Neil?

Mia hesitated, reluctant to stray into potentially painful territory – or so Thomas imagined.

'I hate to say it, but old Fox doesn't hold a candle to Neil. Remember how Bill and I would always ask you to bring him over for a swim?'

Thomas smiled. 'You don't have a pool.'

'That was the point. Something Olympian about that man . . .'

Mia paused, then hastily added: 'Which of course is why he's a fucking raving lunatic. The perfect ones always are.'

It *was* painful territory, Thomas realized. He looked away, at a loss for words.

As always, Mia took up the slack. 'So Sam is hot,' he said, pretending to itemize the proceeds of their discussion. 'You're both covered in pubic-hair burns . . . I hate for you to think I'm nosy, but her car seems to be parked in your driveway more often than not. You guys getting serious?'

Thomas studied the pup-tent in the darkness, imagined his kids bundled like little larva inside. Warm. Safe. According to Sam, information passed on from the NSA indicated that Neil was somewhere in Florida. Ironclad intelligence – something about purchase patterns and several CCTV images. Atta and Gerard were in Florida now, following up with the local authorities, while Sam continued to comb New England for leads, interviewing family, old friends, that sort of thing. Neil's biometric data had been uploaded into almost every realtime digital video network in the country: airports, train stations, subways, even toll-roads and urban intersection surveillance systems. What the FBI lacked in terms of feet on the ground, it more than compensated for with eyes in the sky – or the ceiling, as the case might be. There was nothing to worry about, Sam had assured him.

Not that he could imagine Neil doing anything. Even if Neil was doing all of this for his benefit, it meant that Thomas was the audience . . .

And the audience always got to hide in the dark. Didn't it?

Relax.

It dawned on him that he had caved to the kids more to prove that everything was back to normal than anything else.

'Nah,' he said, suddenly uncomfortable. 'Nothing serious.'

Mia stared at him thoughtfully. 'Why so coy, Tom? I know it's not because it's me. After all the years talking relationship shop, what *haven't* we discussed?'

Mia was right. What was the problem?

'It's just that . . .' Thomas hesitated. 'It's just that everything seems so . . . so fucking fragile, you know?'

Mia nodded. 'Like if you talk about it, you make it real, and if you make it real . . .'

Thomas smiled, recognizing his own advice.

'It *is* real,' he said. 'It's not perfect, but it's real.' Thomas took a nervous drink. 'She *so* wants me to be an active part of the case – you have no idea. I discuss it with her, give her what insights I can, but I can tell she's disappointed deep down. I sometimes worry she thinks I'm a coward. Sounds stupid, doesn't it? But here's Neil on this killing spree, mutilating and torturing innocent people – even children for fuck's sake – and all I can think about is . . . is . . .'

Nora.

Thomas had been looking down at his beer. He dared Mia's friendly gaze.

'I've never felt so . . . so *beaten* before, Mia. All this time, he's been banging Nora, dodging around through the darkness behind my back. All this time, making a fool out of me. And instead of hating him, all I want to do is curl into a little ball.' He blinked, saw Cynthia Powski, sweat-slick and gasping between climaxes. 'Truth be told, I *am* terrified. More frightened than I've been in my entire life.'

'Me too,' Mia said. 'And I'm just the neighbor.'

He wasn't joking, Thomas realized. Psychopaths belonged to movies, salacious news exposés and clinical studies, not quiet Peekskill neighborhoods. Culture had a code for other types of threats, storylines that provided neighbors a measure of comfort. Estranged husbands murdered wives and children, but respected property lines. Fugitive gangsters left town in the middle of the night. Terrorists shaved their beards, forgot to water their lawns but otherwise tried to keep a low profile.

Psychopaths were something altogether different.

'Some fucked up shit, huh, Mia?'

'Fiercely fucked up, my friend.'

Thomas breathed deeply, steepled his fingers about his beer. 'Listen, I know I have no reason to say this, but I need you to keep this stuff under your hat.'

'About you and Sam? Or Neil?'

'All of it.'

Mia snorted. 'I've been wondering why none of this has made the news. Just Chiropractor, Chiropractor, and more Chiropractor.'

'Neil was NSA. I told you that.'

'So why is the FBI hunting him?'

'Because it's domestic.'

Mia nodded in a yah-yah manner. 'With all the madness going on, I imagine they're spread pretty thin.' He tossed a cap, sent it clinking across the patio stones.

'So they keep telling me.'

Thomas had always measured his friendships by the silences they could absorb. As roommates, he and Neil had literally spent hours together without speaking a word. With Mia the gaps between jokes or questions or observations were never as long, but they seemed more profound for some reason, more indicative, a product of common appreciation rather than boredom or distraction.

'Did I ever tell you,' Mia ventured after two or three contemplative drinks, 'that I worked for the Department of Fatherland Security?'

Thomas nearly choked on his beer. 'You gotta be fucking kidding me,' he said, drawing a sleeve across his mouth. The man held more surprises than a magician's pocket.

'Just technical contracts,' Mia said, staring into the night. 'Different stuff, for the NSA, CIA, even helped the FBI with some troubleshooting.'

Thomas gawked. 'A self-proclaimed Marxist, working for the CIA.'

'Don't forget that I'm also an old queen,' Mia said, copping his coquette drawl. 'I've spent the better part of my life undercover.'

Laughter, then another long, but comfortable silence. A million questions crowded Thomas's thoughts, not the least of which was why Mia had never told him about working for the DoHS. But he knew the answer. Everywhere you turned now, you were signing away your right to say this or that, especially in commercial contracts involving the most powerful corporation of all, the US government. It was one of those things the pundits squawked about from time to time, the Commercialization of Speech they sometimes called it. Issues like this genuinely concerned Thomas, but in the way of wars in unvisited countries. It was like the 'Expression Biometrics' issue with retail employees: sure, the idea of computers watching to make sure all clerks and cashiers continually smiled was creepy, but it was kind of nice from the customer's point of view. Even Thomas had to admit that shopping at Wal-Mart was more pleasant than at Target.

And, truth be told, it was nice living in a world where people kept their mouths shut.

'So far it's been all me-me-me,' Thomas said finally. 'How about Mia-Mia-Mia?'

It was an old joke of theirs. 'Great,' his Number One Neighbor said, shrugging his shoulders. 'Bill and I have been great. Too much going on at the Bibles for those little things to seem important.' He paused, frowning as though struck by something both sad and humorous. 'I hate to say it, but back when you and Nora were fighting all the time . . .' He trailed, looking guilty.

Thomas shook his head, chuckled.

'You really should be miserable more often,' Mia continued.

'Things were that good?'

'No, our *sex* was that good.'

Thomas groaned. Though Mia made light of the fact that he was gay, the sheer frequency of his references told him that issues remained. For not the first time, Thomas found himself wondering how open Mia really was. Sure, he was embarrassingly frank about his relationship with Bill, but he almost never mentioned his past before moving to New York. The sheer audacity of his personal revelations, it sometimes seemed, was nothing but a subtle form of misdirection, like the flourish of a magician's hand.

Perhaps this was what made the ensuing silence brittle.

'I imagine you need me to look after the kids next week,' Mia eventually said.

Thomas sighed. 'I'll get something figured out, Mia. It's just—'

'Don't worry about it. School starts soon. Besides . . .'

'Besides what?'

'I never thought I'd say this, but, well . . . I love it.' He looked away with uncharacteristic embarrassment. 'I mean, I love *them*. I never saw myself as the paternal type, you know, what with dressing up like a girl and all, but . . .'

He looked at Thomas apologetically. Sometimes it seemed Mia was always apologizing.

'They get under your skin,' Thomas said.

'They get under your skin.'

Thomas held up his beer. 'Here's to them,' he declared softly, nodding to the shadowy pup-tent.

The clink of bottles warmed the night.

After Mia left, Thomas set his air mattress and sleeping bag across the patio. He'd agreed to let the kids camp out only after crumbling under relentless pressure. He sure as hell wasn't about to leave them alone, even if the FBI thought that Neil had relocated to the Gulf Coast. Besides, it had been a long, long time since he had last slept beneath the stars. And he rather liked the idea of standing guard over his children.

He kicked off his shoes, then crawled in, jeans, shirt, and all. He huddled to conserve warmth, stared at the great bowl of the night sky. Things seemed clear enough, the black gaping between pinpoints of white, so much so it was hard to believe they were abandoning all the earth-based telescopes because of the way jet exhausts hazed the upper atmosphere. There seemed to be plenty of stars.

He stared and breathed. But no matter how deep he peered into the cavernous light years, the sense of awe he was searching for eluded him. Instead, all the lunatic images from the previous week crowded through the turnstile of his mind's eye. Glimpses of Cynthia Powski blurred into images of the widowed Cream writhing about the porn minister's cock. Fingertips pinching nipples. Glass unzipping skin. On and on, no matter how hard he blinked.

Abyss upon abyss. The psychological spread across the cosmological.

He groaned aloud, rubbed his face furiously. What was his problem?

The easy answer was that he was suffering from some kind of mild post-traumatic disorder. The brain actually possessed two ways of laying down long-term memories: a high-resolution, detail intensive path processed through the cortex, and a low-resolution, emotion intensive path processed through the amygdala. Traumatic events usually produced memories of the second variety: it was one of the brain's rapid-response mechanisms. The problem was that the system could be easily fooled, generating intense emotional reactions in harmless situations – which was why so many Iraq War veterans heard gunfire instead of firecrackers, car bombs instead of thunder. For the sake of reaction time, their brains simply weren't taking any chances.

But then why was it *Cynthia Powski* who haunted him in the small moments of his day, and not the horror of Peter Halasz chewing a little girl to the core?

Was it simply because she was a *porn star*?

The idea, Thomas knew, wasn't as preposterous as it seemed. For heterosexual men, simply glancing at a beautiful woman lit up the reward systems of the brain. Neuromarketing firms had funded hundreds of so-called 'endogenous opoid' studies, trying to unravel the alchemy of images and the male erection – adding layer after layer of cultural reinforcement to what was at best a basic tendency. Then there was the unnerving discovery of neural mechanisms dedicated to assessing the sexual vulnerability of women. Or the notorious study that mapped the brains of men watching Jodie Foster's rape scene in *The Accused*, suggesting that they found it even more titillating than run-of-the-mill pornography. The now infamous *Time* magazine headline, IS EVERY MAN A RAPIST? still surfaced from time to time in the press.

Was the image of a porn star slicing her way to bliss a kind of visual narcotic? Could that be it? Had it simply turned him on in some dark and primal way? Hatred and lust, after all, predated mammalian love by a few hundred million years.

Thomas cursed, rubbed his eyes again. What a fucked up animal a human being was. Well and truly.

The Thomas Bible animal in particular.

Stars, he chided himself. *You came out here to enjoy the fucking stars.*

They *were* beautiful, like motes in morning sunlight, forever falling in vast gravitational drafts.

Watch the fuckers, then. Absorb the awe and beauty . . .

Breathe deep.

Absorb . . .

He nearly jumped out of his skin when he heard clicking at the patio door. He cursed himself when he realized he'd forgotten to let out Bart.

Mia was right. He was more than jumpy. Jumpy-jumpy.

'Why couldn't you remind me I'm an idiot *before* I warmed up?' he said, fighting his way free of his sleeping bag. In the gloom, Bartender was little more than an imbecilic, Cheshire grin. Thomas absently scratched the old boy's ears, then crawled back into his cotton and polyester cocoon.

His heart hammered in his ears.

Calm down. Everything's fine. You're safe.

Safe.

So much of the so-called 'modern malaise' could be chalked up to the differences between the modern and the stone-age environment the human brain had evolved to thrive in. What had been advantageous in highly interdependent communities of 200 or so souls had since become at best trivial, and at worst species-threatening liabilities. When energy-rich fatty foods were scarce, a hankering for them was adaptive. When work was mandatory for survival, slacking was recuperative. Most people lived in a kind of media-constructed, virtual stone age, indulging their ancient yens for sex, gossip, violence, simplicity and certainty, flattery and competition – those things humans in small, highly interdependent communities required in the great reproductive scrum called evolution. They lived in worlds that indulged and reflected their weaknesses, and that only incidentally captured the complexity and indifference of the real thing. Disney Worlds. And since ignorance was invisible (Neil used to always say that making ignorance invisible was God's idea of a one-liner), they thought they more or less *saw it all.*

Small wonder, Thomas thought, we humans were so jumpy, so arrogant, so defensive. Small wonder the internet, which was supposed to blow the doors off of narrow, parochial views of the world, had simply turned into a supermarket of bigotries, a place where any hatred or hope could find bogus rationalization. For the human brain, it was like living in a schizophrenic world, a paradise of plenty where any second now, something really bad was going to happen.

In a sense, that's all popular culture was, a modern, market-driven prosthetic for the paleolithic brain. How could such a culture *not* be seduced by the psychopath? By Neil.

Lurking in every shadow, following housewives home from the grocery store, stealing schoolgirls through bedroom windows, pulling over for hitchhikers, scoping out prostitutes through tinted windows . . .

This was a bad thing in a stone-age village of 200 people. A very dangerous thing.

Making up the rules as they went along. Taking no shit no way no how. And of course, getting laid with a capital 'L'.

In a Disney World of 9 billion, few things could be as cool.

For Professor Skeat, psychopaths were nothing less than the horsemen of the apocalypse. Contemporary culture had digested the meaninglessness of natural events, the fact they were indifferent to all things human. A few stubborn fools still shook their fists at God, but most simply shrugged their shoulders. Most knew better, no matter how ardently they prayed. What made psychopaths so indigestible, Skeat claimed, what drove culture to slather them with layer after layer of cinematic and textual pearl, was that they were *humans* that were indifferent to all things human. They were natural disasters personified.

They were walking *gnosis*, secret knowledge, an expression of the nihilistic truth of existence. And this, Skeat insisted, was why psychopaths were the only holy men, the only real avatars left to humankind.

Thomas wondered what Professor Skeat would think of Neil now. Star pupil. Prodigy.

A prophet of the oldest testament of them all.

So many stars.

They reminded Thomas of Neil's crazy seminar in Skeat's class. Rather than present anything of his own, Neil had dressed as the Man in Pink and sung Eric Idle's 'organ donation song' from Monty Python's *The Meaning of Life*. The whole class, including old Skeat, had roared with laughter. But Skeat wasn't about to let Neil off the hook for sheer moxy's sake. Afterward, he demanded that Neil explain the significance of the song.

Neil nodded, smiled rakishly, and said: 'We live in a world where asking about the meaning of life has become a joke. It's no longer just the answer that eludes us. We've lost the question as well.'

The prick received an A, of course.

Staring at the stars, Thomas silently mouthed the lyrics – how could he forget them after enduring so many drunken rehearsals? And it seemed he could feel the entire earth *float* beneath him, wheeling beneath the light of a never-ending nuclear holocaust . . . A sun. A star.

A granule of light drifting in an infinite void.

CHAPTER ELEVEN

August 25th, 7.23 a.m.

'Dad! Daddy, wake up!'

'Wah?'

It was Ripley, sobbing. She had blood on her palms.

'Bart's dead, Dad! Somebody killed Bart!'

Thomas pulled a hand across his face, struggled out of his sleeping bag, stumbled to his feet, at once alert and still sleeping. What was happening?

Bart seemed impossibly black, slumped across the dew-grey lawn between the patio and the kids' pup-tent – so black that Thomas didn't realize the wetness matting his fur was blood until he looked at his finger tips. Brown eyes fogged and open. Tongue slack across the grass.

Ripley stood sobbing, wrist pressed to wrist, hands clutching her cheeks. 'Bart!' she cried.

A terror unlike any he had ever felt clutched Thomas about the throat.

'Sweetie,' he said as calmly as he could manage, 'where's Frankie?'

'I dunno.'

His daughter's words struck him like a hammer. He stood, his stomach bubbling, his limbs as light as styrofoam. *Just adrenalin*, he thought.

He walked over to the pup-tent, calling, 'Frankie?'

He jerked open the flap. Nothing but tangled sleeping bags in orange gloom.

He ran to the house, yanked open the patio doors, crying, 'Frankie!'

The house had the falling-snow quiet of returning from a long trip.

He ran upstairs, hoping that Frankie had crawled into his own bed. Nothing.

'Frankie!' he shouted.

He tried to laugh, to tell himself that Frankie sometimes liked to hide.

'This isn't funny, son!'

He dashed down the stairs through the main floor to the basement.

'Frankie! Jesus Christ . . . This is *not* funny!'

He searched the basement. Nothing.

He exploded through the front door, desperately rooted through the bushes, shrieking, '*Frankie!*'

'*Daddy!*' he heard. His heart stopped.

'Where are you son?' he croaked.

'*Daddy!*' again – from the backyard!

He dashed around the house, smiling through his tears even though he knew.

Oh-you-little-bastard . . .

He jumped the driveway gate, rounded the corner, and saw Ripley still standing next to Bart's inert form. Somehow, it seemed he had known it was her calling all along.

'Daddy, I'm scared!' she bawled.

Thomas knelt before her, tried to grasp her gently, but his hands shook too violently.

'Sh-shush, sweetie . . .' he hissed.

'Where's Frankie, Daddy? Where'd he go?'

Thomas stood, pressed both palms against his brows.

This-isn't-happening-this-isn't-happening . . .

'*FRANKIE*!' he howled.

He couldn't stand. He fell to his knees.

He could hear Ripley crying, feel Mia shake his shoulders, though he had difficulty recognizing his face.

Frankie . . .

Neil had his son.

CHAPTER TWELVE

The following days were a fog of horror. Nothing was real.

Sam, Thomas could tell, was torn between consoling him and doing everything possible to find Frankie. The Evidence Response Team descended on his home once again, doing what Sam called a fingertip search of his backyard, combing the grass and the pup-tent for hairs, fibers, flakes of skin, anything, forensic or otherwise, that might constitute a 'clue'. It made Thomas nauseous just thinking of the word . . . Clue. How had something so silly, a trite Hollywood conceit, become the very hook from which, not today, not tomorrow, but *hope itself* now hung?

This couldn't be happening.

But it was. Thomas watched it from the den window, pacing back and forth, grabbing his hair and thumping his head against the wall. He even prayed – something he had never done even as a child. Please God and all that bullshit. Undo what you've wrought, motherfucker. He watched the technicians stump through the grass, laughing at unheard jokes, rubbing their backs when they got sore. And all the while, Bart just laid there, like an oil-stain in the heart of a tacky carpet. They didn't remove his body until late afternoon. Thomas had cried then, wept for his dog. It hollowed him out, gouged him so deeply he thought he might stop breathing, were it not for Frankie, and the . . .

Possibility.

Word wasn't long in coming. No clues, aside from a superficial match from what seemed to be several of Neil's hairs. DNA confirmation would come tomorrow. The family dog, some genius determined, had been killed at close range by a gunshot to the head.

Case closed. Time for dinner and a handjob.

Sam and Gerard, meanwhile, had canvassed the surrounding neighborhood, searching for potential witnesses. No one saw anything. Of three 'strange' vehicles reported – a black Toyota, a white van, and an aging Ford Explorer – two of them, the van and the Explorer, checked out. The Toyota was too generic to be of much use.

Sam was almost in tears when she came to his door late that evening. 'Sorry, professor,' she said. 'Tom . . .'

The FBI immediately released Nora from custody, knowing that cooperation would no longer be a problem. From what Sam said, she was even more of a basket case than he was. But she cooperated with a vengeance. Whatever hold Neil had over her, it could not compare with her love of her son. She was baying for Neil's blood, Sam told him.

Her tone hesitantly suggested he should be too.

But nothing was real. His son was gone and nothing was real.

Except Ripley.

Ripley had difficulty understanding what was happening. She missed Frankie, Thomas imagined, but the idea that something truly horrific had happened was something she had to borrow continually from adults. Thomas was tormented by the knowledge that for her the trauma lied in *his* manifestations of grief and bewilderment. But for those first three days seeing her filled him with a sense of desperation unlike anything he had experienced. He couldn't look at her without either seeing Frankie or the monstrous shadow of Neil – without seeing his loss or his demon. Even though going to work was out of the question, he still sent her over to Mia's for a few hours during the day.

She didn't complain.

Nora, Sam told him, was too much a wreck to look after herself, let alone her daughter. She blamed herself, Thomas knew.

And perhaps she should.

Using the investigation as a pretext, Thomas found himself interrogating Sam on the details of Nora's statement. As Thomas suspected, Nora had started her affair with Neil *before*, not after, their marriage. Apparently it had been an impulsive, drunken thing, which they had immediately regretted and swore they would never do again because of their love for Thomas.

Thomas wept at this point, and Sam stopped, promising to bring him a copy of the transcript – even though it could mean her job. The important thing was finding Frankie, she said.

It was both easier and more difficult, for some reason, reading Nora's actual words. The intimacy of the transcribed discussion seemed at once shocking, and yet strangely appropriate to a conversation between strangers. What could strangers do with such small and catastrophic honesty?

After a hiatus of years, Nora and Neil had resumed their relationship around the same time her marriage had started to seriously stumble. Nora chalked it up to coincidence, but Thomas knew better. Shared secrets fostered intimacy, while lies deadened it. The spouse being cheated on literally had no chance, outside inertia and the fear of financial ruin. He or she was bound to seem pathetic or judgmental or insensitive or what have you. People always justified their crimes.

The affair was, if Nora's description could be believed, almost pathologically passionate. Neil, she said, became an addiction, and she'd assumed that he had felt the same for her. They met regularly, if infrequently, and though they were strangely reckless in their choice of sexual venues – parks, movie theatres, even a couple of restaurant rest rooms – they were exceedingly careful when it came to Thomas. Poor Tommy.

When the interviewers asked Nora about her feelings for him during this time, Thomas felt his heart slow to what seemed a beat a minute.

sINT 1: How would you describe them?

Nora Bible: My feelings for Tommy? He's a good man. I loved him.

sINT 2: But if—

Nora Bible: But if I loved him how could I . . . betray him? What do you want me to say? That he beat me? He didn't. That he continually psychoanalyzed me, attempting to undermine my self-esteem? No. Not unless we were fighting – but who plays fair in fights? Tommy just couldn't . . .

sINT 2: Couldn't what, Ms Bible?

Nora Bible: Couldn't fuck me the way Neil could. Hm? Was that what you wanted to hear?

sINT 1: Are you saying your husband was impotent?

Nora Bible: Tommy? No. *Hell* no . . . He just wasn't . . . He wasn't Neil.

sINT 2: You know, Ms Bible, your answers seem, well . . .

sINT 1: Imprecise.

Nora Bible: Look. I married Tommy because he *knew* me, he really knew me. But . . . I think I started resenting him for it. For Tommy weaknesses are supposed to be accepted. We're not supposed to punish ourselves every time we screw up, just forgive . . . that, and try to cultivate better habits. But with Neil . . .

sINT 2: Neil didn't know you?

Nora Bible: Oh, Neil knew me.

sINT 2: But then what are you trying to say?

Nora Bible: I was always just a project for Tommy, I think . . .

Tears had tapped onto the transcript page as he read this. Of course, Nora would try to find reasons for what she did; that much didn't surprise him. Owning up was expensive, reasons were cheap. The *causes* were quite clear: women, like men, were pre-programmed for infidelity. The murky alchemy of attraction, from flirt to tingle to climax, was simply a patsy for the biology of reproduction. Given the onerous child-rearing demands of *homo sapiens*, human females were often forced to make pair-bonding compromises. One guy to pay the bills, another guy to ring the bells.

Nora was simply acting out a script inked in DNA, and authored by millions of years of heartbreak and adaptive advantages, unconsciously following an eon-old biological imperative. She had no reason for breaking his trust, his heart. No reason whatsoever.

At least that's what Thomas told himself at first.

He laid in bed all day, transcript pages scattered about, before he realized what he already knew.

Nora fucked Neil because Neil was stronger.

He had been a failure as a husband. As a man. And now he was a failure as a father as well.

Good God, Frankie . . .

Things couldn't get any more real.

August 27th, 1.09 p.m.

Thomas blinked. Both in shock and against the sunlight. When the doorbell rang, his thoughts had leapt to Sam and to the promise of information.

'Hi, Tommy,' Nora said, wincing and smiling beneath her sunglasses. She wore a black skirt and a pearl blouse, like she was dressed for a funeral. 'I was nearby so I thought I'd take a chance and see if Ripley wanted to come home early.'

Thomas wanted to slap her. She had always played little games, but more so after their divorce. 'Seeing what the *kids* wanted' meant unilaterally changing the plan to suit *her* schedule. 'Bring them home' meant bringing them to their *real* home. This shit was bad enough at the best of times. How could she do it now?

Thomas glared at her.

'Where is she?' Nora said, peering around him. 'Ripley!'

'She's still at Mia's,' Thomas explained. 'You want me to go get her?'

She bit her lip. 'No, no, that's okay. I'll come back later . . . when I said I would.'

Two tears streaked from beneath the black lenses. Thomas was struck breathless by remorse.

Always so hard on her.

'Don't be silly,' he said. 'People in Europe are dying because of all our driving. I gotta get her things together anyway, so ah . . .' He shrugged. 'Why don't you come in?'

Just please-please don't mention our boy!

She wiped her eyes, then wordlessly stepped past him into the living room.

He was struck, quite against his will, by the differences between her and Sam. Nora was dark where Sam was sunny, mother-soft where Sam was still school-girl tight. What troubled him wasn't the comparison – both were beautiful in their own way – it was the comparing.

Nothing should be normal.

'Would you like a coffee?'

She nodded, taking off her sunglasses. Her eyes were red, smeared with mascara.

'You remember how I like it?' she asked.

'Two sugars, sub-Saharan black,' his said with phony mirth. 'Do you remember mine?'

'One sugar, Scandinavian white,' she said, smiling – or trying to, anyway.

The joke brought a pang to his throat. It was one of those running gags that couples use to seal the finer cracks of their intimacy. Stupidity made everything smooth.

She lingered at the kitchen entrance while he poured the water, leaning precisely where Sam had leaned the night she'd asked him to drive with her to Washington.

So far so good, he thought. *Pretenses intact.*

'Oh!' Nora exclaimed. 'Where's her album? You know, the photos we gave her from when Bart was a puppy?'

'In the office, I think,' Thomas said. 'On one of the shelves. Do you think that's a good idea?'

She was already halfway into the living room. 'I dunno, Tommy. I thought that . . .' He lost the rest of what she said to the gurgle of the coffeemaker.

He found her still in the office a few moments afterward. She was standing before his Earth poster, with British Columbia and Alaska rearing blue-green over her right shoulder. She was staring at the small photo-album, her eyes obviously overmatched by what they saw. She glanced at him, then closed the album. She set it down on the desk, almost reverently.

'Nora?'

She leaned against the poster and crumpled, not to the ground, but in a direction not described by space. Her sunglasses fell from her fingers.

'I forgot,' she said. She gestured weakly at the album. 'Forgot th-that there were pictures of . . . pictures of . . .'

She started weeping.

Thomas clutched her in his arms without realizing he'd crossed the room. She shuddered, sobbed.

'Oh, Tommy,' she gasped. 'Pleeaase-pleease-pleease . . .'

'Shhh . . . All we can do is wait, sweetheart. Be strong for Ripley.'

'*Ripley*,' she sighed, breathing deeply. 'Ripley . . .' as if she were the only mantra, the only prayer she had left.

He brushed tear-soaked hair from her face, stared into her anguished, vulnerable eyes. She seemed so open, so derelict and exposed. So true.

They kissed. Slow, soft, and yet swollen with promise. She tasted like mint.

Her lips became desperate, even violent. Her hands searched his back. She pressed against him. He clutched her right breast, felt her sigh into his mouth.

He pressed his left hand up her skirt, between her thighs, against warm, powdery cotton. She gasped. She undid his fly, began tugging on his cock with cold hands.

He pulled her panties aside and pressed himself against her heat. She hooked a leg around his thigh, then suddenly, shockingly, he was moving inside her. *No*, something whispered inside of him, far too late.

She cried out, smeared his cheek with wet lips. He thrust harder. '*Ungh*,' she moaned. '*Ungh* . . .'

He'd forgotten that this was what she had felt like – tender, yielding centre, clawing legs and arms. Insatiable mouth.

'*Upstairs*,' she gasped.

He withdrew. Things were moving too fast anyway. He wanted to enjoy her, cherish and remember her. He wanted to make her come the way Neil had made her come.

Thomas scooped her in his arms, carried her down the hall to the stairs. She watched him with swollen eyes. 'I missed you, Tommy,' she whispered.

They undressed slowly, the memory of heat and hardness still thick between them. Then she stood before him, older, but glorious still. How could such a woman . . .

He pressed her down onto the bed. Tears streamed from her eyes.

'*I want my little boy back*,' she murmured. '*My little baby*.'

Lyrics from a different song.

Thomas stared at her, horror-stricken all over again. She rolled onto her side, and he curled naked behind her. He pressed himself between her legs, but not inside. He held her as she wept. Combed her hair with his fingers.

They lay in silence for some time, skin growing slick against the heat of skin. A crease in the pillow bit into his cheek, but he did not move. The pain was like a pin, a place to focus, something to hold him here, pressed against the shuddering body of his ex-wife.

Frankie was *their* boy, the bond that no amount of bitterness could break. The miracle was easily forgotten, and when it was remembered, it so often seemed absurd. A man spilling hot into his wife, the biology of blood and slurry, and then *life*, another dumbfounded soul breaching the surface of the black, the all-encompassing black.

Despite Sam and his feeling of dawning regret, it seemed right that he hold Nora like this. Like coming full circle.

'I always loved this duvet,' Nora said vaguely, running her fingers over the floral patterns.

Adolescent shouts filtered through the windows. The afternoon light possessed a peculiar copper cast. The air was sticky and smelled of guilt.

His gut turned to sand. Her words from the transcript wheeled unbidden through his mind.

'*He wasn't Neil . . .*'

Something savage rattled through him. Suddenly, inexplicably, it seemed he knew, with Old Testament certainty, that *she was to blame.* Not him. Not the father who slept while his son was stolen.

He found himself asking, 'Why, Nora?'

She pressed free of his arms and turned toward him. Her look was hard, almost vicious in its intensity.

But her voice was calm – the pedestrian tone she used to describe grocery lists and co-workers. 'I want you to kill him, Thomas. Promise me you'll kill him.'

Neil. Destroyer of worlds.

Thomas watched Nora from the front door. She put Ripley's things into her Nissan, then after a shy wave, walked across to Mia's to get Ripley. She wanted to 'Say hi to the old fag,' she had said, making Thomas wince. For some strange reason she always insisted she could use the term because she was a woman.

Thomas had told her to give Ripley his love. He didn't feel strong enough to say goodbye.

Out of habit, he flipped the mailbox lid on his way in, fishing out assorted bills and what looked like yet another garbage BD from

AOL – why wouldn't they just die? But the lack of flash and color on the case caught his attention. He pulled it out and froze.

In dark blue marker, someone had written

GOODBOOK

across the transparent plastic. The Blue-ray flashed like a knife beneath.

Thomas backed through the door, hands shaking.

No-no-no-no-no-no . . .

Thoughts of Frankie flooded his eyes with tears.

Please, God . . . Please!

He stumbled on a mat. The envelopes tumbled to the ground.

Not my boy . . .

The BD felt at once insubstantial and like an impossible weight. He raced to the kitchen, yanked the silverware drawer so hard it popped its rollers. Knives, forks, spoons scattered across the floor, making patterns like an augur's knuckle-bones. Thomas clutched a steak knife in a trembling hand, began sawing at the tape.

Evidence! Evidence! something within him cried.

He stopped. Ran a hand through his hair. Dashed to the phone.

'Logan,' the voice on the end answered.

'Sam! He sent a Blue-ray to me. Another fucking BD.'

'Tom? Slow down. What are you talking about?'

'Jesus-jesus, what if it's *him*, Sam?' *No-no-no-no-no-no* . . . 'Sam? What if it's *him*?'

Not my boy, please . . .

He stared at the thing: quicksilver reflecting a stranger's anguished face.

'Listen closely, Tom. Do not, under any circumstances, touch that disc. Do you understand me? You could—'

'What if it's *him*, Sam?' Thomas whispered.

He hung up, dropped the phone on the couch, scrambled across the living room rug. He cut through the remaining tape while crouching before his Blue-ray player. The phone trilled continuously, but for some reason it was nearly inaudible. An unearthly calm had possessed him.

Kneeling beneath the TV, he worked the remote control with numb fingers.

The phone stopped ringing. Shallow breaths. The disc whirred in its chilly womb.
The screen flickered to life.

The couch felt hard, like stainless steel – like a coroner's table.
'Tom?' someone asked gently.
Sam.
He pulled his hands from his face. Sam knelt over him, her eyes filled with tears. Gerard seemed to tower behind her, his expression somewhere between stern detachment and . . . Just what was his expression?
'Was it him, Tom?' Sam asked. 'Was it Frankie?'
He shuddered, exhaled, feeling something like twin incisions across both his lungs. How much more could he take? *Should get my blood pressure checked*, he thought inanely.
'Tom?' Almost a whisper.
'No,' he croaked.
Not yet.
He could remember Neil chiding him during exams. 'Your working memory isn't designed for multitasking, you fucking idiot. It's not as advanced as Windows. You gotta do. One. Thing. Ata. Time.'
'The televangelist,' he explained. 'Jackie Forrest.'
Then my boy.
Tears spilled down Sam's cheeks. She glanced nervously at Gerard, who remained stone-faced. How many rules had she broken, Thomas found himself wondering, by sleeping with him? Certainly fewer than by falling in love.
'What do we do?' Sam asked, sounding curiously helpless.
Gerard scowled. 'Wait for Atta,' he said. 'What else?'

Agent Atta wasn't long in arriving. The August heat seemed to roll in with her – not the brightness, just the heat.
'Tell me you didn't play it.'
Thomas was sitting on the couch, Sam at his side. Agent Gerard stood from his seat at the foot of the stairs, scratching the back of his head.
Thomas looked to his palms instead of the SAC. 'What would you do, Agent Atta? What would *you* do?'

'You seem to be saying that an awful lot, professor,' Atta replied. 'Where is it?'

'Still in the machine,' Gerard said.

'*Zarba*,' Atta muttered, kneeling at the base of the broad screen. Her holster swung into view, gun-metal heavy. The light of the screen flashed across her sweaty cheeks, then the panel framed her in luminous black. Shapes seemed to float in and out of focus, as though they watched things battling beneath black satin sheets. There was a quick glimpse – a shadowy sack of some kind, cement or something – but Thomas was certain he'd glimpsed the name of some kind of farm-supply outlet.

'There . . . Did you see it? The name on that bag?'

'We'll have it checked out,' Atta said, unimpressed.

Thomas looked to Sam, scowling.

'The webcast with Halasz had the same kind of glimpses,' she explained. 'Specialty labels, products from what seemed to be non-franchise outlets. But when we checked them out, they came from places all over the country. The bastard's playing with us, professor. Throwing us manufactured leads to dilute our resources.'

More and more shapes resolved and vanished in the gloom. The image bobbed, as though the camera probed the bowels of some deep-sea wreck. Thomas found himself every bit as anxious as he had on his first viewing. For some reason, knowing he *wouldn't* see Frankie made it seem even worse.

Though if he had . . .

None of this is real. Just things and people in a head that's all in my head . . .

The frame abruptly stabilized. Peering, Thomas saw what seemed to be a chain-link kennel. A kennel in a basement littered with defunct possessions. A human shambled through the murky interior, apparently oblivious to the watching camera-eye. '*Halleluiah*,' hissed from the speakers, as though surfacing from white noise. The figure stumbled backward, then drunkenly fell to its knees. It was weeping now. 'Halleluiah.'

Light splashed the scene, as sudden and bright as a prison-guard ambush. The figure whirled toward the camera. Thomas heard himself sob – the way he had when he first realized that it wasn't Frankie . . .

. . . but Jackie Forrest, hands out, as though fending away

paparazzi. His scalp had been bandaged, like Halasz. Silver braces bracketed his head, fixed with what seemed hardware-store screws. '*You*,' he spat in indignation. 'You can't hurt me! I *know* where I'm going! I have *seen*!'

HOW HAVE YOU SEEN?

The question apparently shocked the preacher. For a moment, anger and terror warred over his expression.

'I walk by faith!' He wiped his jowls, smiled manically. 'Faith is the substance of things hoped for,' he exclaimed in the wavering baritone that so many preachers reserve for biblical quotations, 'the evidence of sights unseen!'

SO BELIEF WITHOUT EVIDENCE IS EVIDENCE?

'You'll never know, you son-of-a-bitch!' Jackie snarled. 'Not until you writhe in the fires of hell! Then your agon—!'

AGONY? YOU MEAN LIKE THIS?

Spit exploded from Jackie's mouth. He went rigid, bent back like a coat-hanger, then fell thrashing onto the floor. Feces and urine darkened his shift. His shriek was choked into gagging by vomit.

Jackie went slack. 'You sum'bitch,' he sobbed. 'You sum'bitch.'

CALL ON HIM.

Jackie curled into a fetal position. '*Pleassse!*' he hissed.

HIM. CALL ON HIM.

'*Pleaaasse, Gawwd!*' he bawled. '*PLEEAAASSSE*!'

A moment of grovelling silence, then the evangelist jumped, as though surprised by someone tapping his shoulder. He glanced around wildly, then slowly turned his face in the direction of the camera's light. He wiped his nose along his forearm, oblivious to shit smeared across it.

DO YOU SEE?

'H-how?' the trembling lips asked. 'H-ho-how is this possible?'

IS IT GOD?

The face crumpled then went blank. 'Y-yessss!' he gasped. 'I can't see . . . but I *feeeel* him . . . here . . . so very close . . .'

HOW CAN YOU BE CERTAIN?

'This is beyond your puny questions . . . beyond . . .'

The evangelist's face floated across the screen, greasy and bloated in the glaring light. Surgical steel gleamed. Blood trailed from the screws. His expression had become plaintive in a wheedling, ingratiating way that Thomas found difficult to look at. Plaintive and joyous.

'I knew it . . . I always knew it!'

A deep shuddering gasp. Fluttering eyelids. A voice capsized by rapture.

'*Sweet Jeeeesusss! Haaaw, praise-praise-praise . . .*'

'Bullshit,' Gerard murmured, only to be silenced by Agent Atta's fierce scowl.

'*Forgive me . . . Haaaw, please-pleas—*'

'It just goes on like this,' Thomas said over the cooing preacher. 'On and on, until the BD runs out.'

'*—I didn't mean to . . . Nooooo . . . Noooooooo . . .*'

The air had become unbreathably thick.

'That can't be real,' Gerard said after a moment. He sounded frightened.

'What can't be real?' Thomas asked.

'He can't make somebody see God.'

Thomas shrugged. 'Why not? That's the whole point: experience, *all* experience, is simply a matter of neural circuitry. Why not religious experience? In fact, these experiences are pretty pedestrian for neuroscientists – among the first to be artificially stimulated.'

Gerard looked unconvinced. No, not unconvinced, *unwilling*. He had been able to shrug off what had happened to Powski and Halasz, but not this. He must be born again, Thomas realized, the proud owner of a personal relationship with Jesus Christ.

But if revelation were simply a matter of wiring . . .

'It's gotta be some kind of trick,' Gerard said. 'Are you telling me he could do that to you, me, *anyone*?'

Thomas nodded. A frantic edge had crept into the agent's tone.

'Easy, Gerard,' Atta said. 'As far as his argument goes, our only concern – our *one and only* concern – is how we can use it to stop the lunatic bastard. Copy?'

Gerard looked at her with dull incomprehension, the look of a man jarred past the point of copying. 'But if it's all just in our heads, then . . . then . . .'

'Then what?' Atta asked.

'Then he's *right*, isn't he?'

Atta rubbed the back of her neck. 'Professor?'

Thomas looked away.

'I could use some help here, professor.'

'Neil's simply showing us facts,' Thomas said. 'When our brains fire in particular ways, we have so-called spiritual experiences. It's as straightforward as that.'

'You think he's right!' Gerard exclaimed. 'You actually *agree* wi—!'

'It's not Neil I'm agreeing with,' Thomas snapped. 'He's not tricking us, or pulling the wool over our eyes. He's simply showing us how it is. If you were Halasz, you wouldn't think, "Oh, that bastard is forcing me to do this." You wouldn't experience his manipulation as a compulsion, as something external you couldn't overcome. You – *you!* – would be like Cynthia Powski. You would *want* to do those . . . those things. Don't you see? That's what you would choose. Gladly. Freely – as freely as you've chosen to do anything in your life. No alien spinal taps hijacking your body as you sit back helpless, paralyzed. Just *you*, because it was your brain he mucked with, and your brain is all that you are.'

'Bullshit,' Gerard said, his face somehow pale and flushed at once. 'Total bullshit.'

Thomas shook his head. 'Everybody thinks they're the exception, don't they? Even after they're diagnosed with schizophrenia, or Alzheimer's. "If I can just concentrate hard enough," they say, "I can conquer this." Don't you see? Don't you see what he's showing us? There's no such thing as the "triumph of the human spirit". There's no such thing as a human spirit! All of them – Gyges, Powski, Halasz, Forrest – have bootstrapped their way to success, more success than any of us here could reasonably expect. That takes *moxy*, doesn't it? That takes a *will to succeed* – far more than you could muster, agent. So what makes you think you'd be the exception?'

'Now look, professor,' Atta said sharply. 'I've done some research on this. It's not the slam-dunk you make it sound like—'

'Research, Shelley? Then tell me, what's Neil's argument?'

She looked at him warily. 'That we're fundamentally biomechanical. That our choices are the result of physical processes over which we have no control, and so –' she shrugged – 'aren't really choices.'

'Then tell me, what are the contrary arguments?'

'Well there's . . .' Atta paused, looking at once angered and uncertain.

'Difficult to express, aren't they? They require rehearsal, training. All those cheesy, pragmatic redefinitions of freedom. All those fuzzy, quasi-quantum speculations on brain function. Blah-fucking-blah-blah. On the one hand, you have flattering hope and the "redefinition of traditional categories in the light of scientific knowledge" – never mind that *anything* can be redefined – and on the other you have Neil's claim which, despite running counter to our most cherished intuitions, is clear, direct, and forceful: consciousness is deceptive to the point of rendering all our concepts suspect, if not bankrupt. The apologists come and go while the unbearable conclusion remains. I'm not a betting man, agent, but—'

Atta had started waving her hands. 'Okay, okay, look,' she said. 'You need to—'

'You people make me sick,' Gerard snapped at Thomas.

'Danny . . .' Atta said.

'What kind of people might those be, Ger?'

'Smart-ass, know-it-all, arrogant pricks, with their terrorist sympathies, their hobosexual neighbors—'

'*Hobo*sexual?'

'*Bum* fuckers! Fags!'

'Are you for fucking real?'

'We're the only *real* thing on this sick planet! Things are going to be all washed away, real soon, trust me. Things are going to be sorted!'

'Danny!'

'Sorted,' Thomas laughed. 'And let me guess which pile you think you're going to end up on.' A derisive snort. 'I feel sorry for you, Ger.' He glanced at Sam, whose look said, *Just leave it alone.*

'Sorry?' Agent Gerard said in a mocking falsetto. 'For *me*? That's rich.'

Thomas shrugged. 'You know how many religions we humans have cooked up over the ages? *Thousands* . . . Thousands! Doesn't that worry you? *Embarrass* you? Think of that feeling you have, that sense of self-righteous indignation that you're struggling to hold onto right now, that you're using to squash the fact of your confusion and fear. I hate to break this to you, buddy, but it's as cheap as fucking dirt. *Everybody* uses it. Everybody thinks the great captain in the sky has picked them for the winning team, and why not? In the absence of evidence, all we have is our psychology, our needs, to anchor our beliefs. To feel safe. To feel special. You can stomp your foot all you want, wave your hands, pray and pray and pray, but in the end, you're just one more fucking Christian-Muslim-Hindu-Buddhist-Jew, just another hapless, dim-witted human, crying out, "Me-fucking-me-me! *I'm* the special one!" '

All three FBI agents stared at him.

Gerard didn't seem either convinced or outraged, just . . . calm. 'And what makes you any different?'

'I know that I don't know shit.'

'But you think Cassidy's right.'

Thomas breathed deep. 'Look . . . How do you argue with science? How? Think of that feeling you get when one of your buddies tells you to "tell him how it is"? Do you *ever* tell him the truth? Not usually. But why? Because you know that he's just like you, that he needs to hear some ego-boosting bullshit, that he just wants to hear his flattering preconceptions confirmed. Left to our own devices, we bullshit, end of story. Humans are bullshitters. So, set aside the fact that science has allowed us to unleash the sun from a few grams of plutonium, the bottom line is that it's the only institution we've ever come up with that's given us *ugly truths.* It's the cruel stranger, the one who lays it out as it is. So tell me, Ger, why would you even *want* to argue against it? How could you honestly think your burning bush trumps thermonuclear tests in the Bikini Islands?'

'You really *think* it,' Gerard grated, 'don't you? You really think Cassidy's right? That it's all fucking pointless.'

Thomas swallowed. The urge to lie was almost overwhelming.

Was this what Neil wanted? Someone to sing the aria for his lunatic opera.

'I don't know what to think,' he said lamely.

Gerard sneered. 'Then why should we, or even *you* for that matter, give a flying fuck about your son?'

Silence.

Tears filled Thomas's eyes. *Not here please . . .*

'You ass,' Sam whispered. 'You pathetic ass.'

'Give me a fucking break, Logan.'

'She's right, Danny,' Atta said. 'You know she's right.'

Thomas sat down on the recliner, feeling numb in a way he had never experienced before. Numb to his fingertips. Numb through to his heart. Even his eyelids felt insubstantial. He knew that he looked broken, but brokenness required substance, and he had none. He had been afraid of crying before these strangers, but crying no longer seemed a possibility. It was as though he'd become a condensed edition of himself, all crises and climaxes abridged.

He thought of Nora, of her residue smeared across his thighs.

Sam's hand settled indecisively on his shoulder. She wanted to comfort him, he knew, but was afraid of what the others would think. She was frail, like the rest.

Only Neil was strong.

Sam said something to him, then began berating Gerard some more, listing a series of recent, almost fuck-ups – including his interrogation of Nora. 'Gerard the Retard,' she concluded in disgust. 'Isn't that what they called you at Quantico?'

'Come on, Sam,' Atta said. 'Danny? Both of you . . .'

'You're such a bitch,' Gerard cried. 'Don't you see what's going on here? Don't you know what this means?'

My son is dead.

'Danny!' Agent Atta barked. She grabbed him by the elbow and directed him to the far corner of the room.

Sam reached out and squeezed Thomas's hand. She tried to smile.

'I thought nothing got to you, Danny,' Agent Atta was saying in low, personal-pep-talk tones. 'What is it you always say?'

'That if you shit on my plate, I'd simply eat around it.'

Atta laughed, but it sounded forced. 'Now that's the Danny Gerard I know . . .'

Then, with the dull spark of revelations outdistanced by catastrophe, Thomas understood. *Neil.* Neil was pulling them under. Starved for resources by the public furor over the Chiropractor, barred from seeking outside help by Neil's NSA past, unnerved and outwitted . . . They were out of their depth. They'd been treading water, and now that Thomas was drowning, they could no longer pretend to see the shore.

Agent Atta turned with a brisk and dismissive air, apparently far more heartened by her words of encouragement than Gerard.

'Listen, professor . . .'

'Spare me the harangue, agent. I'm not one of your troops.'

She stared at him for a thoughtful moment, then nodded. 'Just a question before I go.'

Thomas rubbed the back of his neck. 'Shoot.'

'We already know these abductions aren't random.'

Thomas nodded. 'He's picking tokens, people who represent something.'

'Exactly. With Gyges you suggested he was trying to undermine the notion of personhood. With Cynthia Powski, obviously, his target was pleasure, or suffering I guess, depending on how you look at it. With Congressman Halasz, he was gunning for the will and responsibility. And now with Reverend Forrest, spirituality.'

'Humanity,' Thomas said. 'Each represents a fundamental characteristic of what we think it means to be human. But this is all old hat, agent; why rehash it now?'

'Because it means we might be able to anticipate him. If we can figure out what characteristic or trait or whatever he's gunning for next, we might be able to draw up a list of potential . . .' She trailed, apparently troubled by Thomas's expression.

'What is it, professor?'

'Love,' Thomas said softly. 'His next target is love.'

He pressed thumb and forefinger against his eyes.

'How can you be so sure?'

'Because,' Thomas said to his palm, 'he already has his token.'

My son.

That night he suffered through one of those skidding sleeps, where he fell in and out of dreams, some bizarre, some terrifying – all of them bad. He would wake up, his head and face throbbing, then slip back into a long argument with Neil about nothing in particular, certainly nothing to do with what was happening in the waking world. The prick would shrug and smile his *what-am-I-going-to-do-with-you* smile, then the nightmare proper would begin again. Gunshots. Dead little kids, refusing to behave, always refusing . . .

Then ringing.

His thoughts reeled at the groggy entrance to consciousness. He slapped at the alarm, but realized it was his phone.

His eyes itched, his face felt sunburn swollen – from crying, he imagined. He fumbled in the darkness, managed to grab the receiver.

'Hello.' He coughed to clear his throat.

'Tom is that you?' Someone. Sam. 'Tom?'

'Yeah, it's me, Sam.' He cleared his throat. 'What happened to you last—'

'Listen, Tom, they've found him.'

Breathlessness.

'Frankie?'

'They've found him, and he's alive. The EMTs think he's going to be fine.'

'You found Frankie?' Thomas cried, his voice breaking.

'They're taking him to St Luke's-Roosevelt right now.'

'St Luke's?' His mind raced. Why would they take him there? Then he remembered all the hoopla from the university paper. St Luke's had recently completed a world-class neurosurgery center.

No-no-no—

'I'll be right there!'

An audible sigh. 'Listen, Tom . . . I really think you should wait.'

'Wait? What the fuck do you mean, wait? You said he's fine.'

'Please, Tom. Trust me on this. Give the doctors—'

'You said *he was fine!*'

'He will be. I swear. He's in no immediate danger. You just—'

'The bastard did something to my baby, didn't he? The fucker hurt him, didn't he?'

'Shhhhh. Please, Tom. It'll be—'

'*What the fuck did he do to my baby*?!'

'No one kno—'

Thomas dropped the phone and flew down the stairs.

The drive seemed little more than a crazed abstraction, after the fact. Lights, lines, and menace.

The city, the snaking labyrinth, obdurate and overshadowing, laughing at yet one more white-knuckled father. The parking garage. The smoky concrete. The stupid, surly nurse, asking him to restrain himself.

'Just tell me fucking *where*!'

Elevator doors opening like stage curtains.

What was that noise?

Sam down the florescent hall, glancing, turning, hastening to prepare, to caution. Gerard glaring at the floor.

'Tom . . . Tom . . . *Tom* . . .'

Pressing past her, past all the professional faces, the smart shoes, the crisp white coats.

'Tom . . . He's okay. Okay. H-he—'

That noise . . .

Through a door, down a windowed hall.

'Tom, *please*!'

Past pale-faced physicians.

Pulled up short, as though by a leash chained to his heart.

The lights. The bed. The starched sheets and soft cotton blankets. The restraints.

His boy, his eyes as round as a coin trick, his mouth a yawning 'O', his body riven, curling about some unseen fire . . .

Frankie.

Sam clutching his shoulders. 'He can't stop screaming, Tom. He can't stop screaming.'

That noise.

The weak man wonders why he has been chosen. The strong man knows all along.

Of course there are no words for this knowledge. No books.

I find this convenient.

You cry out when I touch. You gag when I strangle. You try to cover yourself with hands that are too small. It is strange this power I have over you – like a liquid. Your every surface is helpless, even those folds hidden within. And yet I can only pound you into shapes of your making.

I turn you on your stomach, the way I always turn you on your stomach. I run a finger down the cleft of your back. My erection is immediate and insistent.

I reach for the bolt cutters, my fingers sticky. I sever your spine at the base of the lumbar curve. Suddenly you are a doll from the waist down. A doll that shrieks and weeps.

You do not feel me fuck you.

I sever your spine again, this time at the base of your neck. Careful – careful – I must make sure you can still breathe. I roll you over, dab your hands in your blood. I use them to make prints across my body, welts where you never struck.

Theories, please?

I masturbate with your slack hands, your slick palms.

I watch you watching me. Our silence is hooded. I see you realize. *Before you were opaque, but now you are a window, transparent to my desire. Oh yes,* I see *you. As still as a magazine cover. As blank as a porn star between takes. So sweet. So sweet. At long last, you mean only what I want you to mean . . .*

Your blood is not so hot as my semen.

CHAPTER THIRTEEN

August 29th, 10.15 a.m.

Nora squeezed Thomas's hand so tight his fingers tingled.

The office was supposed to be reassuring, to be what some decorator somewhere would call a 'positive emotive environment'. The personal items – the baseball cap, the family photos, the gift-shop knick-knacks – were meant to convey a sense of privacy, to mask the fact that only institutional transactions were possible in this room. The furnishings – the cherrywood bookcases, the vintage desk, the arabesque rug – were meant to convey a sense of affluence, because most everyone conflated wealth with competence. But Thomas knew otherwise. He could picture the cinder-block behind the wainscoted walls, as clearly as he could see it behind Dr Chadapaddai's expression.

This was a room where people were told they were going to die.

After some enigmatic tapping on his keyboard, the Chief of Neurosurgery at St Luke's-Roosevelt Hospital stood from his computer and walked to a series of panels on the wall. They flickered to life with old-fashioned reluctance, illuminating the haggard contours of his face. A three-dimensional fMRI of Frankie's brain materialized on the screen before him, looking far more like a textbook illustration than little Franklin Bible's soul.

'If you look at this scan, here,' Dr Chadapaddai said, 'you can see that a device of some kind has been attached to both amygdalae.' He had the exhausted posture and build of a truck driver, yet he was immaculately groomed and dressed, like a corporate lawyer wearing a lab coat.

'Device?' Thomas asked.

The long-lashed eyes studied him.

'A device,' the neurologist repeated. He pressed the remote and a square appeared on the screen. He zoomed to the base of Frankie's digitally reconstructed brain, then rotated the image. Something resembling a beetle blackened the back of the almond-shaped amygdala. 'It's attached to the central nucleus,' he said, fishing a pen from his pocket to circle the spot. 'As far as we can tell it's anchored to a web of nanotubules, electrically stimulating numerous efferent pathways –' he began drawing the tip out into different regions of Frankie's brain – 'leading to the lateral hypothalamus, the parabrachial nucleus, and so on.'

'All the regions dealing with fear,' Thomas said.

Horror and wonder suffused him in equal measure, prickling him with sweat, swinging his stomach like a bucket. For all the scars Powski, Halasz, and the others had left on his psyche, they were little more than abstractions now. Nothing could be more real than the pastel graphics on the screen before him. His boy (*Frankie!*) rewired by his friend (*Neil!-what-the-fuck-what-the-fuck—*) to cycle through terror after terror after terror.

A soul tweaked like an engine . . . His *son's* soul, programmed like a car stereo, the volume cranked, playing and replaying a misery as profound as anything God could dish out in hell.

'You gotta take it out,' Nora exclaimed. 'It has to come out!'

Dr Chadapaddai's look of compassion seemed a little too professional, and certainly too practiced. 'I don't think we can,' he said. 'The brain's own circulatory system has been hijacked to target various neural subsystems. Nanowires fine enough to thread capillaries . . .'

'Clean in, messy out,' Thomas said.

The neurologist nodded. 'Of course, we'll eventually *have* to try something, and I can assure you that we're studying and preparing for every possible invasive option. But for the moment, Mr and Mrs Bible, your son's best hope lies in finding whoever did this.'

Neil. Thomas could see him, sitting across from him on the couch, an apparition in the flat-screen glow, saying, '*I now know more about the brain than any man alive . . .*'

When neither of them volunteered any information, Dr Chadapaddai bit his lower lip. 'None of us has ever seen anything like this. Nothing.'

Thomas knew first hand what it was like to have a field of knowledge dominate his life: the strange feeling of estate and insecurity, like making home in a far greater mansion. With information reproducing like bacteria, no specialist could hope to master all the details of even their own specialty. Still, you liked to think you had at least a rough sense of the floor plan. You liked to think you at least knew what you didn't know.

Dismay struck the breath from Thomas, almost sent him slumping to the floor. Only Neil. Only Neil could undo this. Only Neil could remove the horror he had planted in Frankie.

'Have you an arm like God?'

'But you're going to do something?' Nora said. 'Right? I mean, someone put that thing in there. You can take it out.'

The neurologist brushed a lick of raven-black hair from his forehead, then lowered his hand in sudden self-consciousness. He was frightened, Thomas realized. Frightened by the FBI and their demand for confidentiality. Frightened by the images on the wall behind him. Frightened by the little boy screaming in the Neurological Observation Unit. It spoke to his professionalism that he recovered his equilibrium so quickly.

'Mrs Bible, look. You have to understand that for the moment, your boy isn't in any danger. That means we have *time*, and that means we have no choice but to be as cautious as possible. Whoeve—'

'But he's screaming!' she shouted. 'My baby's screaming!'

'Nora, please!' Thomas exclaimed. 'You don't understand.' He glanced at the doctor. 'The amygdala simply controls the scream reflex – the *reflex*, honey.'

Nora regarded him with wide, tearful eyes. 'So he's not terrified?'

Thomas shook his head. 'It's just an uncontrollable reflex that keeps firing over and over again. Like the hiccups. Inside he's the same boy we know and love, scared by all the fuss, frustrated by his inability to stop screaming, but nothing more.'

'No,' Nora said, as though chastising herself for her fears. She looked penitently down to her palms. '*No.* Neil wouldn't do that. Not to our baby.' When she looked up, tears coursed freely down her cheeks. 'He was your best friend, Tommy. Your best friend!'

And your lover.

Dr Chadapaddai handed her some tissue, then stepped back, his face professionally blank.

'Come,' Thomas said to her, standing up. 'I'll drive you home.'

Nora wiped her eyes, laughed. 'I'm not leaving him.' She stood, looked about in a witless, frantic manner, then began shaking her hands from her wrists. 'I'm . . . I'm . . .'

'Ask my administrative assistant,' the Chief Neurologist said, opening the door. 'He'll show you to the restroom, Mrs Bible.'

Thomas lingered, telling Nora he'd meet her in the hall. One of them had to go home, look after Ripley. They would have to arrange shifts or something . . .

'You do know—' Dr Chadapaddai began after the door closed behind her.

'I know,' Thomas interrupted. Frankie experienced every iota of the terror expressed in his screams. Thomas had thought his lie well-intentioned, as a means to help Nora cope, but he realized he was primarily interested in managing her response, no different than Chadapaddai, he supposed. It occurred to him that this was something he had always done. Intercept and reinterpret . . .

'Bad idea,' the neurologist said.

'If this was all we had on our plate, I'd agree,' Thomas replied, wiping a tear from his cheek. 'You saw her. Knowing that Frankie actually . . . actually . . .'

The neurologist looked down in embarrassment, pursed his lips. 'But you don't understand. I *have* to tell her. Otherwise I'd be treating her son under false pretenses. It's not simply an ethical matter, Mr Bible, it's legal.'

Fucking lawyers. Even when they weren't in the room, they were in the room, which meant they were everywhere.

'I'll tell her,' Thomas said drily. 'Nora always blames the messenger.'

When Dr Chadapaddai raised his eyebrows, Thomas added, 'She already hates me.'

They fought in the hall, one of those high-intensity hissing matches with the volume just low enough that everyone could pretend not to hear. When he told her she was using Frankie as an excuse to feel sorry for herself, she actually struck him. Driving home, he could swear he felt blood trickling in his right ear, but every time he poked around, his fingertip was clean.

Everything was falling apart.

The plan had been to go to Mia's to collect Ripley. It was important, one of the doctors had said, for at least one of them to spend time with her, so he and Nora had agreed to stay with Frankie in shifts. The thought of his little boy alone and derelict in the hospital was nothing short of overwhelming. It was like someone shoveling hot beach sand into his chest and gut. Wave after wave. Shovel after shovel.

Ripley, he told himself. *Be strong for Ripley.*

But after pulling into the driveway, he found himself walking to his own door, wandering into the air-conditioned gloom of his living room. He sat on the couch, suffused with a body-wide hum of distress, everything wired to the fragility in his eyes. He stared into the silence. The fridge clicked on in the kitchen.

Something . . . He had to do something. Keeping vigil was not an option.

He didn't hear the knocking at first, though afterward it seemed he had jumped at the sound. He caught his breath at the glimpse of a shadow through his window. He rubbed palms across his face, hooked fingers through his hair. The clinician in him laughed, thinking this was what people did when they were about to fall apart: try to clutch themselves together.

He pulled the door open, confused, hot with a cold sweat.

Theodoros Gyges stared at him, a dapper version of the disheveled wreck Thomas had first met several days earlier. He wore the too-studied casual attire of someone wealthy trying to blend with the middle classes: a yellow, short-sleeved dress-shirt and blue jeans cinched too high on his thick waist. He both looked and smelled clean, like a born-again Christian.

'Could I speak to Professor Thomas Bible?' he said politely.

A surreal moment passed, silent except for the sunny noise of birds, kids, and traffic from the nearby parkway – the noise he heard every time he opened his door in summer.

'Yeah,' Thomas replied. 'I mean, it's me, Mr Gyges.'

Something like an anguished grin creased the man's bristle-brush beard. 'I've been waiting for you to return,' he said, nodding toward a Porsche parked on the sun-bleached street. 'I knew it was you, but then, when I saw your face . . .' He hesitated. 'As you know, I only see strangers.'

'How can I help you?' Thomas asked.

'I heard about your son, Professor Bible. I . . .' The billionaire licked his lips in hesitation. 'I wanted to say that I'm sorry.'

Thomas blinked, suddenly found himself despising the man.

'To be honest, I didn't have you pegged as the sorry sort, Mr Gyges.'

The man's eyes narrowed in appreciation. 'I understand, Professor Bible. I really do. You came to me seeking help, and I turned you out.' He let go a thin-winded, patrician sigh. 'But . . .'

'But *what*, Mr Gyges?'

'Listen. You and I know this whole investigation, this task force, is bullshit. They want your friend, sure, but they want him to stay a secret far more. This has nothing to do with justice . . .' He glanced to either side, as though suddenly conscious of eavesdroppers. He leaned close.

'It's a matter of *hygiene*.'

Thomas nodded, felt the hatred drop out the bottom of him. 'So what are you suggesting? That we go to the papers?' Part of his fight with Nora had involved going to the net with their story – something Thomas had dismissed outright. The FBI was all they had, and he for one was not about to fall for the delusional conviction that he 'knew better than . . .' People always thought they knew better, despite the astronomical odds.

'You don't think I've rattled the chain?' Gyges said. 'I'm a connected man, Mr Bible, a man with leverage. What they say about the Golden Rule is true, believe you me. But you'd need the arms of God to ring the bell on this one. I've had old friends, *senators*, tell me to never call them again. And I've been told . . .'

Gyges trailed into frowning silence.

'Told what?' A tingle had crept into his cheeks. 'Just what are you saying?'

The man's face, which was about as handsome as a bearded baseball glove, went blank. 'Nothing,' he said.

'Then why are you here?'

Gyges ran his tongue across his teeth. 'I was just an ante,' he finally said. 'But *you*, Mr Bible, you've been dealt a hand at this game.'

'So?'

'So, I'm a man of resources. More than people like you can believe. I just want you to know that for me this *is* a matter of justice. Fuck hygiene.'

He produced an ivory card from his breast pocket, held it out to Thomas.

'Every player needs a banker, Mr Bible. Every *serious* player.'

Gyges turned and trotted down the steps. Regretting his hostility, Thomas called out to him as he crossed the lawn

'How are you doing, Mr Gyges?'

The man turned and looked at him as though he were a stranger.

'Better, Professor Bible.' His smile was big and Greek. 'I'm trying to win back my wife.'

'Making amends?'

A scowl darkened the broad face. 'You're not a priest.'

Winded by the encounter, he went upstairs to the kids' room and curled into a ball on Frankie's bed. He hugged the sheets tight, as though holding onto a shed skin. He could smell him, his boy, his dancing little body fresh out of the shower, all questions and movie quips. When he closed his eyes, it seemed that he floated in some strange amoebic world, a place where touch and pain were all that was.

So much dark . . . How could anything be so small as a helpless father?

Once again, he prayed or begged or haggled or whatever it was called, offering anything to anyone on the great *Ebay* of the soul. And even though he believed none of it, he did so with more conviction than he had done anything in his entire life. *Please*, uttered with such inner force, it seemed his chest and head and limbs would split open, peel inside-out in offering. Anything! Of course he knew the reasons. He knew that some nameless ancestor had suffered a mutation, a happy madness allowing him or her to extend social and psychological categories to the world, to *theorize*. He knew that Thomas Bible was a human and that humans were hardwired to anthropomorphize.

To see people in dead things.

Please . . . Give me back my boy.

Give.

Him.

Back.

He lay thoughtless for a time, drawing in oxygen, metabolizing. He stirred when images of Cynthia Powski began crowding his thoughts. Pouting pleasure, nipples pressed hard against sail-tight linen . . .

Somehow he found himself on the living room couch, watching news. There was nothing so desolate, it seemed, than watching the tube out of a sense of futility. The drying pupils, the nervous limbs. The stationary dementia, the world flickering so bright and so fast in rooms of silence and gloom. And the *screen*, as supple and as insidious as language, but without any truth-preserving rules, stacking image after image, wiring and rewiring a billion visual cortices.

His own included.

Once again, the Chiropractor dominated the leads, even though events elsewhere were murdering thousands. Apparently several blood-caked vertebrae had been found in a subway car. On the obligatory news conference clip, a task force official described the find as a 'major break'. They were compiling the biometric data even as she spoke, she said, and everyone who rode the car in question would be interviewed within a matter of days.

Thomas felt like spitting.

A quick search found him a forty-five-second piece on Peter Halasz. They were now treating the case as a homicide, a federal agent said. They now believed the 'telegenic congressman' had been the victim of a 'random act of violence'. Clever, as far as bullshit went. Few things had as little meaning as random acts of violence anymore. Thomas wondered if anyone in the Bureau appreciated the irony.

After bouncing around a bit, he stopped on CNN, arrested by some eerie post-apocalyptic footage of southern Moscow. The story covered the furor caused by a company called EA Games that was 'typing' the images for use in its latest 'real-time-topical' first-person shooter game. Soon, for $74.95 you could hunt Dagestanis (or Russians, depending on your sympathies) in the rubble before radiation sickness claimed the last real-world victims. He wondered what the earthly difference could be between that and the newscast itself, with its smoldering blue Volkswagen banner.

The following story chronicled the latest twist in the intellectual property dispute over *Lucille's Balls*, the wildly successful porno that used CGI versions of Lucy and Ricky to explore the mysteries of female ejaculation. Since the makers of the film couldn't be found, the plaintiffs were seeking damages from the sex-toy manufacturers who had paid, via blind offshore accounts, for product placements.

Something about that made him laugh.

He paused to watch Peter Farmer, MSNBC's notorious all-CGI anchor, interview some senator about the recent passage of the Biometrics Integration Act, which would link all public surveillance cameras to real-time online feeds. Certainly the recent Moscow disaster, the senator argued, underscored the need for even greater vigilance. 'Imagine,' he said, 'them making video-games of New York or Washington.'

Thomas lay breathless, pinned by the interplay of furious images and light banter, trying to summon the will to go collect Ripley. Marines with their SMAWS swinging heavy from their shoulders. Formations of drone helicopters sweeping across Iranian hillsides. Bottles of Coke morphing into extreme athletes. He did a search for something on Jackie Forrest and found a piece from a local Nashville station. Sure enough, a spokeswoman for the Nashville police insisted they were treating his case as a homicide. They feared the 'popular evangelical preacher' had fallen victim to a 'random act of violence'.

Thomas almost laughed. Why make the effort to be creative or ingenious, he realized, when you didn't have to?

When he was thirteen his mother had dragged him to church on several occasions, apparently overcome by the need to tame her precocious son. It seemed he could still smell the people and the pews. She forced him, as shy as he was, to sing the hymns with the others. The trick, Thomas had learned, was to pitch your voice low into the background drone – like humming with the tires of a car. That way no one could hear you.

Especially God.

Dreams of backbones and scalpels. He awoke disoriented, frightened.

Frankie?

'Shhh,' a warm voice said. 'It's just me. Everything's okay.'

Sam was kneeling beside the couch, stroking his hair, looking down into him as though he were a pool. She smiled sadly.

'Wha—' He cleared his throat. 'What time is it?'

'Five thirty or so,' Sam replied. 'What time did you fall asleep?'

'Dunno,' Thomas croaked, rubbing his face. He rolled onto his back. 'Oh-oh,' he said sheepishly. 'Everything's fucked up. Truly fucked up.'

'How so?'

'Piss hard-on first thing in the evening . . . See?'

She laughed and reached down, grabbed him through his Dockers.

'This is all wrong,' she said.

'Well, you're the FBI agent.'

'So?'

'So that's your job isn't it? Righting wrongs . . .'

They undressed, and she straddled him. Their lovemaking was tender in the way of weary people, excitement mellowed by familiarity, each movement for its own sake, each touch void of self-consciousness, the way bone-tired museum goers might trail their hands across ivory or diorite – not to get closer, not even to feel, but simply to confirm.

Then she began murmuring, 'That's it,' over and over, 'That's it, mmm,' as though he were a son uncertain of a long and frightening task. For some reason, this both angered and impassioned him. He began lunging harder, faster, until she gasped, 'Ugh . . . Not so deep, please Tom . . .'

He clutched her about the waist and sitting up, leaned and swept everything from the coffee table. He hoisted her from the couch and slammed her across it.

'*Tom?*' she cried.

But he was *fucking* her now, making her whimper and writhe around pounding iron. When she started crying out he clamped a hand across her mouth, rammed into her again and again.

Then she was slapping and clawing. He withdrew. He gripped the coffee table and dumped it. She flopped scrambling onto the floor.

'*Why aren't you wearing your underwear?*' Frankie asked.

'NEIL!' Thomas shrieked. '*NEIL!*'

Then he fell to his hands and knees, crumpled into the carpet, sobbing.

'*I was always just a project for Tommy, I think . . .*'

Sam curled on the recliner, wearing her blouse and panties. With swollen eyes, she studied the Scotch Thomas had given her. She wiped her tears away with her thumb.

‘I’ve been hate-fucked before,’ she said, ‘but that was just too creepy.’

Thomas sat naked at the edge of the couch, elbows on knees, head hanging.

She looked at him, at once angry and indecisive. ‘Just what are you doing, Tom?’

‘I don’t know,’ he whispered.

‘Don’t know?’ Sam exclaimed. ‘*You* don’t know?’

‘That’s what I said.’

‘But you’re the fucking psychology professor, aren’t you?’

He looked at her angrily. ‘Heal thyself? Is that it?’ He huddled against another shiver.

‘Tom . . .’

‘I’m losing my mind here, Sam.’ He wiped his eyes on the back of his wrist. ‘I’m losing my fucking mind.’

Sam set her drink down, clasped Thomas’s hands. ‘Look, Tom. You gotta get a handle on this. You gotta take a step back. You gotta look at yourself as a textbook anecdote, a case study or something.’

‘*I* gotta get a handle on this?’ he replied, rubbing the back of his neck. ‘That’s a fucking joke.’

‘What do you mean?’

Thomas glared at her. ‘You know *exactly* what I mean. The way for me to get a handle on this is for you, Atta, and that clown Gerard to catch Neil.’

‘That’s not fair, professor. You know it.’

‘Do I? You have hundreds hunting for the Chiropractor, and just a handful—’

‘I mean it’s not fair to hold *us* responsible. Do you know how much sleep we’ve been averaging?’

Thomas matched her angry gaze. ‘So just who’s responsible, hmm, Sam? The invisible asses Atta always seems to be kissing?’

She shrugged. ‘I dunno. Maybe. The bottom line is—’

‘You know what?’ Thomas exclaimed. ‘Just fuck it. I’ve been an idiot to listen to you people. My son is *not* a matter of National Security. What a fucking joke! This isn’t about protecting national interests in a time of crisis; it’s about a handful of bureaucrats trying to cover their asses. I should’ve gone to the net with this the morning he went missing. Even earlier!’

‘No,’ Sam said. ‘You shouldn’t have.’

'How can you say that?' Thomas cried. 'How can *you* say that? You know damn well this would have gone worldwide! Sam. *Sam.* What's more important to you, Frankie or—'

'You don't understand,' Sam said, her face blank.

'Don't understand what? That the whole nation could be hunting for Neil right now, instead of a rag-tag band of second-stringers? That Frankie . . .' His voice broke. 'That Frankie could be upstairs arguing with Ripley right now?'

He looked at her beseechingly. *Please be who I think you are.*

'Don't be so naive,' she said in a curiously hollow voice. 'None of that would've happened. Everything's sifted. Everything's flagged. *Everything*, Tom. Nothing about Neil would've made the mainstream net. Nothing will.' She took a drink, stared at him angrily. 'And you'd be punished for your troubles, believe me. Kiddie porn on your computer. Crystal meth in your car. Or worse, branded an eco-terrorist, arraigned and sentenced in a closed court, then *poof*, nowhere to be found. Trust me, Tom, I know these people. I've worked counter-intelligence.'

Thomas simply stared, dumbfounded as much by her tone as by what she said. 'You're just saying—'

'No, Tom,' she interrupted. 'You can't cross these people, not in any of the old ways, and certainly not by running to the papers. This is the twenty-first century, for Chrissakes. Their net-scrubbers can comprehend and collate a billion conversations a second. And the effectiveness of their tools doubles every eighteen months, while we humans just stay the same. Watch the news. There's only martyrs now. That's the only way left. Everything else is just the appearance of conflict.'

Thomas opened his mouth to respond, then closed it. What was she saying? That he was living in a police state? Measures had been taken, certainly, but there was no way—

'Tom, we're all that's been given, and all that you're gonna get. So if you're serious about finding Neil – serious about saving Frankie – you need to get a handle on yourself. You call us second-stringers? Maybe so. But so far you've been little more than dead weight to this investigation. You hear me? Dead. Weight.'

Thomas blinked, as shamed by his own 'second-stringer' comment as by her accusation. He lowered his face into his hands. Women, it seemed, were often desperate in their anger, as though pained by the suspicion that men needed less and so had less to lose. But not always. Sometimes they lashed out with a certainty indistinguishable from honesty – absolute honesty.

For men, honesty was always a matter of degree.

Sam's expression was inscrutable, her demeanor relentless, so different from the hesitancy and ambitiousness that had characterized her until now.

I raped her, Thomas thought.

No, something different. And the same.

'Look, Tom,' she said. 'I'm a spaced chick. It's like I'm continually at war with the urge to please whatever guy I happen to be attracted to. And you know what? I usually find it simple. With most guys, everything can be boiled down to feed me, fuck me, or flatter m—'

'How about,' Thomas found himself saying, 'marry me?'

I'm losing my mind . . .

Sam looked away, blinking. 'That's just the condensed version,' she said.

Neil was doing this. Neil. Neil. Neil.

'You're scaring me, Tom. I mean, you're so fucking complicated. I don't know what to do, I don't know what to say . . . Christ, I don't even know what my *own* motives are anymore.'

Miraculously, it seemed, she was kneeling before him, resting her chin on his naked knee. So beautiful . . .

Take a step back. Think clear. Think straight.

She was right. He knew she was right. Somehow he'd let self-pity get the upper hand. Somehow, he'd allowed himself to start *mourning* his son.

Mourning when he should have been fighting.

He breathed deep, pressed his palms down to his knees. 'I'm suffering what's called a major depressive episode,' he said, clearing phlegm from his throat. 'A common response to bereavement –' he swallowed – 'characterized by morbid thoughts, despondency, irregular sleep . . .'

A sense of worthlessness.

Sam shook her head. 'There's grief, and then there's grief. But with you . . . I mean, Neil keeps kicking you and kicking you, and you just *lie* there. It's like you're suffering from . . . from abused wife syndrome or something.'

Dead. Weight.

Thomas blinked more tears from his eyes.

'It's called conditioned helplessness,' he said.

'What?'

'Conditioned helplessness,' he repeated. 'People stranded in circumstances over which they have no control eventually become conditioned to think themselves helpless. Even when circumstances change.' He looked at her, his heart itching with an odd sense of wonder. All along he'd known what was wrong, but without knowing. 'It's a crucial component of depressive disorders.'

'Well that's it, then,' Sam said. 'Circumstances *have* changed. You gotta shake this off!'

He laughed bitterly. 'But that's the irony, Sam. People simply assume that depression skews a person's outlook. But it's not so.'

'What do you mean?'

'You'd think depressives would consistently underestimate how much control they have over events, but it turns out the exact opposite is true. In tests, they're surprisingly accurate in their estimations. It's the well-adjusted who are deluded. They consistently overestimate their control over events.'

Sam flashed him a go-figure smile. 'Do we now?' she said.

Thomas looked down. 'Turns out you have to be deluded to be happy.'

Could the world be any more fucked up?

He was crying now, and she was watching. It was okay. Expected. There was the grief that clenched, and the grief that let go, that opened all the little cages hidden in our souls. It seemed he could feel things fall through him in sheets, the remorse, the shame, the rage . . . All the little animals.

He could feel himself empty.

Sam watched him. When he looked at her, she seemed to shine with a high-altitude clarity. He held out his hand the way a beggar would, his face his only sign.

She laughed, then did what she always did.

She gave.

He awoke to the light of the television, Sam's naked body crowded against his own on the couch. Images of what must have been the latest Chiropractor crime scene floated in the darkness. For a while he remained absolutely still, watching the parade of images the way tired children sometimes do, blinking and staring thoughtlessly, as though stuck between channels.

He remembered Ripley, cursed himself for an idiot, though he was too drowsy, too numb, to feel any real regret. Mia would understand – even with Sam's car in the driveway. A shot of a harnessed German Shepherd snarling at a French eco-protester stirred thoughts of Bartender. He squeezed tears from his eyes with thumb and forefinger. Poor Bart. What was he going to tell Frankie?

His brain wasn't wired the way ours is, son. He had no awareness, no experience. He was just a blind machine that your Uncle Cass broke.

No, he definitely couldn't say that. What? Tell a boy that his dog lacked the neural integration required to possess experience? That he was unconscious through-and-through, dead all along? Most adults couldn't wrap their heads around that one.

Couldn't save him, son. Just like I couldn't save you. The old man was too busy getting laid.

Shame, like a hammer to the chest. Cold and hard.

Too busy being dead weight . . .

He sobbed into Sam's hair. 'No,' he muttered.

Need to take control . . .

Sam moaned and arched against him. 'Time for bed,' she murmured.

Need to think . . . to take control.

She sat up and stared with eyes that refused to focus. She rubbed a palm against her cheek. 'You coming?'

Control! Control!

'Yes,' he gasped.

He turned off the screen and helped steady her up the stairs. But when she turned toward the bedroom, he continued straight into the bathroom. The light pricked his eyes. He tugged open the medicine cabinet and fished with clumsy fingers through old prescriptions and over-the-counter remedies, remembering how Nora had fairly cleaned the cabinet out when she moved, and wondering how the hell he'd managed to fill the damn thing up again.

Then at last he found it. Control.

The label read:

BIBLE, THOMAS
Lorazepram 1mg
90 TAB APX Dr Bruno, Gene
TAKE HALF TABLET WHEN NEEDED UP TO THREE TIMES DAILY

Once, when things with Nora were real bad, Ripley had caught him taking one. 'Papa's little helpers,' Nora had explained to their daughter, shooting him a scathing glance. Everything had become a pretext by that point. If they weren't sniping, they were scrounging for ammunition.

Thomas cracked the lid and tapped a pill onto his sweaty palm. A jewel of condensed powder against whorls of skin. He popped it and washed it down with water from the tap. He stuffed the bottle behind some Deep Ice, then slapped the mirror shut.

'Nerves of fucking steel,' he promised his haggard reflection.

How Neil would laugh.

There is so much scripture written into little things.

You hear your dog die first, stamped like a can beneath my hard, hard heel. It twitches like a Chinese toy. You come running. Oh-my-God, what's happened? You stop, dumbstruck, when you see me in the living room, unable to make sense of this, *me, the stranger in your home. Your mouth opens, moist and hollow, and I decide to fill it when you're dead. Who? you want to cry, but you already know. You were* born *with knowledge of me, just like everyone else. No! you want to scream, but truth brooks no contradiction.*

Truth brooks no contradiction.

I say the words, knowing their meaning will elude you until your final post-coital twitch. Only as your pupils slacken will you see their bulldozer finality, their crowbar penetration . . .

I have broken into you. There is no refuge remaining.

There never was.

I say the words. 'Just the meat . . . I promise.'

Then comes the beating. Then comes the blood.

CHAPTER FOURTEEN

August 30th, 8.55 a.m.

It seemed like his first sleep in years, decades even.

Morning light filtered through the sheers. He simply breathed at first, blinking and staring at the swirls of white across the bedroom ceiling. From the tangle of cool sheets beside him, he knew Sam was already up. Images of a Toyota commercial he saw somewhere – one of many aimed against the New Environmental Accountability Act – plagued him while he dozed. When he closed his eyes, he saw a fleet of vehicles driving across the back of a great fissured glacier. '*Because tomorrow*,' the voiceover purred, '*is the most important destination of all . . .*'

Then he remembered Frankie. By time he rolled clear of the blankets, he was shaking.

He took another lorazepram before jumping into the shower. By time he was dressed, he could feel the pharmaceutical calm steeping through him, shrinking the horror to a vague uncertainty, the kind that makes you continually check your pockets for your keys. Thomas had always been one to lose things in his pockets, to toss the house looking for things hidden on his person. Always forgetting to remember.

Sam was sitting at the kitchen table reading the paper in lemon morning sunlight. Though dressed in her FBI best – a charcoal skirt and jacket – she still had that fresh out-of-the-shower look. Her hair blonded around the edges as it dried.

'Sooooo?' she asked with an apprehensive smile. Illuminated from behind, the page she held sported the shadow of a giant, inverted 0.9%.

'Fucking forgot Ripley,' he croaked, making for the coffee pot.

Her expression confirmed that she was referring to their argument from the previous afternoon. She was looking, Thomas supposed, for some flicker of something. Determination or resolution.

Not more dead weight.

'I'm sure Mia doesn't mind,' she said as he poured his coffee.

'It's not Mia I'm worried about,' he replied, doing his best to purge the accusation from his tone. 'The last thing Ripley needs is to be d-ditched . . .' His throat seemed to spasm about the word. 'Ditched,' he repeated like an idiot.

The doorbell interrupted her sigh.

Mia, no doubt.

'Time to take my medicine,' Thomas muttered, setting down his coffee. But he heard the doorknob twisting before he'd taken his second step. Mia never tested the door – never. He paused, looked to Sam in alarm. The buried crunch of the key was nothing short of thunderous.

'Does he—' was the most Sam managed to say before the lock clicked. Thomas didn't need to ask who she meant by 'he'. The door swung open on a pale band of sunlight, and for a mad instant the shadow it revealed simply *was* the man who had haunted his every thought since that mad morning mere weeks ago.

Neil . . .

Until it became Nora, digging through her purse as she stepped into the living room. She gasped in surprise when she saw them.

'Tommy,' she said, swallowing, drawing her hand down from her breastbone. Then, after a pause, she added, 'Agent Logan.'

'What are you doing, Nora?' Thomas asked.

There was a long, racing silence. This was bad, Thomas realized – catastrophic, even. Sam could lose her job.

She's going to fuck us, he thought. That was what Nora did. Even when their marriage was good, he used to joke that if she were a nuclear power, the world would have been destroyed at some point in her early twenties. Hand her a lash and she would find an out.

Nora laughed nervously. 'I'm here to pick up Ripley . . . So that we could show her Frankie together like we said . . .' She blinked, brought a finger to her fluttering left eye. 'Remember?'

He did remember – now. Ripley needed to visit her brother before any of her wilder imaginings could take hold. She had always been such a wonderfully skeptical brat, even before the divorce. Words would not be enough. They had thought that if they both brought her, they could cushion the shock somewhat. Even at the time, Thomas couldn't fathom precisely why he had thought it would help. Perhaps he had hoped the illusion of something mended – Mommy and Daddy together – could compensate for the reality of her broken brother.

'Tommy?' Nora asked.

'I'm sorry, Nora. I forgot all about it.' He cleared his throat. 'Rip's over at Mia's.'

'I see.' She looked directly at Sam. 'Too busy, I suppose.'

'It's not what you, think, Nora.'

Nora laughed in the caustic way that always made him ball his fists. 'Now *that's* a relief,' she said. 'Here I was thinking you'd left Ripley at Mia's so that you could bang the lovely agent here.'

Dead silence. Thomas glanced at Sam, thanked Christ she was staring at the floor.

'You have a choice here, Nora.'

'Don't I know it,' she snapped. 'I can't decide which to do first. Call Agent Atta and let her know that one of her underlings is fucking one of the victims' fathers.' She smiled with cheerful malice. 'Or spit in your face.'

The regret struck even before he opened his mouth. 'But that's what you always do, isn't it? Make things worse.'

Her hesitation told him he'd succeeded, struck bone, even though it was the last thing he wanted to do. Nora had more than her measure of secret self-undermining fears. In marriage you shared everything, even the keys to the gun cabinet.

'If that was true,' Nora said blankly, 'I would have told *her*' – she made a point of gazing directly at Sam – 'how you fucked me just last week.'

The two women locked eyes. A truck passed outside. The roar tumbled through the open door, the rattle of ancient cylinders and shafts, then drained away.

Still seated, Sam remained very still, her expression inscrutable save for a look of concentration. Nora sneered, as though unsettled by the woman's refusal to retaliate.

'Nora . . .' Thomas tried once again.

'*Hellooooooo*?' a masculine voice called from the front porch. Mia?

'Mommy!' Ripley cried, her skirts flouncing as she raced through the door. She flew at Nora, wrapped herself about her waist. 'Mia let me watch *Aliens*! Is it true you named me after her, Mommy? The *hero*? Is it?'

Mia followed after a ceremonial knock, dressed in cut-offs and an orange tank. 'Ooooh,' he cooed in his best Alabama gay, 'what *dooo* we have here? A *pawwteee*?' Then he turned to see Thomas and Sam in the kitchen. 'Oh . . .'

Nora crumbled in her daughter's arms. Grimacing, she tried to fumble free of Ripley's embrace. A sob kicked through her, then another. '*S-sorry, hon-honey*,' she gasped as she pulled clear of Ripley's arms. '*Mum-m-mummy can't-can't* . . .'

She fled through the door.

Thomas stood dumbstruck. Somewhere, it seemed, he could feel the remorse, as fingers-to-toes as nausea. But the greater part of him remained remote, as though he were really just part of the audience disguised in the lead's costume.

Control was good.

'Hi, Sam,' Mia said haplessly. He waved with the nervousness of a pear-shaped fourteen-year-old.

Without acknowledging him, Sam stood and walked to the front window, pulled aside the sheers to better look out. She was watching Nora, Thomas realized. Through the gauze he glimpsed the shadow of his ex-wife disappear into the shadow of her Nissan.

'Will she be all right?' Sam asked as Thomas joined her.

'Aw, fuck,' Mia said, breaking for the open door. For some reason, Thomas lacked the will to pull the cotton sheers aside. He watched his neighbor's gracile shadow lope across the lawn toward Nora's car. There was a burst of shrill voices as Mia's form closed on the car. Then the overgunned Nissan pulled away. His Number One Neighbor waved his arms in exasperation, then turned to the house, scratching his head. After a moment's hesitation, he began walking toward the property line, becoming more and more ghostlike with every step.

'Aw, fuck,' Ripley repeated in a small voice. She was sitting on the welcome mat, her legs pulled to the side, her eyes wide and empty.

'She won't say anything,' Thomas heard himself say to Sam.

Agent Logan turned from the window, blinking tears from her eyes. 'How can I be such an idiot?' she murmured.

Suddenly Control was nowhere to be found.

'What's wrong with Mom?' Ripley asked, not the way a child might, but like an adult, with all the cynical intonations of 'wrong'.

'Sam . . . Are you okay?'

She gathered her things with hand-wringing haste. She made a point of avoiding his gaze.

Thomas reached out to press a palm against the wall, did his best to make it look casual. Suddenly his living room felt like the edge of a cliff. 'We should talk about this, don't you think?'

Sam sniffled, paused to pull a tissue from her purse. She did her best to smile at Ripley while she pulled on her heels.

'Sam . . . Please . . .'

She paused for an instant while still looking down. The aura of contrived briskness dissolved. When she looked up, two silver tracks etched her cheeks. She shook her head and smiled in a queer, apologetic way that Thomas found terrifying. 'Sorry, professor,' she said. 'I can't do this.'

Then she was upright, straightening her jacket and skirt with her palms. 'I never could,' she said as she stepped through the door. Thomas listened to her heels tap across the concrete.

Rather than meeting her father's plaintive gaze, Ripley sat listless in the oblong of sunlight, picking fluff from the mat.

'What's wrong with Mommy?' Ripley asked again, this time from the safety of the television's circus glare. To her credit, she had let several minutes pass before repeating the question, apparently every bit as content as he was watching the riot of soundless images.

So much life from so many angles. Explorations of a sea-wrecked world.

'Mom misses Frankie, honey,' Thomas said, somewhat amazed he could say his son's name aloud. Apparently Control was back online.

'But Frankie's just sleeping in the hospital. You said he wasn't dead yet.'

Thomas blinked.

He knelt before his daughter. 'What about you, Ripley? Don't you miss Frankie?'

'Naw,' she said with a shrug. 'It usually takes a week or so for me to miss his sorry ass . . .' Then she exploded in tears.

Thomas picked her up and rocked her in his arms, whispered

loving reassurances in her ear. When she finally stopped crying, he sat with her in the recliner for a time, saying nothing. Soon sorrow became boredom and she began picking at his thumb. He made her giggle by pretending it was an animal ducking in and out of his palm for cover.

'Come,' he said finally, hoisting her into the air as he stood. 'Do you want to join me in my office? Color or something?'

'You gotta work?' she asked.

'Yep,' he said. 'I gotta save Frankie.'

At first, it seemed he had simply awakened with the revelation. But in retrospect, he realized that it had dawned on him talking to Gyges the previous day, only he'd been too rattled to make much sense of it. And even then, he wasn't sure it qualified as a revelation at all.

Ripley swung from his arm as though it were a swimming-hole rope as they turned into the office. She raced ahead to fetch her pencils and books, plopping stomach-first in the middle of the floor. He paused at the doorway, absently studied the great poster of the earth on the far wall.

Neil had loved the thing. He would stand in front of it, his profile turned so that Florida dangled like an obscene goblin dick from his fly, and call out: 'Nora! Ever been to Disney World?'

'Too many times,' she would answer.

Haw-fucking-haw. How many winks had they traded between them? Neil and Nora . . . Thomas wondered how long he'd be rewriting his history. He'd be bled white before it was done, he knew that much.

'Verbal,' he said, settling before the computer. 'Class files . . . Starting from about, ah, five years ago.'

Columns of folder icons unfolded across the screen. Thomas peered at them, looking for likely suspects.

'*Ten* years!' Ripley yelled with a giggle. Everything onscreen flickered out, instantaneously replaced. Thomas scowled at his daughter. She played innocent, smiling down at a blob of poppy red.

'Little bitch,' he muttered with a smile. A 'REPEAT REQUEST' window popped onto the screen.

'Starting from five years ago,' Thomas said.

He studied the icons for a moment. It had to be one of the bigger classes, he decided, the ones he and his colleagues jokingly called the 'hatcheries', where teaching played second fiddle to wowing freshmen into becoming psych majors.

'Open Intro 104a 2010,' he said.

A list of folders, each with a student's name, appeared. He scanned through them.

Nothing.

'Open Intro 104b 2011.'

Again he scanned down the list. Two-thirds the way down, his heart stopped at:

POWSKI, CYNTHIA 792-11-473

She had been his student.

Which meant he had been linked to all of them – all of Neil's victims.

He had once voted for Peter Halasz, had once participated in a pro-labor demonstration against Theodoros Gyges, and had argued several times with Nora over one of Jackie Forrest's books. He supposed he'd never made the link because of the tenuousness of these relationships. They seemed random. Meaningless.

But then this morning it had dawned on him: perhaps *that* was the point. Neil's point.

Only Cynthia Powski had seemed to argue against it.

'Display Cynthia Powski.'

A youthful, innocent version of her face materialized on the screen. Though motionless, it seemed to lean back, eyes fluttering, lips curling . . .

He pushed his chair back on its rollers, ran both hands across his scalp.

'Dad?' Ripley asked. 'Will Sam be coming over tonight?'

Ripley liked Sam. She adored anyone who treated her like a little adult.

'I'm not sure, honey.'

A memory, as insubstantial as gauze in water, came to him: a younger Cynthia, looking Midwest fresh, leaning against his desk and confessing her confusion with the term 'gestalt'. He remembered making a joke – something harmless and clever, he had thought – then immediately regretting it. How frightened she had looked! Bewildered and despairing. It was so easy to forget how vulnerable . . .

His mouse-hand shaking, Thomas scrolled through her record, afraid he would discover what he now thought he remembered.

She had failed. From the looks of her grade breakdown, she had simply dropped out without withdrawing, which probably meant she had dropped out of Columbia altogether. Just one more young, anxious face culled from the herd.

Thomas had failed her. He blinked, saw her licking a red-lacquered nail.

No wonder her image had nagged him with such violent regularity! He *knew* her. Knew without knowing.

But what did it mean?

With the exception of Frankie, Neil had picked his victims on the basis of a random and unwitting connection to *him*. He had ransacked his best friend's life searching for those single degrees of separation that would take him as close as possible to fame. A business magnate, a politician, a televangelist, a porn star. There could be no doubt he *meant* these relationships to be meaningless, accidental, like a scarf or glove 'accidentally forgotten' when visiting an estranged lover. But why? Was it simply part of his larger message? A crude illustration of the meaninglessness of all relationships?

No, Thomas realized. There was something horrifically *personal* in the impersonal nature of these connections. Something meant just for him. He was certain of it.

What was Neil after?

He obviously wanted an audience; the high-profile abductions and dramatic demonstrations had made that obvious from the beginning. He also wanted Thomas to suffer – Frankie and Nora were proof enough of that. But these other people – Halasz, Gyges, Forrest, and Powski – meant nothing to Thomas. Witnessing their pain had horrified him, certainly, but no more than their bit-parts in the script of his life warranted. They were strangers, after all, sharing, as Neil would say, no familial genetic material.

Thomas looked sidelong at Ripley lying on the floor, her heels bouncing against her bum, her head askew as she concentrated on coloring.

For the briefest of instants, she looked a stranger.

Horror. Control faltered, like paint crinkling in the heat of an unseen fire. His skin pimpled in dread.

'*Have you an arm like God?*' Neil had asked that night. '*Have you?*'

All of it, Thomas realized – everything that had happened – was aimed directly at him. The FBI, the clumsy bids for publicity, even the prophet-of-the-semantic-apocalypse routine were simply lies that Neil had told himself, compensatory mechanisms meant to rationalize and conceal his real motive.

Hatred. Psychopathic hatred. Neil wanted his best friend to suffer. Nothing more. Nothing less.

It should have made him laugh, Thomas realized, after agonizing over the Argument, after harboring the chill premonition that Neil could be right. All along the answer could be found in any freshman's psychology course notes – or work of literature for that matter. Neil *hated*, and like any other man who hated, he wanted nothing more than to see the object of his hate destroyed.

'Who hates you?' Ripley asked, looking at him curiously.

Thomas was startled. Had he spoken aloud?

'No one, honey,' he said. 'I was just mumbling.'

None of them were safe. Not Ripley, not Nora, not even Mia or Sam. Neil was coming for them.

Have you an arm like God?

Think clear. Think straight.

Neil wasn't playing Kurtz to his Marlowe, he was playing God to his Job. He was obsessed. For some reason Neil had become obsessed with his best friend. Somehow he had developed, nursed, and concealed some kind of psychopathic affective fixation.

Thomas clutched his trembling hands.

Control had returned. The world had resumed its place outside the fishbowl.

An old professor of his had argued that psychologists were the *true* fishers of men. Great nets of expectation, he said, bound individuals into communities. And when individuals violated those expectations, the psychologist was called to cast further nets about them. That's all the *Diagnostic and Statistical Manual of Mental Disorders* was, he insisted, a way to entangle the unexpected within expectation, to utterly eliminate the threat of surprise. Trespasses became symptoms. Abominations became clinical evidence.

'There's no escape!' he would shout to his class. 'That's the true motto of all psychology.'

No escape.

For the first time, Thomas truly understood what the man had meant. For the first time, he truly understood Neil Cassidy. Neil was a *stalker* – little more than a mutt as far as psychological disorders go. A simple obsessional. Domestic. Delusional. Highly organized. Definitely psychopathic.

There were many ways to crack this chestnut. Any number of interpretative viewpoints suggested themselves: the socio-cultural, the learning, the humanistic, the psychodynamic . . .

Stupid, he thought. *Stupid. So fucking stupid!* How could he have missed it?

He looked to the dust-free square where his brass desk-lamp had once stood. He could almost see Neil bending over it as he scrawled 'www.semanticapocalypse.com' across the green glass. He could almost see the dress-dropping smile, crooked with wicked delight. Neil reveled in knowing things others *should* know, be they facts of character, profession, or women. Nothing tickled him more than irony. In college, he had made an art of stringing along those duped by their own words. Thomas had played as well – but only reluctantly. To witness self-deception was to know someone better than they knew themselves. And even though Thomas had, in a sense, made a profession of the game, he found it far more uncomfortable than comforting. To toy with irony was to toy with the vulnerabilities of others. Since everyone, including Neil, was as much other as self, toying with others' vulnerabilities meant toying with one's *own* vulnerabilities as well. And that was the point. Neil played these games, Thomas had realized, in order to cultivate a sense of invulnerability.

The greatest self-deception of all.

Thomas had tried to tell him this once, but it was part of Neil's peculiar blindness to think he saw everything. He never stopped playing his games, never stopped smirking at the obliviousness of others, at the truth hidden right *there* where anyone could see it – in a wife's flirtatious smile, in a friend's embarrassed silence . . .

Thomas shivered. He turned to his left, to his beaten poster of a world equally hard done by. A landscape of dimples and refracted light obscured the dark, satellite landmasses. He glimpsed a felt-tip 'x' in a finger-shaped gleam. How?

Oh my God . . .

'Ripley?'

'Yeah, Dad?'

'Get your things together, honey.'

Thomas hustled Ripley across the lawn. They trotted up Mia's porch, and Thomas rapped hard on the screen door. 'Mia!' he called.

Ripley was frightened. 'What's wrong, Daddy?'

Thomas pulled on his black-and-green blazer, which he had grabbed on his way out the door. The air had a dry, pre-autumn chill, it seemed.

'When we get inside, Rip, I need you to go out back and watch TV, okay?'

'But nuthin's on.'

'Play with their Gamesphere, then. Or watch a movie. Order any movie you want.'

She squinted up at him, looking so adorable he felt Control momentarily waver. '*Any* movie?'

'Any movie. So long as it's not—'

' 'Ello-ello,' Mia said, little more than an apparition behind the screen. He pushed the door open, and Ripley bolted past him.

'Please come in!' Mia called after her. He turned back to Thomas, perplexed and perhaps a little annoyed.

'I know this is short notice, Mia, but I need you to look after her for a bit.'

'Sure-sure. What's going on?'

'I've been an idiot. A total fucking idiot.'

Mia regarded him apprehensively. He glanced out across the street. 'C'mon in.'

Thomas numbly followed him into the kitchen. The remains of some abstemious dinner – a pot and two plates, a wooden bowl, its insides coated with flattened salad – cluttered the ceramic counter top.

'An idiot, huh?'

Thomas took a seat at their battered antique table. 'Neil. I've been an idiot about Neil.'

Mia winced. 'I had a feeling you were going to say that. How so?'

'All this time I've been taking everything at face value. Reading all his signals the way he *wanted* them to be read.'

Mia shrugged. 'So? He's a man with a message. A psycho with a statement.'

'It's not as simple as that. People rationalize everything they do. The more deviant the behavior, the more colorful the rationalization. And it's almost always bullshit – just like Freud said.' Thomas had yet to meet a Marxist without a smattering of psychoanalysis.

'So you're saying Neil's cigar isn't a cigar?'

'Exactly. The Argument, the death of meaning – all bullshit! Nothing more than a deranged and demented way for Neil to hide from his true motives.'

'True motives . . .'

'Yes! It's *so simple*, Mia!' Thomas paused, struggled to compose himself, his thoughts. 'Neil's "arguing" to deny his hatred. Nihilism is simply an excuse, a way for him to legitimize hurting me.'

'Hatred?' Mia ran a hand along his close-cropped scalp. 'But why would he hate you?'

'To repress his shame.'

'And why's he ashamed?'

'Because he's in love.'

'In love? With who?'

'Me.'

Mia scowled, his elbow up, his hand still on his head. 'Are you sure about this?'

'I know how it sounds. But those three years we spent together at Princeton were pretty intense. It's scary, when I think about it, how many levels we connected on. I came to love him like a brother, but Neil . . . he came to love me more, I think . . . Like a lover.' He found himself leaning forward, as though wanting to grab Mia by the shoulders. 'Don't you see? That's *why* he seduced Nora. Both to avenge himself, and to prove to himself that no vengeance was needed!'

Mia regarded him skeptically, drew his palm down across his stubbled cheek. 'I dunno, Tommy.'

'What do you mean?' The shrill breath that accompanied these words made him realize how desperately he *needed* to be right.

'Neil? Gay?' Mia shook his head. 'No . . . I never got a blip from the guy, and believe me, Bill and I pinged him several times.'

'C'mon, Mia. You guys are always talking about "sticks in and out of water".'

'But that's my point: there was never any question as to whether he was bent or straight – at least not for us.' Mia paused, then shrugged sympathetically. 'He could be some kind of super-stealth homo, I suppose . . .' He trailed, looked at Thomas with dawning scrutiny. 'But what does any of this have to do with dropping off Rip? Why not just call Sam and tell her you have a new motive?'

Thomas swallowed, summoned what seemed the last of his breath. 'I think I *know*, Mia. I think I know *where he is*.'

Mia grabbed the antique back of one of his chairs, as though to steady himself. 'Have you told anybody?'

Something about this question itched.

'No. Not yet.'

'Jeezus, Tommy. Jeezus-jeezus. Wait a minute. Wait a minute. How the hell does Neil having a hard-on for you translate into knowing where he is?'

Thomas braced his forehead in his right hand. He told Mia about realizing his connection to Neil's victims, about discovering that Cynthia Powski had been his student. 'All of them, Mia . . . Neil's not simply hunting half-famous people, he's hunting half-famous people that I've had accidental contact with.'

'But that just doesn't make sense.'

'Not unless it's *me* he's been after all along.'

Mia nodded, but whether in understanding or simply to humor him, Thomas couldn't tell. His eyes remained skeptical. 'So how come you think you know where he is?'

'Because after I realized all this, I thought about the web address he'd written on my office lamp. Then I thought about my map – you know, the satellite photograph of North America in my office? – about how Neil had always loved the thing. Neil's playing these games, I thought, laughing at me, dancing in the darkness where I can't see him, wouldn't it be like him to simply mark his location, under my nose, under the noses of the FBI? So I look at the poster and what do I see? A small 'x' along the Hudson, in the same color pen he used to write the web address.' Fear flushed through him. 'Un-fucking-believable.'

Mia visibly shuddered. 'I got goose pimples. This is too fucked up, Tommy.'

Thomas stared off into space for a stunned moment.

'Yeah,' he finally said.

They both sat silently.

'This is crazy,' Thomas finally exclaimed, patting his shirt and pant pockets as though looking for keys. 'I gotta call Sam.'

Mia looked at him sharply. 'Hold on, Tommy. Think about this.'

'What's there to think about?'

'You *need* Neil, right . . . For Frankie. You said Neil's the only one who can fix him.'

Thomas rubbed his chest. He thought about what Gyges had said the previous day – about hygiene.

'Think about it,' Mia continued. 'Sam's Sam, but what about the others, hmm? If they're so keen to keep everything about Neil quiet, do you actually think they plan on bringing him in?'

'But they gotta,' Thomas said, blinking back tears. *Frankie . . .*

'Do they?'

They locked eyes.

Thomas looked away, down to his all-too-empty hands. 'So what the fuck am I supposed to do?'

Mia glanced wildly around the kitchen, as though looking for a utensil that could solve their problem. 'You gotta do it yourself,' he said distractedly, as though the matter had already been settled. Before Thomas could protest, his neighbor strode to the far end of the kitchen and yanked open the basement door. Without a word, he plunged out of sight.

Thomas followed him to the crest of the steps. He heard boxes skidding across cement, but saw only shadows in the dusty yellow light below.

'Here!' Mia called, swinging into view at the bottom of the steps. He tossed something up through the musty air. Thomas caught it despite the helium in his hands. A roll of duct tape.

'What's this? You think Neil has weapons of mass destruction?'

'No. To immobilize him. You need to bring him in alive, right?'

'So what? I sneak up behind him and pounce on him with tape? He's an armed and dangerous murderer, Mia, not an evil fucking Christmas present.'

Was he actually considering this madness?

Frankie . . .

Screaming and screaming.

'Hold on,' Mia said, disappearing again. This time he returned after only a moment. He began bounding up the steps. Thomas stumbled backward across the kitchen. His neighbor had a gun.

'Mia? What the fuck . . .'

'Take it,' Mia said, holding it out. The gun-metal seemed curiously leaden in the kitchen light, like a dead animal's eyes. 'Take it, Tommy. This is Frankie we're talking about here. *Frankie.*'

His heart pounding, Thomas reached out and clutched the revolver. It was sweaty cold, but lighter than it appeared – giddy light, even though it looked like something carved from uranium.

Thomas began shaking. Where had Control gone?

Your pocket, a voice whispered.

'So I give you my daughter,' he said, swallowing, 'and you give me duct tape and a gun?'

Mia began wagging a reproving finger, but dropped it. 'You're right,' he said. Without explanation, he dashed back down into the basement, nearly toppled down the final steps.

'Mia?' Thomas stood at the crest, dumbfounded. 'Mia!'

Moments later, the wiry man came bounding back up the stairs.

'Here,' he said breathlessly, holding out his hands. Bullets lay cupped like pistachios in his palms. 'Ammunition.'

Thomas clutched them, began fumbling them into his blazer pockets. 'Fair trade, I guess.'

I'm holding a gun!

He had no idea what he was doing. But he was doing it. Dead weight on the move.

Mia watched him, his face pale, his demeanor shockingly stern. 'Now tell me,' he said, 'where exactly do you think Neil is?'

Thomas wasn't sure, not exactly, and the lorazepram wasn't making matters any easier – it made his eyes feel like ball bearings. He found it hard to focus on the surrounding traffic. The I-87 stretched like an endless airstrip before him.

He had double-checked Neil's 'x' against the road atlas, and sure enough, it fell north of the Catskills near a village called, appropriately enough, Climax. Back in their Princeton days, close friends of Neil's grandparents had owned a large cottage near there, which he and Neil had visited three or four times with different women. For an entire summer, drunken one-liners like, 'Would you like me to bring you to Climax?' had been their pub-crawl weapon of choice. Despite the eye-rolling and the indignation, more than a few had taken the bait. (The key, Neil would always say, was to make them feel as though they were on the outside of a *friendly* inside joke). Thomas had enjoyed many climaxes in Climax. The party ended when Neil's grandmother found several used condoms (which, the story went, she had actually picked up, mistaking them for shed snake-skins) behind one of the beds. He and Neil used to jokingly blame each other, but they both knew they had belonged to Neil.

That had been a long time ago. Climax itself was just off the I-87. Thomas had passed the exit on several occasions in subsequent years, each time struck by the strange vertigo of passing a road once taken, the sense of breezing past something better revisited. The question was one of where to go once he reached Climax – his memories of the route had the sound-stage sketchiness of a passenger's. His only hope was that he would remember on the way.

He found the drive at once calming and unnerving, and he distracted himself by pondering this paradox. He had never liked driving, but there was something about the freeway, the surreal quality of whisking through city, field and forest untouched and anonymous; the sense of power exercised, encumbrances shed, of skating along life's catastrophic edge. At a poker game years back, a volunteer firefighter had once horrified him with tales of rural car crashes, of limbs stretched like Play-Doh through twisted metal. 'In the physics of car accidents,' the man had insisted, 'our body is little more than a rubber bag filled with blood. Go fast enough, and it's like throwing water-balloons.' At the time, the comment had made Thomas positively paranoid. But as years passed and the traffic – despite drunks, faulty wheel-bearings, and reckless teenagers – continued to flash by in orderly little rows, his paranoia became a strange euphoria. Somehow freeway driving had become stealing – or a winning streak that could not end.

Small wonder the road had become *the* symbol. On the road, everyone was unencumbered, powerful, fearless. On the road, everyone was an American. What unnerved him, Thomas realized, was the destination.

Neil Cassidy.

His morning revelation had been a reprieve of sorts. Before, Neil had seemed something elemental, more principle than human being.

Every year Thomas began his freshman courses by reading aloud from *The Iliad* and pointing out that Hector, the great hero of Troy, wasn't struck down *by* Achilles' hand as most people assumed, but rather *at* Achilles' hand by blazing-eyed Athena. For the ancients, he would explain, you did not own your words and actions – at least not the way freshmen college students thought they monopolized theirs. For the ancient Greeks, Egyptians, Sumerians, what have you, one was as much a waystation as a point of departure, a channel through which the acts of other, more elusive agencies might be expressed. This was why they regarded madness with as much awe as ridicule. Some madmen were fools certainly, but some were prophets as well. Some spoke in the god's own voice.

This was what Neil had seemed to Thomas: a madman in the ancient sense.

Someone possessed.

Neil had embraced the implacable truth of his existence, and by embracing this truth, he had embraced not only the materiality upon which all experience depended, but all the processes, evolutionary, geophysical, cosmological, that had compelled that materiality. He became the expression of a billion suns winking out, the manifestation of a million wailing births over a million unwitnessed years. He became the conduit of something utterly aimless, indifferent, and incalculably vast.

Before Neil had seemed the terminus of a line that reached back beyond the limits of the observable universe – to the very beginning. A man at one with his myriad and mindless conditions.

A delinquent and horrifying communication: *thou art false.*

And now? Now he simply seemed a sad and dangerous fool.

Or so Thomas told himself.

Most signs – highway, street, storefront – dissolved into the rat-race humdrum of day-to-day life. Everything was For Sale or Next Left or 65 Maximum; everything had a finger you could follow. But for some reason,

EXIT 21-B
CLIMAX
2 MILES

scored in white across generic green, seemed altogether different to Thomas. Not simply ambiguous or fraught with associations, like an ancient parable, or graffiti above a urinal, but slippery in the manner of things sentient and cynical. If it had possessed eyes, he was certain it would have winked.

It took some driving, but soon he discovered a back-road concession he recognized. He found the lane shortly after, a dark opening between radial skirts of vegetation. He turned slowly, listening to his tires snap gravel. Shade swallowed him and the wooded hollows opened, cool yet arid beneath late-summer skies. Though the ground was level, it seemed the Acura rolled forward of its own volition. *Magnetic hill*, he thought inanely. As he remembered, the lane curved to the left, gradually pinched out of existence by screens of greenery. He looked away, to the canopy scrolling along the polished hood – glimpses of sky through tattered black-green. He braked.

Have to stop. Have to surprise him. Have to . . .

He hefted the gun in a sweaty palm.

Frankie.

He wasn't strong enough. Was he?

No. Oh-my-God, no . . .

He leaned his head against the steering wheel. Perhaps one or two sobs escaped him.

My boy. Gotta remember my boy. He rubbed away snot and tears.

But what if things went wrong? Disastrous images cascaded through his thoughts. Thomas wasn't stupid or weak, but in all the years he'd known Neil, he had lost everything to him. From chess to squash to . . . Nora.

Neil always won. Plain and simple.

But not in this!

He was the righteous one, wasn't he? A father fighting to save his son? A father fighting . . .

He pushed open the door, paused. The surrounding woods seemed mossy with humus and motionless undergrowth. The trees defeated the distances, obscuring any glimpse of the cottage.

Thomas turned off the car. Clutched the revolver.

'*Please*,' he whispered. '*Please . . .*'

Everything would be okay. He was a father fighting to save his son.

More images of disaster assailed him, but he clenched his teeth and swung his feet from the car. *Fuck it!* he thought. *Fuck it!* He'd simply sprint through the trees – fucking charge the cabin. Kick in the fucking door! Rush headlong into catastrophe! Who fucking cared what happened? At least it would be over. Wouldn't it?

Not for my boy.

A life of horror. A life spent gagging on screams.

Frankie. How had his name become a prayer?

Thomas pulled his feet in, reached out and slammed shut the door.

Such a fucking idiot!

He dropped the gun on the passenger seat. It seemed he could taste its metal, smell its oily threat.

Idiot! Idiot! The world was a great mindless thresher. Every second, spirits broken, cancers missed, daughters raped, wives beaten, children murdered. Every fucking second, the rules of narrative annihilated. Every second for a thousand years – for a million! Even his hominid ancestors had wept, hadn't they? Raised hapless hands against the dust-rimmed misery of their lives. Even the australopithecines had screamed.

Where was the Book of their Names?

Think clear. Think straight . . . Reason this through for Christ's sake!

With a shaking hand, Thomas tugged his Acura into reverse. He retreated from the lane, barging through bushes like shredded parasols.

Every second some father failed his son.

The world wasn't a fable or an epic or even a comic tragedy.

It was a psychopath.

A red Acura, idling at the side of a country road. Inside, a man leans into a palmtop. He covers his other ear as an eighteen-wheeler roars past.

'Sam . . . Yeah, it's me.'

He looks down to his lap.

'I'm just outside a place called Climax.'

Glances nervously out his windshield, smiles nervously.

'No. I'm not joking. It's a town upstate, north of the Catski—'

He scowls, scratches his chin.

'You alone?'

He blinks tears from his eyes.

'Just following up a lead. Dead weight chasing a dead end.' Another blink. 'You should meet me, though. I could use your help.'

He draws a sleeve across his cheeks.

'No. Not over the phone.'

Again he looks down – an ancient gesture of concentration.

'You're calling *me* paranoid? That's rich. Look, it could be important. Likely not, but it could be. Either way, you need to check it out.'

His eyes unfocus, as though he's counting his pulse.

'Only two and a half hours. North on the 87.'

He glances at a silver sub-compact that flashes past.

'Sure, I'm okay. Just meet me, please. Have a little faith, for Christ's sake.'

Scratches the side of his nose.

'Like I said, go north on the 87, turn off at exit 21B. You'll see me. I'll be waiting in my car.'

He shakes his head from side to side.

'Yes, yes. Look, I gotta go. See you in a bit, okay? Oh, and Sam?' He leans back, seems to glimpse himself in the rearview mirror. 'I . . . I love you.'

Motionless.

'What do you mean?'

He pulls a hand through his hair.

'No-no . . . We'll talk about it later. Drive safe.'

CHAPTER FIFTEEN

August 30th, 6.44 p.m.

From the passenger seat of Sam's Mustang, the drive back to the cottage possessed a surreal, theatrical quality for Thomas. The angling afternoon sunlight, revealing the inner complexities of trees. The war of gravel and thistled grasses along the rushing verge. The epileptic gallop of tires across cracked and quilted asphalt. It all seemed like some impossible show, sharp because it was so blunt, intense because it was so mundane. *Cinema verité.* He could almost believe that Gerard, who sat directly behind him, nursed a bag of popcorn.

The lie he'd told them had come easily, thanks to Control. Shouting above the gust and roar of passing transport trucks, he had even managed to apologize to Sam with his eyes. *No more dead weight,* his look had said. *No more Nora.* But now, as the world parted about the windshield and they drew closer and closer to *him*, the implications of his deception began to accumulate. *Nothing matters except Frankie,* he told himself, over and over, like a curse or a fervent childhood wish. *Nothing. Not Gerard. Not Sam. Not me . . .*

The sunlight followed them a short distance down the wooded lane, but was quickly defeated by the accumulation of shadows. Suddenly late afternoon had become evening. They crawled around the bend and Thomas saw the cottage, almost identical to the way he remembered it: the deep porch, the gabled second floor, the fieldstone foundation. There was light in the windows.

'Someone's home,' Sam said, slipping her Mustang into park. She glanced at Gerard in the back seat, then looked at Thomas skeptically. 'So who's this guy again?'

Thomas had told them some bullshit about remembering an old friend of Neil's, someone called Danny Marsh, who now lived outside of Climax. He'd been deliberately vague as to why he thought this significant, insisting that he had a rare but reliable 'gut feeling'. But he had tried to throw in enough trivial details (such as giving the man a fictitious nickname, 'Perko-Dan') to at least defer their suspicions.

The idea was to simply get them to the cottage.

Here.

'*Helloooo*?' Sam chimed. 'Professor?'

Somehow, Thomas knew his relationship with Sam, whatever it was, would not survive this latest deception. Perhaps it was already dead. Control did its best, but he had to clutch his slacks to keep his hands from trembling.

'I lied,' he said.

'Here we go,' Gerard muttered from the back.

Sam frowned and smiled at once, as though unwilling to believe what she had just heard. Never, it seemed to Thomas, had she looked so beautiful.

'You what?'

'I lied,' he repeated, his voice far more calm than he felt. 'I needed to get you here.'

'I told you,' Gerard said to Sam. 'I fucking told you. Check the best before date, because this Twinkie is out of code.'

'What's going on, Tom? *Why* did you need to get us here?'

He nodded to the cottage. 'Because Neil's here.'

A speechless moment.

'Jesus-fuck-fuck-*fuck*!' Gerard cried from the back.

'Neil's *here*?' Sam snapped scathingly. 'What do you mean? How do you know?'

'You *fucking* fuck!' Gerard continued shouting, genuinely panicked.

Thomas found himself staring at the dashboard. 'He marked this place on my map, just as he wrote the website address on my lamp . . . I think he wants me to find him.'

'Then *you* go knock on the door,' Gerard said.

'Why?' Sam asked. 'Why would you do something like this?' Unlike Gerard, she was all business, and for some reason, this made him absurdly proud. Control slipped enough for him to blink at the sudden hotness in his eyes.

'F-for m-my boy,' he stuttered. He looked at Sam directly. 'I don't trust the others. Not Atta . . . Not even you, Gerard.'

Gerard sneered. 'Funny you should—'

'Shut up, Danny!' Sam snapped. 'You think the idea is to kill Cassidy, not apprehend him. Is that it?'

Thomas nodded, swallowed. 'You said it yourself, Sam. You said you knew these people, remember? If you got on the phone and told Atta you had your SUB cornered, what do you think would happen, huh?'

Sam glanced out the windshield. 'They'd scramble a tactical team,' she said simply. When she looked back, her eyes were bright with indecision – and admission. They *would* kill Neil.

She knew it as well as he did.

'If Neil dies,' Thomas said, 'so does Frankie. You're my only chance, Sam.'

'We can't do this, Tom,' she said, blinking away a tear.

'Fucking A,' Gerard muttered in obvious relief.

Thomas held her gaze, stared deep into eyes that were only beginning to discover him. She was strong, he knew. Strong enough to do the right thing, even if it meant sacrificing the man she loved. Or his son.

'But I wasn't asking,' Thomas said. He reached past her arm, punched the horn.

The surrounding woods seemed to shriek with reverberations.

'You did *not* just do that!' Gerard sang. 'No fucking way!'

Visibly shaken, Sam stared at the cottage. All three of them held their breath.

Thomas saw a shadow bend before one of the golden windows, pull aside the sheers.

It was him, etched in warm interior tones, peering out across cool evening gloom. Neil. He seemed something not quite human, as though he stared through a portal, breathing a different, brighter atmosphere. Then he vanished. Moments later, the cabin went dark.

Fear like a warm bath.

'I guess we do it your way,' Sam said. Her smile was at once sad and fatalistic. She pulled her automatic and turned to Gerard. 'I'll go round back. You keep the front covered. When I give the signal, we both go in, got it?'

'So you're just going to let this prick pull our strings li—?'

'*Do you got it?*'

'Got it,' Gerard grunted.

She turned to Thomas, her eyes bright with fear and excitement. 'You stay here,' she said, then she disappeared out her door. Thomas watched her sprint through the trees, keeping her head low. Kicking up leaves, she crossed a shallow clearing, then hooked around to flank the structure.

Nothing matters.

'You're a fucker,' Gerard muttered as he shouldered open his door.

'And why's that?' Thomas asked – numb words.

The agent stared at him with wide, honest eyes. He looked different in the gloom, contradictory, as though the skin of a handsome man had been stretched across something doughy and stupid.

'Because you fuckered us.'

Thomas watched Gerard shuffle sideways, using the Mustang for cover, then dash toward the cottage. He disappeared in the shadows where the porch jutted from the log walls, but not before Thomas caught a glimpse of grim panic on his face.

They were terrified, he realized. They were *agents*, and they were terrified. In his mind's eye, he saw Sam coughing blood in his arms, accusation like a fading light in her eyes.

Nothing matters!

Thomas pushed open his door, stood and straightened. The evening air was surprisingly cool – hard, even. The smell of charcoal tinctured the bitter of pinched leaves. For several moments he simply scanned the cottage and its damp environs, as though looking for a pet or a real estate agent. Gerard, who had climbed onto the porch and now edged his way to the front door, was hissing something. Even though Thomas couldn't hear him, his expression was clear enough.

Are you fucking crazy?

Blinking, Thomas looked down to his shoes, tried to shake the styrofoam out of his legs. Then he simply walked up the steps.

'He won't shoot me,' he murmured to Gerard on his way to the entrance. 'He's my best friend.'

'And he's my favorite uncle,' the agent hissed. 'Now get back in the fucking car!'

'He won't shoot me.'

Thomas came to a stop before the screen door, breathed deeply. He rapped his knuckles against the ratty wood frame.

'Neil!' he shouted. 'I know you're in there! It's me . . .' He swallowed against his racing heart. 'Tom.'

Silence.

Flat against the wall, Gerard stood poised with his automatic, waiting for the door to open.

'Neil! It's me! Goodbook. I've come alone. I've come to talk!'

Thomas peered into the murky interior beyond the picture window, probed the shadowy depths, did everything but lean his head against the glass. 'C'mon, Neil. For fuck's sake, man. It's *me*.'

The porch light flashed on, rendering the panes opaque. Thomas saw his own reflection stumble backward, saw his face float pale against watercolor-black, bent and pinched in the glass.

What are you doing?

The inner door swung into darkness, and Neil leaned out to push open the screen door. He wore cargo shorts and a skin-tight T-shirt. His feet were bare, his toes dirty. For an instant, everything seemed horrifically normal.

'Hey,' Thomas heard himself say. His smile felt both natural and genuine, even as he watched Gerard raise his gun in the shadows. Oblivious, Neil scowled with *you-idiot* good humor.

'Goodbook? How th—'

'Freeze!' Gerard hissed, pressing his gun-muzzle to Neil's temple.

'*Noo*!' Thomas cried, expecting a shot.

Gerard glanced at him, and Neil grabbed his wrist, thrust the gun away. There was a crack and a flash, and the upper screen-door window shattered. The two men grappled. For an instant, they looked like drunken dance partners, then they fell backward into blackness. Thomas heard grunts and blows, took an unsteady step toward the doorway. The blackness had transformed them into warring animals. Wood-scoring claws. Growls. Frenzied exertions. Spittle whistling through clenched teeth.

Shaking, Thomas edged into the room. *Oh-my-god-oh-my-god . . .*

'Hit the lights!' Gerard suddenly cried. 'Jesus-jesus, hit the lights!' He sounded frantic – hurt.

Thomas swept the walls with his hands. He could hear Sam call 'Danny? Danny?' from somewhere distant.

He stubbed his finger against the switch. The room leapt into existence.

'Uh, professor?' Gerard grunted. 'Could you wipe the mustard off your bud and help me out here?'

Stunned, Thomas numbly fingered his blazer pocket, pulled out Mia's roll of duct tape. He was still blinking against the overhead lights. The front room was exactly as he remembered: an expanse of beaten hardwood floor ringed round by high-backed sofas and dark-stained cabinets. Yellowing needlework decorated the pale walls.

A dead grandmother's room.

Gerard had Neil pinned face-first, hands yanked to the small between his shoulders, across a tangled throw-mat. Shoes and boots lay scattered about them. The room smelled of tracked mud and old insoles, of swelling wood and blankets left out-of-doors. Before he knew what he was doing, Thomas had kicked aside a heavy Timberland and was helping Gerard tape Neil's wrists.

'Logan!' the agent bellowed between deep breaths. 'Got him, Sam!'

'Ookaay!' echoed from some distant room. 'Securing the rest of the structure!' Thomas heard excitement in her voice – even relief. He felt none of it.

Gerard was hoisting him from the ground. *Him.* Neil.

Thomas hit him – hard, like pounding a mattress in a fury. Once, twice, three times. It was strange. Almost like watching himself from over his own shoulder. Only his fists felt real.

'Easy, professor,' Gerard said, staggering as Neil lurched. 'We need him in one piece. *You* need him.'

Neil looked up, his eyes glazed. A line of blood spilled from his nose to his chin.

'Goodbook,' he mumbled.

Thomas felt his face crumple, rubbed his eyes against the rough wool of his blazer sleeve. This wasn't the way it was supposed to happen! He was supposed to be strong, but instead he felt like a little boy again, buckling beneath his father's drunken anger. 'Frankie,' he blurted. '*Neil* . . . How-how could you?'

Something ignited in Neil's eyes – that familiar predatory glint. 'What are you talking about? Frankie what?'

'Nora I can almost understand. But my *boy*, Neil. How could you fuck with my boy?'

'Frankie? No . . . *No.* I never touched—'

'Don't fucking lie! Not now. Not in this. *Don't. Fucking. Lie!*'

His voice pealed through the room.

Neil spit blood onto the hardwood floor. 'Goodbook, listen. I never touched Frankie. Why—'

Thomas punched him again, screeching, 'Liar!'

'He's *not* your boy!' Neil roared. 'Do you hear me? He's *my* fucking son! *Mine*! Why would I use my own son?'

Thomas looked at his knuckles, at the blood smeared like model paint across the veined back of his hand. Something – some kind of wave – crashed through him, splashing all the strength from his limbs. His heart bobbed in his chest. He staggered backward, collapsed against a wall. Gerard, his eyes round with concern, was shouting something at him. Then blood and tissue exploded from the side of the agent's head, and he was slumping forward, falling through a crimson mist, bearing Neil with him to the floor. They landed near Thomas's feet, locked like dead wrestlers.

Unable to scream, breathe, or think, Thomas looked to the lone figure still standing in the room.

Sam.

Sam hooked a toe beneath Gerard's body, rolled him off Neil.

'Hi, doc,' she said, heaving Neil to his knees.

'Jessica,' Neil replied, apparently unafraid.

Propped against pine wainscoting, Thomas watched. Some part of him wanted to move, to run, but his body seemed as heavy as Gerard's looked. *Like dead weight*, he thought inanely.

Sam scooped a chair from a decorative bureau and set it behind Neil. She hooked a finger beneath his jaw – apparently some kind of pressure point, because he grunted and hissed as she pulled and seated him. She smiled at Thomas.

'Well, professor?'

'I do-don't . . .' Thomas paused, scowled. His mouth and tongue felt like clay. 'I d-don't understand what's happening.'

'No,' Sam said. 'I suppose you wouldn't. Disorientation is a common stress response. Especially when you're weak.'

What was she doing? Had Gerard been a threat? Some kind of plant?

Thomas watched as she hooked Neil's arms over the back of the chair and used Mia's duct tape to secure him. She then wrapped his ankles together. 'I was always proud of you,' Neil said to her as she worked. 'Back when those things mattered to me, I always regarded you as . . . well, my masterpiece.'

She replied with the distracted air of a mother dressing her son. 'You might not think so a few minutes from now.'

Neil smiled. 'I'm beyond anything you could do to me, Jess.'

'Are you?' Sam asked. 'We'll see about that.'

She swung her automatic toward Thomas. 'Your turn, lover boy. Stand up and turn around.'

'Sam?' Thomas said. He pressed a palm to his forehead. 'Wh-what's happening? You k-killed Gerard. I mean you *really fucking killed him*!'

Sam glanced at Gerard, slack and grey across the polished hardwood. 'I told the prick he should stay in New York. I had a feeling you were up to something.' She leveled the gun directly at Thomas's face. 'Now stand up, turn around, and cross your wrists behind your back. Otherwise it's beer and nachos with Jesus.'

Somehow, Thomas found himself doing as he was told. He understood none of it.

'She's not who you think she is, Goodbook,' Neil said from his periphery. 'She's NSA, a product of the Flat Affect Neuroplasty Program.'

Thomas understood the words well enough, but they were gibberish all the same.

Sam? NSA?

She slipped something sharp about Thomas's left wrist, pulled his right arm back, looped whatever it was about his left wrist around his right, then yanked it excruciatingly tight.

'She's government owned and operated,' Neil continued. 'A radio-surgical psychopath.'

The room seemed to contort and flatten about her smirking face. Neil's voice fell out of the narrowing corners. 'I performed the procedure, myself, Goodbook. Compassion. Guilt. Shame. I scrubbed her clean, old buddy.'

'Sam,' he heard himself whisper, but he could taste no spit on his tongue.

'Did you hear that?' she cooed close to his neck. He could smell the *Aveeno* moisturizer she used every morning out of the shower. 'I've been *tweaked*. My amygdalas have been stripped down to their predatory essentials.' She licked his ear lobe and whispered, 'Imagine being locked up and helpless with Jeffrey Dahmer.'

The incomprehension evaporated. Thomas became afraid.

'About a decade or so ago,' she continued, pressing him arm's-length against the wall, 'certain planners in certain quarters concluded the human race was trapped in a game-theory nightmare. The Great Scramble, they called it. For resources – peak oil and all that. For food in the face of environmental collapse. For stability in the midst of catastrophic, technologically driven social change. They ran scenario after scenario, and in every projection, the greatest liability turned out to be *you*.'

She brushed some lint from his collar. Her smile was anxious and hopeful – another glimpse of the old Sam.

'Well, not you exactly, but people *like* you. People who think with their hearts instead of their heads. In all the simulations, the only bargainers who survived were those who acted without sentiment. The idea was to create a shadow bureaucracy, to position flat affect bargainers at every level of the government and the military. But where to find them? Mother nature? Please. I mean, look at the Chiropractor. We couldn't have fuck-ups like that running the show, could we?'

Somehow, Thomas had no difficulty with these abstract things. He could see it with B-movie clarity: the generals, the analysts, the money men, leaning over Scotches, exercising their God-given ability to confuse self-interest for natural law. 'So they turned to Neil,' he heard himself say.

'They call us "Graduates",' she explained. 'People surgically unfettered by your stone-age biases. People capable of driving the *hard* bargains, who don't need to bullshit themselves when it comes to choosing the projection of US power over the dissolution of the Knesset, or Orinoco drilling rights over starving Venezuelans. People who protect their own, come what may. And thanks to us, America will survive to pick up the pieces, believe you me.'

She raised her arm, struck him in the face with the butt of her automatic. Thomas toppled to the floor.

She was taping his ankles together before he'd recovered his wits. 'Ordinarily I'd just pop you in the head and call it a day,' she was saying. 'But I figure I owe you one for yesterday afternoon.'

Thomas could only stare in horror. To know someone was to

know what to expect. People were as much trajectories as they were face, form, or voice. And here was Sam, impossibly, moving at right angles to who she was. It seemed she should be bleeding from the impact.

'You're wondering how it's possible,' Sam said, grinning like a tomboy. 'I admit, I didn't think I could pull it off, what with you being a psychologist and all. I just assumed you would see right through me. But after sizing you up in Washington, Mackenzie insisted it would work. "Just be who you were before joining the program," he said. "All the old circuits are still there," he said. And wouldn't you know, the old perv was right: it felt more like . . . more like *reliving* than performing! Good thing I used to be such a twit . . .'

Thomas blinked at the blood and tears, stared at her in numb incomprehension, at the trim manikin nose, the commercial-break smile, the cheek curved to no palm in particular. It was a beautiful face, he realized. It was a beautiful face and it could do anything it wanted. Anything.

She's going to kill us.

He started struggling against the plastic cuffs and the tape. *Fuck-fuck-fuck-fuck-fuck* . . .

Testing her handiwork, Sam winked. She lifted and dropped his taped feet, then turned to Neil, saying, 'And *you* have a few beans to spill, Doc. That was naughty, spiking the database the way you did. Mackenzie nearly had a stroke. He's a heavy smoker, you know.'

Neil spit blood and laughed.

Holstering her Glock, Sam slapped her hands together and surveyed her handiwork. 'All this domination has made me hot,' she said with a heavy breath.

She shed her blazer and began unbuttoning her blouse. Blood pulsed across Thomas's face, wet strings that became more and more tangled in his eyes. No matter how much he blinked he could see nothing more than shapes and insinuations. She was standing over Neil now, a smear of white skin holding the blot of her handgun.

'How about it, doctor?' she asked coyly. 'How much have you unplugged?'

'Enough.'

From the scissoring of limbs he could tell she had continued undressing. 'Your best friend here has a severe case of Franken-brain,' she said to Thomas. 'He's been tweaking and trimming for some time now, haven't you? No more fear. No more love. Of course you must still feel pain – too important a survival mechanism, that. But I'd be surprised if you *cared* about pain anymore. Mackenzie warned me that standard procedures would likely prove ineffective, that I'd have to be creative. "Try the eyes or the balls," he said. "Some reflexes must be intact." '

Thomas jerked and twisted against the restraints, which seemed to tighten.

Think-think-think-THINK!

It was all adaptive wiring, he told himself, some circuits fixed by millions of years of evolution, others molded by a lifetime of coping with environmental and social circumstances. He was out of his depth, caught up in circumstances his brain could not process. For his entire life, everyone had always done what they should, more or less.

But Sam. All her social circuitry had been amputated. Like Neil, she worked in the netherworld between trajectories, in a place neither described nor governed by the rules binding everyday human intercourse. And now she was deliberately acting against the grain, as a way to induce stress, confusion – as a way to punish.

None of this means anything! It doesn't matter.

'Sam?' he coughed as much as cried. *Please don't . . .*

'I almost forgot,' the pale blur said. 'You love me, don't you? Awwwww . . . Isn't that what you said? "I love you, Sam?" '

Thomas swallowed, screwed shut his eyes. *It doesn't matter!* 'Don't . . . Please . . .'

Her voice seemed to wind up. 'All those times you imagined Nora getting fucked – like a knife in the heart, wasn't it? Now you'll see what it's like. You'll actually get to see your best friend fucking someone you love . . .

'Think of it as therapy.'

Heaving breaths. Spit flying from his lips. He opened his eyes, but could see only rose and sting, a bundle of shadows throbbing to the sound of spit.

'Isn't this fucking *wild*?' she said. 'I mean all the energies flying around, all the boundaries being broken! How fucking wild is that? I can remember what I was like. I mean, the thought of doing something like this was just . . . just . . . I'd have a heart attack!'

Neil gasped in her sudden silence.

'But now! What a fucking trip! I'm *sooo* fucking wet!'

Her form detached itself from Neil's shadow. She was standing. 'Anything goes,' the white-and-rose smear said. 'You can see that, can't you, professor? Here, now . . . *any-fucking-thing.*'

Thomas began shaking.

'This is silliness, Jess,' Neil said. 'What do you think—'

The black blot swung toward Neil's bound outline. A gunshot, loud enough to crack plaster.

Oh-my-God-oh-my-God-oh-my . . .

'Neil?' Thomas heard himself croak.

'Watch this,' Sam said, as though she were a seven-year-old about to do a bicycle trick. Her form moved, spilled like sheeted snow, converged with Neil's darker shadow. 'Watch, professor. *There* . . . There it goes . . . that feels good. Can you see it, professor? Imagine Nora . . . *Imagine*!'

'Please,' Thomas said.

'Fucking wild,' she mumbled. 'Oh, God,' – surprised laugh – 'I'm gonna come already. Watch me, professor. Watch me, unnngh . . .'

The running blood had become acid. His eyes screamed, yet he couldn't tear them away from the slurry of light and dark jerking before him. Sam cried out, a primal voice for primal ears, then everything became still, save for the fluttering of anguished eyelids.

'Intense,' she gasped. 'Fuck me. Did you see that? Bammo, and he's still *so fucking hard.* No wonder Nora couldn't get enough!' For an instant, he thought he glimpsed her looking up, searching the ceiling with her eyes. 'Oh, yeah . . . I think I got another one. How many times did your wife say she usually came? Three? Four? What do you say, professor? Wanna watch me toss another load?'

'No.'

Laughter. 'But of course you do! I can see your boner from here. You guys are made for this stuff. Sex and violence. Juice and penetration. Horror versus fantasy, and fantasy wins! Christ, even *Gerard's* got a fucking hard on . . .'

Another gunshot.

More blood he couldn't wipe away, pooling in the spoons about his eyes. Little more than a thicket of overgrown color, Sam and Neil began rocking again. The chair creaked. 'Just so fucking wild,' he heard her murmur. 'So hot! No fucking wonder so many men are rapists . . .' Though he couldn't see her, she became Cynthia Powski sucking on her bottom lip. 'But it's not the same, is it? I mean, if I were a guy and you were chicks, it would be *more*, wouldn't it? The buzz would be bigger . . .'

An oval appeared like light from beneath ice, and he knew she was watching him, her eyes vacant, lethargic. 'Maybe,' she said without a whisper of self-consciousness, 'when I start with the knives . . .'

Shadows behind a widow's veil. Breaths, a male and female counterpoint, wheezing between the creak of floorboards.

'Even still,' she gasped, 'it's unfuckingbelievable . . .' Her voice was doped with pleasure, her words bunched like flannel between compulsive breaths. 'I mean before . . . I was . . . well, not a prude . . . but, you know – like everyone else. Stuff like this . . . like murder and fucking just freaked me right out. So guilty I couldn't pass a fucking bum without digging through my purse! I just . . . just wasn't built for this job. And I wanted it. I wanted it so badly. To be a spook. A real world Lara Croft . . . I wanted to be strong!'

The sound of wood complaining beneath rocking bodies, air puffing through slack lips.

'I remember . . . it was the strangest thing. After the operation . . . I woke up . . . and suddenly I just didn't give a shit. It was like I'd been cringing . . . cringing my whole life . . . skulking like a beaten dog, and then . . . I could really breathe *deep*, you know? Like . . . those first days of spring . . . or that first line of coke. And I realized: *people* . . . People were my problem. I went to bed worrying about people . . . went to work worrying about people – I even worried in the fucking shower! I'd think . . . Why did I say that? or . . . Why did bitch-face look at me that way? or . . . What if Tom tells Dick . . . that I fucked Harry? Cringing. Wringing my hands. Catching my breath. Worry-worry-worry . . .

'But *now* . . . hmm. Now everything is . . .' Pale lines bucked against crowded shadows, and she cried out. 'What can I say?' she continued, talking as though to catch her own drool. 'Anything goes, professor . . . *Anything*.'

There was nothing to see but pain, the bite of blood, his brow crimping to his cheek as though his eyes had become greased marbles. Even still, it was as if a great palm pressed his face back and to the side, his temple to the wall, away from the horror his ears could so plainly see. Sam. Sam.

The creaking stopped. 'Getting close, doc?' she cooed, her voice mother-tender. 'Why is it . . . you all look . . . so lovely the moment just before?'

A faint slapping sound, relentless beneath the chorus of three humans breathing.

'There's a way . . . to get it . . . you know. Just . . . tell me . . . tell me where you stashed the data . . .'

Her voice had become a quavering thread.

'Just . . . tell . . . me . . .'

Again Thomas was blinking, trying to peer past his obscuring blood.

'Never,' Neil grunted.

Another gunshot. A strange noise escaped from Thomas's chest. A cry? The slapping sound, flabby, wet, continued uninterrupted.

'Are you . . .' Sam mumbled. 'Are you *shooooor*?'

'You thought . . .' Neil replied drunkenly. 'You thought screwing me would do it?' Spoken between swallows of spit.

The slapping stopped. Panting filled the silence. 'Mackenzie,' Sam said, like a sprinter searching for her voice. 'Mackenzie's idea. You risked so much banging the professor's wife . . . He thought all your tweaking might have left your executive functions especially vulnerable to sexual stimuli . . . So I thought what the fuck . . .' She laughed at this, and the slapping sound resumed, the tempo more furious. 'But, mmmm, I had no idea it would be so . . . *delicious*.'

Thomas stared blind.

'You've doomed yourself,' Neil croaked. 'You realize. Every Neuropath who's engaged in violent sexual behavior has gone serial. They fall into some kind of obsessive loop. Once they start, they can't seem to get enough.'

'Threshold compensation?' Sam asked.

'Exactly. Once the volume goes up, there's no turning it down.'

'*Crank* it, I say . . .'

A wooden pop from the chair. The floorboards resumed creaking beneath the monstrous patterns, white for feminine skin, indigo for cloth and shadow, the whole shot with filaments of refracted light.

'Watch,' Thomas heard Sam say, a concentrated whisper. 'I'm

going . . . to *shoot* him . . . Shoot him when he comes . . . I'm going to ride him . . . Ride him to the other side . . .'

Thomas had fallen still. It seemed a light blanket of snow covered him, a soundless accumulation. So clear.

Sam, he thought. *Frankie*.

His fingers numb behind his back, he began kneading his blazer.

'So it was all a sham,' he said dully. 'All of it.'

'*Watch*,' Sam moaned. ' Hot steel . . . What a fucking trip . . . Here I . . . Here I . . . ungh!'

The blood had stopped flowing, had become a tacky rind about his still-burning eyes. And at last Thomas could *see*, see her arch her back, see the soundless spasms, see her slump forward, drag the barrel of her Glock across Neil's cheek.

'*Sweet Christ*,' she gasped. Her chest heaved. Hooks and lines of white light gilded her sweaty skin. 'I mean, what is it? The *power*?' She swung her head back in a long, swaying laugh. 'I mean, you guys are *going to die*, to bleed, and all I want is to fuck-fuck-fuck!'

'I told you, Jess,' Neil said, his voice out-of-breath thin. 'Once you do this, there's no turn—'

Another gunshot, this time into Gerard's grey face. It buckled like wax about the point of entry, but did not bleed. 'What is it?' Sam cried. 'What makes this so . . . so . . .'

Thomas stared at the pasty, languorous horror before him. Skin he loved. Limbs he loved. A body he had worshipped, grinding against the pulse of another man.

'So it was all bullshit,' he repeated, still cold. 'A way to dupe me into finding Neil for you.'

Control had regained possession. There was only one question now.

'Of course it was,' Sam said, leaning against Neil's chest in post-coital exhaustion. 'What? Were you still hoping that I might love you? That you could reach some small spark of passion within me?' She laughed, glanced down at herself as though making a point about income brackets. 'Are you for real?'

'I was talking about Frankie.'

Her look became appreciative. She used Neil's shirt to wipe her fingers – knuckle to nail, like a dinner napkin. 'Oh, *that*. Pretty sharp, huh? Had to motivate you somehow, professor. You were fucking dead weight. Had to give you a swift kick – what can I say? I'd like to take credit, but doc's protégé at the plant, Mackenzie, was the prime mover there. The old horn-dog sized you up pretty good, didn't he? Christ, the kid's screams even made *my* skin crawl.'

It seemed he could see it. A figure in black, lithe, fearless, stealing across the humble plate of a residential backyard. Bart's claws scraping the pressure-treated lumber as he ambled toward the familiar smell, then looked up, tongue lolling, into the soundless muzzle-flash. And there she stood, a trick of the eyes, a creature from beneath the floorboards, gazing at the father asleep on the deck, laughing at the pathetic sense of gallantry she knew he must have felt standing guard over his children, over his son. Just another know-nothing huddled in the low circle of his possessions, things prized for an hour before fading into the fog of background shame. Just another father filled with bluster, blind to the tracks that others had cut through his home.

It seemed he could see her, *Sam*, kneeling before the orange glow of the kids' tent.

'*Mackenzie* tweaked Frankie?' Neil asked sharply.

The first shot passed clean through her neck, giving her time to turn around and stare at Thomas in round-eyed amazement – at Mia's revolver shaking in his contorted hands. She raised her Glock in a manikin arm. The second shot took her to the left of her nose, throwing her back off of Neil and onto the floor. She landed like luggage. Her nude body convulsed for several heartbeats, then went very still.

Thomas had swung to his side to aim with his hands bound. His right hand tingled, as though he'd driven a golf ball or a nail. Neil stared at him.

Thomas gagged and coughed. He spat blood and snot across the floor. 'Anything,' he croaked, 'does not fucking go.'

The high-pitched chorus of frogs through the screened windows. The counterpoint of crickets under the beaten trim. Two mosquitos danced like dandelion fluff beneath the yellow light.

Mia's handgun clattered against the hardwood.

Slowly, carefully, Thomas pulled himself to his feet. After hopping precariously into the kitchen and sawing himself free with a steak knife, he returned, gathered the guns, then cautiously began freeing Neil. He held Sam's Glock on him the entire time. Neil watched him with an open, expectant face. Neither man said a word. Breathing, it seemed, was eloquence enough.

Once free, Neil stood, rubbed his wrists. Thomas found himself searching his eyes, although for what he did not know. Unnerved by the flat candor of his stare, he glanced down at Sam. Sprawled like a doll. Cold like rubber. Long pins of blood seeped through the grooves in the hardwood flooring, shining like cherry syrup. Her face was beginning to swell.

Could this be her? It seemed impossible. Once again, the look of her had been cut from the knowledge. Once again she had leapt from the envelope of his expectations.

Thomas began shaking so violently that he stumbled into an overstuffed easy chair. His face tightened, as though bound by rubber bands. With each sob, something seemed to snap within him.

'I . . . I . . .' he tried to gasp.

'Easy, Goodbook.'

Thomas looked up, uncomprehending.

'Frankie?' he hissed.

'Is mine,' Neil replied.

'And Rip . . . Rip . . .'

'The Ripper? She's all yours.'

Thomas could hear them both. *'But Dadeeeee!'*

'But-but . . .' A keening wail escaped him. He blew spit through clenched teeth.

'You're still Frankie's father,' Neil said. 'I know.'

Thomas raised Sam's Glock, aimed at the roaring, looming blur that was his friend.

'Put it down, Goodbook. You need me. You need me because Frankie needs me.'

'N-Nora?' Thomas croaked, jabbing the gun at him. 'She told you?'

Neil seemed utterly unperturbed – terrifyingly so. 'She had the kids tested. But she said she knew all along.'

For some reason, this explanation calmed Thomas. He gazed at his best friend, unable to recognize him, though he could, he was sure, paint photographs of his face. Who was this man, this monster, this friend he knew better than he knew himself?

'My whole life . . .' He paused, feeling curiously empty. Too much trauma. The breakers had been blown. He felt nothing. 'My whole life's been a lie.'

'Now you're starting to see,' Neil replied.

Desolation as insight. Was that what this was all about? Mortification, not of the body, but of the soul.

'You *don't* hate me, do you?'

Neil stared without blinking, his eyes button-black in the dingy light. 'No. Never. Not even when I still could.'

'Then all this *is* about the Argument?'

'Everything is about the Argument, Goodbook. Everything.'

Neil looked biblical in the ensuing silence, angular and statuesque. The man who had transcended the slumber people called consciousness. It seemed impossible that the crimes Thomas had witnessed could be the work of his hand. Impossible and inevitable. Neil had always done this. Moving from rule to sanctity, brushing it all away like so many cobwebs.

'So what happens now?' Thomas asked.

'We save Frankie.'

'But I thought you were past caring. Why should Frankie matter to you?'

'Because he's my son.'

'And that means something to you?'

Neil shot him a curious look. 'Why do you think sex is so pleasurable? It's the way we plug into the *future*, Goodbook. All that heat. All that juice. You think our genes just magically replicate 2 billion years of information? Sex is *survival*, man. What you are, who you are, is the product of a million million fuckings. We're fucking machines.'

'What does that have to do with my son?'

Neil shrugged. 'I plugged into Frankie when I impregnated Nora years ago. Frankie's my future, and I'm his past – a billion years of data! My brain's hardwired to effect his survival.'

That phrase, 'impregnated Nora', was like a blow to the gut.

'That's a reason?' Thomas exclaimed.

'You still don't get it, do you? There's no such thing as reasons, Goodbook.'

Thomas felt like spitting. 'Just causes.'

Neil smiled the way he always would when women propositioned him: as though an obvious truth had been confirmed. He walked over to the bureau and reached for Gerard's automatic. Thomas tried to shout, coughed instead. He held out Sam's Glock; it seemed to rattle in his hand.

Neil paused, turned to his old friend.

'You're going to help me save my son,' Thomas said tightly. It sounded like a cry, a plea.

Neil blinked slowly. 'No. I'm going to help you save *my* son.' He picked up the gun, pressed it beneath his belt.

Since Princeton this had always been Neil's way of avoiding confrontations: pretending they didn't exist. He would stand in the spotlight of others' condemnation and simply act as though he remained backstage. '*People are allergic to conflict*,' he used to say. '*I simply dare them to sneeze.*'

He played the margins of fear and embarrassment to his own advantage. That was a symptom of psychopathy, wasn't it?

Thomas thought of Cynthia Powski masturbating with broken glass.

What am I doing? I can't trust him. He's not even—

'We have to move,' Neil said abruptly. 'They're probably on top of us already.'

Thomas shook his head. 'No one else knows you're here. I tricked them,' he said, nodding to the two bodies on the floor. 'I knew I couldn't trust them not to kill you, so I tricked them.'

'*You* found me?' Neil said.

'Only because you wanted me to.'

'What are you talking about?'

'You marked this place on my poster . . . Just like you put the web address on my lamp.'

'Poster? You mean that satellite poster of the earth?'

'Yeah. You marked Climax with an x.'

Neil shook his head. 'Wasn't me.'

'Right,' Thomas said skeptically. For a second it seemed they were simply older versions of themselves, griping and disagreeing in the same old way.

'*You* put that x there. Don't you remember? Back in the dorm, years ago. We had those two chicks lined up – what was it? Sandra and Ginny or Jenny or something—'

'Jenny,' Thomas said.

'You remember? You were going on about the "world being your pussy" or something.'

Thomas looked at him blankly.

'You remember?' Neil repeated.

So. It was all bullshit. Every square inch of his life.

Even his revelations.

For a time, all Thomas could do was sit and point his gun. When Neil vanished into another room, he would just sit and blink, aiming the gun at the chrome and linoleum spaces beyond the door frame, waiting for Neil to return. When he returned, sometimes bearing rucksacks, other times scuffed aluminum cases, Thomas would watch in wonder as the muzzle tracked him, feeling nothing of the threat it represented, even though tissue exploded again and again in his mind's eye.

Neil simply rattled off instructions. Tac Teams, he said, would arrive shortly, whether Jessica – as he insisted on calling Sam – had alerted them or not. Sooner or later they would aim a satellite at her vehicle's GPS coordinates, just to see what she was up to. The two of them had to get the fuck out of Dodge, as he put it, before Dodge put the fuck into them. Just as men had evolved a preference for young women because of their longer reproductive windows, Tac Teams were attracted to indecisive idiots because of their longer response windows. It took time to isolate, to organize . . .

Apparently Thomas was being an indecisive idiot.

Dead weight.

'What are you taking?' Neil abruptly asked.

'Ativan,' Thomas said mildly.

His best friend rooted through one of his rucksacks, tossed a beer-tinted pill bottle that bounced against his chest, rolled into his lap.

'A neuroleptic,' Neil explained. 'Experimental. Think of it as Pepto-Bismol for the brain.'

'I-I need . . .' Thomas said. 'I n-need to clear my head.'

The gun maintained its vigil.

'Exactly. You have to drive to New York and snatch Frankie. You have to bring him back to me ASAP.'

'Tonight?' Thomas asked, almost overcome by a peculiar drowsiness. His limbs had become heavy – drowning-victim heavy.

Critical incident stress. Need to . . . to . . .

'Goodbook, listen to me. These people are smart; they figure out things quickly. Right now, their disorientation is our only advantage.

But even more, there's Frankie to think about. You know the rule. Neurons that fire together wire together. Even as we speak, Mackenzie's affect feedback implant is wearing deeper and deeper tracks into his brain. It needs to come out *now*.'

There was Sam, over there, cold and nude and unshivering on the floor. Reflections of walls and furniture gleamed upside-down in her blood. Lives, he thought, were like property lines. And Neil was driving cross-country. Who could say where he would turn?

'But you're a madman,' Thomas said.

'You know that's not true,' Neil replied with a shrug. 'You only say it because you find sanity unbearable.'

Pull the trigger. Jesus-jesus just pull the MOTHERFUCKING TRIGGER–

His hand lowered the gun.

CHAPTER SIXTEEN

August 30th, 11.39 p.m.

There was a roaring, and he opened his eyes to the sterile flare of headlights, an oncoming car swerving, something too profound to be an impact, metal imploding, the car frame snapping, air-bag deploying, sharp things sheering, everything whipping about a deranged axis. A crash louder than sound.

He was wet and motionless. Soaking wet.

Something was wrong with his jaw. It was missing.

Thomas awoke to the thud and shudder of his Acura plowing through the median. He cried out, hit the brakes, felt the tires churn up turf and hummocks. He sat there for several moments, idling, weeping, until another car pulling onto the shoulder – some Samaritan making sure he was okay, he supposed – reminded him of the police.

And Frankie.

The car bucked and shuddered. The undercarriage sledged through gravel, then he was accelerating down the highway, cringing at the memory of his dream.

It meant nothing.

'Thank God!' Mia cried, running across the lawn into the yellow circle of the driveway lights. 'Thank *fucking* Gawd!'

Thomas popped the car into park. 'Mia,' was all he could say to the face bobbing in his window. The oil-stain smell of the freeway still hung in the air.

'Fuck, Tommy. Fuck-fuck-fuck-fuck-*fuck*!' His Number One

Neighbor swatted at tears. 'I so thought you were dead. Jesus Christ, I literally thought you were fucking dead!'

Thomas nodded, stared blankly into Mia's frantic eyes. Control was good – for the moment.

'I need—' Something painful hooked his voice into silence. 'I need your help, Mia. I don't think I can do this alone.'

'Whatever, Tommy! Whatever you need!'

'We have to bring Frankie to Neil.'

'Neil—' Mia began but halted, his expression at once astonished and aghast. Thomas studied his face: the thoughtful drift in the line of his nose, the cynical depth of his crow's feet – all those things that Theodoros Gyges could see, but could never recognize.

The face of a friend.

For no reason either could fathom, they took Bill's ancient Toyota 4 × 4. 'Feels like sitting on a toilet,' Mia cracked after settling behind the wheel. The cab's floors were incredibly shallow – to increase clearance, Thomas supposed – forcing them to sit with their knees high. 'No wonder Bill takes a dump on me when he gets home.'

Peekskill was sedate in the manner of shining cars cruising past glowing franchise food outlets. Streetlights kicked like chorus girls across the hood and windshield – a never-ending line of them. Staring into curiously steady hands, Thomas described the afternoon's events the way a journalist might: faithful to the details, indifferent to the implications.

'You *shot* her?' Mia cried at one point. 'Jeezus, Tommy!'

'Pow,' Thomas said, holding his finger out like a gun. He could still see her fall back into the cloud of blood and hair. Her gun trailing ceilingward. Her breasts rising with free-fall buoyancy. It seemed that he both wept and cackled, though his face remained professionally blank and to-the-point.

'Are you on drugs?' Mia shouted, sounding for all the world like a tank driver. '*Nawt* fucking funny!' He always went Alabama when he was frantic. Always went native. 'You killed an— Oh sweet Christ! You killed her with *my gun*!' He pressed a palm flat against his brow. 'An *FBI agent*!'

Thomas found himself setting his teeth in guilt, despite the layers of pharmaceutical lacquer. Mia was a spectator, someone who had tripped on stage from the front row. Only Thomas's firm hand held him in the floodlights. Only Thomas's *need.* And why should that bind him? This was no natural disaster. There would be no correspondents in rain-slickers, no hands-to-the-ear or teleprompters, no camera-eye to impress. The days of overlapping obligations were long gone. The soft tissue of community had shrunk to the bone of property lines; the world had become a great quilt of demilitarized zones. A circumcision for every heart. A burqa thrown over every window. Neighbors need not care, so long as the grass was cut and the volume was turned low.

Thomas was *using* Mia, plain and simple. He was banking on the disconnect between love and its evolutionary rationale, the fact that Mia's brain had confused Frankie for someone belonging to the same genetic cooperative. But giving his Number One Neighbor an out simply wasn't an option. Captain Cassidy had given Thomas a White Whale of a mission. Someone had to row while he teetered with the harpoon.

He continued explaining – why they had no choice but to abduct his son, how Neil had given him a specially scrambled phone, how he was supposed to call to find out where to bring Frankie. He answered Mia's subsequent questions with grim patience, like a clinician deciphering the ghosts of cancer on an X-ray.

When Mia asked *the* question, the question of how he could trust a monster, Thomas simply said, 'Because Frankie's his son.'

His Number One Neighbor said nothing for a long while. The tires hummed, annoyed by the lack of mountains and mud.

Control . . . Thomas could feel it, a cold and clammy hand wrapped about his limbic system. People weren't heroes, he realized. They just weren't.

Only moments of insanity made them seem that way.

Manhattan towered, serene with distance, surreal with innumerable lights. The nimbus of each formed interlocking rings across the windshield, slowing migrating to the curve of the highway. Somewhere, buried among the clefts in the horizon, a little boy lay strapped to his bed, twitching and screaming.

Thomas rocked in his seat, clutched his knees.

'What if he's right?' he asked. It was one of those questions that only became real in the asking. Part of him, he realized, didn't trust Mia to be alone with his thoughts.

‘Who?’ Mia replied. ‘Neil?’

‘We thought we were the center of the universe. We were wrong. We thought we were made in God’s image. We were wrong. Now we think we’re the source of all meaning . . . We think that we’re *real.*’

‘That’s just one more perspective,’ Mia said. ‘One more word game. Look around you, Tom. Nobody has a fucking clue what’s going on. Least of all Neil. It’s just power plays all the way down.’

Thomas shook his head. The tragedy wasn’t that words had no bottom: that was just a way for English professors to flatter themselves into thinking the world was just more Shakespeare, something tailor-made for them and their skills. No. The tragedy was that the bottom was unspeakable.

Unlivable.

‘We have clues,’ he said, gesturing not so much to the rising city as to the knowledge propping it up. ‘We just can’t bear following them.’

Mia snorted. ‘You’re like Woody Allen without a punchline, you know that?’

Thomas pursed his lips. He was pressing Mia when he should be reassuring – he knew as much. But in the glamour cast by Neil’s day-glo narcoleptic, this was simply a matter of course. Something relentless inhabited him, something see-it-through . . .

No matter what the end.

‘You don’t understand, Mia. We’ve come to the limit. We’re standing at the brink. We really are. You know that feeling you have, that feeling of *making* things happen, of being responsible? That’s just a product, something generated by your brain. It simply accompanies your actions, your decisions. Neil’s shut it down. He hasn’t made a decision or willed anything to happen in fucking years. He experiences decisions, just minus the sensation of willing them. They simply happen.’

‘Yeah, well, small fucking wonder he’s gone bonkers.’

‘Has he? Has he gone bonkers? Or has he gone sane in a world of madmen? This isn’t speculation, Mia. It’s *fact.* The will is an illusion – fact. No different than the facts that make this car possible, or New York possible, or vaccinations or nose-jobs or polyester pants. We’re the illusion! That’s how fucking crazy the world has become. And Neil is the first man to see his way past it, to see his way—’

‘Look, Tommy,’ Mia interrupted, his eyes clicking between him and the freeway. 'You've been through a lot so I'm going to say this gently, okay? Three words . . . Shut. The-fuck-up. Cocksucker.'

Thomas looked back to the city piling black and gold on the horizon.

'Did you hear that, Tommy? Do you understand what I'm saying?'

'You know that virtual news anchor on MSNBC?' Thomas continued, 'Peter Farmer, the one they morphed using real-time brain imaging feedback to give him the most pleasing voice, the most pleasing appearance, and so—'

'Shut-the-fuck-up,' Mia sang. 'Shut-the-fuck-aaawwwp—'

'No. Look, Mia, fuck. *Just listen.* Our society is basically a giant version of Farmer: an immense flattery feedback mechanism, a machine tuned to cater to our wants, spiritual, social, material. Our *wants*, not our needs. So we run around, sticking our dicks into mouth after mouth, and whenever someone comes along wanting to talk, not suck, we say, "Excuse me, buddy, but I'm like, getting a *blowjob* over here." How can facts compete? We think we can believe whatever we fucking want, that reason and evidence are simply different sections of the grocery store, that we don't have to answer to those scratching their heads, let alone to the world. And because we can't *see* what we don't know, we all think that we more or less have it sewn up – never mind that in three thousand years, we'll sound every bit as ludicrous to our descendants as our ancestors sound to—'

Thomas stopped, shouted down by the roar of the Toyota wandering across the rumble-strips.

Mia jerked the SUV back into the centre of the lane. 'It's not that I don't find this interesting, Tommy. Hell, I pretty much agree with you, word for fucking word. It's just that right now I really don't give a flying fuck.' He hit the blinker, slowed onto the exit ramp. 'We got bigger fish to fry, neighbor. And *this* illusion, for one, does not want to find his taut, athletic ass in prison.' A quick glance. 'We clear?'

Thomas blinked, surprised by the hot tears that dropped down his cheeks.

'Clear,' he said, looking to the road. The trash in the concrete sockets. The endless oil-stains, blurred into bands of smoke by the speed. The off ramp seemed to peel him away from something essential, like skin from the stalk.

That noise. He would do anything to stop hearing that noise. Even if it meant driving on the rumble-strips for the rest of his life.

No more screams, Frankie.

Daddy promises.

When they pulled up to the hospital, Thomas half-expected Mia to tell him to get out, then peel down the street. When he didn't, when he actually led the way toward the white, fishbowl world beyond the glass doors, Thomas could feel the ground wobble.

We're coming, son . . . Both of us.

'Lordy-lordy,' Mia murmured as they paused in the hospital's gothic shadow.

Their plan was simple, but it depended on who-knew-how-many-variables going their way.

'Ready?' Thomas said, biting his lip.

'Like spaghetti,' Mia replied.

The lobby was all but abandoned. He felt almost no apprehension approaching the metal-detector and its bored, sleep-deprived guard. Mia strode through briskly, with nary a second glance from the bull-chested man, who seemed more interested in the small backpack Thomas carried. Thomas swung it across the detector's threshold, dropped it into the guard's waiting hand, before stepping through himself. The guard had already peeled it open when the metal detector chirped in a polite yet insistent way.

Thomas felt his heart stop.

'Again,' the guard said without even looking at him. He pawed through Frankie's clothes with a big black hand. Thomas took two steps back, then once more stepped across the threshold. He heard the second chirp more with his skin than his ears.

Still not making eye contact, the guard simply murmured, 'Arms out,' then began waving his wand along the contours of his body. Thomas could swear he was being beaten with sticks, though at no point did the man touch him. The wand followed the X of his form, starting with his right arm, then moving down to his right ankle. The guard then panned up along the outside of his left leg. The wand let out a wiry whistle as it passed over the left pocket of his blazer.

Eye contact at last, though the man looked far more bored than concerned. 'Your pocket, sir,' he said. 'Do you have anything in your pocket?'

Breathless and immobile, Thomas said, 'Not that I know of . . .'

The guard reached in with thick fingers, withdrew what Thomas mistook for a handkerchief, then recognized as Sam's white cotton panties.

The guard smiled and scowled at once.

'You *dawwg*,' Mia drawled.

Then a bullet rolled from the panty-liner, made a perfect, tuning-fork ping against the tiled floor.

The guard frowned at it for a moment, raised hard eyes . . .

Mia's foot took him in the jaw. He staggered back, uncomprehending, utterly unprepared for the second foot, which sent him toppling. His keys jangled, then all was silent.

Thomas gaped at his neighbor, who rolled his head from his left to his right shoulder.

'A little piece of advice,' Mia said, kneeling next to the unconscious guard. 'If you're a man, learn how to kick ass before you put on a dress.' He held out his hand, snapped his fingers impatiently.

'What?' Thomas asked, scarcely able to breathe.

'The duct tape,' Mia said. 'Remember?'

Numb, Thomas pawed his empty right pocket, looked to his neighbor helplessly. He'd forgotten the tape at the cottage. Cursing, Mia grabbed the panties, brandished them as though making a statement about his priorities. '*Boxers* are too big to stuff into pockets,' he said. 'C'mon. We have to get this lug out of sight. If anyone's monitoring those cameras' – he nodded at an abstract point above and behind Thomas – 'we might be fucked already.'

They tucked the guard in an out-of-the-way bathroom.

'It's not like the movies,' Thomas said, standing over the slumped form. 'He needs to see a doctor as soon as possible. He could be reall—'

'I don't know about you,' his neighbor said, 'but I came to bet on Frankie.'

The most Thomas could do was nod. Control was slipping.

They passed two nightshift nurses who seemed too caught up gossiping to notice their presence. The air in the elevator was fever-hot. They stared like idiots at the Air France commercial on the screen. Thomas found himself looking for the embedded sexual cues that all advertisers used to catch wandering eyes. A millisecond glimpse up a business traveller's skirt. The background cleavage of two teenage backpackers stowing their overhead gear. All of it sealed with a family-friendly smile.

Like an idiot, Thomas found himself thinking, *Come fly the fuckable sky . . .*

The elevator doors rattled open.

Thomas beamed a tired smile at the neurological observation unit's duty nurse – a once-pretty woman named Skye, if he remembered correctly. He leaned over the counter to swallow as much of her periphery as he could. He could neither hear nor see Mia, which was a good thing.

'Professor Bible,' she said, her voice silky with compassion. She knew he was divorced, and with professional women now vastly outnumbering men – the 'Great Gender Role Reversal' the pundits were calling it – guys like Thomas, ones who had actually studied in college rather than turfing out in a haze of dope and video games, were something of a rare commodity.

He played the part. The exhausted father, the grieving father, desperate for feminine comfort and support. One who flirted because he had nothing else, no other spark to warm his thick, ringless fingers . . .

A monitor alerted her that Frankie had been disconnected. She looked up in almost comical alarm.

'Is that Frankie?' he asked with feigned horror.

'H-his sedative must have worn off.'

He chose that moment to swing the backpack onto the counter before her.

'Don't move!' he barked.

Of course she froze; it was instinct.

'You know about directed motion detectors, don't you, Skye? – don't nod! Just blink if you understand me.'

Two tears fell when she did so, inking her cheeks with mascara.

'Well, one of them is aimed right at you . . . and it's connected to a bomb in this bag. Any movement or loud noise could set it off. Even your lips. Do you understand?'

Again tears accompanied her blink. She was shaking like a little human centrifuge, enough to trigger a dozen shopping-mall doors. Nausea wheeled through Thomas – from the shame, he imagined, though Neil's pills had Saran Wrapped his every emotion.

He leaned back from the counter, slowly, as though scared of his own diabolical device. He saw Mia running down the hall with Frankie. He took his unconscious boy in his arms.

He held his little body tight. Kissed his cheek. Sobbed against his shaved scalp.

So long as I hold him. So long as I never let him go.

They dressed Frankie in a fumbling panic. Thomas silently thanked nobody that he had remembered to bring his velcro shoes. They did a passable job making a discreet, nonchalant exit. Every nurse they passed smiled at the sight of Frankie slumbering in his arms. One man, a custodian, whispered, 'Long day, huh?' An attractive doctor said, 'He's a beautiful little monkey, isn't he?' She even laughed and wiped drool from Thomas's shoulder with her sleeve. 'Such a *sound* sleeper.'

Once again, Thomas silently thanked nobody, this time for having the foresight to bring Frankie's Jersey Devils cap. With his scalp shaved and bandaged, she would have realized something was up.

It was strange, strolling and smiling while his heart lunged in terror. His skin tingled, as though rubbed raw by the catastrophic possibilities that surrounded him. But by the time they made it to the unattended lobby, Thomas felt something akin to criminal glee.

Twenty steps, he thought, staring at the doors and the concrete darkness beyond them, *and we're home free . . .*

Fifteen steps, and we're home free . . .

They trotted down the stairs.

Ten steps . . .

They passed the metal detector, waded through the turnstile.

We made it, Frankie! This is going to work!

They pressed through the doors into the hot night, stopped dead in their tracks. All they could hear was the deep, over-the-horizon thrum of the surrounding city.

The police cruiser's lights seemed to click as they spun, but it was just a trick of the eyes.

'Sorry-sorry!' Mia cried, bounding to the curb. The officer, who was probing the Toyota's interior with a flashlight, turned in alarm.

Thomas could only hug his boy's tiny body tight. Control had evaporated. He kissed his warm neck, then sobbed once, twice, against his little shoulder. He could hear Mia's insistent voice, then suddenly he was blinking against the flashlight.

'Not cool,' he heard Mia say to the cop. '*Nawt* cool.'

'Sorry,' the officer said. 'You two take care.'

Then Mia was beside him, disentangling Frankie from his arms. 'C'mon. It's okay, Tom. *Ups-a-daisy* . . .'

Somehow Thomas ended up behind the wheel, while Mia tried to secure Frankie in the back seat. Wiping his nose on his blazer sleeve, Thomas slowly accelerated down the street. He felt like an ant pulling away from a tombstone. *Please* . . .

The first police cruiser picked them up before they hit the fourth city block. The siren fairly kicked the breath out of Thomas's lungs.

'Not-good-not-good-not-good,' Mia muttered.

Thomas turned the vehicle slowly, not quite able to process what was happening.

'What are you doing?' Mia cried.

'I hit the blinker.'

'I can see that. You afraid we might lose them or something?'

Thomas sped down the side street. Then swerved to the right down a thoroughfare. Again he hit the blinker.

'Are you kidding me? You worried about a traffic ticket?'

'I can't help it!' Thomas cried. 'It's habit. Conditioning.'

He screeched to the left, this time without hitting the blinker.

'Faster!' Mia cried. 'Faster!'

Thomas hit the blinker and yanked the SUV right.

'Jeeesuz fucking Christ!' Mia howled. 'Tommy, I love you like a neighbor, but I will so fucking tear you another asshole if you don't. Fucking. Speed. *Up*!'

'I can't help it! I'm a little neurotic when it comes to driving.'

'A little? You make OJ look like Jimmy Dean!'

'So I'm a lot neurotic.'

'But you're a psychologist!'

'What? You think I went to school to figure out why *other* people are so screwed up?'

'Pull into that alley there! Pull into there!'

At least this time he didn't hit the blinker. The alley was narrow – too narrow to open doors. Thomas drifted into the left wall, cried out as the mirror exploded from the side of the Toyota. The exit neared.

'Brake!' Mia was shouting. 'Brake! Stop the fucking car!'

Thomas stomped on the brakes. The police cruiser screeched to a halt behind them.

'Now pull forward until our doors are clear,' Mia said. 'Pull forward!'

Thomas did as he was told. When the doors were clear Mia opened his. 'Get the fuck out,' he cried. 'Switch seats! Quickly!'

Thomas popped from the driver's seat, glanced back at the cops stranded behind them. They looked thunderstruck in a shaft of streetlight. He rushed past Mia in the headlights, rounded the hood, grabbed the door only to have it yanked from his hands. He heard a crunch and squealing tires, then toppled to the pavement. The cops had decided not to wait, had bulldozed the SUV clear. Mia pulled the Toyota to the right. Thomas stood just in time to get knocked onto the cruiser's hood.

Frankie, something inside him cried.

He rolled off the hood as the cruiser braked. He scrambled to his hands and knees, ready to dash off on foot. But there was a thump, the whish of exploding glass, and the cruiser's headlights were replaced by the Toyota's profile.

'Get in! Get in!' Mia was crying. 'Get the *fuck* in!'

Then he was in the passenger seat, his whole body shaking, the whole world flashing past the windshield. Another cruiser screeched into the intersection before them, blocking it. Mia gunned the SUV.

'*Nooooooo*!' Thomas cried.

The impact threw him against the dash, but for some reason it seemed miraculously minor. The Toyota wobbled, then barreled down the street, stable as a spinning pigskin.

'Frankie!' Thomas cried, nearly diving into the back. Frankie had slipped through the belts, fallen onto the floor behind Mia's seat. He was still unconscious, but seemed otherwise unhurt. Thomas sat him upright, did his best to buckle him in. He glanced through the rear window, saw flashing lights through dark, canyon streets.

'Fuck,' Mia was saying, 'they're green-lighting us!'

'What?'

'All the lights in Manhattan are run by AI now. To improve response times they red-light interfering traffic and green-light emergency vehicles. And in situations like ours . . .'

'But that's good, isn't it? It means we won't hurt anybody.'

'But it means we're fucked too. So long as they keep feeding us greens they know exactly where we are, where we're going.'

'What are we going to do?'

'You see a grey leather case back there? You know, Bill's case!'

'Yeah, why?'

'Open it up.'

Thomas fumbled behind his seat, fished out the case. He clicked it open.

'Is his TV in there?'

Thomas pulled the panel out. 'TV?' he asked.

'Birthday present,' Mia snapped. 'Don't ask. Just turn it on.'

Sure enough, he saw a helicopter shot of Manhattan, alternating between dark natural light and the whites and greys of FLIRR – forward-looking infrared radar. '. . . *to recap, then,*' a tinny voice was saying, '*we're following an old model, black Toyota SUV along—*'

'How did you know?'

'Got another bad OJ vibe,' Mia said sourly. 'But this is good. It gives us information.'

'They're setting something up ahead of us!' Thomas shouted. 'Something to take out our tires.'

'Like my papa always said,' Mia cried, ' "Son, ya cain't outroon the frickin' ray-deeooo . . ." ' Without warning, he yanked the Toyota right so hard Thomas nearly rolled onto his lap. ' "Unless ya gawt woon yerself . . ." '

The city was a whirring tunnel, a cylindrical swarm of light and streaking blackness.

'Mia! What the fuck! What are you doing?'

'Is this for keeps?' Mia shouted. 'Are we playing for keeps, Tommy?'

'My son . . . What are you talking about?'

'This is for keeps, right?'

'Yes . . . Yes! But what are—'

'Look. I'm so scared I'm blowing bubbles out my ass, but if this is for keeps, if we really have to do this to save Frankie, then we're going to hafta take some risks.'

'Take some risks? What the hell do you call this?'

'Softball,' Mia muttered, yanking the car hard right once again.

*

Oh my word, a miniature voice chirped.

What do you make of that, Delores?

Well, Jim, things seem to have become more desperate. It was almost as though they sensed the trap the NYPD had set for them. I gotta tell you, though, the fact they're driving an SUV makes me that much more nervous.

And why's that?

Because of the higher center of— Jim? You got the bird's eye view up there? What are they doing now?

I'm not sure, Delores. It looks like they've . . .

Static punctuated by voices in the background.

Jim? Jim? For those of you just joining us, our Fox 5 Newsnet Chopper is covering a dramatic police pursuit through the Upper West Side. Reports say that the two men in the vehicle have abducted, I repeat, abducted, a child patient from—

Delores? Delores?

Yes, Jim, we can hear you.

I just asked Johnny Pharo, our expert chopper pilot, and he agrees that yes, the vehicle has entered the 207th Street Subway Yard.

Why would they do that, Jim?

We're not sure, Delores . . . Perhaps to take advantage of their four-wheel capability.

I see them, Jim. My word, are they on the tracks?

Yes, Delores, it would appear that they're on the tracks. Johnny seems to think—

Put Johnny on for a moment, if you could, Jim. Johnny Pharo, for those of you who are not familiar with our Fox 5 Skyteam, is an expert pilot and a decorated veteran of the Iraq—

Oh my . . . Are you getting this, Delores?

Yes, Jim. What's happened? Did you lose them?

No, Delores. They lost us! It would seem, ladies and gentleman, that they have entered the subway. I repeat, the black Toyota SUV being pursued by New York's finest, has just driven into the subway . . .

They'd barreled down 10th Avenue so fast that the Toyota began shaking from the inside out. Then Mia was yanking them right down some side street, then left, smashing through a parking gate. Thomas cried out as he gunned the 4 × 4 across a lot peppered with parked cars and into what seemed a towering chain-link fence. It fell away like rotten fabric, though for an instant, razor wire looped and thrashed across the hood and windshield. There was an instant of zero gravity, the Harlem horizon dipped out of view, then a deafening thud, and they were bouncing over gravel and weeds, between stacked industrial spools, chattering over tracks, past night-silver subway cars, and Mia jerked them left once again, into a square maw of black cut into a cinder-block wall . . .

The SUV danced like a stub-legged bronco. Pale lights lined the darkness before them, falling away like pearls dropped into the abyss. They were in the subway! Each time they careered into a wall, glass shattered, worlds screamed.

'Mia-Mia-Mia-Mia!' Thomas cried.

'Shut-up-shut-up-shut-up,' he exclaimed. 'I'm trying to think!'

Without warning they passed through a station. It opened like a white-tiled miracle. Thomas glimpsed a handful of astonished faces, gaping in the drab light.

'Did you see it?' Mia exclaimed.

'See what?'

'The fucking station! Did you see which station?'

'No . . .'

'Fuck!' Mia began bouncing up and down in his seat, punching and slapping the steering wheel. 'We're fucked!' he cried. Tears of frustration glittered in his eyes. 'We are well and truly fucked!'

Then Thomas remembered.

'Stop,' he said.

'What?'

'Stop the fucking truck! Stop!'

The Toyota slid sideways. Metal popped and crunched. They were wedged to an instant stop.

'We've bought ourselves a window,' Thomas said, reaching back to unbuckle his son. 'We have to hurry.'

Dumb luck. They left the Toyota a ticking ruin behind them, headlights squashed against looming tunnel walls. They humped over the soot-enameled tracks, then followed a series of closeted service tunnels to a miraculously unlocked door. The next station. Trying not to blink against the antiseptic light, they ambled beneath the security cameras with the other exiting travelers.

They climbed to the mighty surface, New York, then walked with urban purpose.

Breathless, they sheltered in an alley next to some kind of defunct club. Sirens seemed to claw the air from every direction. Mia held Frankie against his chest, rocking him and rubbing his back. He watched Thomas apprehensively. Like him, Thomas imagined he could see *them* – whoever they were – in his mind's eye, running biometric searches using various search criteria, replaying images from all the traffic cameras surrounding the subway exit they took – which they *knew* they took, because of the AI security system installed in the subways three years earlier.

Terrorist counter-measures. They had pinned the world down like a butterfly.

Thomas pulled an ivory business card from his inner pocket, used the phone that Neil had given him.

'Mr Gyges,' he said, shocked to hear his own voice distorted in the ear piece. 'It's me. It's Tho—'

'Don't say a word!' the billionaire snapped. 'Their networks can recognize names, even rudimentary contents, as easily as they can voices. And try to stay calm. They can even detect vocal stress patterns. They'll be scouring everything looking for you. Everything.'

'I-I don't understand.'

'I think you do. You wouldn't be using a modulator otherwise.'

'Listen . . . Mr Gyges, what you said back—'

'I don't need this kind of exposure. Not now.'

His thoughts raced. *Something-something—*

'Then why are you up? Why are you watching the news coverage?'

Silence.

'Look . . . Mr Gyges. I don't know where he is, but I will, very soon—'

'Just tell me where you are,' the gruff voice said. 'I'll send a car.'

Thomas gave him the nearest intersection and a description of the boarded-over bar. 'Please,' Thomas added, 'hurry.'

But the line had already clicked into silence.

He crouched in the darkness, astonished that he would ever find this much comfort in the absence of light. Then he sobbed, thinking of what Sam had said not three days before.

'*There are only martyrs any more . . .*'

'Shhhh,' Mia murmured to his son. 'Shhhh, laddie.' The look he gave Thomas was wide and scared. He knew nothing would be the same after this, Thomas realized. He knew the stakes. 'You trust this asshole?'

'Yes,' Thomas said after a moment. 'In a sense, he's lost more than I have.'

They heard the roar of a wound out six-cylinder. A police cruiser flashed across the mouth of the alleyway, whipping up litter like leaves in its wake.

'I gotta feeling,' Thomas added lamely.

The car arrived several minutes afterward, a black beemer with tinted windows. It coasted to a stop at the mouth of the alley. The driver was East Indian, very smartly dressed. He simply stepped out of the still-running vehicle and began walking.

'I'm driving,' Mia said, hoisting Frankie to hand him over.

'No,' Thomas said. 'Once we get out of the city, I'll drop you off.'

'Are you fucking kidd—'

'I can't afford to spook Neil. You know that.'

Mia nodded, hitched Frankie higher onto his shoulder. They walked to the car together.

Neil was right. It took time to assess and to organize. You could still slip through so long as you didn't hesitate. They used Bill's television to guide them through the police cordon before it could be effectively closed. Then they tossed it out just to be safe. Who knew what the Feds could do?

Perhaps it was the beemer's soundproofing, or simply their post-adrenalin exhaustion, but a deceptive sense of normalcy crept into their drive out of the city. The sky was brightening in the east. Early-morning commuters were beginning to populate the roads. The world suddenly seemed orderly – servile even.

Thomas found himself thinking about coffee, even though he knew that his horror was likely just beginning.

'I hope they pick out a nice one,' Mia murmured at one point, staring out over the dark Hudson.

'Nice what?' Thomas asked.

'Picture. Sooner or later they're going to start flashing pictures of me and my old act.'

Thomas glanced at his Number One Neighbor.

Mia snorted. 'What did you think? That the morning *Post* would read "PSYCHOLOGIST AND *NEIGHBOR* ABDUCT BRAIN-DAMAGED SON"? It'll be "PSYCHOLOGIST AND *CROSS-DRESSER*", trust me.'

'I hadn't even thought about it.'

'I'd bet my pink panty paycheck. Psychologists? Everyone knows you can't trust psychologists. You can't trust anyone who actually *knows* the rules. Once you know them, you can manipulate them. And cross-dressers . . . Well, they're just fucked up to begin with. They can't even dress right, let alone aim at the right hole.'

Thomas stared at the road in the headlights, at the lane-marking lines roping to either side, thinking of that word, 'right.' Humans were judging machines, hardwired to conserve the beliefs and attitudes that were required to keep stone age communities afloat. They condemned so quickly, so regularly, because once it was imperative for their survival. Now, it was little more than psychodrama, yet another set of maladapted reflexes. People like Mia were mocked and ridiculed not for *loving wrong*, but because *someone* had to be mocked and ridiculed.

'It could be a good thing though,' Thomas said after a pause.

'What are you talking about?'

'Not the ridicule. I mean the publicity. So long as we turn *ourselves* in, I'd be surprised if any of this made the courts.' Thomas breathed deep for what seemed the first time in weeks. 'There'll be threats, certainly. But there's a good chance we could simply get away with this.' He smiled, glancing away from the road. 'All thanks to your peculiar choice of evening attire.'

Mia didn't look convinced. 'You don't have family in Alabama,' he said.

The sun was full and low in the east when he dropped Mia off at an Exxon just outside Tarrytown. Everything, the dull-shining pumps, the gum-freckled pavement, possessed the air of cold things warming to the rush of daily life. Cars shot past, roaring as though driving across paste.

'Take care, Tommy,' Mia said, leaning into his window. He glanced at Frankie slumped in the back. 'That goes for him too.'

'I will.' Thomas swallowed at a pang in his throat. 'Remember, lie low for a day or so. Keep away from cameras – anything connected. Then turn yourself in.'

A pensive nod – reluctant even. 'Watch out for that bastard. Remember the Neil you knew is dead.'

Thomas gazed at the man, found himself, in spite of everything, begging with his eyes. 'Tell me this is going to work.'

Mia flinched. For a moment, he managed to smile in reassurance, but his expression faltered, became slack with admission. He looked like someone turned inside out for giving.

'What the fuck do I know, Tommy.'

A numb and breathless nod.

Mia pulled his arms from the door, backed away. 'This is crazy,' he said, his eyes brimming with tears. He pulled a hand through his hair. Though he stood straight and motionless, he looked as though he might be falling. 'Crazy-crazy.'

Thomas clicked the window, watched the tinted glass swallow his Number One Neighbor. He dropped the shift into drive, began pulling away. He didn't notice that Frankie's eyes had popped open.

Not until he began screaming.

CHAPTER SEVENTEEN

August 31st, 8.26 a.m.

All that separated luck from grace, Thomas's grandmother had told him once, was the sincerity of the prayer beforehand.

Car after car slipped past the shining black BMW, weaving between the elephantine eighteen-wheelers. Beautiful coeds, yakking and laughing on their palmtops. Resentful punks with buttoned lips, staring and scoffing at the German engineered lines. Old women, eyes fixed religiously forward, their hands 10 and 2 on the steering wheel. Sleek mothers. Wizened golfers. Cockpit businessmen. All of them propelled by soundless engines, skating the lines of utterly disconnected lives.

All of them oblivious to the leather-padded sarcophagus that whistled in their midst, sucking up scream after scream.

The road was little more than a whisper, the countryside a wobble, the world a brief windshield glare. Thomas Bible reached back to soothe his only son. Little-boy limbs cringed from his adult hand.

'You are mine, you know.'

Screaming, his mouth pulled into a chimpanzee grimace.

'They used me as bait to find Uncle Cass. Do you remember Sam, honey? Daddy's friend?'

Coughing, convulsing.

'Sam was going to sacrifice me.' He swallowed hard. 'When it seemed I might die on the altar, she sacrificed you as well.'

Small, warding hands scraping the leather-backed seats.

'You *are* mine, you know. No matter what Uncle Cass might say.'

Eyes rolling in bovine horror. Screaming.

'Sacrifice,' Thomas wept. 'Sacrifice makes fathers.'

He called Neil when he was supposed to. He always did what he was supposed to. According to Nora, it was one of the reasons she had left him. He was too much a part of the machinery – the fucking machinery.

With the road an abstraction in his periphery, he scrawled down the directions to the new location on a Taco Bell napkin – some place in Connecticut. 'How can I trust you?' he asked the distorted voice.

'It all comes down to guesses, Goodbook,' Neil said. 'The trick is deciding which ones are worth dying for.'

Thomas hung up, glanced at his shrieking son. He looked back to the summer-shining road, stared at the passing promised land, the parallax of asphalt and brick. As always, the horizon held the distances motionless while what was near whipped into the funnel behind him.

Control was long gone. All he had was a weeping litany: 'Frankie-shh-shh-please-Frankie-shh-shh-please.'

Empty words. Pathetic words. Words that could only wheeze and grovel before his son's terrible scream, before the most ancient prayer of all. The first great transmission.

Everything. Everything was stuck on absolute transmit. The mountains. The oceans. Even the stars. Nothing listened. Nothing. The skulls of a million lambs cracked in the jaws of a million lions. A billion human screams, and each one unheard. Nothing more than a flicker in the abyss. Even less . . .

No consequences outside the inevitable. No point to yank short the knife's never-ending edge.

Only children died–Thomas understood that now. Small. Helpless. Uncomprehending.

Everyone was an infant in the end.

It seemed almost normal. An old, upstate friend, waving from the porch. A summer wind whisking through the trees. A child who had to be lifted from the back seat.

Whatever voice Frankie possessed, he had screamed away a long time ago. Now he simply rasped and twitched the way a dying addict might. Only rolling eyes and an old-man grimace spoke to the horror that cycled through his soul.

This could not be his son.

This could not be.

Thomas climbed the cement steps, looked up across the white, colonial facade, squinted at the sparking sun. He blinked at Neil, his thoughts beyond hope or hate.

Buff smile. Pained eyes.

Neil pressed open the door so that he could carry Frankie into the polished gloom. Thomas felt a reassuring hand fall on his shoulder as he passed. There was a faint prick against the nape of his neck. Thomas turned, too exhausted to be alarmed, let alone startled. He simply looked at the monster who was his best friend. His knees cracked like wax. Frankie slid from his arms. Everything swayed, dust bunnies dancing about a vast existential broom.

'Ah, Goodbook,' the shadow said. 'You should know by now. No matter what the rule . . .'

The world collapsed into milk and watercolor.

'*I go sideways.*'

'The central nervous system of homo sapiens,' Neil was saying (though just when he had *started* saying this Thomas couldn't recall), 'isn't like the heart or the stomach. It isn't a distinct organ with discrete functions. So much of our brains' structure is determined by *other* brains. In a certain sense, there's only *one* brain, Goodbook, sprawled across the face of the planet, busily rewiring itself into a key that will unlock the universe. One central nervous system with eight billion synapses.'

Thomas was bolted to some kind of apparatus, almost upright. Something held his head immobile – profoundly immobile. There was no play of skin or hair against restraints. It was as though his skull had been screwed or welded into a building's architecture. Looking up, he could see some kind of metallic rim beyond his brow, but nothing more. The room before him was spare and spacious: cinder-block walls painted white, an unfinished ceiling above glaring florescent lights. From the surrounding angles he could tell he occupied the centre of the room, but he could see nothing behind him. Cases had been stacked in a corner to his right, next to a fat-wheeled dolly. Two tables filled the space immediately before him, crowded with flat-screens, keyboards, and several devices he could not recognize. Wearing sandals and shorts, Neil had turned to hunch over an open case. Tubes glinted from dark foam slots.

Neil walked up to him, holding a syringe upright in a latex-sheathed hand. 'And right now, my friend, you and I are the only synapse that matters.' He leaned forward and Thomas felt a brittle prick in his jugular. Neil rubbed the spot with a cottonball. He winked. 'A little something to quicken your recovery from the anesthetic.'

'Frankie . . .' Thomas croaked. It seemed the only language he knew.

The handsome face darkened. 'There's been a small change in plan, Goodbook.'

'*Frankie*!' Thomas screamed. He began spitting and straining against the vice that held him.

Neil's look silenced him. It was something without limbs or prehensile appendages, something belonging to a snake soul, as unreachable as a grinning Nazi commandant or a glaring Hutu machete-man.

'There's no need to worry.'

'Wuh-worry?' Thomas cried, tears spilling from his eyes. 'What-the-fuck-do—'

Neil turned to a keyboard on the nearby table, began tapping keys. Thomas heard the hum of something overhead, like a printer standing by.

'You son of a bitch!' Thomas raved. 'You fucking *cunt*! I'll kill you! Kill yo–!'

But he paused, first in confusion, then in dawning realization. Neil was right. There was no need to worry. He breathed deeply and smiled. How could he be such an ass?

'Better?' Neil asked.

'Yes,' Thomas said, grinning. 'Much better. What did you do?'

'Not much. So you're not worried about Frankie?'

'Fuck him. He'll be fine.'

Neil shook his head. 'No, Goodbook, I'm afraid he won't.'

'No?'

'No. Actually he's dead.'

Thomas laughed. 'No kidding?'

'No kidding. There's only one procedure that can undo an affect feedback loop – at least the devilish way Mackenzie does it.'

'What's that?'

'A bullet to the head.'

Thomas snorted with genuine laughter. Intellectually, he knew it shouldn't be funny, but it *was* . . . And it seemed the most natural thing in the world that it should be. 'You always were crazy.'

Frankie. Poor little kid. He was going to miss the little bugger . . .

'So all this,' Neil asked curiously, 'seems normal to you?'

Thomas tried to shrug. 'Well, I suppose to an outsider it would *seem* strange, but it really is quite normal when you think about it.'

'How so?'

Thomas flashed him a bright *Are-you-stupid?* smile. 'We're long-time friends. We always play gags on each other. Though I suppose we're getting a little too old for this.'

Neil scratched behind his ear with a pen. 'But at some level you *know* what's happening, don't you? You know that I'm stimulating the neural circuits responsible for your feeling of normalcy and ambient wellbeing.'

Thomas frowned, happy and perplexed. 'What can I say? You always were elaborate.'

Neil shook his head the bemused way he always did whenever his cynicism was confirmed. 'This,' he said, wagging an I-told-you-so finger. 'This is the part that sold me, that made me *realize*.'

'You've lost me, Neil.'

'The confabulations. I mean, think about it, Goodbook, *I just shot your son in the head*, and you genuinely believe everything is right as rai—'

'C'mon,' Thomas interrupted, trying to shake his head. 'You're over-analyzing again. I-know-I-know, listen to the neurotic psychologist talking about over-analysis, but sometimes it really is just that simple. Sometimes you just gotta—'

'It was the same with the first terrorists I tweaked in this way,' Neil continued. 'You know I actually spent two days arguing with one, trying to get him to see how dire his situation was? Two fucking days! It was like the guy only had two buttons, shuffle and repeat. Did you know the brain has an entire module dedicated to the production of verbal rationalizations?'

'Yeah-yeah,' Thomas said, realizing how much he missed shooting the cerebral breeze with Neil. 'Yeah, Mackenzie babbled about that for a bit.'

An appraising look. 'Well, trust me, if you want to get a sense of just how much consciousness – *life* – is simply a mechanistic output, try going toe-to-toe with a rationalization module. I could literally spend the rest of my life arguing with you, and you would just come up with reason after reason why me shooting Frankie in the head is the most normal, sensible thing in the world.'

What was he talking about? Life was filled with contingencies – demands – that no one had any control over. Even the craziest shit in the world could be reasonable, given the right circumstances. 'Look,' Thomas said, 'I understand how it looks. But Neil, you of all people know that there's always more than what meets the eye.' Even as he said this, Thomas realized it was for naught. Neil was watching him with inward eyes, the look he always had when he was busy thinking about what to say next rather than listening. 'There's always more! Neil. Neil! That's all I'm saying. *Look deeper.*'

Neil waited with mock politeness, as though wanting to make sure it was safe to continue. 'Would you believe it was dinner at my parents' that finally let me put it all together?' he said. 'You know my Pop, always railing on about this and that, never letting you get a word in edgewise, and never, *never* acknowledging that he could be wrong. I was just sitting there – Mom had cooked a turkey – and I suddenly realized that his rationalization module was on overdrive, that the only real difference between him and my subjects was that he'd been *accidentally* wired. I realized he was just another machine. And Mom too, clucking about how she didn't baste the bird enough. I sat there watching them cycle through their behavioral routines. Can you imagine, seeing your *mom* as a machine?'

Thomas cackled. 'C'mon, Neil. Listen to yourself! Your mom is *not* a machine. She's too fucking nutty!'

But Neil wasn't listening. 'I'd reached some kind of threshold, I think, working for the NSA. It had been happening for a while: I would just notice certain behaviors, and think to myself, their caudate nucleus is lighting up, feeding information forward to the prefrontal cortex, yadda-yadda. But after that turkey dinner, I began understanding *everything* others did in those terms . . .'

His look drifted inward.

'That was when I reread your book.'

Thomas snorted, though the absence of the accompanying head

and hand movement made it sound odd. 'Now you're really scraping the bottom, don't you think?'

Neil's smile was at once skeptical and genuine. He turned back to the nearest table, lifted a beaten hardcover from a sheaf of papers. Thomas glimpsed *Through the Brain Darkly* embossed in gold across its black fabric spine. Neil opened it to one of several orange sticky notes that drooped like tongues from the closed pages. Holding it out and up like a preacher, he read, ' "If we know anything, we know this: the regions of the brain implicated in consciousness can only access a minute fraction of the information processed by the brain as a whole. Conscious experience is not simply the product of the brain, it is the product of a brain *that can only see the merest sliver of itself.*" ' He looked up, eyebrows raised. 'So you no longer agree with that?'

Another unsuccessful attempt at a shrug. 'Facts are facts. Look, Neil—'

But he had continued reading.

' "The magician's magic depends on the audience remaining oblivious to her manipulations. As soon as we look over her shoulder, the magic vanishes. Consciousness is no different. Oblivious to the manipulations that make it possible, experience makes do with what can only be called illusions. Consciousness is always 'now' because the neural correlates of consciousness, though quite adept at processing time, cannot process the time of this processing. Consciousness is always unitary because the neural correlates of consciousness, though quite adept at differentiating environmental features, cannot differentiate their own processes. Again and again, the fundamental features of experience only make sense when we construe them as the result of various *incapacities* . . ." '

Neil closed the book, recited the rest from memory. ' "And this is why consciousness disappears whenever we dare look over the brain's shoulder. We are little more than walking, talking coin tricks." '

A silent moment passed between them, filled only by the drone of some fan buried in the machinery above Thomas's head. The smell of ozone and cooking rubber soaked the air.

'Um,' Thomas eventually said, 'is there any way I could get a beer?' Games were games, sure, but he was getting fucking thirsty.

'That,' Neil said, obviously referring to the passage, 'was the kicker. It was easy enough to see other people for what they were – even Mom and Pop. But how could I do the same with myself? I mean, *look at you,* trying to cajole the man who murdered your son into having a beer – and thinking it as natural as natural can be! Ultimately, I'm no different. I'm just as much a mechanism as you, just as much the output of processes over which I have no control. And back then I was just as apt to be deluded, to be certain that I *knew* otherwise, that if I were plugged in the way you were, things would somehow be different, that some spark or some residue of spirit would light up and allow me to transcend my neurology . . .'

Neil raised the book, shook it so that it wobbled in his hand. 'It just couldn't be. And yet, *there it was . . .*'

Thomas stared at him skeptically, even as he marveled at how good it felt to be hanging out and debating again. 'Am I actually allowed to talk now?' he said smiling. 'Are you ready to yield the podium?'

Neil shot him one of his famous squinting scowls. 'By all means.'

A sudden itch afflicted Thomas's nose, reminding him of the restraints. But he knew the routine with Neil and his gags: so long as you ignored whatever it was, Neil would eventually relent out of boredom. That was why asking for a beer had been a mistake. 'So you're saying,' he began slowly, 'that all this craziness, the abductions and the mutilations and the recordings, *is about my book*?'

'The Argument is *yours*, Goodbook. You always were better at the theory.'

'And you're just a practical man, right?'

Neil shrugged. 'I prefer working with my hands.'

Thomas laughed, though the shaking jarred his skull. 'So riddle me this: how could you be interested in my argument, any argument, if you think *reasons* are illusory?'

Neil grinned and shook his head. 'You can do better than that. Reasons may be deceptions, the result of a brain stuck at the tail end of its own problem-solving, but they're still *functional* – as you might expect, given that they're a product of the real deal. While you and I argue, experience the world of meaning and justification, our brains are simply producing and responding to various auditory inputs and outputs, literally rewiring themselves in response to each other and their environments. *That's* where the real action is. The projector, as opposed to the screen. That's why we stare at an interpretative abyss whenever we try to use reasons to get behind reasons, while we find it quite simple to dismantle the machinery that makes it possible.

That's why philosophy is bullshit, while science has transformed the world.'

Thomas chuckled. Were it not for the restraints, he would have held his hands out in surrender; instead he simply said, 'Ouch.' Neil had simply paraphrased his own response in *Through the Brain Darkly*. 'What page is that from again?'

'Three eighty-two, actually.'

'You *memorized* the fucking thing?'

Inexplicably, Neil frowned and reached into his pocket, withdrew a small black remote. Click.

Suddenly all was misery and agony, as if each of Thomas's innumerable pores gave birth to white-hot pins. Something mewled and screamed, bucked against iron restraints. Somewhere, something defecated.

Click. Then he was happy again.

Neil smiled. 'Try to avoid changing the topic,' he said.

Through a fog of good humor, Thomas could feel his body shivering, as though about frozen bones. 'Sure thing . . . Where were we?'

'I was explaining how the brain simply isn't equipped to keep track of itself, how it lacks the processing power, the evolutionary pedigree, so that even though it's remarkably proficient at modeling its external environments, the best it can do is scribble cartoons of itself.'

'Ah yes,' Thomas said. 'You mean the mind.'

'Exactly. The cartoon extraordinaire.'

'But it doesn't seem that way.'

'Of course not. It *has* to seem as deep as deep, as wide as wide, as sharp as sharp, simply because "deep", "wide",' and "sharp" are part of the cartoon. We can't step out of our minds and take a walk around them, like we can the brain.'

'Which is *why*,' Thomas cried with what he could only describe as drunken good humor, 'you'll never convince anyone that you're anything but crazy!'

'Who said anything about convincing anybody?'

'But then why do any of this?'

'Why?' Neil repeated. Once again, he began thumbing through Thomas's book. ' "Our brains," ' he read aloud, ' "are able to track their own prospective behavioral outputs, but are entirely blind to the deep processing that drives them. Rather than doing things because of this or that feed forward mechanism, we do them 'for reasons', which is to say, for desired outcomes. Causality is turned on its head for consciousness. Results and consequences – goals – become the engine of our actions because the neural correlates of consciousness have no access to the real neurophysiological movers and shakers down below." '

He popped the pages shut as though snapping at a fly. Thomas flinched. 'Purpose?' Neil said. 'Point? These things are ghosts, Goodbook, hardwired hallucinations. They only seem real because we're riding the neural horse backward.'

Thomas snorted, equally amused and unimpressed. 'So then what's your *illusory* point? What does the cartoon called Neil think it's doing?'

These words seemed to catch Neil by surprise. For a heartbeat, he stared at Thomas with almost lunatic intensity. 'Neil,' he repeated, as though his name were some absurd Chinese expression. 'That cartoon no longer exists.'

Thomas would have shaken his head if he could. 'Then what does exist?'

'I've disconnected certain performance-inhibiting circuits,' Neil said with what seemed to be reluctance. 'What you folk-psychologists call anxiety, fear; all that bullshit. They're little more than memories to me now. But I've also shut down some of the more deceptive circuits as well. I now know, for instance, that I *will* utterly nothing. I'm no longer fooled into thinking that "I" do anything at all.'

Thomas could only stare at his friend in wonder. Where did he find the *balls* to do the things he did?

'And I've gone deeper,' Neil continued. 'So much deeper.'

Pause.

'You see through the cartoon,' Thomas said. The words tingled on his tongue.

Neil nodded, as though at some inevitability only he could fathom. 'Only partially. I still experience things, after all. It's just a radically different experience, one far more sensitive to the fragmentary truth of our souls. One without volition, purpose, selfhood, right or wrong.'

Thomas frowned and whistled. Part of him understood the monstrous implications of what Neil was saying, but it seemed little more than an amusing abstraction, like boys with sticks playing guns. The greater part of him wondered, even *revered.* What would it be like to walk without self or conscience, with plans indistinguishable from compulsions, one more accident in the mindless wreck that was the world? What would it be like to act, not as something as puny or wretched as a person, but as a selfless vehicle, a conduit for everything that came before?

'Fucking wild, Neil. Too fucking wild.'

Neil's grin was genuine and contagious – one brain communing with another through the ancient choreography of facial cues. Looking at him, Thomas thought of the intervening years, the fine chiseling about his eyes and dimples, the painstaking brushwork of his salting hair. And it seemed to Thomas that he always knew this moment would come, from their first meeting in their dorm room. From Neil's first sly and appraising smile.

It was so good to see him!

'I'm the world's first neuronaut, Goodbook. And you're about to join me.'

Neil bent over the keyboard, peered into a computer screen. 'As much as I'd like to keep you in a happy place,' he was saying, 'some things have to be done the old-fashioned way.' An affable glance. 'Especially if you want them to *stick.*'

Clickety-click-click-tap-*tap* . . .

Thomas's ebullient mood slowly faded away. Then the dread came, slowly, oddly, as though some inner, oxygen-starved limb were prickling back to life. What was happening? What was going on? The memories of moments ago suddenly seemed impossible, like a graft from some more innocent chapter of his life. But they were real: the thoughts, the feelings, all of them as real as real could be. The words . . .

Frankie! Frankie? No-no-please-dear—

'Neil!' he cried.

'Shhhh,' his old roommate said. 'It's totally natural that your brain's in high alert. All it has are its evolutionary defaults, and lord knows the environmental stressors have been piled high—'

'You didn't!' Thomas cried.

'Right now it's cycling through million-year-old circuits, producing various failsafe behavioral outputs. Grief. Panic. Christ, it wasn't designed to recognize itself for what it is, so how could it possibly recognize its own potential? As far as it's concerned, this is nothing but a stone-age confrontation.'

'Tell me you didn't *kill my boy*!'

Neil pinched his brows in a friendly frown. 'There you go. A perfect example of those defaults in action. The brain generates bonding outputs, or "parental concern", because those outputs once assured the replication of its genetic material. We're just stinky Xerox machines in the end, Goodbook. Only we use spunk and love instead of ink and paper.'

'Where is he? Tell me where he is! Neil! *Neil*!'

Shrug, followed by a drowsy smile. 'These are just facts, Goodbook. If you want to embarrass yourself arguing against them, be my guest.'

Though Neil had him clamped face-forward, though he could see nothing beyond the oblivion of his periphery, in his mind's eye he could see Frankie splayed across the basement floor, his eyes dark, his tongue dry, his face grey against the crimson pool. Like Gerard. Like Sam.

'Jesus, Neil! Oh my God! *What have you done*?'

Neil glanced back at his flat-screen. 'Your brain's fight or flight systems are in full arousal. It's testing the restraints now, realizing the futility of physical behavioral outputs. Now the frontal cortex is processing hypothetical alternatives, doing its best to inhibit and cope with signals it's receiving from its more primitive limbic cousins below. Now it's starting to realize that linguistic behavioral outputs are its—'

Thomas gagged in panic. He needed to think – think! There had to be some way – some way to reach him!

'Neil,' Thomas said, trying to squeeze the terror from his voice. 'Just take a step back, buddy. Just ask yourself *what you're doing*.'

'But I already told you, Goodbook. I'm just along for the ride, same as you. The only difference is that I know which way the horse is pointed.'

'Neil! This is my *family*! My family! This is Frankie we're talking about!'

But the madman had turned back to the bright, computer-screen schematic. 'Now if I dampen the linguistic circuits, your brain should return to its most basic failsafe output . . .'

Tap-click-click . . .

Suddenly talking didn't matter. Crying out, Thomas threw himself at the restraints again and again. He wheezed, blew spittle through clenched teeth.

'Physical struggle,' Neil said.

It was like trying to lift the floor. It was like warring against his own bones. The grip was seamless, as though he had been fused to the world's implacable frame, as though the meat of him had been wrapped around mountains.

Neil drawled on. 'Now it's registering the futility of its efforts, beginning to form what you psychologists call negative generalizations.'

An inarticulate roar. He was trapped – trapped! It was hopeless. Frankie! Frankie! Dear sweet Jesus, what was he going to do?

Desolation yawned, swallowed him entire. He let go. He simply hung, like clothing stapled to the wall, sobbing.

Frankie's dead.

His boy, smiling, clean, and safe. The horrible Scottish accent. The obsession with everything 'sooper'. The dog hair on tiny T-shirts. The band-aids pressed across the carpet in front of the TV. The wide-wondering eyes. The farts on Ripley's pillow. The words, *I love you, Daddy*, pinned to a million different expressions, a thousand different events. *I love you, Daddy*, scribbled in clumsy crayon, declared through a hundred skinned-knee sobs. The one sure thing . . .

Gone.

'And there we have it,' Neil said, his face graphed by the cross-sectioned brain on the screen before him. 'The neural fingerprint of learned helplessness.'

Through the roaring, watery blur, Thomas saw the monster turn and smile.

'Beautiful,' it said with his best friend's voice. 'Textbook.'

My little boy.

For a time Thomas simply breathed, leaned against his absolute immobility. Everything seemed distorted, as though viewed through a fisheye lens. Neil flicking through handwritten notes, scratching the corner of his eye with the butt of his pen. The luminous brain on the computer screens, slowly revolving beneath windows of text. The overhead florescent lights, casting haloes over the dark slots between ceiling joists.

A kind of claustrophobia gradually overcame him. It was more than the simple fact of his paralysis, more than the suffocation of hope or movement. Neil had nailed him to a single, myopic perspective, and for some reason, it rendered the ring of nothingness that encircled his visual field *palpable.* Ordinarily he need only twitch his head and it would be shattered – what was peripheral would become focal, and the world would be better known. But now it seemed as though he carried the void itself on his shoulders, that a great disc of blackness leaned against him like a slaver's yoke, choking him with insinuation and implication.

What kind of horrors had Neil draped around him?

This was how it happened, Thomas realized, for real and not in the movies.

Fathers failed.

Monsters won.

Quite without curiosity, he watched this realization soak the computer graphic of his brain with various colors, cream to scarlet.

When he finally spoke, it seemed he did so from a coma. 'So what is it?' he rasped. His ensuing cough rattled the bolts screwed into his skull. 'You have me strapped into some kind of transcranial magnetic stimulator?' TMS devices, as they were called, had been in common use since the 1990s, employing magnetic fields to alter neuronal activity at targeted points in the brain. They were common as dirt at most neuroscientific research centres.

'No-no,' Neil said without looking away from his screens. His fingers clicked across the keyboard. 'TMS can't reach nearly deep enough.'

'So what is it?'

Neil turned without looking at him, walked up, and began tinkering with something just outside his periphery. Thomas tensed, felt his eyes roll like a horse's.

'It's a Homeland Security special,' Neil said, like a dentist talking to keep his patient preoccupied, 'called Marionette. We adapted her from stereotactic neuroradiosurgical devices – you know, the ones that use overlapping particle beams to burn out tumors? We found a way of doping the blood so that we could exercise pinpoint metabolic control at multiple points in the brain . . .' Thomas heard the tinkle of a small wrench. 'We call her Mary.'

'Doesn't ring a bell,' Thomas said, more out of hatred than humor.

Neil's laugh tickled his neck below his left ear.

'Oh, she will soon enough,' he said, standing upright, then ducking out of his periphery. Thomas rolled his eyes, trying to follow him, but the fringe of blindness was absolute. Neil's next words, 'Trust me,' seemed to fall out of nowhere.

Thomas could hear him root through what sounded like a toolbox behind him. Suddenly he reappeared, glanced at him on his way back to the computer terminal. 'I actually have several screen savers,' Neil said, sitting. 'Would you like to see?'

'Screen savers?'

Grinning at the flat-panel, Neil tapped something out on his keyboard. Light gleamed along the curve of his teeth. 'That's what we call them. They're programs that play on the neural circuitry responsible for consciousness.' He swiveled toward Thomas. His chair whistled. 'It's the final frontier of art, actually. The most fundamental canvas of all.'

'Canvas?' Thomas asked dully.

Remember . . . he murdered your son . . .

'Existence,' Neil said. 'Existence itself.'

He turned back to his keyboard and screen. 'You know how we used to always debate SETI back at Princeton, the question why, despite decades of searching the skies, we haven't been able to detect any ET version of *I Love Lucy*. After this, it becomes pretty clear why.'

'I don't under–unngh!'

His groin exploded in pleasure, tidal and blistering. He gasped, stared at Neil in drooling panic. Orgasms passed through him in sequential waves, clenching his anus like a fist, shuddering through the rebar of his body, slathering him with bliss. It was as though something divine and electric lunged about his cock.

'This one's my favorite,' Neil said, laughing. 'Blow your load right away, so the symphony that follows unwinds in a drowsy post-coital haze . . .'

Suddenly the pleasure was gone. The silence crackled. He gasped. Even though his skull remained bolted to Marionette, he could feel himself floating in and out of his body, as if he had become a flag hanging in a humid breeze. He tried to clutch. He tried to hold on. But he had become insubstantial.

'Of course,' Neil was saying, 'the obligatory oscillating OBE – out of body experience – followed by a slow, crawling absence in your visual field.'

Parts of the scene began to . . implode before him, as through his visual field were a thing of rubber, being sucked through holes into a greater vacuum behind. The absences scrawled in wandering lines, at one point collapsing Neil's head into jaws and hair. And it looked as real as real . . .

'Pardon the descriptive monologue,' Neil was saying as first his torso then his leg vanished, 'but the next sequence requires someone talking—'

'—because,' Thomas said, 'it mucks with the neural circuits that distinguish the origin of voices.' What was Neil doing? Fucking *lip-synching*? 'I imagine that right about now,' Thomas added, 'you're wondering why I'm mouthing your words. The thing that freaks most people out is that it really seems *they're* the ones talking, that they're deciding to say what, in fact, someone else is saying.'

Neil's lips stopped moving, and Thomas assumed that he'd given up his stupid mockery – why bother, when he had degraded him in so many more profound ways? But when Thomas found himself adding, 'You should brace yourself for this next sequence; it's pretty intense,' Neil mouthed the identical words once again.

Then all was free-fall, a crazed vertigo of being . . . the room soared, yawed and pitched, even though it remained sun-stationary.

'I call this Dante's Bungee,' Neil said, glancing from Thomas to the screen again.

Something chainsawed into his chest, while something else tongued his cock with lightning. Rage overcame him, only to be swamped by love, by the tender melancholy of awakening before a lover in early light. He wept, and he howled in fury and joy. Never had he so loved. Never had he so hated. Never had he so yearned, as though a chasm had cracked open within him, an endless clutching abyss, suddenly filled with divinity, with a resounding, weeping unity, pinged by twinges of anxiety that grew like bloodstains, that blackened into a thrumming dread, with claws like capillaries, peeling muscle from the inside of skin, while the world before him flapped back and forth like wings on an interdimensional hinge, dragging the world that was his right into the world that was his left.

'This sequence,' he could hear Neil saying, 'fucks with the construction of extrapersonal space. Some funky shit.'

Place crumpled and bloomed. Hollows collapsed into solids. Movement collapsed into stuttering instants, as though his heartbeat had become the very strobe of being. He could recognize everything about him – the man, the table, the chair – but he could see none of it, only movements, devoid of substance, whirring in the corners like quantum clockwork.

And he ached with reptilian wrath, with mammalian tenderness . . . Expect-yearn-hope-pray. Memories, pulsing like glands, fading, fading . . . Somehow he forgot how to breathe.

Then nothing.

No feeling. No sensation. Just a trembling, a teetering blacker than black.

Death.

Bursting into pounding groins and howling fear-fuck-love-fuck-hate-fuck-horror-joy-jealousy-rage. Canines bared. A million women and a million rapes. Claw-kill-you-fucking-cunt-pussy-cunt-I-will-fucking-kill-kill-kill-kill! Aggression. Aggression.

Then a spinning head. The sound of Neil chuckling. The creak of his chair.

'I don't believe in happy endings,' he said.

Thomas cried out, unable to think, to sort . . .

'Mary give you a good ride?'

Resentment, fear, and indignation.

'You prick,' Thomas gasped. 'You fucking bastard.' He blinked the tears from his eyes, wondered why his mouth seemed so disconnected from his voice. 'Somehow,' he managed. 'Somehow I'm going to kill you, you fucking bastard.'

Again . . . Neil was lip-synching again.

Hollow and heavy, as though resuscitated from a drowning.

'We call endings like that "blurs",' Neil said. 'Little reminders that Mary simply does what the brain does anyway, just minus all the environmental red tape. Since the feeling of being compelled is as much a product of your brain as anything else, you only feel compelled when Mary tickles it. Mackenzie cooked up these little "will inversion" algorithms – I'd show you if you weren't in restraints. They're creepy. You think you're willing your right arm to move, and your left arm starts waving instead. All sorts of little mindfucks like that. One of his screen savers even has a short omnipotence sequence. No matter what you're looking at, you're convinced that you're *willing* it to happen. Even if it's thunderclouds rolling in on the horizon. It's quite a trip, believe me.'

Neil laughed, looked appreciatively to the largely invisible apparatus that held Thomas. 'You can see why we used to call her Mary, Mother of God.'

Thomas tried to speak, but could not.

'Some things are untouchable, though, just as you predicted in *Through the Brain.* The experiences are always unitary, and they're always now, as you would expect, given that they're the by-products of what the brain lacks.'

Thomas tried to speak again, but could only cough.

Neil smiled. 'Nothing to worry about. Just a little neurotransmitter backwash. You might feel dopey for a couple of days, but nothing more.'

'Ah . . .' Thomas rasped. 'Ah-ah . . .' He breathed deep, shuddered, and tried again. 'Ah . . . *bomination* . . .'

'Yesss,' Neil drawled. 'The future.'

His body buzzing, boneless and immobile. Neil humming some tuneless song, swinging his chair between computers.

C'mon, Goodbook. Get a handle . . . Think clear . . .

Think straight.

Frankie was dead. As hard as that thought clenched his chest, Thomas knew he had to seal it away, concentrate on the *now.* Neil was mad. In-fucking-sane. That meant his priorities were all his own, that his thought processes possessed their own alien logic. If he was going to survive, Thomas knew, he would have to figure out what that logic was. Everyone was predictable, in the end. Even lunatics followed rules.

'You—' he started, only to be interrupted by a fit of coughing. He could feel Mary's screws bracing his skull. He cleared his throat, blinked tears from his eyes.

Frankie . . . The little king, pronouncing his love through a mouthful of Cheerios.

'*I have powers, Daddy . . .* soooper *powers. If there was a truck, and it was going to run you over, I would save you, Daddy. I would punch that truck and BOOM!*'

Thomas glared at Neil's back. 'So what do you gain, huh, Neil? What does your brain win?'

Neil spun about in his chair. 'You're supposing the world can be divided into winners and losers.'

'A game without winners or losers is theatre,' Thomas said in a tone void of all spirit. 'You know that.'

'Game?' Neil chortled. 'Dude, there's no one keeping score.'

Thomas leaned against the screws that bound him. 'We are, Neil. I am.'

His best friend's face became blank with something resembling pity.

'Like I said. No one.'

At that instant, Thomas suffered a kind of power outage of the heart. He felt like a dead man breathing.

He murdered my son . . . His son . . .

'You,' Neil continued, his voice thinned by an implacable sincerity. 'You're the illusion. Think about it, Goodbook. You want to believe I'm doing things *to* you, when in fact I'm doing things *with* you. The only reason I can play your thoughts and experiences like a sock puppet is because *that's what you are.* I'm just slipping my hand over the world's knuckles.'

Neil had turned away to enter yet more cryptic command strings into the keyboard. 'You *want* to think,' he was saying, 'that I'm some kind of invader, that ordinarily *you* occupy the control room. But you know better. The control room's empty; it always has been. Since it lies outside the information horizon of your thalamocortical system, it simply doesn't exist for your consciousness, which is why your thalamocortical system thinks itself an unmoved mover, the floating origin of all your actions.'

And these seemed the most heartbreaking words of all. It was the Blind Brain Hypothesis, his own argument from *Through the Brain Darkly,* not simply paraphrased, but *enacted.* Neil had transformed him into the demonstration of his own outrageous claim. All of it, everything from meaning to self to morality, illusory artifacts of a brain duped by its inability to see itself as a brain. Even *these* thoughts . . . Even this very moment!

He was nothing more than a fragment of something vast and terrible with complexity – something dead. A fragment that could not but see itself as a whole. A ruin that styled itself a little god.

No-no-no-no-no . . .

He couldn't be right. No. No. Not in this!

'Why are you doing this? Neil! Neil! It's *meeeeee.* It's fucking *Tommy*! Why are you doing this to me? What did I do?'

A vice clamped his throat. Something animal sobbed and snuffled from his chest.

'Shhhh,' Neil said. 'Easy there, Goodbook. C'mon. Look at me now. No crying. *Look* at me.'

Thomas raised his bleary eyes.

'This isn't punishment. This isn't the expression of some pathological hate or repressed sexual desire. This is *love*, Thomas. True love – love that knows it's an illusion. I can plug myself into the low-field if you want to see. This brain loves you, that's why it's gone to all this trouble. I think it thinks your brain is its brother, its only brother. I think it's trying to set your brain free.'

'But Frankeeee,' Thomas keened in a low murmur.

Frankie . . .

'Come,' Neil said. 'It's time you understood why I sent you for Frankie.'

A moment of heart-stopping hate.

Neil disappeared behind him. 'You see, I needed time,' he said from the blackness. 'You caught me before I had everything in place.' There was a snap – the release of some kind of mechanism shivered through the apparatus. There was a high-pitched squeal, and Thomas watched the room spin about his axis. Neil had turned him some 30 degrees to the right . . .

. . . so that he could see her laying unconscious on an upright bench like his own.

Nora.

He began shaking uncontrollably.

'No,' Thomas said, but what he heard was little more than an inarticulate gurgle.

She was dressed in her cougar best: a silky red tank-top and white 'pubic plunge' shorts that were all the rage among college girls. Like him, she was strapped to what looked like a stainless-steel mortuary table spot-welded to a revolving base. A device resembling an upside-down toilet finned with exposed circuit boards hunched over her, obscuring part of her scalp. A cage set with thumbscrews rimmed its nethers, fixing Nora's skull in place. Little lights glared like gargoyle eyes.

Another Marionette.

'She's quite all right,' Neil said, opening her eyes and checking her pupil dilation with a pen light.

'Y-you said,' Thomas managed to exclaim. 'B-but you said! Tha-that this wasn't puh-puh-punishment!'

Neil frowned. 'I told you already. Our brains are social. They wire themselves in response to the brains around them. Why do you think divorce or bereavement is so disorienting, so painful? Our brains form networks. What do you think happened to us at Princeton? Why do you think it took me so long to see my way past the illusions? It was *you*, Goodbook. My love for you. Despite all my work, despite Professor Skeat and your book, despite everything, my brain simply couldn't accept that my love for you was meaningless – not for the longest time, anyway. The evolutionary defaults governing loyalty and solidarity, the cooperative bonds that allowed our stone-age ancestors to survive, were too strong.'

'What the fuck?' Thomas cried. 'What the fuck does that have to do with anything?'

'Well, that's why I started sleeping with her, for one. I knew that as strong as those evolutionary defaults were, the ones governing sex were even stronger. All my brain needed was an excuse. I seduced her, knowing that afterward, the defaults governing rationalization would take over. I literally played various modules of my brain against one another. Its hardwired tendencies toward infidelity and self-justifying rationalization against its hardwired tendency toward loyalty . . . It wasn't much of a fight, I'm afraid.'

Thomas's thoughts raced. *Something. Something. I have to think of something—*

Neil smiled the way he always did whenever he caught himself in an inaccuracy. 'Of course, it wasn't "me" doing any of this. I was little more than along for the ride. In point of fact, my brain overcame itself.'

'And my brain can too, Neil. *Neil!* You don't need all this elaborate hocus pocus. Look, let her go, shut the theatre down, and let's you and I get down to business.'

'Nice try,' Neil replied with a chuckle. 'You need to be decoupled, Goodbook. The others – Powski, Halasz, Forrest and Gyges – they were meant to get your brain processing the Argument again, to reacquaint you in the most urgent and intimate way with the force of your own logic. I had to let you steep, like a cup of fucking tea.'

'No,' Thomas murmured, thinking of the gallery of obscenities he had witnessed, of all the arguments he had made *for* the Argument in between. Neil had known he would do this, that he, like most everyone else, would be seduced by the sound of his own voice. 'Never!'

Neil crinkled his nose, as though smelling a bad joke. 'C'mon, Goodbook. I'm tracking your cortical processes as we speak. You know the score: MRIs tell no lies, my friend.'

If he could have hung his head, Thomas would have. Even the posture of defeat was denied him.

Neil grinned with canine pity. 'Your brain needs to process the actual loss of its network, it needs to *see it crash*. Only then will it be able to accept, to see through the cartoon mind it confuses for itself.' He squinted as though in sorrow. 'You're just too attached to your imaginary family.'

Family? The thought almost punched vomit from his stomach.

Ripper.

'It was easy enough to lure Nora up here,' the madman continued. 'I left an old cell in her junk drawer a couple of weeks back, something I knew the Feds would overlook. Called her. As you can see, she entertained some notion of seducing me – for Frankie's sake, I imagine. She was part of the plan all along . . .' He said this last with a preoccupied air: something on the screen to his left had snared his attention. 'Every rebirth requires a baptism, Goodbook.'

Something strange happened then, something he, as a psychology professor, should have been able to recognize, but could not. A strange buoyancy filled everything, made candy of all the sharp edges. It suddenly seemed that he watched a rubber world, a place filled with foam simulacra.

That wasn't the woman who had cried tears of joy at their wedding. That wasn't his old roommate. None of this actually *happened* . . . There was simply no way. There were no roads between this place and where he lived.

Neil had returned to his computer terminal. 'Suffering some kind of dissociative fugue, are we?' he called over his shoulder. 'You're lucky I didn't rotate your rack the *other* way.'

What was he talking about?

Then Nora said, 'Tommy?'

She was weeping.

He suffered that old rush of protective instincts. Once, before the kids had been born, they had gone to the fair drunk. At the end of one of the rides, she had simply jumped the fence rather than queue with him and the others at the exit: for an instant she had teetered at the blurred fringe of the neighboring Tilt-a-whirl, a bug in the shadow of hammers, and Thomas had felt her peril with more immediacy than he could ever feel his own. He had literally doubled over with relief when she stumbled back out of harm's way.

But there was no place for her to stumble this time. And he could only double into himself, into a haze of panic that would not let go.

She was dead. As dead as he was.

'Shush,' Thomas gasped. 'We'll figure something out.'

'No . . . No. There's something you need to know. Something I have to tell you.' Her voice cracked with tears. 'I *love* you Tommy. I love you so much! How could you ever forgive me?'

Thomas clamped his eyes shut, tried to will her out of this nightmare. 'He's controlling you.'

'Who? What do you mean? This is me saying this, Tommy. *Me.*'

Thomas felt his face crumple. In the corner of his eye, he could see new lights flicker across the schematic of his brain on Neil's computer. 'But you said you didn't love me. You said you never loved me.'

'I . . . didn't. I couldn't . . .'

'He's just fucking with you, Nora. Manipulating you.'

'No-no! You just have to listen for a minute. Okay, Tommy? This is something I have to say. I have to, Tommy, please! I *do love you.* I don't know why or how, but I can see it now. I can feel it. Oh, Tommy, my heart feels like it's going to explode I love you so much!'

'Nora. Listen to me carefully, hon—'

'Why do you do this? Every time! Like it's a mechanical reflex or something. Every time we start exploring our feelings, it's like you . . . you shrink. Like you're allergic.' Her smile was both persecuted and beatific, as though she were a mother trying to share the glory of Jesus with an atheist son. 'Thomas John Bible,' she cried in a *goddamn-you* tone. 'I'm telling you that I love you! All you have to do is listen.'

'But where's that feeling coming from? Huh, Nora? You're bolted to a machine for Christ—'

'Stop, Tommy, *stop*! Who cares where it comes from? Really! If you found a winning lottery ticket in your pocket, what would do you do? Fret about where it came from, or *cash it in*? Really, Tommy. It's as simple as that!'

A cold pit of realization. You spent your whole life with a person, sharing the same inside, too immersed in the intricacies of the relationship to ever clearly comprehend it. It was as if a kind of *incapacity* was the true measure of belonging to another person, an inability to see the other against the frame of larger events, an inability that found its culmination in the self. All humans belonged to one another in this sense.

But the woman speaking to him from across the room – she was not his wife; she was not the bundle of encompassing hopes and anxieties that populated his memories. She was scarcely human.

She was a doll. A machine plugged into a machine.

'Nora. Please. This is madness.'

'All the important things are, Tommy! You know that better than anyone.'

He looked to the monster, his friend, who had turned in his chair to watch their exchange. 'Neil. Stop this, Neil.'

'You're going to throw *that* in my face?' Nora cried. 'Him?'

Thomas paused, struggled with a confusion that was at once a recognition. She wasn't simply a doll. She was a broken one.

'He's right *there*, Nora.'

A kind of concentrated desperation had seized her expression. 'Look. I know I fucked up, Tommy. I know I don't . . . I don't deserve you. Please. Please, you have to forgive me. I'm not that . . . that . . . person. That wasn't me! It was just some lonely, fucked up insecure version of me.'

'Nora . . .'

'She can't see me,' Neil said. 'I've shut down the left hemispheric circuits involved in constructing extrapersonal space. That means she can't see anything on her right side. She can't even see that she doesn't see. Where I'm standing simply doesn't exist for her brain, not even as an absence.'

'Neil?' Nora said, her passion crimped by alarm. 'Where are you?'

'Do I need to tell you what you already know?' Neil continued, watching Nora but obviously speaking to Thomas. 'Everything that happens in the brain of someone who truly loves is happening in her brain right now. Every neurochemical transfer. Every storm of synaptic firings.' He smiled as though she were a prized zoo exhibit as he said this. He turned to Thomas, his eyes bright with arrogance and jubilation, the way they always were when he scored some incontrovertible point.

'True love, Goodbook. She's offering you true love.'

'Neil?' Nora said. 'Where are you? I'm . . .'

'There's nothing true about this,' Thomas spat. 'Nothing. You're controlling her. *Forcing* her to love.'

His friend shrugged. 'So? What earthly difference does that make? If it wasn't me who tipped the equilibrium in her brain toward the manifestation of bonding behavior, then what would it be other than an accidental collection of stimuli? A rose brought to the door. A lingering kiss. Heartfelt words. A smile. What does it matter if the world pulls her strings directly, or if it pulls her strings through me?'

'I'm confused,' Nora murmured. 'I . . . I . . .'

'It matters,' Thomas said.

'Does it?' Neil sprang from his seat and walked toward Nora, paused just to her right. Nothing about her eyes or expression registered his presence. 'There's a million circumstances that would produce this particular output with this particular brain . . . love. This –' he held his hands out to the room – 'is just one more. Just as natural. Just as meaningless.'

'Neil? You're close. I can hear you! Where are you?'

'Natural?' Thomas asked with savage incredulity. 'What could be natural about this?'

Laughter. 'Our brains are manipulating machines, Goodbook, each the result of millions of years of evolutionary adaptation to its environment, its world. That it should reach out and manipulate itself is as natural as can be. Just think! After grasping and grasping through hundreds of millions of years, it's finally touched the bottom of the bag. Don't blame me if it's empty.'

'I don't . . .' Nora called, her tone eerily like the one she had used to break into their debates back in the old days. 'I don't know what's going on. But I *am* feeling these things, Tommy! No one's forcing me. Especially not Neil.'

'Nora . . .'

'Aw, sweetheart,' Neil said. 'It just seems that—'

'But I feel it! It's the most certain thing I've ever . . .' Her face was pinned beneath looming circuitry, lines of blood trailing from the bolts that fixed her skull, and yet her expression was one of maudlin yearning, as though she were some teenage diva emoting for the camera. The absurdity of it jarred a wave of nausea from his gut. 'I mean, why did it take me so long to see? I love. I *love*!'

Experience, she was saying. Pure and bone deep. What could be more true than that? What could be more true than the feelings that underwrite our very existence?

'*Amor vincit omnia*,' Neil said. 'Is that it, Nora? Is that your theory? Love conquers all?'

'Leave her out of this, Neil!'

He stood directly before her, lingering just far enough to her right to remain entirely unseen. 'I suppose you think that *you make meaning*, right?' He stepped back to his worktable, leaned over one of the vermillion-screened laptops. 'Tell me,' he said, his fingers sprinting across the keyboard, 'which "you" would that be, Nora?' He turned to beam a vicious grin that she could not see. 'This one?'

Click.

Something changed. There was a hole . . .

"This is what it's like," Neil was saying. "This is what it's like when the *self* is shut down."

No, hole wasn't the right word; it assumed a subtraction from some greater sum, when it was the sum itself that no longer existed.

'So tell me, sweetheart, how can you make meaning when you're simply another output? Just like the feeling of making. Just like the feeling of love. How can the "feeling of being you" anchor anything, when it can be shut down with a flick of a switch? Hmm?'

Neil was speaking, but no one listened. There was simply this clearing, this space, a manifold of things and happenings, articulated in time, and belonging to no one.

'You like to think you have all these experiences, that you author all your actions, but the sad fact, my dear, is that you simply accompany them.'

There was this voice, humming with a familiarity so profound it terrified.

'No,' it said. 'No.'

Neil laughing. 'Strange, isn't it, Goodbook? To finally hear your voice as it truly is. A stranger, speaking with your lips.' He stood, and from within the clearing, seemed to gaze at the clearing itself, at the angle of its opening. 'You don't know how long I've wanted this . . . how long I've ached . . . for an opportunity to speak with you. The *real* you.'

And in the parallel weave of existences, there was a stinging that was also a knowing, an understanding that he spoke not to 'Goodbook', not to the cartoon, but to the brain behind and beneath. And it heard him.

Neil drifted back to his worktable, a kind of torpor in his movements.

Click.

Then *Thomas* was watching him, reeling with something deeper than dismay.

'I'm confused,' Nora was sobbing. 'I don't . . . I don't understand what's happening. All I know is that *I love you*, Tommy. That's all I know!'

Neil spoke before Thomas's speech center could generate any words. 'And you know what you feel, huh, Nora?'

'I told you!' she cried. 'It's the deepest, the most awesome feeling of . . .' She trailed into silence. Her eyes fluttered. She swallowed, then let out a long, groaning sigh. 'Ungh,' she gasped. 'You *are* doing something to me, aren't you? Are you *touching* me? Are you-you-you-*yooooooo*—'

'You can see it, can't you?' Neil said, glancing at Thomas. 'See her for what she is.'

No, something said. *Yes*.

'Mmmmm,' Nora murmured in a tone that stabbed for its familiarity. 'Ohmi*gawd* . . .'

Thomas felt his voice crack. 'She's no different than us.'

'Exactly,' Neil said, grinning. '*None* of us are real. Unable to see itself, our brains continually cook us up. It's just that at the moment, her brain finds itself one step lower on the causal food chain.'

He winked and added, 'Just like you.'

*

Neil made her weep. Neil made her scream, and he made it so that Thomas thought it funny – sublimely funny. The more ragged, the more tortured her scream, the more uproarious it became.

Then afterward, Neil laughed at his shame, and showed him every cubit of that monstrous emotion.

This time it was Nora who laughed.

Neil made her forget the minutes, then even the seconds, so that every breath she would say, 'Where am I?'

'Where am I?'

'Where am I?'

'Where am I?'

Between each game Thomas tried to soothe her, this jerking mechanism that had once been his wife. He tried to whisper reassurances that possessed no meaning in the ringing tin of his own ears.

But she could only weep, 'Ripley,' over and over again.

'Frankie . . .'

Neil made her come, then transformed the data signature of her voice into an algorithm that made him come. He stood between them and cackled as they cried out again and again, driven to orgasm after orgasm by the sound of the other's climax.

And Thomas did not want it to stop.

Then Neil did the same with pain, so that her wagging shrieks made him buck and howl, over and over again. A pain beyond weeping. A pain beyond succor or reprieve.

A pain only fallen angels could know.

And something began to understand.

Something . . . not him.

He was nothing more than an output, a kind of holographic speaker system that generated experience like sound. He had lived the abstract force of the Argument for too many years for it not to be rote, reflex. But this . . .

The nimbus of white ringing all points of illumination. The ache murmuring through teeth cracked for gnashing. Flexing rage. The battering love and horror. Arching lust. The glimmers of hope and beauty. And the pain, the overriding pain.

All of it falling from his best friend's fingers.

He was but a moment, something deeper than him realized.

Nothing more than a fragment, fooled by blindness into thinking itself whole. Notes contemptuous of the instrument.

Music oblivious to the score.

He was still screaming when Theodoros Gyges appeared at the very edge of seeing.

Impossible. But there it was, the coarse beard climbing acne-scarred cheeks, the bearish eyes far too sharp for such a blunt face, *there*, hanging on the verge of visual oblivion, motionless, watching with the blank fascination of a tourist who had wandered through an EMPLOYEES ONLY door at Disney World.

Thomas spared him no thought.

He had no thought to spare.

The billionaire strode into the blurred circle of his agony. Thomas did not care when he raised the crowbar. He did not rejoice when Neil looked up from his monitors too late. He did not start at the watermelon-thump.

He did not thank God.

The crowbar fell again and again. Screens and equipment danced to spitting sparks.

Then the pain was gone.

Nora twitched across from him, her eyes rolled back into her head. Neil lay stretched across the concrete floor, his face bent toward Thomas, his body broken-doll still. He seemed to blink and work his mouth. Somehow Thomas knew that his neck was broken.

The burly man stepped up to Thomas, peered into his face. Thomas tried to say, 'It's me,' but he had screamed his voice to blood.

With thick thumbs, Gyges unscrewed the bolts holding his head in place. The pain of unthreading the bone seemed almost a joke. Thomas let his chin loll against his chest as the man unbuckled the remaining restraints.

'It's me,' Thomas finally rasped. 'It's me, Mr Gyges . . . Thomas Bible.'

The billionaire nodded. 'And that's him?' he said, nodding to Neil across the floor.

'It's him . . . Neil Cassidy.'

The billionaire held Thomas's elbow as he stepped clear. Even still, he fell to his knees.

'You followed me.'

'The GPS in my car,' Gyges said.

It seemed to Thomas that he had known all along. That he had waited. Everything had coordinates, nowadays, even roads unmarked on any map. Everyone could be found.

'You get your family,' the man said. 'Then you leave.'

'I-I do-don—'

'You leave!' Gyges barked. 'You do not want to hear . . . to see . . .'

He turned from Thomas, pulled a long knife from a sheath strapped to his left calf. He kneeled, placing his right knee in the small of Neil's back. He used the knife to scratch an itch on his bearded cheek. Thomas saw dried blood marring its sheen.

He felt no surprise. He lacked the neurotransmitters.

'The spine is the door, the connection . . .' Gyges said, looking at the task before him. He turned to Thomas, his piggish eyes rounding in a kind of wonder. 'Cut it and the soul is preserved, kept safe, wrapped in a box . . .

'Don't you see?' Gyges hissed, staring down his cheeks like some ancient chieftain. 'I only fuck the *meat*.'

Thomas backed away from the madman, knowing there was no reason, no connection . . .

He was just noise. One more senseless output.

'I only fuck the meat!'

Thomas glanced at Neil's face, saw the brain behind it reaching for him through the pose of facial musculature, clutching with primeval visual cues. He could see it *looking*, peering through keyhole eyes, buzzing with anguish and information, trapped by the severing of a single cord.

It pulled Neil's lips into a rueful smile, pinned his face into a pathetic grimace.

Goodbook, it mouthed.

Please . . .

'What I do,' Gyges gasped with coital intensity. 'They know . . . but they do not *feel*.'

Untouched, Thomas turned to free his ex-wife. In his periphery, he could see Gyges hunched over Neil's broad back. But he dared not look. The billionaire had become a thing of blood and sawing shadows. A monstrous tabloid horror, murmuring as he worked . . .

'Look at you.

'Boned like a fish . . .

'Like a prom queen with low self-esteem.

'I will fill you like a cup . . .

'Like something holy.'

The false premise in Neil's argument.

After freeing her, Thomas held Nora's face to his chest so that she too would not see.

'Look at you . . .'

The Chiropractor brooked no witnesses.

They held hands as they climbed the basement stairs. A series of colorless images assailed Thomas with each and every blink. He saw Cynthia Powski, her skullcap drawn back like the curtains of a theatre stage. He saw the Museum of Natural History diorama that had so impressed him as a kid: male and female australopithecines walking side by side across a vast plain of volcanic ash. He remembered asking his father what had happened to them, whether they had gone to heaven. 'Do you see wings?' his father had snapped.

My son . . . Thomas thought as they crested the final steps.

My son and daughter are dead.

All was dark upstairs. Nora's face, bruised and bloodied by Mary's screws, seemed to float in the gloom. Neither of them spoke. When they turned on the lights, it seemed they could see too much. Cobwebs in the corners. Hardwood floors that seemed to creak beneath the weight of their gaze. No furniture. No pictures. No obligatory antiques. Thomas knelt and picked a small white card from the floor, studied the painted real estate agent smiling from the corner photo.

WELCOME HOME!

the gold-embossed letters shouted.

He let the card flutter from his fingers. Then he wondered where Neil had hidden the bodies.

Nora began testing doors, gingerly, as though feeling for fire beyond the blank wood panels. Thomas followed her lead, more out of some instinct to mimic than out of agreement.

They found the children thrown like luggage across the floor of a spare bedroom. The heads of both were dressed, Ripley with gauze clotted with small spots of blood, Frankie with the original bandages from the hospital. Feeling the flutter of their pulses, Thomas wanted to weep, but there was a gaping hollow where his joy and anguish should have been. He gathered his unconscious son in his arms instead, rocking him the way Nora rocked Ripley.

Both were sedated.

They took Nora's car, which Neil had pulled out back. Thomas was too numb to care that she had willingly brought their daughter to her monster lover.

The way he had brought their son to his monster friend.

She sat in the back with both their children, gently weeping. It seemed fake, somehow. Thomas drove, entranced by the apparitions that swept up and around his sensorium.

The headlights illuminated too little road, a wedge of gravel rimmed by bracken and flailing trees. They rolled into the black. Everything flying outward, into the black beyond and behind them.

'Gyges was the Chiropractor,' he whispered to her image in the rearview mirror. 'Neil made him . . . A diversion, a way to strangle the resources devoted to finding him.'

Not that explanations mattered anymore.

'How?' Nora croaked.

Everything would be shadows after this – simulations. No fear, no pain, no joy or love would be as profound, as *true*, as what Mary had shown him. Neil was gone, and the world was back behind the controls. Only the familiarity of the things Thomas thought and felt set them apart. *He* was the difference, which meant he was nothing at all.

Like this very moment.

'Mommy?' a little girl's voice whispered.

Thomas heard the sharp intake of Nora's breath.

'I love you, Mommy.'

'I love you too,' she rasped.

'Yesss,' Ripley said. 'I really, *really*, love you . . .'

The words were right, but the world that gave them meaning was so very wrong. Soon, Thomas realized, his son would awake also.

Then the screaming would begin.

'I luvvvvvv . . .' his daughter cooed in a smiling, teary-eyed voice.

'Shhhh,' Thomas croaked. 'Time to sleep, honey.'

Experience, unspooling like a movie, qualms for color, hopes for shape, decisions for the illusion of movement, waiting for the bulb to burn through, for the celluloid to boil into black rings, so that it all could vanish into the hidden frame, leaving only catcalls and white light on a white screen.

'So much it hurts, Mommy.'

AUTHOR'S AFTERWORD

Since this book turns on an intricate combination of fact and fiction, I thought I should try to clarify, at least in general terms, which is which. In so many ways writers are the least trustworthy of sources, not only because of the sheer breadth of the ground they cover, but because they spend so much time alone with their opinions. Love affairs are inevitable.

Of the myriad details regarding psychology and cognitive science that appear, the majority are either fact or close extrapolations of fact. Some, however, are what might be called 'future facts', results that have not been obtained, but very well might be, given a pessimistic interpretation of existing trends. The stuff regarding free will is a primary example. To my knowledge, researchers have yet to determine rudimentary choices before any conscious awareness of making them. The notorious findings of Benjamin Libet, I think, are too freighted with ambiguity to say one way or the other. By the same token, it seems very likely that free will, certainly the way it is generally understood, is in for a very, very rough ride. For those interested in an accessible overview of recent trends in consciousness research, I highly recommend Susan Blackmore's excellent *A Very Short Introduction to Consciousness.*

There is of course no such thing as Marionette, but since it's simply a deep-reaching version of Transcranial Magnetic Stimulation, a technology that has already entered its maturity, I'm inclined to think it's more a matter of *when* we'll see such devices than if. Of course, all the glimpses of what Thomas experiences while in Marionette are sheer speculation, but entirely possible in principle, which is all the Argument really needs.

The same might be said about the novel's central 'novum', low field fMRIs. These have been in the research pipe for some time now; the question is how long that pipe will prove to be, especially when it comes to scanning individuals' brains as they go about their business. I want to say 'very long', but the resources gathering on the horizon are more than formidable. Marketers are taking that fateful step from training us like animals (via associative conditioning) to treating us like mechanisms. There are tremendous amounts of money to be made.

As for the marriage of technology and the brain, that day has already arrived, and the therapeutic possibilities are nothing short of breathtaking. Forms of depression, blindness and deafness that seemed incurable only years ago now seem destined to become maladies of the past. But since I wanted *Neuropath* to be a thriller, one that strives to be intellectually as well as viscerally disturbing, I primarily focused on the more frightening implications of our 'post-human' future.

As a result, the book will no doubt smack of alarmism and techno-phobia for those who see a cornucopia of possibility in the 'post-human'. For my own part, I think we have every reason to be more than a little paranoid. Fiddling at the edges of brain function to relieve suffering seems an obvious good. But the stakes change drastically once we begin manipulating the machinery of consciousness. What happens when *experience itself* becomes as pliable as paint? What happens when the only measuring tape we possess becomes as elastic as a rubber band? Altering our own neurophysiology means altering the very structure of our experience, the shared bedrock of our humanity, not to mention the tools required to decide further alterations. There's good reason to believe that self-modification at such a fundamental level will send us looping out into different directions of insanity. Either way, we quite simply *cannot imagine* what a world without this common frame of reference would be like. And if it were the case that things like meaning, purpose, and morality are kinds of illusions, then there's no reason to expect any of them to survive the post-human future to come. Post-human optimists generally base their arguments on the very experiential staples they intend to render obsolete. They assume that some 'humanist center' will hold when their arguments imply precisely the opposite. They are literally advocating what they cannot conceptualize, which in a sense means they are advocating nothing at all.

When it comes to the post-human, we really have no reason to be anything other than profoundly uncertain. And profound uncertainty regarding essential matters warrants excessive care.

Or as I like to call it, paranoia.

Recent years have seen a number of popular works written by philosophers trying to head off the nihilistic implications of contemporary neuroscience. Someone like Daniel Dennett, for instance, wouldn't so much argue with the science of *Neuropath* as he would argue with the interpretation. It's not that freedom or morality don't exist, he would say, only that they're not what we take them to be. Rather than wringing our hands, what we should be doing is reinterpreting our old concepts in the light of new scientific evidence. So something like 'freedom', for instance, could be redefined as 'greater behavioral versatility'.

To me, this amounts to reassuring mourners at Grandma Mildred's funeral by telling them to simply name their household pets 'Mildred'. I don't know about you, but my experience of freedom is not the experience of 'greater behavioral versatility' or however you want to scientifically redefine the term 'freedom'. It really does seem as though I'm confronted with choices, and that I could at any moment do otherwise. The problem isn't that our concepts are out of date, but that our *experiences* are out and out deceptive. But even if it were a matter of terminology, then why bother with the old nomenclature at all? Why, outside of the tendentious desire to eat one's conceptual cake and to have it too, not just say, 'Well, you're not FREE, it's true, but you sure are VERSATILE'?

But of course, the real difficulty is that despite their business-as-usual appeal, 'reconciliations' of our popular and intuitive understanding of human nature with recent discoveries in the sciences assume that we actually know what these discoveries mean, when it is painfully obvious that we do not. All we have are trends, which seem to point to a continued undermining of apparent experiential verities, and the knowledge that we are not what we thought we were. We really have no reason whatsoever to think that science will offer us anything remotely recognizable, let alone, as Owen Flanagan argues in *The Problem of the Soul*, 'preserve much of what it means to be a person'. The fact that we can cook up his kind of reassurances should come as no surprise; we're hardwired to rationalize, after all.

Personally, given our all-too-human ability to pluck conviction out of abject ambiguity, I think philosophers should strive to be gadflies, not apologists. If you take your arguments beyond the pale of empirical testability, you're pretty much bound to arrive at the conclusions you want, *especially* if you're as brilliant as Dennett or Flanagan.

The 'Blind Brain Hypothesis' that I give to Thomas is actually a creation of my own from several years back, when I was still actively pursuing my PhD in philosophy. It's little more than a hunch that the basic structure of conscious experience would be far better understood by reference to what the brain *lacks* than by what the brain has. Since this is one of the most crucial and contentious 'future facts' presented in the book, I thought it might merit some more explanation.

Take one of Thomas's favorite examples: the Now. It is the lens through which we experience time, yet it somehow remains outside of time. Each Now is in some mysterious manner both different and the same – a paradox that has exercised intellects as far back as Aristotle. Given the Blind Brain Hypothesis, however, the Now might be seen as a temporal version of our visual field, the boundaries of which somehow just 'run out'. We receive no visual information beyond the scope of our retinas, so we see nothing beyond that point, nothing *at all*, not even the absence of seeing. We literally see, in other words, against an undifferentiated frame of sightlessness, which is why the edges of your visual field just . . . end. We rarely register this because of all the other systems that stitch our keyhole glimpses into an entire world. But from the standpoint of sight, our visual field literally hangs in oblivion.

The same might be said of our 'temporal field', what William James famously called the 'specious present'. In the same way we can't see the limits of seeing, the idea runs, we can't *time* the limits of timing, so we literally experience earlier and later against a frame of timelessness. This would be what generates the illusion of before and after, the strange bundling of the past and future within the Now. Time passes in consciousness, but in a strange sense it can't pass *for* consciousness. The bulk of the brain, after all, lies outside the information horizon of the thalamo-cortical system, churning away in timeless invisibility.

For structural and developmental reasons too numerous to elaborate here, the brain can only 'see itself' in blinkered terms. According to the Blind Brain Hypothesis, this not only determines what is conscious and what is unconscious, but the very structure of consciousness. The Now is no small feature of lived experience. It also means that for many features of consciousness, it makes no more sense looking for 'neural correlates' than it does looking for 'visual drop-off circuits' to explain the strange limits of our visual field.

According to the Blind Brain Hypothesis, conscious systems like humans should have an exceptionally difficult time understanding themselves – as indeed happens to be the case. Since the brain only glimpses slivers of its own processes, small fragments that it can only see as wholes, we should expect it not only to be baffled by the findings of neuroscience, but to insist those slivers *really are wholes*, and as such require some mechanism in the brain to explain them. If the Blind Brain Hypothesis is true, then much of cognitive science could very well be a wild goose chase, a search for 'magic coin circuits'.

The upshot seems to be that consciousness is illusory through and through, as opposed to just here and there, which is why I find myself in the strange position of wanting my own theory to be wrong. We now know that much of what we take for granted, experience-wise, is simply not what it seems, more than enough to ask all the hard questions covered in this book. But if consciousness is fundamentally, structurally deceptive, then the reason we have so much difficulty trying to figure it out could be that we have no way of knowing just *what it is* we're trying to figure out. And perhaps we never will.

Personally, I am neither an eliminativist nor a nihilist; I genuinely believe that what we *experience* should trump what we know. But like Thomas, I just can't figure out how to argue this honestly, let alone convincingly. We, as a species, have an exceedingly difficult time with claims we don't like, and we typically muster all the power bias and ignorance have to offer to confirm our preexisting intuitions. (For a sobering tour of just how bad things are, check out David Dunning's *Self-Insight*, or Cordelia Fine's splendid *A Mind of its Own*.) Humans are believing machines, credulous to the point of comedy, be they priests, philosophers, or assembly-line workers. Once you come to appreciate this fact, it becomes very hard to credit anything in the world of competing claims, and very easy to understand why, despite thousands of years, so few of our innumerable theoretical disagreements have ever found conclusive resolution – outside of science, that is.

This is not to say that science is the end-all be-all, only that if you believe, as I do, that not all claims are equal, and you appreciate just how inclined we are to dupe ourselves, then science, which is institutionally and procedurally structured to combat (as opposed to exploit) our shortcomings as believers, quickly starts to seem like the only remotely reliable game in town. And as the book suggests, science doesn't give a damn about what we *want* to be true. In a sense, this is the key to its power.

The world of *Neuropath* is a world where these 'unwanted truths' have reached critical mass, both socially and spiritually. It's a world where the pace of technologically driven social change has outstripped culture's ability to cope, where the black box of the soul has been laid bare to the appetite of irresistible institutional forces. And it very well could be *our world*.

Whatever the case, knowledge and experience have come to a crossroads, and things don't look so good for experience. What used to be the abstract worries of philosophers have been covered with skin and hair. Neil, I'm afraid, is alive and well – at least in embryo.

We should be prepared.